DEATH IS GOLDEN

THREE FEET OF SKY

BOOK THREE

STEPHEN AYRES

Website: http//www.stephen-ayres.co.uk

"Time is a game played beautifully by children": Heraclitus

LITTLE BASTARDS

Crawling out of the dense clinging undergrowth, Jomo Tikolo shuddered with relief as he felt a hard concrete surface beneath his hand. If this was still Australia, then he was far from the parched empty landscape of the west coast. The twisted maze of wet fronds and fuzzy creepers had seemed endless under the barely broken darkness of the rainforest canopy. All manner of insects had chanced a run across his naked body, some lingering to bite and sting, but they invoked little worry compared to the nightmare from which he had escaped.

Unable to hear his pursuers, Jomo dragged his naked body onto the wide highway and lay on his back, catching his breath. He winced as his injured leg scraped against the cracked and pitted concrete, slightly scuffing his makeshift bandage of grey duct tape. A trickle of blood escaped from under the tape, glistening crimson against his dark brown skin.

Jomo only allowed himself a couple of minute's rest, before struggling to his feet. The pain from his deep leg wound grew increasingly intense as he hobbled along the road without a stick or crutch for support. Every few faltering steps, he cautiously looked back, sweat building on his forehead, fearing that they were following.

After a few hours walk south along the old road, stopping only to drink rainwater from some conveniently low bowed leaves, Jomo noticed a subtle change in the climate. Despite being the height of the day, the temperature was slightly milder and the humidity less cloying. Looking up to the sky, there was a pronounced gauze-like effect bisecting the view. With luck, it might be the weather filter for the slerding plains.

In amongst the thick vegetation, a touch of cold grey caught his eye. Reinvigorated by the cool water, Jomo tore away some coiled vines, revealing a bare metal pole with a large rectangular sign at the top. Sitting about ten feet high, partially obscured by leafy branches, the sign was roughly eight feet long and half as tall. The surface was covered in a protective transparent layer, undamaged by neither time nor nature, behind which a three-dimensional display still flickered, welcoming visitors to the prestigious Bullara Slerding Station.

The sign was a shock, and Jomo staggered backwards onto the road. If the sign was correct, then this was Western Australia, but the thick rainforest either side of the highway was new and unexpected. Could this really be the route that Jomo had taken in 3012? Back then, the road had a powered glide coating with nightlights, and was busy with people eagerly travelling for their induction into The Experience. The land had been a featureless sandy expanse then – a dry barren wasteland. Was the change due to an extensive greening scheme, or had Jomo been slerding for far longer than he ever thought possible?

As the head of a wealthy Kenyan family, Jomo had inherited land, and a number of lucrative licences and patents. He was the first in his extensive social network to sign up for the Orchard Elite's simply titled, 'Experience' – the latest alternative-life package from the all-powerful global corporation. Within hours of running the 30-day trial period, a limited virtual version of the highly addictive mind sequence, Jomo was completely hooked.

Jomo chose a first class passage to the Slerding Plains. Whereas his less wealthy relatives would spend eternity sliding around in the dense human herds of Australia's interior, he and his closest friends and family would enjoy the exclusive and less crowded expanse of the west coast. The luxurious Bullara Slerding Station was the western gateway, offering a champagne induction day and a two android white glove placement on the smooth floor of the plains – unlike the crowded interior, where those poor wretches unable to afford a first class ticket were roughly pushed onto the plains by industrial shover trucks.

Once mentally shuttered inside the Experience, sliding around in their new, almost featureless, all-weather bodies and slime suits, it was the same for everyone. However, Jomo felt comfortable and smugly superior knowing he would spend a splendid eternity blindly rubbing shoulders with the rich and famous.

Looking ahead, Jomo expected to see the vast expanse of the Slerding Plains, a smooth floored vista with humanity's billions sliding around, but instead a dense wall of forest blocked the way. Stumbling on, he noticed the road turned a sharp right, and vaguely remembered it led to the Bullara Visitor's Centre.

Jomo stood for a moment at the junction, unable to decide whether to cut through the foliage in the hope that the plains were just beyond, or head for the visitor's centre, which was certainly derelict and held in the sturdy grasp of nature. Whichever route he chose, Jomo longed for The Experience. To slip back into that expertly crafted endorphin symphony, the perfect addiction, eclipsed all other concerns. It was then that another terrifying concern jumped to the front of the queue. An ominous noise erupted not far behind Jomo, peaking his fear.

Turning too quickly to face the source of the sound, an eerie high-pitched whine from thousands of tiny mouths, Jomo twisted his ankle in a crack in the concrete. Pouring like a glittering river of liquid silver from the undergrowth, a horde of miniature creatures moved almost as one towards their prey. From painful experience, Jomo knew that the metallic sheen was the sunlight bouncing off thousands of blades – smaller than pins but easily able to deliver the proverbial 'death by a thousand cuts'.

Survival instinct and blind panic overcame the pain in his leg and ankle, and Jomo managed an ungainly lope towards the relative safety of the forest. If he could reach the slerding plains, then perhaps he could mingle amongst the crowds. Their relentless sliding would surely deter his tiny pursuers. Like so many bugs, the little bastards would be trodden on and squashed.

The surging torrent of tiny jump-suited humans, men and women, all about an inch tall, skipped and leapt across the cracks in the road with the disproportionate speed and agility of ants or spiders. Shrieking with furious delight, brandishing a small sword in each hand, they rapidly closed the gap on their beleaguered quarry.

Before he reached the forest, the horde swarmed around Jomo. Using their blades as handholds, stabbing into the exposed flesh, like demented mountaineers they began scaling his naked legs. As they climbed, the skin was sometimes pierced deep enough for blood to seep out, and soon Jomo's legs were wet and glistening.

Jomo screamed and writhed, trying to shake off the expanding coat of little people. He shuddered and gasped as he felt someone, or something, crawl up into his anus. Feeling another uncomfortable incursion underway, Jomo frantically reached around and grabbed the second insidious potholer.

Glancing briefly at the contents of his sweaty hand, Jomo spied a tiny man wearing what looked like makeshift breathing apparatus and a grey wetsuit. The faecal diver wiggled and moaned, perhaps begging for mercy. Without a thought, Jomo tossed him to the concrete below.

Hurtling into the undergrowth quickly dislodged many of the climbers. Most fell to the ground, but again, like insects, were only stunned by the impact rather than injured or killed, and promptly re-joined the chase. With seemingly boundless energy, the horde pursued, but the thick vegetation made it almost impossible for them to resume the climb. Having no regard for the pain or his well-being, Jomo crashed hard against any tree trunk in his path, squashing and scraping away those resilient souls still stubbornly clinging to his body. The foliage was definitely thinning, and slivers of daylight cut through the gaps in the bushes ahead.

Suddenly exiting the soft light of the rainforest brought a searing sunlight that caused Jomo to close his eyes. He could feel the reassuring hard surface of the slerding plain beneath his feet as he stumbled on, and fought to keep his balance on the low friction coating. Daring to open his eyes, now accustomed to the light, he breathed a sigh of relief as the monotonous smooth plain spread out into the distance. Not far away, maybe a few hundred feet, was a large cluster of slerds, engrossed in the Experience, oblivious to the real world around them. If he could reach them without incurring another tide of vicious mini-mountaineers, then he stood a chance.

Tentatively looking back, afraid that his pursuers were close behind, Jomo saw the horde appear from the undergrowth. Rather than follow, they spread out like a metal kerb along the edge of the plain, watching their prey from the forest. They began screaming, thrusting their blades in the air. After a few minutes, the high-pitched venting rage became a distant whine as Jomo approached the silently sliding slerds.

Slowing down, reassured that the miniature army were no longer an imminent threat, Jomo became aware of an unusual weight and biting pain in his groin. He stopped and carefully inspected his genitals. Holding his penis out of the way, Jomo saw two tiny humans hanging under his scrotum like some darkly gothic genital piercings – their sharp blades, lodged in the sac, acting as rudimentary handles. Perhaps they were members of an elite squad, but who on Earth trains an elite squad of testicle hangers?

Expressing anger rather than fear, Jomo tore the miniature humans from his balls. Holding them up to his face, one in each hand, squinting hard at their unrepentant snarling faces, Jomo spat at them:

"I should drown you in my spit for what you have done. Why did you do this to me? Why did you do this, when you live in paradise?"

Unrepentant, the little men struggled against Jomo's grip, and furiously stabbed at his hand with their blades. Though tempted to crush the life out of the savages, Jomo instead displayed a humanity perhaps alien to his unyielding attackers. Crouching low, he bid them farewell, and deftly skimmed them across the smooth slerding floor in the direction of the forest. He watched as they came to a skidding halt, sprung to their feet, and began sprinting back to their compatriots.

With the light beginning to fade, finding shelter and medical assistance was a priority. The only structures he knew of on the Slerding Plains were the melding tunnels – useless for shelter unless he wished to become finely ground sausage meat. Scanning the horizon, his hope almost lost, Jomo spotted a small grey structure about a mile away. Looking out of place on the plains, it stood like a concrete carbuncle, partially obscured by crowds of slerds. There was no other choice. Stumbling on once more, Jomo headed for the mysterious building.

DOWN BY THE RIVER

Early morning, Adam Eden lounged by the river, wearing only a blue dressing gown, and drinking his third highball of freshly squeezed orange juice. The deep red Moro, a sweet tasting blood orange with a hint of raspberry, shared the glass with rich Rioja, and a generous splash of Bobadilla brandy - a refreshing, though boozy, staple of Adam's long standing morning routine.

A contrast to the meadow-banked, gently meandering stream that once gracefully wound its way through the miniature environment, the new improved wide fast-flowing river boasted a grandiose, five arch, stone bridge. Cool grey flagstone paved promenades cut a sharp edge to the water, bordered by imposing five-storey luxury apartments. The buildings, an eclectic jumble of 20th and 21st century architectural styles, were always pristine, without grime or signs of wear, lending the area a just-built quality.

Dramatically imposing on both sides of the bridge, huge utility buildings served the social needs of the 500 strong community - archetypally postmodernist, copious expanses of glass, framed with grey stone, and topped off with striking steel gables. On the promenade, you might mistakenly believe you were in a large city, but either side of the river, behind the single row of apartments, were hedge-rowed fields and dense woodland.

Nestled comfortably into the generous cushioning of his chair, in his favourite spot on a short jetty near the bridge, Adam enjoyed the bustle of the promenade. People emerged from their buildings, perhaps to enjoy breakfast with friends, or jog to the gym for an early morning workout. Some headed straight for the river to navigate a kayak along the swift waters – beginners and casual kayakers sped safely through the wide central arches of the bridge, whilst experienced or foolhardy souls rushed through the treacherously narrow outer arches.

"Hey, Eden, you lazy bastard, why don't you grab a kayak and get paddling?"

Nonchalantly placing his glass in the chair's cup holder, Adam cast an uninterested glance down at the river. Below, Stern Lovass, first-life media sensation and renowned hindreader, frantically padded backwards against the current. Bare chested, long black hair wet and swept back, Stern did not wait for a reply.

"Come on Adam, get your ass outta that chair and let the river take you for a ride!"

"You go show off your muscles and wear yourself out," Adam shouted, grabbing his glass from the cup holder and raising it high. "I'm just going to sit here enjoying my drink, whilst I soak up the early morning sun."

Stern battled against the incessant current for a few more seconds, bronzed muscles popping, veins pumped, but the kayak began moving down river.

"Adios, muchaco, but if this was your first-life, you'd be one obese mother, and rockin' your coffin with liver damage!"

With an effort and a groan, Adam heaved himself from his chair and thrust a middle finger to his perpetually ebullient friend – now shooting out of sight through one of the narrow outer arches, accompanied by a stream of Mexican expletives.

"But this isn't my first-life!" Adam cried out to no one. "I can stuff myself with every toxin known to man, but still wake up fit and healthy every morning." Adam took a large swig of his potent Sangria. "And this won't give me a headache, make me sick, or violently drunk! All hail the Viroverse! Whoever designed this man-made afterlife obviously enjoyed the good things in life."

Faintly dizzy, Adam sat slowly back into his chair, careful not to spill his drink, and let out a louder than expected fart. He chuckled childishly for a moment, then, slightly embarrassed, looked around for witnesses. The immediate vicinity was clear, but a figure crossing the bridge caught his attention. Thin, wearing skinny black jeans, a tight fitting black t-shirt, and a red baseball cap, the bearded man brought a smile to Adam's face. Despite the disguise, the man's silver-topped cane and familiar purposeful stride immediately gave away his identity.

After crossing the bridge, the man headed straight for Adam, and except for a subtle tip of his cap, remained silently impassive behind his mirrored sunglasses.

"Good to see you again, John," Adam said, holding back a belch. "What's it been; about 300 years, give or take a decade?"

"But ... but ... how did you see through my disguise? I spent all of yesterday researching your time period."

"Well, for a start, you need to lose the cane, and stop marching."

John Langdon Down, the eminent Victorian physician, who described and gave his name to Downs Syndrome, looked around nervously, like an enemy finding himself deep behind enemy lines.

"Look, just relax and pull up a chair." Adam pointed to a stack of folded wooden deckchairs nearby.

John took a chair and unfolded it, frowning.

"This does not look as comfortable as the plush armchair in which you are sitting. There isn't even a cushion."

"This is my favourite recliner," Adam said, rubbing his cheek decadently against the memory gel filled headrest. "One of the perks of being a local."

Once seated, John explained that he had orders from the Captain – the android leader of the Terminal, a secret security organization that lay outside the viro walls. Only a few select people knew what lay outside the viro walls – the rest living their lives in blissful ignorance.

"Where are my manners," Adam said, realising that John was dry. "What can I get you?"

"Is that wine you are drinking?"

"Orange juice with just a touch of wine and brandy," Adam slurred, betraying his inebriation. Sangria without the disgusting fruit chunks."

"A touch? Adam, I can smell the alcohol from here. Ten in the morning and you are already drunk. You have only been awake for two hours."

"Aw, come on, what does time matter when you are immortal? These days, time seems rarely important, and never of the essence." In an act of boorish defiance, Adam downed the remaining Sangria in one gulp, and burped as loudly as he could. "Well, I'm getting another one of these from the dispenser by the bridge. What can I get you?"

With a judgemental huff, John pulled the knees of his jeans and crossed his legs.

"Assam tea with milk and two sugars please … and not in one of those vulgar mugs that people in your time period inexplicably find so acceptable. Are you sure you wouldn't like me to fetch the drinks? You look so, hmm, settled."

"John, you just kick back and watch the kayakers. In here, you're my guest."

Without moving his resting head, or any body part except his right hand, Adam slid open a cover on the chair's arm, and deftly ran a finger over a small touch pad. With a soft hiss, the chair swivelled around and promptly sped off on its tracked wheels towards the bridge.

"Never, never, never, have I witnessed such a slothful display, Mr Eden!" John called out to his host, waving his cane as if to emphasise the point.

Upon Adam's return, John wasted no time in admonishing Adam's drunken laziness. Defending himself, Adam pointed to the farthest apartment building.

"I live on the top floor of that yellow brick building," he explained. "I don't want to walk all this way every morning just to soak up the atmosphere."

"Hmm, well at least you get to walk up and down a few flights of stairs."

"Uh, there's a lift about ten feet from my apartment."

John Down removed his sunglasses and stared hard at Adam.

"So, it's just the short walk to the lift then?"

"Actually, my chair fits easily into the lift."

Adam handed his esteemed guest a cup of tea in a dainty porcelain cup with a silver stirrer. John nodded appreciatively and sipped the hot drink. Tasting the steaming brew, he again nodded his approval, and even smiled. Adam had chosen well - whether from the 18th or 21st centuries, a decent black tea was the perfect bonding beverage.

"So, how are things out there in the halls?" Adam asked. "It's been so long since I've been on a mission that I've lost touch."

"Regrettably, it is getting rather dangerous out there. Only last month we lost an operative in an ambush. Over the past fifty years, we have lost nearly a fifth of our number."

"Good God, is Kimberly all right?" Adam gasped, shocked at the news, and surprised that no one had told him until now.

"Do not worry; she is fine. Though, without operatives of her calibre and fearlessness, we might have retreated from the halls long ago."

"I can't believe the Captain hasn't called me to action. What's going on? What are you facing out there?"

"For now, that is classified," John said calmly. "Things have died down lately. The Captain has recruited new blood, fiercer types, and we have retrained and reequipped to meet the threat. We were on our knees, but now we stand tall, or at least upright."

"So, you still rule out there."

John rapped his cane on the jetty defiantly.

"We certainly do!"

Sitting back in his uncomfortable foldout chair, John took another slurp of tea, then nestled the cup in his lap.

"Now to business, Adam. Your orders are to visit the Psychoviro, and recruit Stardust and one other … um … psychopath for a possible mission outside the Viroverse. The Captain stipulated that the other psychopath must not be Ziggy. He is too unpredictable."

"You mean outside the viros, out there in the halls. You don't actually mean …?"

"Yes, I mean outside the Viroverse itself. I have no idea what lies outside the Viroverse or the nature of the mission, but the Captain said this is of the utmost urgency."

"If you have no idea about the nature of the mission, then what do I tell them? They are psychopaths you know. They're not the easiest people to deal with."

"You tell them that the Captain might need them for an operation outside in the real world, and that when the time comes, they will be properly briefed. Until then, the Captain requires only a yes or no. Your job is to secure a yes. I am sure they will enjoy a short break from their unpleasant concrete environment."

"When do I have to go?"

"Arrange the visit today, and wake up in the Psychoviro tomorrow. As I said, the mission is of the utmost urgency."

"Why me? Why can't you talk to them directly? Their leader, Stardust, can be reasoned with. Well, up to a point."

John grinned:

"Because, dear friend, you are the legendary Copacabana, and you have a way with these murderous fiends. I know you only fight them once a month, but nobody else has their ear as you."

Adam thought for a moment, taking time for a gulp of Sangria. In truth, he could not imagine John Down negotiating with any of the Psychoviro's insane inhabitants – even though the venerable Victorian had spent a lifetime studying many mental maladies. At least, by Wednesday, Adam would be back in his favourite chair.

"Ok, I'll do it," he said. "It's Tuesday tomorrow, and they never fight on a Tuesday. Might be interesting to see what they get up to on a 'normal' day. By the way, how did you get in here without being spotted, and, more importantly, how are you getting out?"

"I have spent nearly a thousand years slipping in and out of viros without arousing the local's suspicions. Once you are in, they think you are just another guest. None of the windows in your viro has a direct line of sight to the portal, so a couple of Terminal operatives lowered me down on a rope before anyone left their buildings. To get me out without being seen, Marcus will set up a small fog bank. They will haul me back up behind the cover."

"A fog bank sounds a bit suspicious."

"Not at all," John laughed. "Your viro is fully populated – 500 residents plus visitors. People will think it a harmless prank by the usual suspects. Every viro has a number of such reprobates."

Adam chuckled, knowing that he was one such reprobate. He remembered tipping a vat of blood red dye into the river two years previously. The sight of the terrified kayakers, including the usually cool Stern, frantically paddling for the safety of the promenade was a moment of uncommon joy.

John stood up and straightened his baseball cap.

"Not leaving already?" Adam said. "Thought we might sit, drink, and reminisce. Plenty more tea where that came from." Adam quickly came up with some small talk. "I mean, how's your family these days?"

"There is an urgent matter I need to attend to." John looked at his digital watch. "I need to get to the trees below the portal before Marcus activates the fog canisters."

Adam took a drink of Sangria and heaved himself out of his chair.

"At least let me escort an old friend to the bridge. I'm not the perfect host, but I do have some standards. After all these centuries, it wouldn't be polite to just sit on my arse waving you goodbye."

Grasping clumsily for his drink, his usual companion, Adam caught the tie of his dressing gown on the arm of the chair. As he pulled it free, he fell backwards and landed on his back. Sprawled on the jetty, gown wide open and everything on display, Adam noticed his glass standing upright without a drop spilt. Oblivious to the disapproving faces glowering from nearby apartment windows, he laughed loudly, sat up, and grabbed his drink.

"Bugger those who say this is a godless place. Praise be to the divine hand of fortuitous gravity!"

John reached down a hand and helped Adam back into the cocooning comfort of the chair.

"Mr Eden, much as I enjoy your company, in light of your present state, I think you should stay here. I cannot afford to attract any attention."

After a final reminder to arrange the visit to the Psychoviro, emphasising the urgency of the matter, John left the faded legend slumped in his comfortable chair, and headed for the bridge. As John crossed the river, Adam blinked open his bleary eyes. Still sitting on his arse, he waved a weary goodbye.

UNWELCOME VISITOR

Immediately awake, alert, and with no need to rub his eyes or exhale the briefest yawn, Adam Eden threw off the garish quilt – groovy orange globes and yellow sunbursts – and leapt out of bed. A lesson in retro 1970's glam decor, the psychoviro wake-up cubicle was very different from the utilitarian box of his first visits: chrome swirls on the walls, a multi-hued glitter ceiling, and the plushest faux-fur carpeting. Stardust, the relatively pleasant psychopath, ruled the notorious environment with a lighter and significantly camper touch than his predecessor, but, as always, the killing continued.

Avoiding the pink hibiscus Hawaiian shirt and tight white trousers – his expected 'uniform' for the hunt – Adam pulled on a pair of blue bell-bottomed denims and a tight brown t-shirt with a scratch 'n' sniff banana motif; glossy black platform-heeled zip boots completed the 70's ensemble. Acquiring a tub of hair wax from the cubicle's dispenser, he slicked back his shoulder length brown hair – a look he had sported for the past eighty years. Before stepping outside, Adam cast a sparkling toothed smile in the illuminated vanity mirror. He was ready to face the psychos.

As expected, Stardust was waiting outside the drab concrete visitor building, his arms crossed, face frowning. Blitz, the latest and meanest member of the glam gang, stood close behind, poised to attack. Standing tall on oversize silver platform boots, turquoise sequined jumpsuit dazzling under the Psychoviro's artificial sun, Blitz's pointed face flared with two red curls of fire extending from his cheeks to his hairline – hair dyed a vibrant red, blazing in a hairspray demi-wave.

"Why are you here, Copout?" Blitz yelled, clenching both his teeth and ring festooned fists.

Adam, still smiling, held up a hand, displaying the two-fingered peace sign.

"No fighting today, gentlemen," he said. "I'm here with a request."

Keeping his arms crossed, Stardust did not return the smile, or even make a signature sweep of his long ultra-blonde wig.

"You know the deal, Copa," he said. "We fight from Tuesday to Saturday every week, and you're only supposed to turn up on the last Friday in every month. This is our day off. It's our chance to get out of these uncomfortable clothes." Stardust gestured to his crimson sequinned shirt and shiny black leather trousers with his black-velvet gloved hand. "You turn up, and we are forced to dress the part; rules of the viro."

"These boots really chafe the ankles," Blitz seethed, shaking a fist. "Bloody chaffing, I tell you."

"I see you aren't dressed for the hunt," Stardust noted. "We've made the effort, so I expect you to do the same."

"No, no, no, I haven't come here to fight. I have a request, from the Captain no less. For the first time in nearly a thousand years, I guess you could say I'm paying you a social call."

Finally, with a subtle shake of the head, Stardust offered a friendly smile:

"Regrettably, time makes no difference, dear Copa. We are sociopaths not socialites. I like you a lot, more than you know, but ... we must feed our needs. What we want and who we are always comes first. The hunt starts at three, and you are the prey."

"But ..."

"I rule here!" Stardust glowered darkly behind black eyeliner, striking a dynamic pose, and pointing a gloved finger at Adam. "You get back in that cubicle, and change into your beach wear. If you don't, then we'll finish it right here right now. I promise ... you ... will ... suffer!"

After feigning a moment of fear, Adam started laughing, and offered a polite clap. "Hah, you're getting better at the leader business, Stardust. You nearly sold it, but the pose is a little too rock-star. Give it another century or two and you'll have people quaking in their high heeled boots."

"I do try," Stardust sighed, holding his hand against his cheek. "I guess it means you can't be both fearsome *and* fabulous at the same time. Still, I meant what I said. If you don't change into your fighting clothes then we will make you suffer."

Not wanting to push Stardust any further, Adam nodded and reached for the door handle. Stardust put a hand gently on his shoulder. "Hey Copa; before you change, do let me scratch your banana."

Back in the wake-up cubicle, Adam quickly changed into his Aloha clothes, supple and light as if for summer, but combat evolved to be as tough as hard leather. Ignoring his host's unsubtle advances, his banana had remained unscratched and unsniffed.

Heading along the tarmac path towards the steel canal bridge, a short walk taken many thousands of times before, Adam fell silent. The Psychoviro had changed little over the centuries, yet despite the years, it still evoked a sense of dread. Compared to his own environment – green meadows, cool riverside walks and gleaming apartment blocks – the concrete estate was an unrelentingly brutish fist in the face.

Up ahead, under the bridge, the narrow urban canal with its concrete sides, thin ledges, and dark water, did nothing to soften the landscape. Looming tower blocks, grey and utilitarian, now sported shiny steel balconies – added flair courtesy of Stardust – but still cast dark shadows over the snaking pathways and the slab-floored central square.

A place of pain and suffering, time had ensured that every surface of the Psychoviro had drunk the blood of the hunted, and, sometimes, the hunters. Adam

Eden was the constant guest star, the only person to defeat the glam gang single-handed. He could have stopped his involvement long ago, retiring to a life of eternal comfort and gradually diminishing celebrity, but continued the vicious ritual for two reasons. Firstly, as part of a deal where the psychopaths promised to fight volunteers rather than luring unsuspecting resurrected to their deaths. Secondly, was that Adam secretly enjoyed the killing, revelling in his ability to deploy deadly skill and dispense righteous justice.

Like a veteran rock group, the glam gang had changed its line-up a few times over the years. Stardust and Ziggy were the only original members, joined by relative newcomers, Ricochet, Jet, and Blitz.

Though Adam despised all of the psychopaths, he held a special hatred in his heart for Blitz. A secondary school maths teacher in his first-life, real name Trevor Wintock, Blitz was by all accounts mild mannered, orderly and law abiding. However, he stunned both colleagues and pupils when he fatally poisoned almost the entire arts staff. Trevor never gave a motive for his murderous actions, but a few weeks previously, the head of the arts department had engaged him in a staffroom discussion about the application of advanced mathematical graphing techniques in digital art. Out of his depth, Trevor looked a fool as the shallowness of his mathematical knowledge was laid bare.

For the past few months, Adam made it his goal to annoy Blitz. It was an easy task, playing on the psychopath's innate sense of superiority and self-delusion. Like many of the psychoviro residents, Blitz strolled around with a permanent condescending sneer.

Stardust had gone ahead to talk to Ziggy by the bridge. Grinning and drooling thuggishly, Ziggy, the mirror top-hatted psycho, and Stardust's loyal deputy, waved enthusiastically at Adam. Adam and Blitz waited uncomfortably and impatiently together. Blitz attempted to engage Adam in small talk:

"I suppose you don't really want to be here today?"

"That's true," Adam said, "but I'm under orders."

"One should always follow the rules. Without rules, there is no order. Nothing would make sense."

"Like mathematics, then."

"Just like mathematics."

Now was the time to pounce. Adam casually adjusted the collar of his Aloha shirt and cleared his throat.

"You know, my good friend Stern and I discussed a very interesting math's theory the other day. I thought you might be interested."

Blitz sniffed:

"Yet again you were discussing mathematics with your arse-smelling friend. I find that hard to believe, Copout. This is just another childish trick, isn't it? You have as much interest in mathematics as I do in your welfare."

"Ok, I understand, forget it; you're a bit rusty. It's been centuries since you've taught the subject, so it's no wonder you're a bit reluctant."

Turning to face Adam, Blitz took the bait.

"Is this secondary school level?" he asked. "I taught to secondary level remember."

"Yes it is. I swear to God." Adam crossed himself.

"Swearing to an imaginary being does not count."

"OK, cross my heart and hope to die!"

Blitz leaned forward, invading Adam's personal space with a cold stare:

"In a few hours, that's going to happen anyway." Blitz gently rocked back on his platforms. "So, what's this interesting theory?"

"The Hamiltonian Cycle," Adam replied nonchalantly. "See, I told you it wasn't anything difficult."

A light blush rose in Blitz's normally white skin, his cheeks pinking rapidly. "Ah yes, the Hamiltonian Cycle, that rings a bell. Yes, very interesting indeed."

"Then why don't you tell me about it," Adam asked.

"If you already know everything about the theory then it would be a waste of my time, and I most certainly don't want to waste my time on you."

"Aw, don't be like that. We've got an eternity here, so there's plenty of time to waste." Adam tugged an arm of turquoise sequins.

"Don't you dare touch me," Blitz growled, pulling his arm away. "I never taught that theory to my secondary school pupils. I'm sure it wasn't on the curriculum."

"So, you're saying you don't know about the Hamiltonian Cycle." Adam affected surprise. "You know, now that I think about it, it may have been primary school level."

"I …I …"

"No wonder your students failed their exams."

"They didn't …"

"They say there's always one bad teacher in every department."

Blitz's skin flushed way beyond a healthy rosy hue. "Of course I've heard about the Hamilton Cycle!"

"Hamiltonian," Adam coolly corrected.

Blitz's anger grew, the colour of his skin blending in with the lightning flashes on his face and the vivid red of his hair. His face, fit to burst, took on the appearance of a demented killer tomato sitting atop the most glittering blue green vine. Even as his stress levels peaked, Blitz always held himself back; ever observant of the viro rules, he never lashed out. With a hurt squeak, he slipped into victim mode and ran over to his leader.

"Please Stardust, can I be excused for a moment?" he sulked, pointing to Adam. "Copout's insulting me again. I really want to hurt him right now, but … the rules."

"Course you can go," Stardust replied. "Take more than a moment. I need to talk to Copa alone."

Blitz disappeared behind one of the drab grey amenity buildings, perhaps to cry.

"Come, Copa, walk with me," Stardust said. They slowly walked towards the bridge. "Now, what do you want from me? I am surprised John Down didn't come here himself."

"Just as well he didn't, considering your attitude to unscheduled visits."

"But he doesn't mind you getting killed?"

"Seriously, John knows about our 'special relationship' and thought I might persuade you."

"Couldn't this have waited until our usual meeting – last Friday of the month?"

"No; although I really, really wish it could. Apparently, whatever's happening is happening soon."

"You mean you don't know what's going on?"

"John either didn't know or wouldn't say. I only know that the Captain requires our services. I just need you to agree to help when the time comes."

They reached the middle of the bridge, and Stardust suggested they sit on the low steel railing.

"Does the job involve leaving the viro?" Stardust asked, sitting down on the cold metal.

"Yes." Adam shuffled slightly along the railing, making sure there was adequate distance between himself and his unwholesome host.

"If we die out there, then will we be resurrected?"

"You know, I hadn't thought of that. Truthfully, Stardust, I can't say. However, we need one other gang member."

"Oh, I'll take Ziggy."

Adam shook his head:

"The Captain gave specific instructions not to choose Ziggy. He's not right for this job. No disrespect, but he wants someone with more … mental capacity."

"Fair enough. Hmm, then I choose Blitz. I dislike the man as much as you do, but he is intelligent and very capable."

"I just knew you'd choose that bugger," Adam groaned, wishing Stardust had instead chosen Ricochet or Jet.

Slouching silently against a dispenser at the far side of the bridge, avoiding eye contact, Ricochet wore a weather-beaten suede cowboy hat, embroidered beige jacket and well-worn jeans. At first glance, the clothing seemed more hippy than glam, but a vivid red bandana around his hat, silver tassels hanging from the jacket arms, and the ubiquitous silver platform boots provided ample sparkle.

In combat, Ricochet favoured a black leather slingshot with half-inch stainless steel balls as ammunition. Two centuries of training and a quietly ruthless attitude made Ricochet the most formidable long-range huntsman Adam had yet encountered, easily surpassing Rhapsody's mastery with a bow. With a hard stare and a sudden whip of leather, the soft-suede slingster brought his deadly brand of pinball wizardry to the fray.

A few feet from Ricochet, sitting awkwardly on the bridge railing, hands pressed hard on the cold steel, Jet kept her head down. A black patent leather jumpsuit, low-zipped and glossy, with matching platform boots gave her a rock-chick persona – strengthening the image, a silver bandana kept her jet black hair under control, and a chrome guitar pendant hung over her cleavage. Pouting her glossy red lips, she muttered quiet profanities, a Tourette's style symptom of her deep psychosis.

Encountering Jet on the hunt was always a sensually close experience. Slinking silently in for the kill, the first and sometimes only warning was her warm breath on your skin. For Adam, the experience might have been pleasurable, except for the two intentionally blunt daggers Jet so ably employed. Her blade-work was intricate and precise, targeting particular nerves, veins, and arteries; she dubbed it 'sub-dermis detailing'. The calm intimacy of Jet's attack meant she often died in the process, usually the victim of a last gasp counterattack. She seemed strangely relaxed about the risk, as if dying in an enemy's warm embrace made her passing less brutal and somehow darkly romantic.

"It will good to get out for a while," Stardust said. "Much as this place has grown on me, it is still a prison, not a home; and a prison is still a prison, even after a thousand years. I spent the last fifty years of my first-life in a cell, so I know what I'm talking about. You see, this is just …"

"Please, please don't say gilded cage, Stardust. You don't know how many times I've heard you say that line over the years. Anyway, what I really wanted to ask was whether you could break the rules just this once. I'll stay in the wake-up cubicle for the day and you lot can enjoy your day off."

"We need our rules," Stardust said. "Without our rules and rituals, this place would quickly descend into chaos. We had a bloodbath a few centuries ago just because I added some quality wines to the picnic menu."

"Yeah, I was there remember. That was all out civil war – over half the viro killed or mortally wounded in a battle over Liebfraumilch versus Chablis. I backed you all the way with the Chablis, even though I prefer a cold beer."

"It took months before things completely settled down."

"OK, but I really, really didn't want to fight today."

Stardust thought for a moment, gently stroking his chin with his gloved hand:

"There is one rule I can bend, given the circumstances. How about we make the hunt a one on one? Five against one will be over all too soon. Just remember that with a one on one I won't allow hiding for anything more than a few minutes, or a long drawn out chase. Sneak around if you must, but we want to see a fight."

"Well, I would prefer *none* on one, but that sounds better than facing the whole gang. I guess it's me against Blitz."

"He's the best swordsman the Psychoviro's ever produced," Stardust said. "He's a true artist with the cutlass. You know, sometimes he reminds me of dear old Rampage."

"I've always rated your rapier work as superior to anything I've seen from Blitz."

"Oh, you flatter me," Stardust sighed, shuffling over and resting his wig swathed head on Adam's shoulder. "I do take a certain pride in my thrusting abilities."

Suddenly, Ziggy's guttural voice cried out:

"You … come back! Not allowed … on bridge!"

Both Adam and Stardust looked up as a short man, sweaty, with an angry stare, positioned himself impudently in front of them. Ziggy lumbered up to apprehend the intruder, but Stardust ordered him to stay back a few feet, hoping not to create a scene.

Wearing a white apron, and sporting an immaculately starched chef's hat, the thin faced individual addressed Adam in a breathy yet high pitched voice:

"Will you be enjoying the buffet today, Mr Copacabana?"

"Most definitely," Adam replied warily.

"And, will you be eating the prawn cocktail vol-au-vents or perhaps the chicken and mushroom? We use the flakiest of pastry."

"To be honest, I'll probably have both. I can't get enough of them."

"So, no sandwiches for you … again." The man's voice took on a darker, yet still disturbingly high pitched, tone. "I haven't seen you touch a sandwich in many months. Do they not please you?""

"I like sandwiches, but I find them a bit heavy," Adam said honestly, patting his stomach. "Mustn't be too full for the hunt."

"Mr Copacabana, I only use the lightest of loaves. 'Nothing but Nimble' is my motto when it comes to bread. I know you like egg and cress. There was a time, last year, when I stood close to you as you ate one. I studied you. I watched as you took every bite, every chew, and I could see the approval in your face. This morning, I'm making some egg and cress just for you."

Adam never humoured the locals. They were all unrepentant psychopaths: a vile collection of murderers, rapists, and assorted sadists.

"Think I'll stick to the vol-au-vents," Adam grinned. "Somehow, they seem so superior to plain old sandwiches. Anyway, I don't want eggy breath."

"Do you realise how many slices of bread I butter every fight day?" the man shouted. "Do you realise or appreciate the skill that it takes to spread the butter without tearing the bread or the precision necessary to remove the crusts and cut the sandwiches into perfect triangles?" He gritted his large teeth and narrowed his eyes. "Do you even know my name?"

Adam, still grinning, shook his head. Stardust raised his hand in light protest:

"Back off, Mutilator; I've had enough of this. Copa's our guest today and you will treat him with respect."

Mutilator thrust his hand forward, and aggressively waved a butter knife in front of Adam.

"What about my respect?" he shrieked.

Eyes wide, Ziggy pointed at the fast developing situation:

"Look out! Mutilator's got … a butter knife! Butter knife!"

"Watch me spread Copa's jam!" Mutilator screamed, raising his arm for a fatal slice.

Instinctively, Stardust threw himself sideways, out of danger, whilst Adam futilely shielded his face with his hands.

A silver gloved hand suddenly gripped Mutilator's hair from behind, viciously pulling his head back. Glittering turquoise and a flash of cold steel slipped smoothly across the sandwich maker's neck. Immediately, a wash of blood burst forth from a wide gash, covering Adam in a warm crimson glaze. Mutilator gurgled sickeningly, blood spluttering from his gaping mouth as Blitz heaved the dying butterer over the bridge railing.

As the body hit the water, Stardust picked himself off the ground. Adam wiped a sticky slick of blood from his face:

"Why the Hell didn't you let Ziggy grab that psycho?"

"I am so sorry, Copa. I just wanted to avoid an incident."

"Well, good call, Stardust," Adam said with sarcastic scorn, holding up his bloodied hands. "Why would someone called Mutilator be a cause for concern? I mean, are there any more disgruntled chefs out there? I haven't eaten the sherry trifle for a few years; should I watch out for an attack with a large spoon?"

Stardust stood up and helped Adam to his feet:

"I can only apologise once more, Copa." He turned his attention to Blitz. "Couldn't you have just restrained Mutilator? He's such a puny fellow."

"He had a knife," Blitz replied coldly. "That was Mutilator's weapon of choice in his first life. The rule, your rule, states that guests are not to be harmed before the hunt, unless absolutely necessary."

"Then, I guess I owe you my thanks," Adam said, blinking his eyes as Mutilator's blood dripped from his forehead.

"I guess you do," Blitz said. "And, I look forward to killing you later. I won't let anyone deprive me of that pleasure."

Stardust slapped Blitz on the arm:

"Then I have two pieces of news for you, Blitz. Firstly, today's hunt is one on one; you against Copa." Stardust paused and called over to Ricochet. "Hey, Ricochet, take Copa back to the wake-up cubicles. Make sure he gets cleaned up and get him a change of clothes. Then, I want you and Jet to keep him under close guard until the hunt. I don't want anymore 'incidents'."

Dutifully, the two gang members escorted Adam to the cubicle block.

"What was the other piece of news?" Blitz asked eagerly.

"Since you are so talented with a blade, you can finish making the sandwiches."

NEVER TRUST A PSYCHOPATH

Firmly gripping the leather hilt of his machete – his ever faithful ally in this dark den of psychopaths – Adam took steady breaths as five hundred maniacs shouted out the ten second countdown from the tower block balconies. Waiting silently at the edge of the central square by the canal bridge, Adam refused to look at Blitz, who stood by his side. Silver gloves casually on turquoise glitter hips, Blitz stared and grinned with smug disrespect at the legendary fighter in the pink hibiscus shirt.

Atop a large chrome plated dais furnished with orange globe swivel chairs, Stardust stood resplendent in black glitter with a cape of lustrous red faux fur. Balancing skilfully on the tallest of platform boots – a psychoviro tradition – he carried a glossy black sceptre in one hand and a matching megaphone in the other. One step down from his flamboyant leader, Ziggy sat slouched, burping a simple tune whilst fastidiously scratching his groin. On the lowest level, Jet and Ricochet struck dynamic poses, pointing and gesturing like minor Gods.

The countdown reached one and Stardust waved his sceptre in the air. He raised the microphone to his lips:

"Five minute head start, Copacabana! G ... G ... Get it on!"

The towers immediately erupted into loud roars and cheers as Adam thrust his machete high above his head and walked coolly onto the bridge.

On cue, sounds of a loud scream and explosion burst from the huge loudspeakers on the tower roofs, followed by a fast stomping glam beat. *Hellraiser* by The Sweet was a psychoviro staple to start the proceedings, and Adam began walking rhythmically to the familiar tune.

During the five minute head start he usually hurried away from the square. The warren of alleys between the utility buildings or the hedgerows and woodland on the northern boundary were the usual destinations, but today he believed that fortune favoured the brave. One-on-one gave him the chance to publicly humiliate Blitz.

Stopping in the centre of the bridge, Adam turned to face his insane adversary and started dancing to the music – a well-practised energetic routine combining early breakdancing, glam stomp, and aggrotech punching and kicking. In their towers, the psychos sang along to the tunes, and even Stardust and his deputies stood stamping their feet to the beat and punching their arms in the air – apart from Ziggy who sat trying to control a stream of burp induced hiccups.

Adam's moves brought him closer and closer to Blitz, who stood like a statue, refusing to be phased by the goading aggression. As they passed the three minute mark, Adam slowed his gyrations. Though he wanted to unnerve his easily infuriated opponent, he did not want to wear himself out for the fight. Somewhere in his mind, in a niche held for extremely unlikely hopes and dreams, Adam liked to believe that Blitz's sandwich making session had impaired his abilities with a blade. Perhaps, in a world dictated by such positive self-delusion, Adam might face limp buttering swipes rather than the deadly slashes and stabs of the Psychoviro's greatest swordsman.

With thirty seconds to go, Adam stopped dancing and slowly backed off towards the centre of the bridge. He slashed his machete threateningly at Blitz, who remained immobile, but whose red faced betrayed the fury building inside.

Once more, Stardust lifted the megaphone:

"Times up, Copacabana! Blitz, make us proud!"

Finally off the leash, Blitz howled like a tortured wolf and rushed towards his prey, his cutlass raised for attack. Adam stood in a defensive stance, side-faced, machete held forward. Inside, he congratulated himself for successfully enraging his opponent. Angry and unbalanced, Blitz would lack precision and coherence, leading to inevitable mistakes.

"Fuck you to Hell, Copout!" Blitz shouted as he tore across the bridge.

In the final second, Adam braced himself and adjusted the angle of his machete to block the coming strike. Even as he completed the manoeuvre, he realised he had been fooled. In a stunning display of timing and physical ability, Blitz slammed down his leading boot, using his powerful momentum to pivot on the tough silver toe.

Adam had a fraction of a second to react as Blitz spun around to his defenceless side, the sharp blade of the cutlass scything towards his head. Managing a half-step back, Adam narrowly avoided a fatal cleaving, though the blade still made contact, grazing from cheek to cheek, and slicing through the bridge of his nose.

Blitz immediately followed up with a swift shoulder chop. Adam, still staggering backwards, blood welling up from his facial wound, awkwardly deflected the blow with his machete. Desperately looking for a way out, he regretted taking the direct approach. Stealth and sudden in-and-out attacks were his preferred and usual method of combat.

Keeping up the pressure, thrusting and sweeping, Blitz grinned ecstatically:

"What were you thinking facing me like this?" he seethed through gritted teeth. "Hoping the buttering had dulled my swordplay, eh? Well, the only dull thing around here … is you!"

Adam, taking a chance, dropped his defence and lunged wildly at his glittering green tormenter. The sharp edge of his machete sliced deep into Blitz's hip. The psycho cried out in pain and whacked his assailant in the side of the head with the ornate hilt of his cutlass. Stunned by the sudden impact, Adam reeled sideways, his legs knocking against the low bridge railing. Breaking one of the original and most respected rules of the Psychoviro Hunt, Blitz delivered a powerful steel toe kick to Adam's genitals, painfully forcing one of his testicles up into the groin – 'nothing below the belt' went the well-worn mantra but with the psychopaths' bloodlust fully aroused, no-one would stop the fight on a technicality.

As a cacophony of booing resounded around the urban core, Blitz slashed open Adam's left leg, sending him tumbling backwards over the railing. Falling towards the dark water of the canal, he threw out a desperate hand, and managed to grab the lip of a steel bridge girder. He held on to the cold metal, grip tenuous, his wrist wrenched hard.

Fearing he might lose his hold, Adam carefully clipped the machete to his belt and slowly reached for one of the inner struts. Pulling himself across, Adam hung onto the strut with two hands. He licked his lips, tasting the blood dripping down from his nose. For a moment, he gently swung back and forth, testing his wrist for injury. Once certain there was not a problem, Adam began a slow monkey swing from strut to strut. With luck, Blitz would head for the wrong end of the bridge, giving Adam time to climb back up and disappear into the alleys.

Taking Adam by surprise, Blitz climbed down from the bridge wall about twenty feet ahead. Crawling, Blitz hurried along the outer girder, cutlass in hand, a harsh scraping of steel on steel. As the red headed menace shuffled nearer, Adam tightly gripped the cross-strut with one hand, whilst unclipping his machete with the other – one easy action via a well-placed popper and a swift flick of the thumb.

"You need good strength to weight ratio if want to fight like this," Blitz said, moving over to a cross-strut. He hung for a moment, and then leaned backwards, raising his legs high until they touched the underside of the bridge. "I'm the only one who can do that, and I'm carrying a cutlass. Meet the King of the Swingers!"

Adam tried to appear nonchalant, but he doubted he had the strength to hang on much longer:

"Well swing over and fight, you overdressed clown!"

Blitz slowly swung towards Adam, careful not to drop his cutlass, which the cup enclosed hilt allowed him to keep in his hand. As soon as the psycho was in range, Adam lashed out with his machete, hoping to gain an early victory. Blitz laughed, swinging back out of harm's way, before swinging back with a forceful swipe of his sword. The blade struck the side of Adam's Aloha shirt slightly off angle, only lightly scuffing the materiel.

"Damn your body armour!" Blitz seethed. "That should have easily cut through! Bloody cheat!" He swung away from another attack.

Adam's 'evolved' clothing often made the difference between life and death or, at the very least, agonising wounds. Every week, for the first two years of fighting – now almost a millennium ago – his clothing strengthened yet remained lightweight. Now, it had the look of flimsy cotton, but the strength of medium leather. A pointed stab might easily penetrate the material, but a swiping blow with a blade often had little effect. Realising it made for a better hunt, Stardust allowed Adam to wear his Aloha ensemble much to consternation of the other gang members.

Exchanging blow after blow, each expertly parried, both men felt the pain growing in their hands as they hung grimly onto the steel struts. To ease his discomfort, Blitz showed off his superior 'monkeyness' by switching his cutlass to the other hand. As he deftly enacted the motion, Adam mustered all his strength for a last ditch attack. Swaying forward, he thrust the point of his machete at Blitz's face, only for overwhelming fatigue to cause him to lose the weapon. It flew out of his weakened grip and sailed passed Blitz's head, nicking his ear. Though an insignificant wound, it proved effectively unsettling. With a demoralised groan Blitz let go of the strut and plummeted into the canal below. For a fleeting moment, the sight of turquoise glitter and long red hair sinking into the murky depths put Adam in mind of Ariel the fairy-tale mermaid. The spell was broken a couple of seconds later as Blitz resurfaced, spitting, spluttering, and swearing, thrashing his cutlass wildly in the water.

Wasting no more time, and ignoring the pain, Adam heaved himself onto the outside girder and crawled towards the canal wall. Every shuffle left a thin smear of blood on the girder from the gash in his leg, like a snail leaving its sticky trail across a window sill.

Reaching the grey concrete canal wall, Adam climbed the side ladder. Once at the top he stumbled over the low railing and limped into the central square. He wanted a weapon and hoped the cold hearted psychopaths on the platform might provide one.

As Adam approached the chrome dais, blood soaking his lower face and left leg, Stardust and his deputies stood up, menacingly wielding their weapons.

"Copa, what do you want?" Stardust demanded. "If you're wise you'll keep your distance!"

Respectfully, Adam stopped some feet away from the dais:

"For God's sake, Stardust, lend me your sword!" he pleaded, peering anxiously over to the bridge.

"Away with you!" Stardust scoffed with a dismissive wave of his gloved hand. "You still have your knife; use that!"

"A combat knife against a cutlass? I'm good with a knife, but I thought you wanted some real entertainment."

Tight in her squeaking glossy black leather, Jet leaned forward provocatively and spun her black daggers in her hands:

"Mmm, is the pink baby scared?" she said softly. "I only use knives … *shit* … and you never hear me complaining … *fuck*. Are you compensating for … *bollocks* … *shit* … something?"

What about you Ziggy?" Adam asked desperately, ignoring Jet's insults and involuntary profanity. "Surely you'll let me use your cricket bat?"

"No-one use … my bat!" Ziggy snarled, brandishing the infamous willow wood. "Maybe … I use it … on your head!

A surround sound of expletives and boos came from the towers, the balconies heaving with vilely gesticulating figures. Adam held up his hands, urging the maniacs to swivel on his middle fingers.

"You are going to suffer for making me swim!" Blitz yelled, climbing over the bridge railing. "I'm going to teach your body all about long division!" His shock of red hair a dark sopping mop, turquoise glitter suit weighed down with water, the failed maths teacher turned psychopathic sword master suddenly loped across the square to finish the fight.

Adam insolently pointed a finger at Stardust and his deputies:

"You are nothing but a bunch of motherfucking bastards!" He clicked open his Benchmark combat knife and hobbled towards the warehouses. Stardust held up his megaphone:

"What went on between me and my mother is none of your bloody business!"

A few metres into the alley that lay between the two huge warehouses, Adam stopped by a sturdy iron downpipe. Grimacing in pain, he squeezed his leg wound, covering his hand in blood. Hastily, he wiped his dripping hand over the downpipe, reaching as high as possible, making sure to lightly stain the wall either side for effect. Adam wished that for once, just once, the arrogant psychopath would prove as stupid as he liked to believe, thinking Adam had climbed up the pipe and onto the flat warehouse roof. Stifling moans as he scaled a large stack of wooden crates next to the downpipe, Adam spread more blood higher up. Once satisfied he could do no more, he lay face down on the crates, and silently waited for his quick tempered adversary.

The soft sound of footsteps alerted Adam that Blitz was close-by.

"Why make this so difficult, Copout!" Blitz shouted. "You are going to lose anyway so we may as well get this over with!"

Adam gripped his combat knife, cleared his mind of unnecessary emotion, and carefully controlled his breathing. The sudden unexpected strike was his speciality, and a stone cold demeanour was essential.

Blitz began chuckling and clanged his cutlass against the downpipe:

"So, you're up on the roof again! Could you be more predicable? You know you can't win in a face to face showdown, so it's your funeral!"

Adam listened intently, and heard the faint sound of metal scraping against metal. Knife held firmly in a downward grip, Adam raised himself and leapt from the stack of crates.

As Adam carried out the desperate leap, he realised once again that Blitz had fooled him. From a low defensive stance, Blitz brought his cutlass round in a wide arc, maximizing the force and catching Adam in mid-flight. The savage impact sent Adam slamming to the ground – the blade cutting through the side of his Aloha shirt and slicing open the flesh beneath.

For a few seconds, Adam lay on his back, waiting for Blitz to administer the final blow.

"Well, Copout, it seems true talent wins out again," Blitz said, leaning casually against the stack of crates. "If you had really climbed onto the roof, then the audience would have started cheering." He swiped his bloody cutlass contemptuously through the air. "Look, if you promise to behave, I'll make this quick. Oh, and by the way, of course I knew about the Hamiltonian Cycle. I was just teasing you earlier, and you fell for it." Blitz laughed uneasily, failing to cover his lies.

"Prove it then," Adam croaked, agonisingly lifting himself into a kneeling position. "Tell me the damn theory and I won't put up a fight."

Lowering his cutlass, Blitz began in a tediously measured drone, "The Hamiltonian Cycle, also known as The Hamiltonian Circuit, is a graph cycle that …"

Adam whipped his hand forward, releasing the knife he had held hidden behind his back. The blade remained true to the intent, wedging itself tightly into one of Blitz's eye sockets and some way into the brain.

Blitz whined dementedly, wobbling on his high platforms, tugging at the stuck blade as the blood poured down his cheek. Taking advantage of the situation, Adam leapt to his feet and snatched the cutlass from Blitz's other hand. Unexpectedly, the move brought the glittering psycho crashing face down onto the hard concrete path. With a sickening splinter and squelch, the impact drove the knife deep into Blitz's skull.

The expanding puddle of blood around Blitz's head was obvious proof of death. Adam was in too much pain to offer a witty remark – or even the most hackneyed pun. Dropping the cutlass, he limped slowly to the square. Weak from loss of blood, Adam held a hand over the fresh wound in his side and used the grey warehouse wall for support.

Eerily quiet, the psychos stared from their balconies, all eyes fixed on the legendary Copacabana as he emerged from the warehouse alley. The expected cheering or, at the very least, satisfied applause, was absent, replaced by quiet muttering.

Adam stood defiantly at the edge of the square, struggling to appear unphased by the unusual reaction. Stardust and Ziggy sat on their trendy orange globe chairs, neither one making a sound. Raising both arms, Adam addressed his audience with as much strength as he could muster.

"Not for the first time, the great and mighty Copacabana has earned the right to sit at your illustrious table! I have come to your ship of fools and defeated your champion. Today I shall feast on a prawn cocktail starter and a main course of Steak Diane – the dish of the huntress! I demand the finest buttered Jersey Royals and my filet mignon perfectly red and bloody" Receiving only silence from the high towers, Adam noticed too late that Jet and Ricochet were absent from the dais.

A faint whooshing of air and a steel ball ploughed through Adam's left cheek, cracking the top off a molar before settling on his tongue. Blood rose quickly from the wound and Adam stumbled sideways, letting the ball fall from his mouth. Hoping to avoid another strike, Adam turned towards the alley, only for another ball to ricochet off some nearby pipework straight into the same gory cheek-hole. The cold hard projectile lodged in the back of his throat, but mercifully without enough energy to cause further damage.

From his vantage point on one of the warehouse roofs, Ricochet thrust an arm majestically in the air, waving his leather slingshot like a flag of victory.

"Ric … O… chet! Two in one; suck on my balls, Copa!"

Choking up and spitting out the second ball, along with a phlegmy hawk of blood, Adam stumbled backwards. He winced as he held his hand over the wet hole in his cheek.

A gentle 'mmm' from behind, and an arm snaked around his chest. Before Adam could react, something thrust deep into his armpit, followed by sharp pain. Through the agony, almost paralysing in intensity, he heard Jet's quiet expletive-laced words.

"Copa, *shit* … *shit*, there's no point in struggling. I'm rough-housing the brachial plexus; mess of fucking nerves. You may not remember, but we've been here before, and you … *cocks* … lose every time. Mmm, the pain is excruciating, isn't it, and this arm is out of play."

"What's going on?" Adam choked with short wheezing breaths. "This was … one on one!"

"Well, we're one on one now, aren't we, my love? Can't you … *fuck* … feel me?" Jet breathed softly on Adam's neck, and pressed up close behind him. "Life's a bitch and shortly yours will end."

Adam tensed and nearly vomited as Jet pushed her other blade into his lower back, twisting it hard between two vertebras, cracking them apart like an oyster shell. Quickly, she dragged the point of the blade across the exposed spinal cord, and lowered a shrieking Adam face down onto the ground. Blind with pain, Adam could do nothing as Jet withdrew the blade from his back and promptly shoved it into his other armpit for another brachial roughhousing. Her work completed, she wiped the blades clean on Adam's trousers, and then casually slipped them back into her belt sheaths.

Jet rolled Adam onto his back, intensifying the pain for a few seconds, before offering her prognosis. "At this point your wounds are not fatal. Your legs are paralysed and your arms are totally fucked up. You still have control of your head and torso, *shit … shit … shit*, so feel free to wiggle about and pull faces. Scream if you must, but that will not help." Cruelly emphasising the point, she poked a finger into the bloody hole in Adam's cheek and scraped her gloss-black fingernail over the raw nerve of the cracked molar.

Jet stood up and stepped back, her eyes never leaving Adam – like a surgeon taking pride in their work or a satisfied lover drawing away after sex. Through increasingly blurred vision, Adam watched helplessly as Stardust loomed into view.

Standing tall over his prey, slender rapier already drawn, Stardust was obviously here to deal the killer blow.

"What the hell is this?" Adam croaked, coughing a sputter of blood through his cheek-hole. "You broke the rules … your rules."

As if in shame, Stardust bowed his head.

"Oh Copa, I am sooo sorry for lying to you. You won fair and square, but I just couldn't let you live. You see, I had this arrangement with …."

Perhaps mindful of giving too much away, or his psychopathic associates sensing weakness, Stardust hardened his tone.

"No… no, I do not need to explain myself to you! I am not sorry at all! I am leader of this environment, and I do not answer or apologise to anyone!"

Gesturing for all to fall silent, Stardust raised his rapier and kissed the flat of the blade

"Copacabana, with a single thrust of my trusty steel, I commit you to the darkest night." Eyes brimming, the over-sentimental leader of the psychoviro almost shed a tear as he plunged the point of his rapier into Adam's heart.

Death followed – yet another never remembered journey into the resurrection void.

Coldest Mountain

Back to life, as expected, Adam woke up clean and refreshed. Sitting up, he flung out his arms … 'smack'! He yelped in pain as his right hand struck against a hard wall next to the bed. Taking better notice of his surroundings, he looked about the room, quickly realising that this drab bunk was not his usual sumptuously comfortable king-size bed, and that this was definitely not his own bedroom. Though the room seemed vaguely familiar – starkly functional, no-frills concrete and steel – the distant memory remained stubbornly elusive. The rules of resurrection guaranteed that Adam would wake up in his own viro, so this utilitarian space was unexpected and disturbing.

Adam got out of bed and rummaged through a thick pile of clothes placed on a trestle table near the basic white ceramic sink. The clothes – all thermals, including a lightweight arctic-grade parka coat – were giveaway clues to his present location. Mindful of the temperature that might lie outside, Adam put on some socks, threw the parka around his naked body, and slowly opened the wake-up room door.

Howling wind accompanied by a raft of icy sleet was evidence that he high up in the Sonador mountain range; the secret interface between the Viroverse and the outside world. Adam closed the door, shutting out the biting cold.

Without bothering to eat breakfast, he put on the clothes and took a few deep breaths to steady his nerves. Before braving the treacherous mountain ledge, with its sheer drop of hundreds of feet, Adam attempted to obtain a flask of whisky from the room's dispenser. Despite a number of attempts, he remained alcohol free. Either this dispenser was different from those in the rest of the Viroverse or someone wanted him sober. The deep breathing would have to suffice.

The clothes blocked out the worst of the weather, but the chill wind dried Adam's throat and hurt his squinting eyes. With short steamy breaths, he looked for a welcoming committee.

"Adam, over here!" a voice called out over the noise of the wind. "Over here, by the vehicle!"

Through the relentless sheets of sleet and snow, Adam noticed a figure standing at the far end of the wake-up block, next to a small tracked ATV.

"Is that you, John?" he called out. "What in Satan's name is this? I should be in my nice warm apartment!"

John Down, snug in furs like an early Antarctic explorer – but with his signature silver topped cane – waved, and marched over to greet Adam. Unaccustomed to the conditions, he paid little attention to the icy rutted road and caught his cane in a snow filled crack. The ebony shaft snapped clean in half. Without its support, the heavy clothing unbalanced the startled Victorian, and he began an ungainly slide towards the edge of the ledge.

"Oh Lord, please help me!" he wailed in terror, slipping towards the precipitous drop.

With little regard for his own safety, Adam rushed forward in a chaotic skipping skidding motion. John shouted out a stream of unintelligible sounds as he tipped over the edge – perhaps speaking in tongues on the verge of meeting one's maker, or more probably just fearful gibberish.

Lunging after his friend, in true action-hero style, Adam one-handedly caught hold of John's wrist – the other clung on to a small rocky protrusion. John hung twisting in the whipping wind, the green valley far below obscured by the weather.

"Argh, my sodding arm!" Adam screamed, as he felt the weight almost pull the straining limb out of its socket. "Take your bloody coat off!"

Normally, Adam's language would have provoked a sharp rebuke, or at least an offended sniff, but John obeyed without question. A few seconds of gritted teeth, painfully stretched joints, and frantic finger action, the heavy fur coat fell free, fading from view as it swirled and spiralled down as if a helpless bear sucked into a violent whirlpool.

Without the coat, Adam found the weight manageable, and breathed a sigh of relief. Then, casting a wry grin, he decided to let his helpless comrade dangle.

"You know," he said, "if this was a movie, I would pump you for information in return for not letting you drop."

"Just pull me up, Adam! A sudden squall and we're gone!"

"However," Adam continued, "I seem to remember that after getting the information, you still let the poor bugger plummet to their death. Hmm, then I have to come up with some witty remark."

Adam chuckled, and heaved John up onto the ledge. They both carefully crawled away from the edge.

"Lucky for you, the dispenser was all out of drink, so I'm sober and all out of witty remarks."

They sat against the wall of a wake-up cubicle, catching their breath and silently contemplating their close brush with death. Adam stood first and helped John to his feet – a noticeable quiver of fear remained in the Victorian's well-insulated legs. Not wishing to hurt a friend's pride, Adam said that four legs were better than two, and put a supportive arm around John's waist. Slowly, cautiously, they made their way to the ATV.

"Is there resurrection in this place?" John asked, shakily. "I may be a religious man, but I don't want to die just yet?"

"I have no idea," Adam replied. "I've been here before, a few times, but I never thought to ask the Captain. The weather up here has never been this bad." Adam paused and pointed to the snow-capped mountain peak. "From up there, you can see the city of Sonador on the other side. The Sonadorians think these mountains are just viro wall projections, thanks to a transparent wall between here and the city. We could climb up and take a look if you want."

Both men spent a few seconds weighing their chances of survival in the raging ice storm of the peak. They shook their heads and continued on to the ATV.

"I'm driving," Adam said, ignoring John's protestations. "I know my behaviour by the river has given you doubts, but I am stone cold sober. You may be a demon in those Terminal airport carts, but I have spent the past few decades nipping around the viro on my tracked chair. Drunk or sober, I've never had an accident – not even a squashed pinkie."

Safe inside the warm compact vehicle, Adam and John relaxed – the noise of the storm outside seemed as quiet as a household fan. The only reminder of the raging elemental power was the occasional strong gust, which gently rocked the cabin on its stubbornly steady tracks.

Running on fuel cells, the vehicle made unhurried silent progress down the winding mountain road. Adam drove slowly. Safety was a motivation, but he also wanted answers.

"First things first," Adam began. "How are Mary and your sons?"

"They are well, thank you. My sons, Percival and Reginald, took first place again in the annual pedalo race, and my daughter Lillian won a silver trophy for her beautiful rendition of 'Abide with Me'."

"What about you and Mary; did you win anything?"

"Mary and I provide medical aid at these events. I always say we should win a gold medal for our efforts."

"So you should, so you should," Adam agreed, nodding, and then raised his voice. "And, you should also tell me what the bloody hell I'm doing here!" Adam swerved the ATV from left to right on the narrow road, purposefully veering close to the edge.

John jumped in his seat at the sharp change of mood. He flustered and hesitated before offering a coherent reply.

"The Captain did not tell me why we need to travel outside the Viroverse. I have honestly never been here before. After leaving you the other day, I surfed here as fast as my short board allowed with only a two-man security escort. The doors to this particular viro were always barred before, but this time they responded to my palm. For centuries, my colleagues and I have wondered what lay inside. I got here late last night and slept in the end cubicle. You obviously know the rest."

"Do I?" Adam said angrily. "You floated here on a surfboard with your Terminal buddies. No doubt you stopped off on the way for a rest and a light lunch in some delightful Italianate viro."

"Actually, I had a rather heavy pasta dish. A smidgeon too much cream if you …"

I got killed in the Psychoviro!" Adam shouted. "I even remember Ricochet putting a ruddy great hole in cheek and knocking my teeth out. Thank fucking Christ I have no memory of what happened next, because those evil bastards play hard."

"Please do not take the Lord's name in vain, Adam. I … I apologise for what you went through, but I promise it was necessary."

"Then you better tell me why, or I'm going to blaspheme so hard that I guarantee we'll turn into salt by the time we get down this mountain!"

"The truth is that it was the only way to get you here safely. I told you about the danger in the halls, and the Captain believes you are too important to lose."

"Hmm, that sounds reasonable," Adam agreed, pride temporarily trumping anger. "So, what's so dangerous out there that I couldn't travel with you?"

"Spanish conquistadors," John said, his hatred unmistakeable.

"Conquistadors?"

"More specifically, those loyal to Hernán Cortés."

"Hah, I remember doing a project on him at school. He's the one who crushed the Aztecs."

"The same. Specifically, they are Rodeleros, armed with sword and buckler. When they first broke free from their viros, some 100 years ago, we were unprepared for their skill and ferocity. Nobody in the Terminal organisation had familiarity with martial arts involving sword and shield. Only our knowledge of the halls, and our ability to reinforce quickly via surfboard, saved us."

"You should have recruited the Psychoviro populations. They would have relished the fight."

"The thought did cross my mind on a few occasions," John admitted, "especially when our backs were to the wall. However, in truth, we had enough lunatics on the loose."

The ATV bumped over a particularly rutted patch of road. Both men fell silent, clenching their teeth, but Adam maintained skilful control of the vehicle. Green grass up ahead signalled that their mountain ordeal was near its end. Another half-mile and they would reach the safety of the smooth, wide, valley road.

"So, have you caught Cortés?" Adam asked.

"Hernán Cortés is not a resident of the Viroverse. There is no record of his resurrection. His involvement is a mystery. The Rodeleros often cry out his name in battle, and swear they are following his orders, but there is no evidence that he exists – at least in this mortal realm."

"But, you say you have the situation under control."

"We recruited a number of Khevsurian warriors and Italian sword and buckler masters, and all Terminal operatives have undergone intensive weapons retraining. Whenever the devils reappear, we engage them in numbers, backed up by tranquilising crossbows. Then, we erase any memory of the portals or the halls and return them back to their viros."

"But, they keep coming back."

"We do not know how they keep finding the portals or how they obtain the shards necessary to open them."

"Maybe you should constantly monitor their viros directly," Adam suggested. "Find out what is going on."

John shook his head:

"Sadly, that is against Viroverse rules. An operative might visit one of their viros for the day, listening for idle gossip, but any permanent surveillance is prohibited. The AI will not allow such an invasion of privacy, despite the obvious benefits."

"Sounds like you're fighting with an arm tied behind your back."

"As you know, there is no resurrection in the halls. Over the years, I have lost so many colleagues; so may good friends. They will never return." John sighed and wiped away a tear. "Why the system protects such murderous criminals is beyond me."

"Same as it ever was," Adam muttered, and turned the ATV onto the valley road. "But, did I really have to die in the Psychoviro first? Couldn't I have just woken up here?"

"There are only a few locations where the Captain exerts some control. The Terminal and the psychoviros are such places. As far as I am aware, there are no links between this place and the normal viros. You had to die in the Psychoviro to wake up here. To save you the pain, you could have been signed up as a client of the Terminal, and woken up in a five-star suite, but that would have taken nearly a few weeks to arrange and the Captain could not wait that long."

"So, this was all a set-up. Are Stardust and Blitz really needed for a mission, or is that just part of the lie?"

"I believe their services are required, but I arranged all that the day before I came to visit you."

"You mean you visited the psychoviro?" Adam gasped, imagining John hanging under the bridge, desperately fighting off Blitz with his cane. "Did you have to fight?"

"Not at all," John enthused. "I had a most agreeable day. Apparently, it was one of their days off so there was none of that glam nonsense. Everybody looked quite casual in common twentieth century attire."

"So, no hunting?"

"There were a couple of scuffles, which were swiftly dealt with, and some poor fellow jumped off the roof of one of the towers. Other than those little wrinkles, I experienced nothing but warm hospitality. In fact, Mr Stardust himself took great care of me for the day – the perfect host and quite the dandy. We had a wonderful meal in one of the utility buildings. Such ugly structures on the outside, but rather elegant once you get inside. I had the venison. Oh, and did you know they have the most marvellous French waiters?"

"I'm so glad you enjoyed yourself," Adam said. "I'll think of you tucking into your venison next time one of them cuts my throat or kicks my balls up into my stomach." Adam put his foot down, and sped towards the interface.

Crossing the steel and concrete bridge that spanned a deep ravine, the full majesty of the temple-like structure, set into the grassy side of the valley, loomed into view.

"My goodness," John gasped. "It seems transported from ancient Rome itself. Those magnificent Doric columns, and the superb statuary – humbling indeed."

Adam parked the vehicle close to the entrance. Once outside, John stood motionless, staring in awe at the interface and the grey craggy mountains. Adam grabbed John by the arm.

"Come on, John," he said. "It may look like the valley of the Gods, but it's still just a viro."

Side by side, dwarfed by the immense columns and sweeping triangular portico, they ascended the wide marble steps. As they reached the top step, the black lacquered, double doors swung open on silent hinges.

"You say you have been here before," John said, wide-eyed and obviously overwhelmed. "So many years and you have kept your tongue. You have certainly honoured the trust that the Captain placed in you."

"I'm just as surprised at that as you are. Usually I'm the git who ruins a film by telling you what happens at the end, or ruins a joke by blurting out the punchline."

Despite three previous visits, Adam still caught his breath when he entered the vast cathedral-like hall. With elaborate golden columns, a painted ceiling depicting a lurid bacchanal of ancient gods and goddesses, and a perfectly tiled chequerboard marble floor, the Hall of the Gatekeepers never failed to impress.

A white-robed gatekeeper, its face a mysterious swirl of green gas, seemed to glide across the shiny floor. John gulped as the figure slowly approached.

"Adam, I consider myself of open mind, but this all seems far too satanic!"

Unaccustomed to the grand hall's acoustics, John shook in fear as his voice echoed loudly around the room – the word 'satanic' reverberating like a summoning chant at a black mass.

"Calm down," Adam urged, "it's all just for show."

Enigmatic, androgynously elegant, the gatekeeper raised a slender robotic hand, also swathed in verdant vapour.

"Follow me," it crooned.

"Don't we have to negotiate?" Adam asked, remembering the procedure from his past visits. "You know, I put up arguments and you put up counter arguments."

"Due to extreme circumstances, the rules of passage have been set aside." The gaseous face breathed red for a second, before returning to green. "Your journey is preapproved. I am here to expedite your swift transference to the surface."

The gatekeeper swivelled around, his robe fleetingly rising, offering a brief glimpse of hard titanium, and beckoned for Adam and John to follow.

"I'd better warn you," Adam whispered, "that, up on the surface, the Captain looks quite menacing. He is roughly human shape, with legs and arms, but he is all micro-pistons and polished metal. He doesn't have skin, eyes, or anything that makes him look like a real human."

"Why would he need to appear menacing? Is there danger outside?"

"There might be danger, but that's not the reason. The terrifying android look is simply a resource saving measure. Why waste resources on window dressing when there is no one to see it. Unlike us humans, he can just upload into the waiting android body from anywhere in the Viroverse. However, I get a brand new full-size Adam Eden body every time I go up there. Even though they recycle anything they can, the procedure is still heavy on resources."

"A full-size body," John said, marvelling at the prospect. "It will be such a pleasure to be truly human again … if only for a few hours."

Entering the Conversion Chamber – rows of identical columns, each with a statue of the Greek God, Hermes, standing to the side – Adam was surprised that two of the columns were already open, revealing the conversion capsules inside. Usually, the statue of Hermes would point his winged staff and utter some suitably dramatic words before the capsule opened, but now the stone effigies remained silently immobile.

Adam helped John into the steel capsule, reassuring the worried Victorian that the conversion process was quick and painless, and not related in any way to satanic rituals.

"You did not pick your nose this time," the gatekeeper remarked, as Adam settled himself in his own capsule – the cloud face now silver with sparkling points of light.

"You're not going to let that go, are you?" Adam said, remembering the nose related altercation he had nearly a thousand years ago. "I guess that sparkly silver is your humour colour. You know, I didn't even find it funny the first time round. And, as I keep telling you, I was rubbing it!"

"Safe journey, gentlemen," the gatekeeper said, and the capsule doors slid shut.

Body of Evidence

Standing upright, head bowed, Adam slowly awoke with a warm sensual friction of skin on skin. Before opening his eyes, his mind foggily unfocused, he shuffled around and gently writhed, enjoying the experience. Like a lover's soft caress, his hands enjoyed the smooth texture, softly running his fingers across the flats and curves of the bare flesh. He groaned contentedly, his thoughts a vibrant kaleidoscope of his many sexual encounters throughout the centuries.

"What in blue blazes are you doing, man?"

The loud voice, unmistakably John Down, tore Adam from his sleepy pleasure. Opening his eyes, blinking once or twice, he realised they were sharing a wake-up capsule – naked. Both men immediately pulled away from each other, covering their genitals with their hands.

"I was still half asleep," Adam protested. "I thought you were a woman."

"You fondled my buttocks!"

"I … well, you have very feminine buttocks. Oh god, did our … you know … things touch?"

John screwed up his face in disgust.

"Mr Eden, even if I knew that sordid fact to be true, I would never tell you. Never!"

The capsule door suddenly hissed open. Both men stood awkwardly as the Captain welcomed them to the surface outpost. Unexpectedly in humanoid form, complete with realistic skin, eyes, and hair, Captain Andrews smiled and straightened the cuff of his dark blue pilot's jacket. The Captain oozed charm with his soft gravelly voice and his irresistible smile of brilliant white teeth.

"Gentlemen, welcome to The Outpost, the Viroverse's only physical link with the outside world. Sorry you had to wake-up together in the same capsule, but time is of the essence, and there is only one capsule up here. I trust you weren't too inconvenienced?"

"Not at all," Adam said, quickly shaking his head.

"No inconvenience, Sir," John agreed. "I absolutely did not experience any inappropriate touching."

The Captain raised an eyebrow, and then pointed to two piles of clothes placed over some pipework.

"To save time, I took the liberty of choosing your clothes. Get dressed and meet me up on the mezzanine."

Whilst the Captain took the industrial lift up to the first floor, Adam and John quickly dressed – grey zip-up overalls, and sturdy combat boots. Looking around at the concrete and steel of the small outpost, John looked disappointed.

"Not what you were expecting," Adam said, lacing his second boot.

"After that magnificent building in the mountains, this drab place is decidedly underwhelming. Did they run out of money?"

"A grand interface was planned here on the surface, allowing the miniaturised resurrected to visit their descendants, but humanity chose a different path and it never got built."

"A different path?"

"You'll find out soon enough."

Once dressed, Adam sauntered casually over to the outpost's heavy industrial styled dispenser.

"Double Laphroig 10 year old … Cask Strength," he said, making the appropriate hand gestures.

The unblinking red light indicated the request denied. Adam tried again, but the red light remained.

"No single malt whisky for you, Mr Eden," the Captain called down from the mezzanine, "or any other kind of alcoholic drink. Today, I need you sober."

As they ascended to the mezzanine, Adam quietly cursed his inability to obtain a hard drink, and John grumbled that his full-size body felt heavy and sluggish. The lift came to a halt, and Captain Andrews came over to greet them.

"Before I tell, or rather, show you why you are here, I think Mr Down should see the outside."

"That sounds very exciting," John said. "I have so many thoughts on what the outside world might look like, and how the human race is coping. A veritable utopia, I would suggest, given the technological wonders I have seen in the Viroverse."

Not wanting to spoil the surprise, Adam remained silent. He really wanted to see John's reaction to the slerding plains.

"Do we have to wear the slime suits," Adam asked.

"We will only be viewing from the terrace," the Captain replied, "so there is no need for them. We are really pushed for time, so we won't stay out there for long."

Without fanfare or introduction, Captain Andrews ordered the wide, metal-shuttered door to open. It rolled up on smooth rails like a wide garage door, and a fetid stink blew in from the outside. Adam and John covered their faces with their hands.

"Positive pressure!" the Captain shouted, and hidden fans spun into action, preventing any more smell from entering.

"That stunk like an open sewer," John complained, taking his hands away from his face.

"Plenty more stink outside," Adam said, grinning.

"Here, take these breather clips," the Captain said, handing out the small nasal filters.

After fitting the devices, they walked outside onto the concrete outpost's large terrace. John slowly stumbled forward and grasped the steel railing – his grip tightened, hands whitening, as he beheld the baffling horror of humanity's chosen future.

Shaking his head in disbelief, John stared at the unending sea of slime covered naked humans. Zombie-like, unspeaking, the final generations of humans slid across the flat, almost featureless, landscape in huge stinking herds.

"Oh my goodness," John cried, "this is a hell spawned from the feverish dreams of Danté himself. They are like cattle! Why would mankind choose such degradation?"

"I'll give you the quick version," Adam said, enjoying John's shock. "One huge company and some old dynasties ruled the world. They came up with an addiction that fed straight into the minds of its customers – like the best dream you ever had, but from which you never wake up. The company sold the addiction in exchange for all their customer's worldly possessions, and plonked them here, in specially made bodies. The entire population of the planet was suckered into the deal. The poor buggers slide around in great herds; hence the name, 'slerds'. I was shocked the first time I saw the slerding plains. I even rubbed shoulders with them. Officially, I am Humanity's Representative. I speak on their behalf, although really it's just a handy legal trick to enact changes in the Viroverse."

"Can they be woken?"

"Only by the company, but they are also addicted and slerding; so no luck there. They will do this for eternity, or until some bloody great comet breaks through the Earth's defences and obliterates us all."

With a hollow expression, eyes unblinking, John turned to Adam.

"For these pitiful creatures, that might be a mercy."

The Captain slapped a firm hand on each man's shoulder – they both jumped.

"When you have quite finished killing off humanity, I have something you need to see – the reason you are here. Follow me, gentlemen."

Back inside, on the wider, far side of the mezzanine, Captain Andrews directed their attention to a white glossy cylinder. Like a designer coffin or high-tech medical monitoring casket, the cylinder had a number of control icons and multi-function indicator graphs. A steel table covered with various instruments, and a wall mounted cabinet with a green cross logo, set this part of the outpost as an ad-hoc medical unit.

The Captain pressed an icon of a black cross. The cross turned pastel blue, and the top half of the cylinder swivelled open. Inside, rested a humanoid figure. Apart from a smooth white cast over the right upper leg, and a bare patch of light brown skin on the shoulder, the body was almost completely covered in a shiny blue material.

"Gentlemen, I would like to introduce you to Mr Jomo Tikolo, erstwhile citizen of the wealthy East African federation – more specifically, Kenya – and, until recently, a carefree inhabitant of the slerding plains. He turned up outside the outpost, unconscious, and close to death. Given the severity of Mr Tikolo's condition, I have placed him in a chemically induced coma until his wounds are fully healed. You will notice there is no blue healing material on the left shoulder. The wounds here are stabilised but not healed. These are indicative of similar wounds I found across Mr Tikolo's entire body."

"Including his …" Adam asked.

"Everywhere, Mr Eden."

Adam studied the wounds, which appeared as red dots – little more than tiny pinpricks, but the sheer number was disturbing. John admitted he had never seen anything like it, and suggested it may be a new micro mutation of measles. The Captain shook his head.

"Pick up a magnifying glass from the table and take a closer look."

Adam and John each picked up a magnifying glass, and leaned in as close as possible. Up close, the red dots appeared as tiny straight cuts, each scabbed over. Something caught Adam's eye. Protruding from one of the cuts was what looked like the wooden hilt of a miniature sword.

"Is that what I think it is?" Adam asked.

John moved his magnifying glass in front of the object.

"Hmm, interesting; it looks like our Mr Tikolo has the tiniest of swords in his shoulder. Would it be all right to remove it?"

"You're a renowned physician, Mr Down, so go ahead," the Captain said. "Just remember to be gentle."

With a pair of sterilised tweezers, John carefully pulled out the miniature blade and held it up for all to see. Adam recognised the weapon as 15th century in design.

"Could this be the work of the dastardly Rodeleros?" John asked.

"Possibly," Adam said, squinting to see the details of the blade and pommel. "Did you ever recover any swords of this style during your skirmishes with them?"

"It is hard to tell, given the scale," John admitted, straining to study the details. "If I was miniaturised, I could hold the blade in my hand, and answer with a higher degree of certainty."

The Captain handed Adam a bottle of disinfectant spray.

"Give it a good clean then put it with the others in that plastic tub on the table. And, you should know that the Rodeleros have never used these particular swords."

After cleaning the blade, Adam was surprised at the contents of the tub.

"Good God, there must be hundreds in here! How is this man still alive?"

"There are exactly 72, including the one you just added," the Captain said, moulding a shiny blue pad over the exposed shoulder. "Fortunately for Mr Tikolo, the blades weren't long enough to cause any serious damage. The real injury, the one that almost killed him, is what I am going to show you next."

Captain Andrews lifted the smooth white smart-cast from Mr Tikolo's upper left leg, revealing a terrible wound. A large portion of the outer thigh was missing – a few glimpses of bone were shocking proof of the depth.

"Ugh, I … I was never a thigh man," Adam mumbled, trying to make light of the stomach-turning sight. "More of a breast man, myself. I'm talking about fried chicken of course."

"That is highly inappropriate, Mr Eden," John said. "Especially since this may be cannibalism or, even worse, ritual cannibalism. There are dark forces at work here."

Adam looked closer and was struck by the patterned structure of the wound. Stepped, squared, and layered, a miniature Giant's Causeway sprung to mind:

"It looks like a tiny quarry – a leg quarry." He suddenly imagined cubes of juicy red steak. "Shouldn't there be a mess of blood."

"A hardener has been injected in to the flesh," the Captain explained, "allowing the quarrying of meat without a bloodbath or killing the victim. If you look closely, you will notice that the major blood vessels are intact, protected by surgical insulation tape, and supported by tiny clamps and posts. When he arrived, the entire wound was securely wrapped in duct tape, without which Mr Tikolo would certainly be dead. Take a much closer look at the wound."

Adam leaned in close with his magnifying glass and studied the gruesome excavation:

"I can see shoe prints! Lots and lots of tiny shoe prints! And, that looks like a handprint. Do you think you could lift some fingerprints?"

The Captain shook his head:

"Too small I'm afraid. However, I did find a DNA signature. A quick analysis revealed the owner to be Marie Antonin Carême."

"Who's she?"

"He is a famous 19th century French chef, and an early exponent of haute cuisine; not something you will be familiar with, Mr Eden. Carême is not a resident of the Viroverse, so his involvement is something of a mystery."

Adam stood back, disgusted with himself for licking his lips:

"Hey John, it looks like those cannibals of yours are dining in style. I bet the chef sautés the meat in lots of butter and garlic."

Captain Andrews replaced the smart-cast back over the gruesome wound and pressed a yellow sad face icon on the control pad – the face smiled and turned green, indicating activation.

"Though Mr Tikolo is thoroughly clean now, when he first arrived at the outpost his skin was covered in green plant stains and dried mud. That suggests he has been beyond the plains."

"There's no greenery in this part of Australia, is there?" Adam asked.

"A lot has changed in the 3000 years since you first stepped outside. If I use enhanced vision, I can see the edge of a vast jungle bordering the northern limit of the plains."

John Down interrupted.

"Did you say 3000 years? Surely you mean 1000 years."

"Another secret of the Viroverse, I'm afraid, Mr Down," the Captain said, "At midnight, you think you fall asleep for eight hours before waking. The truth is that the sleep is more akin to an enforced coma, which lasts 56 hours, or two whole days longer than you are led to believe. The time is necessary to take the pressure off the recycling and repair systems."

John Down's silence and bewildered expression evidenced he was suffering from information overload. Adam gave him a friendly nudge:

"Oh dear, you have missed sooo many wedding anniversaries. What exactly is the material for 3000 years? Lithium? You look like you could use some."

A soft sealing sucking sound accompanied the closing of the white cylinder. Captain Andrews turned to his shocked, sickened, but attentive audience.

"This is where I should say, 'and now for my next trick', because I have one more thing to show you."

DARK CANAL

Each stomach-turning revelation made Adam increasingly suspicious about the nature of the forthcoming mission. Given the stains and mud on Mr Tikolo's body, he automatically assumed that it involved a journey beyond the slerding plains – the threat of cannibals and the absence of resurrection made for an alarming combination, especially given Adam's present sobriety. He listened intently as the Captain revealed the final violation of Jomo Tikolo. How could this possibly be worse than the limb quarrying?

"When I first brought Mr Tikolo into the outpost, I conducted a full 3D body scan. My main concern at the time was internal injuries. Thankfully, there were none, except minor dehydration damage. However, I discovered something unexpected, and a whole lot stranger. The scan revealed a foreign body lodged in Mr Tikolo's anal canal. Linked to this, there was unusual tearing around his anus, and small flecks of a rubbery material."

Adam screwed up his face – this could be worse.

Captain Andrews continued:

"Let me show you the 'foreign body'. I have it preserved in Galgaeic Gel."

The Captain opened the glass door of a wall mounted medical refrigerator. He carefully reached past the various plastic containers, preloaded syringes, and withdrew a small container. Adam noticed that the metal container was roughly the size and shape of a small tin of sardines. The Captain gently clipped off the airtight lid, and placed the container on a nearby tabletop. Adam and John peered in, eager to see the contents. Beneath a translucent gel, which smelled faintly of brine, lay a tiny naked figure – about an inch tall, the same scale as Viroverse inhabitants. Captain Andrews smiled mercurially.

"Gentlemen, meet Edgar Allan Poe."

After a round of gasps and mild expletives, Adam picked up his magnifying glass and studied the tiny man. He frowned, seeing no sign of life.

"This goo makes it hard to see any details. Is he dead?"

"I'm afraid so," the Captain said. "A slerd's anal canal is a treacherous place for someone so small, since the interior sphincter does not automatically relax. Otherwise, Mr Poe may have been naturally … ejected. Deprived of oxygen, he didn't stand a chance."

"So he died of …"

"Yes, Mr Poe died of asphyxiation."

Tuned-in to toilet humour, a first-life remnant of both nature and nurture, Adam's mind quickly brimmed with crude puns and jokes. Reluctantly, he kept them to himself, but failed to contain a grin followed by a snigger.

"A man is dead, you degenerate," John Down harrumphed, casting a withering glare at his immature colleague.

Controlling himself, Adam coughed into his hand and attempted to appear serious.

"Are you sure it's him?" he asked the Captain. "Are you sure this is the man who wrote 'The Raven'?"

Captain Andrews clipped the lid back on the tin and placed it back in the refrigerator.

"Everyone in the Viroverse has the DNA signature from their first life, plus an I.D code and profile biologically embedded in their bone structure. There is no doubt that this really is Mr Edgar Allen Poe, the famous 19th century American author and poet."

"Such irony," John whimsically mused. "It is as if the esteemed Mr Poe now rests in his very own 'Cask of Amontillado'."

"Didn't think you liked that sort of thing," Adam said.

"In a thousand years, or should that be three thousand years, there are those rare times when I have strayed into darker reading material." He turned to the Captain. "Sir, will you resurrect Mr Poe for questioning? It seems he has a great deal of explaining to do."

In customary fashion, Captain Andrews coolly tipped back his pilots cap, and sighed.

"That will not be possible, Mr Down. Despite being standard scale, and having an official I.D code and profile, Mr Poe has never been a resident of the Viroverse. There is no record of his resurrection, so we have no contractual obligation or authority to bring him back. We need to find out where he came from and how he was able to crawl up into a slerd's anus. Mr Tikolo's slime suit should have protected him from any such intrusion. But, then again, Mr Tikolo has no slime suit." The Captain rummaged in his pocket and pulled out a small transparent zip-lock evidence bag. He passed it to John.

"Mr Poe was wearing those clothes when I extracted him from Mr Tikolo."

"This looks like an underwater diving suit," John said, before handing the bag to Adam, who studied the contents with his magnifying glass.

"Yes, this looks like scuba gear. It's crudely made, amateurish stitching and probably not as waterproof as it should be. The facemask is cracked and I think the air tank is ruptured. Poor Poe didn't stand a chance."

"I feel this is connected to the Conquistador attacks," John said. "They keep mentioning Hernán Cortés, and he is not a Viroverse resident either."

The Captain ushered Adam and John towards the lift.

"I have considered many possibilities, Mr Down, and that seems likely. It is also highly likely that the attacks and Mr Poe's arrival are linked to our problems in the Via Sacra."

The lift slowly descended to the ground floor. John and the Captain carried on their conversation. Having never heard of the Via Sacra – another secret of the Viroverse – Adam interrupted.

"Hey, what is this Via Sacra? I didn't come all this way to be kept in the dark."

John explained, whilst the Captain fetched some refreshments from the dispenser.

"The Via Sacra, the Sacred Road, is where the dead bodies go before recycling."

"What dead bodies? We're all immortal here, aren't we?"

"Mr Eden, it may have slipped your mind, but you were killed yesterday. You woke up in the mountains with a new body ... and even that tiny body was replaced with the full-size one you now inhabit. By now, the body you lost in the Psychoviro has already passed through the Via Sacra, and the other is on its way as we speak."

"So what goes on there? I'm getting an image of burning torches and guys in black robes and hoods chanting?"

"Nothing like that goes on in the Via Sacra!" John said gruffly. "It is a multi-faith vault where last rites are performed. However, you will be no doubt pleased to know that Satanists like yourself are catered for."

"Calm down, Down. I was only joking."

"For some inexplicable reason, you are Humanity's Representative, but I am the Overseer of the Dead. Monitoring the Via Sacra is one of my many, many duties, and I take it very seriously."

"Oh, then I apologise to the almighty Overseer of the Dead," Adam said mockingly. "So, what's the problem with the Sacred Road – council not filling in the potholes?"

Before John could vent his anger, the Captain returned with food and drinks.

"Ginger beer, Herefordshire beef and horseradish sandwiches for the Overseer of the Dead." He handed John an earthenware bottle and a lunch-tin lined with red gingham cloth. "And, for you, Representative of Humanity, a large coke and a chilli cheese burger from your favourite chippy."

Adam opened the yellow polyurethane container, and nodded appreciatively at the sight of the huge Tabbas half pounder – salty, greasy, and dripping with blazing-hot chilli sauce, the limp salad always took a backseat to the neon-cheese covered mystery meat patties.

As they hungrily devoured the food, and knocked back the drinks, the Captain explained the problem.

"For the past 100 years, bodies have been going missing from the Via Sacra – exactly 1086 to date. The disappearances always coincide with conquistador incursions, which we believe are prearranged distractions. However, the losses from the vault each time are relatively small compared to the daily throughput, so the matter has never been properly investigated."

"Oh deary me, John," Adam said, spluttering a laugh of burger and sauce, "Looks like someone's slacking off. I thought you took your duties seriously."

John shot forward, standing toe to toe with Adam, who calmly munched another bite of burger.

"Why is everything a joke to you?" John raged, eyes wide with fury. "We are dying in those halls so you can live a life of slothful drunkenness in your Viro! One in five of us gone, dead, never to return, and you insult their memory with your insatiable need for yet another snigger! Eden, you are nothing but a worthless, gibbering …" A vein on John's forehead bulged as he struggled to say the word, "… runt!"

Adam creased up with laughter, struggling to keep his food in his mouth.

"Hah, nice try. Replace the first letter with a 'C' and you might have surprised me."

"Damn you!" John cried, and swung his arm around.

Adam reeled from the sudden impact of the earthenware bottle. It shattered against the side of his skull, soaking him in an explosion of ginger beer, and sending a gob of half-chewed food flying from his mouth. He fell to the floor in a daze, and lay still for a moment, moaning incoherently.

John stood over Adam, and dropped the end of the bottle on the floor.

"I used to believe that you had a good heart and a strong inner integrity. You are a pathetic shadow of your former self."

Rubbing the side of his throbbing head, a small cut seeping blood, Adam slowly sat up.

"Why didn't you stop that?" Adam asked the Captain.

Captain Andrews helped Adam to his feet.

"To use a phrase from your own time, 'you were asking for it, mate'. Mr Down, you are wrong about Mr Eden being a shadow of his former self. He is back to his old self – the weak willed drunk of his first-life. A thousand years of idle pleasure and he has reverted to type."

"So why the Hell did you want me here?" Adam asked, whilst proffering a hand to John Down.

John Down snubbed the handshake: "That is earned, Mr Eden."

"Why do I want you here," the Captain replied. "I have my reasons, but I also have serious reservations."

John handed Adam his handkerchief, and told him to hold it against the wound until the bleeding stopped. Adam thanked the famous physician. The absence of further 'Eden humour' soon lightened the mood and eased the tension.

"You two need to kiss and make up," the Captain said. "After leaving here, you will wake-up tomorrow morning in the Terminal. I want you both to visit the Via Sacra, and conduct a thorough search. It is only a few hours ride from The

Terminal to the utility level entrance. A security surf formation will get you as close as possible, but after that, you are on your own."

"You could do it yourself," Adam suggested, as the fear rose in his body. "You're an android – virtually indestructible. No need for us to go."

"Only humans are allowed to enter the Via Sacra," the Captain admitted. "I cannot even enter the halls."

"I know there's no resurrection in the halls, but the Via …."

The Captain shook his head.

"There is no resurrection anywhere on the utility level. Only two people at a time are permitted in the vault, and that is why I wanted the legendary Copacabana to accompany Mr Down. If there is trouble I am sure you and your machete can handle it."

"Can I say no?" Adam asked, hopefully.

Adam flinched as John Down stepped forward again, standing toe to toe.

"Mr Eden, it depends if you want to earn that handshake."

SHARK SURFING

In the old world, the world before immortality, many who espoused atheism spent their final years, months, minutes, increasingly petrified by the anticipation of nothingness, a non-future that they embraced so assertively in their youth. Even those who only paid lip service to their supposed faith, revelling in their church's dogma rather than the faith's true message, faced the icy fear. Once resurrected in the Viroverse, death's dark horizon blurred into insignificance with the promise of a blissful eternity - ironically, it was often the true believers, those that lived their first lives certain of a heavenly hereafter, that felt lost and betrayed in the manufactured paradise.

In his first life, Adam Eden never faced the fear of death. His demise was sudden and unexpected, drowning after falling off the harbour wall in Portsmouth. There was no time to contemplate mortality, nothingness versus the immortal soul. He went through a painful dark limbo and resurrected as a miniature human in an artificial environment. Fighting against the psychopathic glam gang regularly for nearly a thousand years, and usually meeting his demise at their evil hands, did nothing to instil a mortal dread. Adam always resurrected the next day, warm and snug in his own bed, with death no more than a forgotten night journey between lives.

Now, Adam felt the fear. A thousand years of idle pleasure had addicted him to life itself, rendering him hopelessly unable and unprepared to face the prospect of non-existence. The fear uncoiled from the pit of his stomach, was heard through a faint tremble in his voice, and revealed itself in fevered beads of sweat on his forehead.

The seemingly endless halls outside the Viros were as minimalist and foreboding as Adam remembered. Set into the grey floor, the ten white lines – a maglev system facilitating the use of surfing-style hover boards – stretched into the far distance.

Despite the presence of the battle-hardened personnel of the Terminal's security team, busily preparing for the journey to the Via Sacra, Adam shuddered, thinking of the mortal danger that might lie ahead. Giving the team space to work, Adam and John stood further down the hall, opposite the Terminal waiting room door.

"Stop worrying," John said, more out of embarrassment than true sympathy. "You're the great Copacabana, fearless killer of those awful psychopaths. Please, do not let the security team see you like this. Fear can be contagious. Let them see you as an asset, not a burden."

"Then get me a soddin' drink," Adam seethed, having been denied access to alcohol in the Terminal. "Damn, I hope these warriors are as good as you say. And why aren't they here yet?"

Dolph Zabel, the Terminal's chief security officer, strode up, wearing standard Terminal light-blue fatigues and grey lightweight body armour. Tall, muscular, he towered over everyone else in the team.

"Any problems here?" he asked – deep voiced, Germanic. "The boards are waxed and ready to ride the lines. We leave in 20 minutes."

"No problem, Commander," John said. "Adam and I are positively raring to go."

"That is good. It should be a straightforward run, but still, be prepared. Keep your weapons at hand at all times."

Putting on a brave face, Adam triumphantly raised his machete and John swished his new cane – ebony with a steel core and claw handle. Dolph grunted his approval and returned to the Terminal team for final preparations.

"Do I really have to wear the Copacabana clothes?" Adam asked, tweaking the collar of his pink hibiscus Hawaiian shirt, "I feel like a bloody clown or, even worse, a tourist."

"We all wear uniforms of a sort, and your clothes go hand in hand with the legend. Anyhow, I thought your clothes had mysteriously evolved over the years fighting the psychopaths. I believe they have special defensive qualities?"

"Yeah, they're tougher than they look, but … this shirt, and the white trousers and blue deck shoes; I should be drinking Pina Coladas on the beach and soaking up the sun."

With a familiar hiss, the Terminal's waiting room door slid open.

"Oh God, yes!" Adam cheered, giving a thumbs up to the twelve, grim-faced Khevsur warriors filing out of the waiting room and into the hall. Gaunt faces, moustached and bearded, their eyes stared piercingly from under spiked-topped chainmail helmets. Wearing rugged leather strapped boots, and titanium chainmail bodysuits, the Khevsurs proudly displayed the crimson cross of Georgia on their broad chests. From their steel-studded, black leather belts hung sabres sheathed within brass and leather bound scabbards, and similarly sheathed krindjal daggers. Each held a steel buckler in one hand – a small circular shield with a metal handgrip, serving both offensive and defensive purposes. Adam grinned appreciatively, seeing they each held a silver hipflask in the other.

"They really, really look like Crusaders," Adam said, in awe of the hard-faced swordsmen. "The cross, the chainmail … the beards and moustaches. You know, the guys that always turn up at the end of Robin Hood films."

"A common and romantic attribution, but probably untrue," John replied, nodding respectfully to the warriors, and tipping his top hat, "since many of their traditions predate the crusades. To a man, the Khevsurs are fiercely loyal to the Georgian Kings. That was the key to our recruiting them. If the conquistadors forced us out of the halls, then the Spanish devils would rampage unopposed throughout the Viroverse. Before long, the wellbeing of every citizen, including most of the Georgian royal lineage, would be in jeopardy. Their fight is our fight."

The Khevsurs formed a circle, facing each other with sombre expressions, and began singing. A low droning bass, sacred in tone, soon gave way to higher pitches, and haunting polyphony. Like enthused choral monks, their passionate highland voices touched the hearts of all present.

"That's … beautiful," Adam said, transfixed by the vocal skill and dexterity on display. "It sounds both sad and uplifting at once. Is it a hymn?"

"No, it is a love song, 'Shatilis Asulo', 'Daughter of Shatili'. They sing it before every mission, in honour of the wives they leave behind."

Reaching the end of the song, as one, the Khevsurs turned to face Adam. They flipped open their hipflasks, and cried out, 'Copa, gaumarjos!', and then took a swift drink. Making their way to the surfboards, they chattered, swaggered, and swung their swords with confident bravado.

"What did they just say?" Adam asked, respectfully clapping his appreciation.

"Copa, victory," John translated. "Their way of saying, 'cheers'."

"Excellent; I guess that's not tea they're drinking."

"Probably Chacha, a strong Georgian brandy. None for you, I'm afraid."

"Bollocks!"

Arranged in escort formation, ready to ride, the hover-boards were unlike any Adam had previously seen. Formidable, redesigned for combat, a single silver 'T' emblazoned each board – the de-facto insignia of the Terminal.

Two Tigersharks – enhanced three person longboards – each with one rider and two seated passengers, made up the core of the group. Titanium grey, sturdy, with menacingly spiked fronts and armoured sides, the huge boards looked like trackless Mad Max style bobsleighs. Adam and John sat as passengers in the rear board, whilst Dolph and another operative – both equipped with lightweight cutlasses and tactical knives – sat in the lead.

Smaller, sleeker, two-man Nightsharks sat to the rear and either side of the Tigersharks. Gloss black low-profile boards, with a front tapering to a blood red spike, the twelve Nightsharks were considerably faster than their relatively ponderous cousins, and tuned for rapid acceleration. Behind each Nightshark rider, stood a Khevsurian warrior gripping onto a steel-meshed bungee cord for balance, whilst holding their buckler at the ready. Should the need arise, the board riders also carried 6" tactical folding knives, and could rapidly deploy a compact crossbow, conveniently clipped to the front of each board.

Favouring the traditional method of starter motion, the riders began pumping up and down with their legs – slowly, softly at first, then with increased speed and vigour. Suddenly, the sharkboards began twitching backwards and forwards, like vicious attack dogs straining on the leash.

"Ready to ride these sharks!" Dolph thundered, his deep voice echoing along the halls. "Tsunami!"

As usual, Adam was unprepared for the bullet-like acceleration along the white lines. With an undignified, 'whoa' he fell back against John Down, who cursed and heaved him back onto his small nub of a seat. Adam clung tightly to his seat side-straps as the surf formation raced down the perfectly straight hall. Looking to his side, Adam marvelled at the nearest Nightshark – the mirror-visored rider crouched low at the front, whilst the stoically silent Khevsur stood to the rear in a dramatically heroic combat stance. The warrior briefly turned his head and, unsmiling, offered a brisk nod to the man in the pink shirt. Returning the manly gesture, Adam put on his sternest face, and even managed to furrow his brow.

"What happened to the jellymen?" Adam asked, shouting to be heard above the constant rush of air. "I know they're pretty easy to deal with, but surely they cause the conquistadors some trouble."

John leaned forward, and spoke over Adam's shoulder.

"Being part of a redundant system, they, like the temporary hall barriers, had a finite resource supply. Those resources completely ran out centuries ago. Even when you encountered the jell … Osmotic Guards, they were insubstantial shadows of their former selves."

"Anything else not working?"

"The lines are still powered, and we have lighting. Be grateful for that."

After every ten viro stretch of hall, approximately eleven miles in length, the convoy encountered a large crossroads and the risk of ambush. Experienced and highly trained, the sharkboard riders automatically carried out a standard defensive procedure before reaching the danger point.

Firstly, using enhanced goggles, the rider in the lead Tigershark scanned the junction ahead for wire and obstacles – John explained that in the early days many Terminal operatives were bady injured and some decapitated by wire stretched across the hall. Though it seemed the enemy had long since abandoned this particularly gruesome practice, continued scanning was considered a prudent measure.

Once given the all clear, the six jet-black Nightsharks either side of the Tigersharks immediately pulled ahead of the pack. From behind, the remaining six moved up to take their place.

As the first six Nightsharks silently shot off into the distance, Adam strained to see the crossroads manoeuvre. Three boards either side, riders and warriors crouching low, the Nightsharks skid-turned around the corners of the crossroads – leaning through the turn, the Khevsurs' bucklers stabilised the boards, scraping hard against the floor.

Seconds later, the rest of the convoy passed safely through the intersection. Adam witnessed the halted Nightsharks guarding the right and left halls – the Khevsurs stood in front of the boards, sabres unsheathed and held waist high, while the riders knelt by their sides, crossbows loaded and ready to fire.

Less than a minute later, John tapped Adam on the shoulder. He looked around, and saw the Nightsharks speeding up from behind, taking up their new positions at the back of the pack.

Minutes turned into hours as the sharkboards headed further along the halls. The defensive cycle constantly repeated, and soon Adam became bored of the intricate and daring skills on display. Yawning, he asked John to slap the back of his head if he fell asleep.

ADAM AT THE CROSSROADS

The likelihood of danger remained constant, yet Adam's fear of danger gradually subsided with the monotony of the journey. The never changing architecture, smoothness of the ride, cool rush of air, and the faint hum of magnetics, were powerful sleep inducers. Adam struggled to keep his eyes open. Leaning his elbow on the Tigershark's side-armour, he rested his cheek on his hand and stared at a Khevsur's boot – for no reason in particular, other than it was there.

Mile after mile, crossroads after crossroads, Adam lazily stared. The fact that after each cycle, the next Nightshark – and another boot – lined up only within a few centimetres of the previous board's position should have amazed Adam. However, such precision went unnoticed amid constant yawning, bleary-eyed blinking, and a childish urge, so far unacted upon, to shout out, 'are we there yet'?

"Only another hour and we should reach our destination," John said, as if reading Adam's mind. "And please try to look alert, if only for appearances sake."

Adam mumbled an unheard reply, smiled comfortably, and slightly tilted his head:

"Hang ten, dude!" he yelled to the Khevsur warrior to his right.

The Khevsur – Mr Gigauri as Adam would later learn – slowly turned his head, like a statue stiffly come to life:

"Hang ten what?" he asked, his deep voice tinged with a pronounced rustic rasp.

"Err, hang ten toes."

"Why must I hang my toes?"

"It's an expression; a well-known surfing expression. Like Hang Five."

"Hang five what?"

"Toes."

The Khevsur snorted loudly, clearing his nose:

"Are you finished?"

"Yes, um, that's it," Adam said, embarrassed.

The Khevsur nodded respectfully and turned his gaze frontwards. Seconds later, the Nightsharks pulled away for yet another defensive cycle. Watching them speed ahead, Adam spied a small black object with a tiny red light by the side of the hall. Opening his mouth to yawn, he suddenly realised that nothing should be in the halls. The half-formed yawn mutated into a loud demented warning as he sat bolt upright in his seat.

"It's a trap! It's a trap! Stop the bloody boards! They know we're coming!"

In the lead Tigershark, Dolph stood up, holding onto the rider for support, and watched as the forward Nightsharks disappeared around the corners of the upcoming intersection. From actions and sights unseen by the convoy, an eruption of noise immediately broke the dread silence: a multitude of sharp yells and the furious clash of metal on metal.

Speed and momentum demanded a quick decision – a split-second, the faint luxury of time available to the steadfast Commander. Waving his hand forward, Dolph urged the pack onwards.

"We push through!" he ordered. "Brace yourselves, stay low, and prepare for bolts!"

Everyone tightly gripped their seat-straps and bungee cords. The remaining Nightsharks kept perfect pace with the Tigersharks, the Khevsurs facing out to the walls, anticipating the crossroads and imminent attack.

There was no stirring slow motion cinematic glide-past, but instead a frantic high-speed dash through the visceral cut and thrust, blood and screams, of battle. As the lead Tigershark raced through the intersection, a rogue, stolen Nightshark shot out from the right hand junction – two whooping Rodeleros riding the deadly spiked board. It reared up over one of the escorts, bowling the rider and Khevsur warrior onto the hard floor. The enemy board rammed into the side of the lead Tigershark, impaling the rear operative on the blood red spike. The impact sent the Rodeleros hurtling through the air, and sent the speeding Tigershark careering across the intersection in a perilous propeller-like spin.

Adam and John looked on in horror as the front teeth of the spinning Tigershark shredded the legs of those on the left side escort, and then crashed into the brutal swordfight taking place at the left hand junction. Taking evasive action, the rider of Adam's Tigershark braked hard using reverse magnetics, attempting an emergency sliding stop.

"Shit!" Adam cried, as the side of the Tigershark slammed into the huge transparent tubes that stood at the corners of each junction. Fortunately, the tubes, carrying the liquid effluent from the slerds up above to the Viroverse bioreactors below, remained solidly intact.

The last four Nightsharks braked and skidded into the intersection without incident. The Khevsurs leapt from the boards, drew their sabres and rushed into the fray. Thrown from his Tigershark, Dolph Zabel heaved himself off the floor as a Rodelero broke through the line and thrust his sword at the partially stunned Commander. Instinctively, Dolph leaned sideways, fell onto his hands, and kicked the legs out from under the startled attacker. The Rodelero flipped over and crashed to the floor, his steel morion helmet slamming against the hard surface.

Dolph leapt back to his feet, kicked away the Rodelero's rapier, and stamped viciously on the dazed enemy's quilted chest armour, pinning him down. With a sharp shout and a beckoning hand, the Commander called to one of the board riders. The rider sprinted over and stood over the Rodelero. Taking careful aim with her crossbow, she shot a fast-acting tranquilizer bolt into the man's leg.

Dolph lifted his boot off the unconscious enemy, and turned to see another Rodelero storming forward, crying out the name, 'Cortés'. Dolph drew his folding tactical knife, clicked it open, and met the threat. The Spanish warrior blocked with his rodela shield – larger and heavier than a Khevsur buckler – hiding his sword arm and tactical intent.

Quickly reloading the crossbow, the panicking board rider fired prematurely, causing the bolt to glance harmlessly off the enemy's shield. The Rodelero made his move, thrusting low from behind the shield, aiming for Dolph's unarmoured thigh. Anticipating the strike, a skill learned from many such attacks, the tough German brought up his leg. The tip of the sword hit Dolph's knee protector and slid safely sideways. Dolph closed-in with his tactical knife. With brute strength, he knocked away the shield, and shoved the 6" black blade straight into the Rodelero's neck – the blade severed the carotid artery and sliced open the internal jugular vein.

The Rodelero slipped easily off the blade and slumped to the floor in an expanding pool of his own blood.

"No resurrection for you," Dolph said unemotionally. "Now you must explain yourself to your God."

The relatively minor skirmish at the left hand junction was already over – a Terminal victory. Seven operatives, disregarding their own injuries, clothes dripping with the blood of friend and enemy, hurried over to the right hand junction to support their beleaguered colleagues.

With Adam reluctantly following close behind, John raced over to join the fight – brandishing his walking cane like a fighting stick, the oversize steel claw raised high.

"Where do you think you're going?" Dolph asked, holding John back with his hand.

"To let those devils feel the weight of my steel claw," John said, eyes ablaze with martial fire.

"No, I want both of you to stay behind the Tigershark. Take the spare tranqbows strapped to the sidings. If you get a clear shot, try not to kill … unless there's no alternative."

"But … but, my cane and Adam's machete could turn the battle," John protested.

"We are fighting so you can get to the Via Sacra. If you die, then our sacrifice is for nothing."

"Err, we should listen to him," Adam said, tugging at John's sleeve. "Let them do their job so we can do ours."

The sturdy Commander nodded, but narrowed his eyes and stared, as if looking deep into Adam's soul.

"I must join my team," Dolph said, picking up a discarded Spanish rapier. "Get behind that board and stay alive! That is an order, Mr Down!"

Dolph joined the battle, spurring the Terminal team to fight harder and meaner. Standing taller than anyone else in the bloody melee, he was both a rallying figure to his troops and a target for the enemy. Showing not a hint of fear, the veteran Commander obviously relished the combative attention, shouting out stirring battle cries as he lifted a Rodelero clean up above his head, before hurling the shocked Spaniard to the floor.

Nearly thirty fighters remained standing, giving no quarter as they stepped around the bodies of the fallen. For a moment, Adam and John stood motionless, engrossed in the vicious spectacle of blue, grey, and glints of sharp steel. Grisly spatters and sharp spurts of crimson soaked the unrelenting combatants – the floor beneath their feet slick with blood, its warm ferric aroma heavy in the air. An enemy bolt embedded itself in John's top hat, persuading both men to seek immediate cover behind the Tigershark.

Keeping low behind the armoured board, warmed by the gentle surface heat of the effluent tubes, Adam grabbed the crossbows and a quiver of tranquiliser bolts. He gritted his teeth and struggled to cock the weapon.

"It's always a bit tight the first time," he said.

"Is that an attempt at crude innuendo, Mr Eden … at a time like this? Just cock it."

Adam shook his head and cursed as his finger slipped across the bowstring, opening up a small cut. He sucked his finger:

"No, it's just that I always forget how much force it takes to cock these buggers."

John handed Adam a pair of leather gloves.

"Use these to protect your hands."

"These weapons are so outdated!" Adam fumed, lining up the primitive iron sight. "Just why are we using swords and crossbows anyway? This isn't the psychoviro! The Terminal must have access to more advanced technology. I realise that nothing combustible is allowed, but you could send remote controlled drones out into the halls: load them with gas, knock out the enemy, and collect them later. If that fails, then fit the drones with high-powered gas guns and take them out permanently. What the hell's stopping you?""

"Because, there is no honour in using such cowardly devices." John's voice ran rich with scorn. "The Captain thought it best that we battle the conquistadors using weaponry similar to their own. We want them to fear us, but we also want them to respect us. When this war is finally over, the Terminal will not be tarred with the stick of tyranny."

Surprised at the noble goal, Adam confessed that he had believed the non-deployment of overpowering force was due to some petty Viroverse contractual smallprint. John coughed uncomfortably, admitting that legal impediments may have played a part in the decision.

The Khevsurs fought the Rodeleros one-on-one– sabre and buckler versus rapier and rodela. Almost evenly matched, the swordsmen thrust, parried, and blocked like some violently enhanced variation of rock, paper, scissors. Serving as weapons, the small shields smacked aside sword arms and smashed into faces. Sword attacks were rapid and varied – the motion viciously dynamic, but brutally short of balletic – each fighter seeking that rare though inevitable mistake in their opponents defence.

Adam aimed his crossbow at one of the Rodeleros. The fast moving conquistador was getting the better of his Khevsur adversary – the Georgian forced backwards under the relentless sword strikes hammering against his steel buckler. Taking the shot, the tranquiliser bolt struck the Spaniard in the upper arm. The Rodelero dropped his shield and keeled forward, but not before lashing out one final time. Sweeping high, the rapier slashed across the Khevsur's forehead – unheard above the noise of battle was a sickening scrape across bone.

Reeling around, the Khevsur cried out in pain as a thick veil of blood poured down his face. Unable to see, the warrior staggered around, thrusting and swishing his sword. Another Rodelero lunged forward with his rapier, taking advantage of the enemy's blindness. The tip of his sword broke through the tough titanium chainmail, the blade burying itself deep in the Khevsur's stomach.

Steely eyed, John raised his crossbow and let loose a shot. The bolt struck the Rodelero in the heart – an intentional kill or simply off-target, John would never tell. Meanwhile, the Khevsur lay screaming on the floor, his writhing body spreading the blood that spurt from the wound.

"Though I sense victory," John said, looking away from the suffering warrior, "I fear it will be sorrowfully pyrrhic. However, even now there is a small chance that the Terminal will lose this one. Perhaps you would prefer to run, Mr Eden. I could stay here and cover your ignominious retreat."

"Don't pin this on me," Adam muttered, unable to look John in the eye. "The Commander told us to stay here. How would us dying help the mission?"

"A thousand years ago, when we faced the Dreamers in battle, you were told to stay up on the ledge, out of harm's way. I seem to remember that you ignored that order and refused to hide. You fought side-by-side, tooth and nail, with the rest of us. Your selflessness ensured our victory."

Adam grunted, cocked his crossbow, and loaded another tranquiliser bolt. "This … this is different."

"Or, sadly, perhaps you have become that tourist in a ridiculous pink shirt."

No more bolts were necessary. The Rodeleros resistance crumbled as their numbers dwindled. Surrendering, knowing that they would be drugged, memory wiped, and transported back to their Viros, the Spanish warriors threw down their arms, dropped to their knees and accepted their fate.

A quick head count confirmed that out of an original Terminal force of thirty, including Adam and John, only seventeen remained standing. The injuries were many and often gruesome, but nobody complained. Tending to the less fortunate, to those desperately clinging to life, was the immediate priority. The next priority, a task that brought even the most hardened fighters to tears, was to drag the dead into a line. Within hours, a transport team would arrive to bag the deceased, both friend and foe, and take them back to the Terminal refrigerators.

Saloni Mehta, the second in command, approached with a disturbing discovery, her blue uniform and dark olive skin glistening with sweat and blood.

"Commander, the Nightshark that the enemy was riding was not taken from our team. It is a genuine Terminal board – has all the right markings and the latest refinements – but I have no idea how they got hold of it. Mr Eden was right that they knew we were coming. We've recovered a couple of laser sensors – again, official Terminal issue."

Rubbing his large square chin, Dolph walked over to the kneeling prisoners.

"Where did you get the Nightshark and the sensors? This equipment belongs to the Terminal! And, don't pretend you don't speak English!"

The nine surviving conquistadors ignored the question, mumbling catholic prayers, refusing to look up. Dolph squatted down and spoke quietly.

"You will all be taken to the Terminal for questioning. They have the means to make you talk. We have operatives well trained in your tricks and schemes."

As Dolph stood up, the conquistadors began sniggering, as if sharing a private joke. Disregarding the pathetic slaps of the defeated, the Commander organised his exhausted team.

"Deputy Mehta, I want you to remain here with Scott, Arabuli, and Xun. Guard the prisoners – drug them if necessary – and do all you can to keep our wounded alive. When you get back to the Terminal, inform Captain Andrews about the Nightshark and the laser sensors."

"And if more Rodeleros turn up?"

"Then no one would blame you for abandoning the prisoners and the wounded. I believe most of the Nightsharks are still operational."

Deputy Mehta raised her head and stood to attention.

"We'll fight like fury, Commander."

The Terminal operatives spent the next 30 minutes busily checking their equipment for damage. Gently pumping the boards, the surviving riders slowly cruised around the large intersection, testing for problems and white-line worthiness.

Dolph spoke frankly to Adam and John:

"We haven't had an ambush like this for decades. How the enemy knew to place the sensors on this particular route, on this particular morning, is very disturbing. I am also very concerned that they had access to Terminal equipment. Very suspicious."

"Sounds like you have a traitor at the Terminal," Adam said.

"We shall see," Dolph replied. "For now, it is my mission to see you safely to the Via Sacra. I can spare one Tigershark with a four Nightshark escort. I will personally ride the Tigershark. Any questions, gentlemen?"

Adam raised his machete: shiny, undented, and free from the crimson stains of battle.

"John and I took out a couple of the Rodeleros. One each."

Dolph wiped the gore from his rapier with the sleeve of his slashed and torn combat jacket.

"Good for you, Mr Eden," he said politely. "I am sure your contribution turned the tide of battle in our favour. Be ready to ride. We leave in 10 minutes."

As the diminished convoy sped towards the utility level entrance, Adam sat quietly at the back of the Tigershark, contemplating his gutless inaction. As they rode, the Khevsurs either side of the board, their red Georgian crosses almost invisible beneath the dried blood, retained a hard won heroic bearing. Though the warriors never mentioned Adam's cowardly behaviour, he caught the cold glances and scornful expressions. Now, his fear was gone, replaced with the deep hurt of humiliation. Using a childhood analogy, to everyone at school, Adam was now the 'precious' kid who crapped his pants in class.

THE VIA SACRA

Tired and bloodied, the Khevsurs and board riders guarded the hall. Dolph and Adam stood by the entrance to the utility level, weapons unsheathed, as John Down placed his hand on the palm scanner. In a second, the wide door slid open, revealing a large empty room beyond – two more doors at the far side of the room the only visible features. Adam peered into the space, looking for hidden adversaries.

"Even though the panel accepts anyone's palm, the conquistadors never enter the utility level," John said, walking confidently into the room. "If they appeared in the halls right now, you could stand in here taunting them and they would not cross the threshold – although they might let loose a bolt or two."

"The conquistadors are not necessarily the threat," Adam cautioned.

A strong hand grabbed Adam's shoulder and pulled him back into the hall. Adam turned to face Dolph. Using one hand, the towering Commander roughly grabbed Adam by the shirt and lifted him to eye level.

"I expect you to defend Mr Down with both your blade and your life. They say you are a man of rare qualities, but so far, you have shown us nothing." Dolph's expression remained neutral and unmoving as he lowered Adam back down. "What you do here will not be forgotten."

Lost for words, Adam nodded quickly and hurried into the room, the door sliding shut behind him.

Oblivious to the confrontation, John stood by the two rear doors.

"We can take the elevator, or the stairs. The corridor to the Via Sacra is some 300ft below us, so I would suggest the elevator."

"Definitely the elevator," Adam agreed. "Not just because I'm lazy, but we might need all our strength for whatever lies ahead."

They stepped into the bland steel lift – up and down arrows, one blue button, and a welcome absence of muzak.

"Going down, Down," Adam joked, pressing the down arrow.

The button glowed green and the lift began its descent.

After a few minutes, with little sensation of movement, Adam asked how long it would take to reach the utility level floor.

"About twenty minutes," John said. "The elevator is very slow. Perhaps I can somewhat relieve the tedium."

John pressed the blue button and the back panel of the lift became transparent, revealing the austere landscape of the utility level.

Stretching out into the far distance, the city-sized utility level had a disturbing geometric monotony – soaring towers, deep trenches, and colossal cubes – a stark construction of concrete and dull metal. Snaking down from the impenetrable dark of the vast sky-wide ceiling, profusions of pipes carried the murky effluent flow of the slerds to the gigantic domed bioreactors – anaerobic digestion, breaking down the waste into carbon dioxide and methane, satisfying the voracious power demands of the Viroverse.

Other pipes, gleaming white, crisscrossed below the dark, like extruded surrealist representations of clouds. Here and there, the white pipes combined, and thrust downwards into the floor far below, perhaps to the lower level of the Viroverse.

"Those must be the transport tubes," Adam said. "That's how we travel to other viros during the sleep phase."

"Highly probable," John agreed. "I used to think the brown tubes were for our conveyance, but since seeing the slerds I now believe they serve a far filthier function."

The lift maintained its slow descent to the utility level floor. Sucking up his pride, Adam decided to apologise for, and attempt to explain, his recent cowardice. Whilst he mulled over the best way to broach the subject, John took the conversation in an unexpected direction.

"It occurred to me that I have not asked about the lovely Jennifer."

"The lovely who?"

"Your fiancée; when we dealt with the clone catastrophe, she was all you could talk about."

"That was over 300 years ago," Adam laughed, trying to place the name. "What did she look like?"

"Well, I was never introduced to the young lady, but I recall you describing her as a radiant angel with ringlets of gold and a smile that could brighten the darkest day."

"Hah, I said that? I must have been in love." Adam clicked his fingers as an image sprung to mind. "Ah, now I remember her; crazy, crazy. We were together for about two years. Far too intense about the legend. Tried to talk me into fighting in the Psychoviro every week, so she had to go."

"Hmm, no matter how long I live in the Viroverse, I will never understand some people's total lack of commitment."

"So, you've never strayed … or at least been tempted?"

"Never, never, Mr Eden!" John said adamantly, exaggerating his shock at the accusation. "I will admit I have certain female admirers, some remarkably comely, but I draw strength from God and my undying devotion to my beautiful wife. Temptation is for the weak. Do you have a lady in your life right now?"

"Not right now. Me and Louise split up a few months ago."

"Humph, so you are quite the philanderer."

"We were together for nearly 90 years! Before Louise, it was … err … Carol; I was with her for 25 years. "

"My point exactly. What did you not understand about, 'Till death do us part'?"

"Hah, I'm off the hook then; I die about eight times a year in the Psychoviro."

"That is not death," John said.

"I still think 90 years is a pretty impressive achievement."

Reaching the ground floor, the lift door slid open. John hurried out and took a left turn down a long narrow corridor. Since walking two abreast was an uncomfortable squeeze, Adam stayed in front, machete in hand.

Brightly lit, the tough grey vinyl flooring and plain whitewashed walls seemed too cold and lacklustre for a place so reverentially titled, The Via Sacra.

"Dare I ask if your parents are still married?" John asked, continuing the conversation. "The way you always described their relationship, I detected more than a touch of volatility."

"Yeah, they're still married … at the moment." Adam wished John would change the subject before anger got the better of him.

"At the moment? What on Earth do you mean by at the moment?"

"I mean they're always falling out. Over the centuries, they've split up, met other people, split up again, got back together, split up … You get what I'm saying."

Walking behind, John remained silent.

"Thing is," Adam continued, "no matter how long they're apart, sooner or later they always get back together. It took thirty years one time, but somehow they found their way back into each other's hearts. You know, despite all their arguments and insane behaviour, they really, really need one another. I guess you could it true love."

"I believe serial adultery is a more appropriate term," John sniffed.

Clenching his grip on the machete, it took all of Adam's resolve not to lash out the sanctimonious Victorian. However, in his head, he kept telling himself that their strained bond of friendship was deep enough to survive such trivial conversation.

"There it is, up ahead!" John exclaimed, pointing over Adam's shoulder. "The door to the Via Sacra."

An almost non-descript door – flat, white, with a simple steel handle – stood between the corridor and the secrets of the sacred road. Adam turned the handle and opened the door.

Darkness obscured the true size of the vault, its extremities unseen in the inky black. In contrast, part of the room, illuminated by bright directional spotlights, revealed the cold reality of the Via Sacra – far removed from the illustrious mausoleum erected in Adam's imagination. Experiencing a sickly unease, he lowered his machete and took slow steps down the industrial steel staircase.

"This is terrible," he murmured, reaching the bottom of the stairs. "Why didn't you tell me the Via Sacra was like this?"

"Perhaps I wanted to see your reaction, Mr Eden."

Walking into the harsh light, the air filled with the loud hum of machinery, Adam walked to the end of a fast moving industrial conveyor belt. Behind the long conveyor, ran another, almost as busy as the first. Three more, further along, stood silent, and non-operational.

"Are those what I think they are?" Adam asked, referring to the steel containers travelling along the conveyor belt. "They look like futuristic coffins."

Like a huge ammunition belt fully loaded with human sized silver bullets, the coffins lay across the conveyor, smoothly, relentlessly heading for the end of the line. Adam watched in silent horror as container after container tipped over the end of the belt, gravity flipping the top open, depositing a naked corpse into a gaping hole in the floor. Adam leant over a waist high metal barrier surrounding the hole, and looked down into the darkness. Accompanying the swift descent of each body came a subtle hiss some metres below. Somehow connected to the belt, the containers carried on under the conveyor in the reverse direction – perhaps to collect another customer.

John tapped Adam on the shoulder with his cane.

"Quite shocking, is it not? Come, let me explain the process."

They walked to the other end of the conveyor, stopping short of the darkness.

"The conveyor starts outside The Via Sacra, on the other side of the wall. This part of the journey is to pay final respects before recycling."

"You call this respectful?"

"Considering that the essence of the individual, the remaining fragment of brain from their first-life, has already been saved via time channelling, it could be argued that we are dealing with soulless shells. However, I maintain that these are still human beings worthy of a final consideration."

"I say it looks like a production line in a fridge factory. This is death rites on an industrial scale."

"The sacred road handles over 20 million bodies per year," John explained. "The figure used to be much lower, but with the Viroverse population standing at close to 140 billion, two of the conveyors are in almost constant use. At certain times of the year, usually in mid-January, conveyor number three sparks into life. As far as I am aware, the other conveyors have never seen any use, and I pray it stays that way."

"So, how many go down the chute each minute?"

"The road only operates during the human conscious phase, so that's 16 hours per day. Obviously, the numbers vary, but the maximum limit per conveyor is one body every two seconds. The first conveyor always runs at full speed, with number two often reaching its limit. If I remember correctly, last year we ran an average of about 60 bodies per minute."

Shocked at the scale of the operation and the number of bodies involved, Adam remained silent. John moved along the line, pointing out a black metallic stalk overhanging the belt, firing an intense stream of particles at the lids of the coffins passing underneath.

"This device prints the symbol of the deceased's belief onto the coffin lid. The symbol is based on the subject's true beliefs, gleaned from an in-depth analysis of their profile, not necessarily their professed religion."

Adam watched the device print a scarlet 'A' onto a passing coffin.

"I guess that one's an anarchist."

"An atheist; although there are a few competing symbols for each belief. I am told there is another machine somewhere which erases the symbol as the coffin is readied for another body."

Adam noticed a similar black stalk further along the line. No particles fired from the device, but an annoying click sounded every time a coffin passed underneath.

"That noise is so fu ... irritating."

"What you are hearing is a 30 minute spoken funeral service, appropriate to the deceased's beliefs, played in a second; the pitch is transposed to avoid a high-pitched squeak. Beyond this point there is only the recycling chute."

"So, what you are saying is that, in your final moments before oblivion, you get a sticker and a click. Hell, I got more than that when I took the kids to Alton Towers."

John tilted his top hat and brushed his hand over a coffin lid like a car dealer presenting his 'star buy'.

"You also get to ride in a luxurious silver-plated coffin."

"Yeah, but getting dumped down a recycling chute is a pretty shitty end to any rollercoaster ride."

John sighed, and leant against the recycling barrier, watching the unceasing stream of flesh.

"The hissing noises are the recycling filters pre-processing the bodies," he explained. "Beyond that, all I know is that the bodies are recycled into the resource vats for general use. The exact process of destruction is a closely guarded secret."

"So your old body could come back as anything and everything."

"Who knows," John said, smiling, "perhaps that revolting food you ate in the outpost may have contained vestigial remnants of your previous bodies."

Adam leaned out, and slapped the head of a falling body.

"I'll still eat them," he said defiantly. "In my first-life I had no idea what went into a Tabbas burger, so I don't care if these guys are part of the mix – I'm sure they'll turn out real tasty."

THIS IS WHAT WE ARE

Leaving the dark areas until last, John and Adam searched around the brightly lit conveyors and the steel staircase for clues. Since high-powered directional cleaning jets, set into the ceiling and floor, activated once every two months, Adam rated their chance of finding anything significant as near impossible.

As he approached the fifth conveyor, Adam wrinkled his nose, detecting a musty odour in the air.

"Smells like stinky socks," he said. "John, shine your torch over there, behind the last conveyor. I think there's something on the floor."

John took a long sniff, wafting the air towards his nose like a wine connoisseur.

"Unfortunately, I know that smell. I would describe it as wet dog, but stinky sock is close.

Cautiously, they peered behind the last conveyor – the ancient machine, silent, unmoving, redundant. John shone his powerful torch at the misshapen heap on the floor. Adam retched, and grabbed the side of the conveyor for support.

"Oh shit, what the hell is that?"

Fleshy translucent pink, with crumpled distortions of bones within its gelatinous body, the mound resembled a reject from a life-size human shaped jelly mould. Hideously twisted, the almost tentacle limbs bent out unnaturally. The glob-like head, its features compressed against the floor, oozed a milky white slime from what was once a mouth. Perhaps most disturbing of all, was a thin film of red liquid spread under and around the body. Realising he was standing on the liquid, Adam raised his foot – his stomach heaved at the accompanying gluey sucking sound.

"What the Hell …?" Adam turned away and vomited violently over the conveyor. Suddenly, the conveyor jolted into life – the sick spilling over the edge of the belt and disappearing down into the darkness of the recycling tube. Wiping his dripping chin, Adam heard the faint hiss of a recycling filter many metres below.

John handed Adam an embossed calfskin covered spirit flask.

"Martell cognac. In this place, I often need a certain liquid fortification."

Adam took a generous swig, swished the warm amber liquid around his mouth and gulped it down.

"What is that thing?" he croaked, the spirit and bile burning his throat. He took another swig. "Is it … was it human?"

"This is what we are," John explained. "When I became Overseer of the Dead, the Captain explained the truth of us. This is what happens to our dead bodies if we are not recycled."

"Looks a bit like one of the jellymen, only more disgusting."

"A shrewd observation, Mr Eden, since the osmotic guards are made from the same material. In the early days, well before you found your way into the halls, the guards were denser and only slightly jelly-like – quite formidable foes. As their resource stream exhausted, they became increasingly dilute. These days, I still discern a stain here and there on the hallway walls."

"We're made of jelly?"

"Algae; synthetic, with additional meta-materials, but we are predominantly algae based. A rather versatile material, capable of multiple densities and textures, and even powers our tiny bodies via microbial fuel cell technology."

"So, you're saying we're basically pond scum?"

For the first time since leaving the Terminal, John cracked a smile.

"Basically, yes."

"Hah, I think that's pretty much what we deserve. After all, didn't we originally crawl out of the primordial swamps?"

"Had he been resurrected, no doubt Mr Darwin would enjoy the irony."

John poked the end of his cane into the putrid blob, and lifted up a gummy strand. Pulling off the sticky mess with his gloved hand, he rapped one of the outstretched hands – a dull thud indicating a harder substance.

"This is quite recent," he said. "After the moisture has leached or evaporated from the body, the material dries out to a consistency not unlike a hard-boiled sweet. That so much is still wet and pliable indicates that this poor soul has only been dead for a few days, at most a fortnight. There was a loss of a few bodies about ten ago, so we have our timeframe. The real question is who or what placed him here."

"How can you be sure it's a 'him'?" Adam asked.

"Our records show that apart from a handful of females, the vast majority of missing bodies are male. If you so wish, we could turn the body onto its back to check for remnants of genitalia."

Taking another swig, Adam shook his head.

"No way. I'll trust you on this one. I guess the body was grabbed from one the working conveyors and dumped here, maybe accidently if the body snatchers were in a hurry."

"And, so what we are looking for might well be in this part of the vault."

Opening a long box beneath the conveyor, John pulled out two steel-shafted shovels, and a small shiny object, which he popped into his jacket pocket.

"I apologise for the low tech – a personal preference – but we need to shovel the unit onto the conveyor." John paused, leaning on the black steel handle. "Oh my Lord, I just called this poor soul a unit. When did I become so cold hearted? Perhaps I am finally losing my respect for humanity?"

"You haven't," Adam said, thrusting the spade under the blob's chest. "You're just trying to rationalise pure horror. I do it all the time in the Psychoviro. Now, shove your spade under his belly and see if we can lift the bugger in one go."

On the count of three, both men, legs bent to take the strain, heaved as one. The wet mess lifted far more easily than expected, the large central section too liquid to adhere to the floor. Before they could tip the body onto the belt, the resistance increased due to the long gummy strands still attached to the dry stuck down extremities. Faces red with effort, they heaved with all their strength, until finally the body plopped onto the belt.

"Phew, that was exhausting," Adam wheezed, dropping the shovel.

The conveyor yet again sprang into operation, but the gelatinous mass remained unmoved on the frictionless belt, anchored to the floor by the tough elastic strands. Slowly, alarmingly, the front half of the blob began slipping off the side of the conveyor. Adam reacted immediately, pushing it back onto the belt with his bare hands, engulfing his arms up to the elbows. Lending his assistance, John used his spade to drive the mass towards the end of the conveyor.

In a sudden lurch, the blob slopped over the edge of the belt, the weight snapping the anchoring strands. Adam lifted off the floor, one arm still stuck up to the elbow. He cried out as he slipped towards the recycling chute – after thousands of recycled Adam Edens, the thin filament of his true identity, that sliver of brain that contained 'the self', was about to join the resource pool.

John Down intervened, grabbing Adam around the waist. He wedged his knees under the conveyor and held fast. The sticky mass slowly flopped down the chute – sucking away from Adam's arm. Once free, John shot backwards, taking Adam with him. Shaking from his near-death experience, Adam picked himself up and helped John to his feet.

"I owe you for that," Adam said, controlling his breathing. "I can't remember when I was that scared. But, at least I left with a consolation prize." He brandished a long femur bone like a sword. "En garde, Monsieur Down!"

Grumbling quietly to himself, John tidied the crease of his grey stripe trousers. Adam apologised and held the bone against his chest.

"In nomine Patris et fillii et Spiritus Sancti," he solemnly intoned, crossing the bone before throwing it down the recycling chute. Picking up the shovels once more, they scraped up the dried remnants.

Resuming the search in the darker areas of the vault, Adam decided to check the walls for hidden passageways. The elevated grey stone walls reached some 20 feet up to the ceiling – an imposing interlocking array of large solid blocks, reminiscent of the inside of a medieval castle. John held the torch whilst Adam checked the blocks for hollows, rapping the hard stone with the hilt of his machete. Without a ladder, they could only check the bottom two rows. Making swift progress, they soon made their way around the room, from the fifth conveyor all the way round to the staircase.

"Nothing," John said despondently. "Perhaps if you stand on my shoulders we could check the next two rows."

Lightly scraping his machete against one of the blocks, Adam came up with another idea.

"Do you have anything with a straight edge? I thought I could use my machete but there is a curve on one side and the hilt juts out slightly on the other."

"Would this do?" John asked, producing a magnifying glass from the inner pocket of his jacket. "The handle is perfectly straight and conveniently unscrews from the lens frame."

Adam took the thin metal shaft and placed it over the join between two blocks – perfectly flush as he expected. With John following, shining the torch where needed, Adam repeated the test on the other blocks. Nearing the fifth conveyor, Adam stopped and smiled.

"This join isn't flush," He quickly checked the join on the other side of the block. "And, neither is this one."

"Not to dampen the spirit, but just how do you propose we move a stone block of that size?"

Adam pushed the end of his machete into the thin gap and began wedging left to right.

"I don't think this is one of the blocks. It's some sort of thick panel made to look like one of the blocks. It looks too tough to smash, but I might be able to prise it loose."

Working the blade further into the join, Adam gently opened up a tiny gap.

"This is no good." He withdrew the machete. "I can wedge it open a little, but at this rate I'm going to snap the blade. When I say 'now', stick the claw of your cane into the gap and give it a really good pull."

Replacing the blade into the slit, Adam carefully wedged open the panel as much he dared.

"Now!" he cried.

John jammed the silver-plated steel claw into the opening and pulled hard, gritting his teeth and grunting as his muscles took the strain.

"It's working," Adam said, as the gap slightly widened. "Wait, I can see what's holding the panel on; some kind of very thick material. There are two strips on this side, could be two on the other side. Pull with all your might; I'm going to try something."

John leant back, making a supreme effort, whilst Adam sawed through the tough material with his machete. It took only a few seconds to cut through the material. John staggered back as the panel swung open, the connectors on the other side acting like rudimentary hinges.

Instinctively, Adam thrust his machete into the darkness beyond the opening, whilst John brought up his torch. Cut deep through the thick wall and beyond, a smooth tunnel angled steeply downward. A ramshackle metal stairway sat tight in the gap, offering an easy yet precarious descent.

This is the northernmost edge of the Viroverse," John said, leaning in and running his hand across the smooth surface of the tunnel. "There are no tools in the Viroverse powerful enough to cut through these outer walls. Perhaps this tunnel was excavated during the initial construction."

Adam examined the back of the hanging panel. Two metal handles jutted out, held on with more of the strange grey material. The unexpectedly strong adhesion made peeling off a piece extremely difficult. Using his tactical blade, Adam chiselled off a sliver.

"You know, I think this is duct tape," he said, trying to shake the piece from his hand. "It's much thicker than usual, and really, really sticky, but I'm sure its duct tape. You know, I think it might be full-scale, like you'd find in the real world."

"I recall the Captain mentioning that Mr Tikolo had such a tape around his leg when he first arrived. Could there be a connection?"

Adam ripped the tape away from his hand, losing a little skin in the process. With his machete held outstretched, he pointed down the stairway.

"I guess our answer lies down there."

Sturdy enough, the rough stairway consisted of odd lengths of pipe and metal plates crudely tied and bolted together. Anxiously, Adam and John carefully tested each step as they progressed ever downward. Reaching the bottom, relieved the structure had not collapsed, they walked out onto a grey paved floor. Shining the torch around the space revealed they were standing on a short platform in a wide tube – reminding Adam of a small underground station. He peered over the blue tiled edge of the platform but saw no rails, grids, or power lines, just more grey paved flooring. To the south, in shadows under the Via Sacra, the tube ended some twenty feet away. Shining the torch to the north, the tube carried on into darkness.

"Should I call out," Adam asked, straining to see further along the mysterious tube.

"No, and I suggest we talk quietly. The Captain supplied us the means to search a place such as this." John placed his top hat on the platform floor, and reached in with both hands.

"I guess you're not going to pull a rabbit out of there," Adam quipped, hearing the sound of unzipping.

"The upper part of the hat has a reinforced compartment. I was not to bring this out unless we were beyond the Viroverse." John stood up, a black dagger-shaped object in one hand, his hat in the other. "A scout drone."

"I thought you called that type of technology cowardly."

John placed the top hat back on his head and rubbed the device with his thumb – the sharp tip glowed red.

"The drone has no offensive capabilities, and the red light confirms that we are outside the jurisdiction of the Viroverse. It will map and record anything it detects and return here." Holding the tiny drone up to his face, John whispered,

"Heathrow Six," and launched the device into the air, like encouraging a bird to flight. With a high-pitched whine, the drone shot off into the darkness.

"So, what do we do now?"

"Unless you have a pressing engagement, I suggest we sit and wait for the drone's return. That may take a few minutes or perhaps a few hours. At the latest, it will return by 8pm. That should give us enough time to get back to the team and to a nearby safe viro where we can sleep."

Adam looked at his Tommy Bahama Hula watch – 3.47pm – and groaned. John took a pack of playing cards out of his jacket pocket.

"Beggar Thy Neighbour?"

THE BEAST WITHIN

The scout drone returned after only 30 minutes. John secured the precious device inside his top hat, and the two men hurried out of the Via Sacra to meet the security team – glad to leave the gruesome vault and the never-ending stream of bodies. As the lift ascended to the upper halls, Adam marvelled at the brutal magnificence of the utility level. The beating heart of the Viroverse, its colossal structures and very existence were unknown to the miniature immortals cosseted within their comfortable environments.

Once out of the lift, John straightened his hat and tidied his silk cravat. Adam strolled to the main door, quietly relieved to be alive, and looking forward to further sunny days idling by the river.

"You know, I was actually looking forward to some action," he claimed, with retrospective bluster. "Only a one-on-one, but enough to get the juices going. I know there's no resurrection, but a showdown with some crappy guard would've been OK. Oh well, at least I got to see where all my dead bodies go."

"I have every confidence in your courage and fighting skills," John admitted. "The Captain picked you, and I always trust his judgement … though I admit there are times I cannot initially see his wisdom."

"Behold the wisdom," Adam laughed, theatrically brandishing his machete as he pressed his other hand against the palm scanner. "Well, I hope I never see that damn creepy place again. No wonder you're reading Dante and Poe …"

The door slid open, and a steel sword hilt punched hard into Adam's face – the elaborately engraved finger guard shattering his cheekbone. Stunned by the attack, Adam dropped his machete and fell sideways, knocking his head against the side of the door. For a fleeting moment, he regained his bearings, and swivelled on a fast failing balance to face the enemy. The Rodelero raised his blade, intending to cleave his opponents skull, just as Adam closed his eyes and fell back against the doorframe, hand held out in feeble defence. Fortunately timed unconsciousness meant the strike missed its intended target – the swift descending blade severing Adam's outstretched thumb, slicing off an ear, and biting into the collar of his shirt.

Falling to the floor, Adam entered a familiar world of silent black, where time had no meaning save for the beating of his heart, and pain was but a distant thud on a locked door. The passing of seconds, minutes, perhaps hours, were an unknown and unappreciated quantity to the man in the pink hibiscus shirt. Eventually, cold reality, the irritating condition of the conscious world, trickled into his dulled mind – the smell of blood, the noise of clashing weapons, and the screams and groans of frantic combatants.

Intense pain flashed into unwanted existence as Adam blinked open his eyes. He tried to feel the right side of his head but the excruciating pain in his hand and neck stopped him from raising his arm. Using his left hand for support, he sat up, and looked around the hall.

About ten feet away, John Down battled ferociously against a Rodelero, striking the thin end of his cane into the Spaniards stomach, before viciously cracking the silver claw handle into his jaw. Taking a step back, the Rodelero spat blood contemptuously and quickly responded with a bluff swing of the rapier, throwing John off his guard. The Rodelero immediately followed with a hefty sideswipe of his rodela. Knocked to the ground, John had the skill and dexterity to roll onto his back and held up the cane with both hands just in time to block the lethal down sweep of the sharp edged blade.

Bleary eyed, Adam picked himself up off the bloody floor. Two other Rodeleros lay nearby, motionless – dead or at least close to death's door – and a badly wounded Khevsur, Mr Gigauri, groaned quietly, slowly dragging himself towards his sword. Adam caught the eye of the Georgian warrior and both men exchanged a mandatory manly nod. The message was clear. It was time to unleash the wrath of Copacabana.

Adam reached down with his uninjured left hand and picked up his machete. Taking in a deep breath, puffing out his chest, he mocked the Rodelero for hitting a man when he was down.

"Steel against steel!" Adam cried, aggressively whipping his machete through the air. "But hey, you can keep the shield if you need it, you coward!"

Turning away from John Down, who shuffled backwards to relative safety, the Rodelero rapped his rapier against his rodela, and dared Adam to make a move. Raising his machete, he dared, swaggered forward … and slipped up on his own severed ear.

Unfortunate unconsciousness left Adam in the same dark silent place as before. He awoke abruptly, lying on his back, and witnessed the ongoing battle between John Down and the Rodelero. Without assistance, John now had the upper hand, raining blows down on his hapless opponent – the Spanish warrior forced into a slow blocking retreat behind his rodela. In a sudden reckless quest for supremacy, the Rodelero came out fighting. Letting down his guard, he swiped a wide arc with his rapier. Anticipating the move, timing the sweep of the sword, John thrust his cane onto the floor and pole-vaulted over the blade towards the enemy. Legs together, the eminent physician performed a perfect landing on the Rodeleros left knee. Despite his own pain, Adam winced, hearing a loud cracking of bone.

A groan prompted Adam to glance to his side. The bruised and bloodied Mr Gigauri was a couple of feet nearer his sword. Once more exchanging looks, the Khevsur's glaring expression now seemed to scream, 'get off your lazy arse and fight!'

John Down stood over the surrendered enemy, threatening to hit him in the face with his cane. The Rodelero lay on his back, grinning smugly, hands behind his head. Adam limped over, the blood from his ear wound soaking into his shirt and matting his hair.

"Leave him be," he told John, noticing the portentous fury in his friend's face.

Spotting a discarded tranqbow near the intersection – bolt loaded and ready to fire – Adam advised John to stay calm. He ran over to collect the weapon, but came to a skidding stop as two more Rodeleros appeared from the right junction.

Talking animatedly, the Rodeleros pointed at Adam, perhaps baffled by his unusual clothes. One of them walked forward to confront the Aloha warrior, whilst the other stood back, wryly stroking his immaculately manicured beard. Exuding the fearless bravado of the forces that brought down the mighty Aztec Empire, the conquistador laughed haughtily, and honoured Adam with a light flick of his rapier.

"Many, many years ago, señor," he began, his speech heavily accented, "I heard a tale of a man such as you – a fairy tale of course. They say he came from the land of Eden and slew the monstrous silver beasts. That man also wore a shirt of lady's flowers. If you are that man, then I …"

Without warning, not even a facial twitch or the blink of an eye, Adam leapt forward, curving his machete towards the enemy's throat. Revealing lightning fast reflexes and frighteningly accurate anticipation, the Rodelero raised his rodela and stepped backwards, maintaining his distance. Skilfully synchronised with the move, the Rodelero's slim rapier thrust down from above the shield.

Frantically evading the plunging sword, Adam awkwardly rolled backwards. As he fell, the point of the elegant Spanish rapier slid under the skin of his scalp, slitting open a two-inch gash – an unwanted centre parting. Despite the blood soaking his hair into a wet-look redhead, he immediately sprung into a crouching stance and slashed out with his machete. Blind luck was on his side as the blade clashed against the Rodelero's rapier, defeating the deadly follow-up strike.

Struggling to his feet, wiping his bloodied face with the back of his thumb-less hand, Adam moved warily. He stayed on his opponent's sword side, diminishing the hiding and blocking qualities of the rodela shield. Now, sharpness of mind and eye were the most potent weapons. For a few minutes, both men sparred with slow caution, toying with each other's defences, looking for any weakness or opening.

Seizing his chance, Adam feinted fast to the left, leaving the Rodelero's inner shield arm wide open. Bringing down the machete, he sliced through the quilted armour and deep into the bicep muscle. The Spaniard gasped in pain as his shield arm fell limply by his side, hanging uselessly as a dead weight.

Keeping up the pressure, ensuring the Rodelero had no time to unstrap his shield, Adam danced around, forcing his foe to wheel and lurch. Without the use of the shield, the Rodelero's sword attacks were exposed and easy to counter.

"Necesita asistencia, Javier?" the other Rodelero yelled, witnessing his comrade's struggle.

Grunting a negative, the defiant Spaniard stepped up a gear, engaging in fast footwork and intimidatingly precise sweeps and thrusts of the rapier. Adam easily parried the blows and skilfully sidestepped the attacks. Looking beyond the enemy, he suppressed a smile as he noticed a familiar figure emerge from the intersection.

With a stealth belying his size, Commander Zabel rushed up behind the second Rodelero. In a brutally rapid two-handed movement, he snapped the Spaniard's arm at the elbow – the rapier falling to the floor amid its owners screams. The Commander wrapped a brawny arm around the Rodelero's neck and held him in a vicelike chokehold. After only six seconds, the body went limp and Dolph carefully lowered the man to the floor.

Arms crossed, Dolph stood watching Adam fight. Casually walking around the furious encounter, the Commander studied each move, assessing the legend of Copacabana first hand.

Adam did not disappoint. In a bold and bloody end game, he piled forward, blocking his enemy's rapier with his machete, whilst grabbing the Rodelero's wounded arm. Digging his fingers deep into the gaping flesh, right down to the bone, Adam squeezed and wrenched, causing the Rodelero to scream out in agony and drop his sword.

Adam quickly withdrew his hand from the bloody hole and moved up close, feeling his shocked adversary's warm breath on his face. Despite missing an opposable thumb, Adam still managed to grip his unfolded tactical knife in his right hand, and pressed the tip hard against the Rodelero's groin.

"Time to end our little dance, don't you think?" he whispered menacingly. "I've lived with my boys long enough to know what hurts." He gently twisted the blade. "Let go of the sword or you will know real pain."

Sweat formed on the Rodelero's forehead as he considered his options.

"There is no honour in this, señor," he spluttered.

Another tender twist of the knife and the proud Spanish warrior promptly relinquished his weapon.

"Nighty night," Adam said, viciously punching the hilt of his machete against the Rodelero's head.

Dazed, the Rodelero fell to the floor. Dolph walked over with a loaded tranqbow and administered a swift bolt to the enemy's arm. As Adam sheathed his blade, two Nightsharks cruised in from the right junction, riders and warriors stooped with fatigue and the scars of combat.

Adam became aware of a constant thumping noise, punctuated by the intermittent clash of metal. Looking around, he saw John Down standing over the dead body of his opponent, battering the man's face and helmet with the steel claw of his cane. Adam ran over to his distraught friend. For a moment, he stood in horror as the cane slammed down once more.

"John, for all that's sacred and holy, you've gotta stop! He's dead!"

Repeatedly, the steel claw smashed into the Rodeleros face, crushing the bone structure, and pulping the once dashing features. The warrior's luxurious 'Van Dyke' moustache was as a greasy rat's tail snaked into coarsely ground raw mince. Ignoring Adam's pleas for him to stop, John boiled with rage.

"You fiend, you are not coming back! You will take up your position in Hell! No more shall perish at your murderous hands!"

Adam tried to wrestle the cane away, disregarding the agony of his bloody thumb stump, which slipped painfully across the ebony shaft.

"Devil! Devil! Devil!" John screamed at the dead Rodelero, his voice increasingly hoarse.

Finally losing the cane, he let out a distressed howl and slumped against the wall. Slipping down, he sat with his head buried in his hands.

"Devil," he sobbed, slowly lowering his hands revealing tearful eyes, face haggard with grief. "I ... I ... have become the Devil."

Adam crouched down beside his distraught friend:

"You? The Devil? I don't think so. I fight Devils every month, so I know what I am talking about. You are a man of the very highest standards and morals – a man of peace amongst the beasts." He pointed to the bloody mess that was once a face. "This is not the John Down I know. This is the product of true horror."

"They show no mercy; they fight to kill," John croaked, throat raw, words indistinct. "Every time they attack, our numbers grow fewer, whilst we send them back to their homes, to their friends and families. Like banished spiders, they eventually find their way back to test us once more. One day, when we are vanquished, what will become of my own family?"

Dolph threw over a small water bottle.

"Drink this," Adam said, passing the bottle to John.

Taking a large gulp, John sighed, and wiped his mouth. Adam held out his hand.

"Have I earned that handshake?"

"Of course you have, but I do not deserve it."

"Then just take my hand."

Adam firmly clasped John's hand and pulled him to his feet.

Unexpectedly, for second time that day, the Commander grabbed Adam by the shirt, lifted him up, and faced him eye to eye.

"Before we leave, there is something I need to know," Dolph said, his face as unreadable as stone. "Did you kill Kevin?"

"Kevin?" Adam choked.

"The inkman."

"Err … yes."

"How did you kill him?"

Adam knew that Dolph Zabel had been the inkman's best and probably only friend. Now, nearly 1000 years after the inkman's death, what were Dolph's motives? Was he looking to execute a long held revenge? With a minimum of movement, Adam slowly reached for his knife. Dolph's eyes subtly narrowed, and Adam obediently brought his hand back without the weapon.

"He challenged me to a duel," Adam explained. "He thought he had the better of me, but I was faking. Arrogant bastard did a victory cartwheel. I simply walked up and disembowelled him while he was in mid-turn. While he lay dying, I cut his head off."

"Why did you kill him?"

"We were just about to face the Dreamers in battle. I couldn't let him jeopardise our lives and the future of the Viroverse."

"Fair enough," Dolph said with a contented smile. "There are so many rumours. I just needed to hear the truth from your own mouth." He lowered Adam to the floor and patted him on the arm. "He was my friend, but that crazy guy was always trouble."

Traumatised and bloodied, the few survivors gathered around their steadfast Commander.

"Leave the wounded and the dead where they lie," Dolph ordered. "We have no time to grieve, pay final respects, or transport the enemy. We must get to a safe viro before midnight. There are seven of us, so we will take the Tigershark with a two Nightshark escort."

"What about our own wounded?" Adam said, gesturing to the fallen Khevsur.

Still unsteady on his feet, John knelt down and checked the warrior's pulse.

"I am afraid Mr Gigauri is dead."

Leaving the dead and wounded behind, the three sharkboards surfed away from the carnage. Though the Terminal had won the day, there was no triumphalism – not even a whoop and a high-five. Without exception, the silent pain of their losses revealed itself in the deep furrows of their brows and the length of their hollow stares.

TERMINAL DESTINATION

Adam awoke the next morning atop a steep grassy bluff overlooking a humble hamlet of thatched cottages. The viro was unmistakably 'olde' English. A black and white pub sat by the small market square, cosily enticing with lead-lined bottle glass windows and a gently swaying wooden sign of a smiling sun. Alongside the pub stood a grey stone chapel – prayer and a pint, for many millennia the sedatives of the masses, and still often effective in the confined worlds of the tiny immortals.

Lying comfortably on the soft grass, Adam rested his chin on his hands and pondered leaving the mission. A fast sprint and he could be sitting at an oak table, supping a mug of strong frothy ale, and tucking into a hot pie. A night's sleep and he would wake up in his own bed. Better still, if the Captain could wipe his memories, then he could spend eternity blissfully ignorant of the dangers that lay beyond the walls.

"Tempting, isn't it," Dolph remarked, startling Adam from his daydreaming.

"I could kill for a pint right now," Adam replied, "even if it's a warm one."

"Dolph slapped Adam on the shoulder:

"That is good, my friend. Keep that attitude for our enemies. Now, stay low and follow us through the portal. We need fresh clothes and some food for our bellies."

"Wouldn't you like to stay … forget about all the troubles out there?"

"Of course I would," Dolph admitted, his voice darker, deeper. "Only maniacs, and those with something to prove, love life on the frontline. Most of us fight for our communities, friends, and families. If we withdraw from the halls, then who is to say that places like this won't become the new frontline." Dolph gestured to the viro's invisible perimeter. "These are not the walls; … we are."

Adam nodded, feeling slightly stupid for extolling the merits of deserting to the fearless Commander. Without warning, Dolph grabbed Adam's chin, turned his head, and stared coldly into his eyes:

"And, if you do decide to run, I promise to make you my personal project. Every morning I will send an assassin to kill you as soon as you leave your house. Your eternity will be nothing but breakfast followed by the painful cycle of death and resurrection. Do you understand me?"

"I do," Adam confirmed, blinking under the intense gaze. "Although, I'll admit, breakfast is my favourite part of the day."

The survivors crawled through the rubbery portal back into the viro waiting room. Healed and refreshed, the horror of the previous day still scarred their minds. They ate heartily, filling the aching void in their stomachs. After a rousing pep talk, Dolph slammed his palm on the scanner and the waiting room door hissed open.

As the two remaining Khevsurs, Mr Arabuli and Mr Oriauchi, stood guard, the others hauled the three sharkboards out into the halls. Within minutes, they were speeding towards the Terminal.

Cruising along the monotonous corridors, unable to defend the potentially perilous intersections, each member of the team successfully disguised their fear. They stayed vigilant, looking for any sign of the enemy, realising that death might lie in wait around any corner. Shivering occasionally, John sat silently in front of Adam, his top hat bowed. As the miles sped by, Adam grew increasingly concerned for the mental health of his Victorian friend.

A few hours into the journey, Louise Samson, one of the Nightshark riders, spotted something in the far distance:

"Sir, there's something coming towards us! Looks like a basic long-board: one rider, male, and …," Louise stared hard; her shades switched to full zoom, "not wearing a Terminal uniform or shades."

On Dolph's orders, they reduced speed – slow enough to step off the boards if required, yet just fast enough to allow for rapid acceleration. The Commander brought his lumbering Tigershark to the front of the group and zoomed in with his own shades:

"I recognise the man. That is Professor Krantz, the interrogator. He should not be out here, not without an escort."

"Perhaps he's the traitor," Adam offered, saying aloud what everyone was thinking.

"A possibility, but we must not jump to conclusions. That said, if Krantz does not slow down, we will turn the sharks sideways and block the hall. Wait for my signal."

Once within two hundred metres of the small convoy, Krantz brought his board to an abrupt halt, nearly pitching himself over the front. Visibly panicked, the professor slowly manoeuvred the board around, executing the embarrassing line-surfing equivalent of a nine-point turn.

"Damn fool's going to run," Dolph said. "Miss Samson, can you catch him before the next intersection?"

"Definitely, Sir, he's got no real speed – doesn't know how to pump and glide. I'll be on him in a few minutes."

"Excellent; then you and Mr Arabuli chase him down and detain him until we catch up. If he gets to the next intersection, I want you to hold off. For all we know, he is leading us into a trap, and I doubt we will survive another ambush."

"Let me do this," Adam said, unclipping his machete and nimbly jumping from the Tigershark. He jogged easily alongside Louise's Nightshark, and slapped Mr Arabuli's chain-mailed arm.

"Mr Eden, what in God's name do you think you are doing?" Dolph demanded, unable to leave his position. "Get back in your seat! I have orders to get you safely back to the Terminal."

Defiantly, Adam kept pace with the Nightshark:

"And, I want to make sure I do! You said only maniacs and those with something to prove love it on the frontline. Well, I really, really don't love it here, but I do have something to prove. Too much blood has been spilled on my behalf."

Perhaps impressed by Adam's heroic words, Mr Arabuli immediately stepped off the board. Taking Adam's place in the Tigershark, the smiling Khevsur warrior took a swift swig of Chacha and raised his flask:

"Kill da filthy bugger, Copa! Avenge my brothers!"

Adam stepped onto the Nightshark, tightly gripped the bungee cord, and leaned back. Louise looked to her commander for guidance; her surprised expression partially hidden behind her dark shades. Dolph remained impassive for a moment – his jaw set so hard it might shatter teeth – then waved on the Nightshark.

"We must take Krantz back to the Terminal for questioning!" he yelled, as the board rapidly accelerated into the distance. "There will be no killing!"

Exhibiting the skill of centuries, Louise subtly pumped the board for increased speed, her lithe body moving in a slow motion of muscular restraint. Leaning back behind the mesmerising figure, Adam found it hard to concentrate on the line ahead – 'thank God I'm not an arse man,' he thought.

Less than two minutes later, they caught sight of Krantz's board. Louise warned Adam to hold on tight, and jumped the board across the hall onto the same white line that Krantz was using:

"This way he won't see us coming! We'll be on him in less than 30 seconds!" She made highly skilled fast twitch muscle movements, increasing the speed beyond what Adam thought possible. "I'm going to skip lines again, and draw alongside! Be prepared for rapid deceleration after the jump!"

The Nightshark rocketed along the white line, catching Krantz so quickly that it seemed as if he was not even moving. His teeth gritted, Adam held in a scream, thinking the board was about to plough into its prey. With less than a second to spare, Louise jumped the board to the left hand line.

Unprepared for the powerful lateral force of the high-speed jump, Adam lost his machete and nearly slipped off the side of the board. Only a determined grip on the bungee cord kept him from flying across the hall and into the hard marble wall. The Nightshark drew alongside Krantz's board and the startled professor lashed out with his fist.

Adam grabbed Krantz's arm and held on. Losing his footing, the professor fell against Adam and lost control of his board. The two boards collided, sending the Nightshark careering across the white lines. Louise furiously performed what looked like an Irish jig, trying to bring the board back under control. Krantz's board, now in an uncontrollable slide towards the wall, clipped the front of the

Nightshark. The impact sent Adam to his knees but he managed to stay on the board, gripping firmly onto the cord. Clasping a strong arm around Krantz, he held the squirming captive tightly until Louise brought the Nightshark to a smooth gliding halt.

"Stop bloody struggling!" Adam shouted at the professor, roughly dragging him off the board and onto the cold hard floor of the hall.

Like a lunatic, Krantz shrieked foul insults, both in English and Spanish, and viciously lashed out at Adam with his fists. After a particularly hard punch to the stomach, Adam reached for his combat knife – a little extra persuasion was necessary. He slapped his belt and gulped; the knife was gone.

"For Cortés!" Krantz shouted, whipping the razor sharp blade into view. Instinctively, Adam shifted into a defensive stance, ready to knock away the attack. He mistook the professor's intent, as Krantz plunged the blade into his own stomach, screaming as the pain shot through his body.

"Oh, you stupid bastard," Adam said, moving forward and catching Krantz with a hard punch to the side of the jaw. With an arm and a knee, he pinned the howling traitor to the floor.

"You are the stupid one. I die; you lose," Krantz seethed breathlessly, spitting out a tooth.

"Then you're out of luck, idiot. You completely missed anything vital. Anyone knows that a neck wound is the sure way out. You're going to suffer pain you won't believe, but no way you're dying before we get you back to the Terminal. I'll bet they'll be queuing up from one end of the concourse to the other to 'interrogate' the interrogator."

Here, Copa," Louise called from a few feet behind, "take these wrist ties! Get him secure before the Commander arrives."

For a second, Adam released his hold on the professor, and turned to catch the ties. Sometimes, a second makes all the difference: the difference between success and failure, and that fateful moment that kicks a hero down to a fool. As he caught the ties in his hand, Adam heard the ominous sound of fleshy suction followed by the familiar rip and squelch of a stabbing blade. He turned to see the consequence of his misjudged second.

His face paralysed in shock and agony, bug eyed and open mouthed, Krantz managed a convulsive splutter in place of a final word. He still gripped the hilt of the knife in a quivering hand – the blade buried deeply in his neck, blood spraying out like crimson water from a perforated hosepipe.

"Shit, shit, shit …" Adam quietly muttered, holding his fingers around the wound in a futile attempt to staunch the flow. Louise walked up and held her hand over her mouth, stifling a surprised gasp:

"What have you done?" she asked.

Adam drew his dripping hand away from the bloody wound and rose to his feet:

"Stupid bastard stabbed himself. I only looked away for a second."

"But you told him…"

The soft hum of magnetics interrupted the conversation, heralding the arrival of the other sharkboards. Dolph was the first on the scene, jumping from his Tigershark and marching straight over. Shaking his head, and casting a dismissive glance at Adam, he asked John Down to join him. Obediently, with a fatigued sigh, John came over and carefully inspected the blood soaked figure.

"Is there anything we can do?" Dolph asked.

"Fetch a mop," John said dryly, before slowly ambling back to his seat.

"Miss Samson, please tell me what went on here. Specifically, I want to know why Professor Krantz was able to stick a knife in his neck."

"After a near collision, Copa…, I mean Mr Eden, attempted to restrain Professor Krantz. I believe the professor acquired Mr Eden's knife in the struggle and stabbed himself in the stomach."

Dolph looked once more at the body, noticing the blood around the professor's abdomen:

"Then can you tell me why the knife is now in his neck?"

"Mr Eden…" Louise cleared her throat, "suggested that a neck wound would be more effective."

Dolph drew in a sharp breath and glowered at Adam:

"You suggested a neck wound would be more effective? Did you also hand him the knife and show him the perfect angle of entry?"

"No … I … looked away, just for a second, to catch the wrist ties!" Adam stammered, offering a feeble defence. "This was all Krantz!"

"So, you looked away, after suggesting that a neck wound would be more effective?"

"In retrospect, I should have probably taken the knife, but I didn't want to open the wound and cause him to bleed out."

"Well, we certainly wouldn't want Professor Krantz to bleed out, would we?"

Dolph turned his back on Adam and walked back to the Tigershark:

"Mr Eden, get back in your seat. Mr Arabuli, I will deal with you once we are back in the Terminal. For now, take your usual place behind Miss Samson. I will have no more of this nonsense."

"What about Professor Krantz?" Louise asked the Commander. She screwed up her face as Adam pulled his knife out of the professor's neck.

"We will leave him here. If we make it back, I will send out a clean-up crew to pick up his body."

Everyone took their respective places, and the three sharkboards continued on their journey. Adam sat quietly at the back of the Tigershark. For a few minutes, thoroughly ashamed of himself, he felt yet again like the embarrassing kid in class, until Mr Arabuli drew alongside:

"Hey, Copa, I must thank you for killing da devil. My brothers can sleep well now."

"I didn't kill him," Adam admitted. "He killed himself. It was suicide."

Mr Arabuli shook his head and pointed his sword at Adam:

"No, da tales do not lie. You have da spirit of a true warrior. You killed da devil with only your words. I salute you!"

"I too salute you, Copa!" Mr Ochiauri cried out from the other Nightshark, prompting a swift rebuke from Dolph.

With a bemused smile, Adam pondered his new status. Was he right to ignore Dolph and chase Krantz for a cheap grab at restoring his shattered pride? Moreover, did the faded legend of Copacabana really need topping up now and then, even if by accident? He decided it was best to accept the strangely fortuitous turn of events. His legend somewhat enhanced, Adam was now the cool kid in school who defied the teacher and sorted out the class snitch.

RETURN OF THE QUEEN

Relief and safety waited an hour down the line – a team of ten Sharkboards guarding either side of an intersection. The formation leader waved on the survivors, as the other operatives clapped respectfully – hard expressions giving away their bitterness and sorrow at the few numbers returning. The ten sharkboards quickly caught up with Dolph's team, moving in front, to the rear and the sides, providing a protective shell.

At regular intervals along the route, more forces joined the convoy. By the time they reached the door to the Terminal's waiting room, a formation of over sixty boards filled the hall.

Entering the replica airport, complete with commercial jetliners parked by the Terminal as well as realistic three-dimensional wall projections of takes offs and landings, Adam felt relief as he walked into the warm air-conditioned comfort of the departure lounge. A number of smartly dressed airport staff – all androids, specially prepped by the Captain – stood ready to greet the survivors, and a fleet of airport carts quickly whisked the weary warriors to the huge bustling central atrium for a private barbeque and soft debriefing in the upscale hotel.

After a well-earned grill and grilling in the Vesuvius Pit Room, Captain Andrews warmly thanked everyone for their valiant efforts. Whilst the board riders and Khevsurs headed to their rooms, with a long stop-off at the piano bar, the Captain ushered Adam, Dolph, and John into a small conference room.

A number of high-ranking Terminal operatives were already present, some seated at the large round oak table in the centre of the room. Adam recognised Deputy Commander Mehta amongst the faces, and waved, glad that she had made it back alive. Before Adam took his seat, the Captain shook his hand and beamed the most joyful of smiles – a perfect 'Duchenne' with the optimum amount of crow's feet around the eyes and an almost sparkling luminescence to the teeth.

"I would like to thank you for accompanying Mr Down. You were a real asset to the team."

"Well, I only fought one of the Rodeleros. Oh, and I brought down another one with a crossbow."

"It only takes an extra drop to make a cup overflow. You made a difference."

"Well, then I'm glad to be of service. And, you know, that's the most awesome smile you've ever flashed."

The Captain raised an eyebrow:

"The product of intense calculation, Mr Eden. It is the furthest I can push the expression before looking like a complete lunatic. My smile is much like my relationship with the Viroverse rules. It walks the line.

"Yeah, and I guess I crossed that line when I killed Professor Krantz with just the power of my words. I don't suppose Dolph spoke too highly of me in his debriefing."

"Despite your little mutiny, Commander Zabel still thinks you have some potential. Concerning Leonard Krantz, it is unfortunate that we lost him, as he was a shining star in the field of rare Spanish dialects. I have been able to access his recent profile and I can now see his involvement. Simply, he was obsessed with the legend of Hernán Cortés. He agreed to supply the conquistadores with some equipment now and then in the hope that he would one day meet his hero. However, his profile revealed that he never met him and knew little about the operation. With all that has happened over the last few days, his part would have been over anyway."

Adam bent his head to the Captain's ear and whispered:

"So, who's keeping an eye on Mr Tikolo whilst you're here?"

"Considering you professed to be an IT expert in your first-life, I am always amazed at your lack of knowledge on the subject. I'm here and there, running in both devices. I am always using multi-location multitasking, inhabiting various devices at any given moment, but it hardly registers on the difficulty scale. As for Mr Tikolo, you'll be happy to learn that he has regained consciousness and is almost fully healed … physically at least." He patted Adam on the arm. "And, you don't have to whisper; I'm about to reveal the secret of the outside to everyone here. It's a brave new world."

Everybody sat down around the table, waiting for the Captain to start the meeting. He sat silently, waiting, gently tapping his fingertips together. The door eventually slid open. Elegantly sashaying into the room with a long practised regal bearing, Queen Boudicca Chang, a former English monarch from the 22nd century, turned everyone's heads. Wearing an understated grey shimmer-suit, her long cherry-blonde ponytail bound in silver-filigree, she offered the ghost of a polite nod to her surprised audience.

Skin like soft snow, black-lined Asian eyes sharply focused, Boudicca smiled as she recognised Adam. Not returning the smile, Adam tightened his lips, angered by her presence. In addition, he expected the resident of the semi-autonomous miniature city of Soñador to be taller. The Dreamers, as Soñadorians were known, were usually twice the height of regular Viroverse inhabitants, and had a superior attitude to match. Obviously, Boudicca had awoken in the Terminal that morning, shrunk to regular Viroverse size – over inflated ego excepted of course.

Almost everyone around the table, including Captain Andrews, stood up as Boudicca walked to her chair. Adam and Dolph, the only exceptions, remained seated with their arms tightly crossed – as if uncrossing them would lead to unwanted involuntary deference.

"So, you are a fellow republican?" Dolph asked.

"Well, possibly; though it's more that Boudicca had my eye pulled out of its socket over and over again, and then trapped me in a metal casket for a few decades so that the entire city population could suck my memories. No matter how much times passes, I just can't quite forgive her for that."

"Ya, crazy inbred nobility."

Ever the perfect host, the Captain formally introduced the illustrious Dreamer, pulling out a chair. Boudicca took her seat without a nod or thank you, and everyone sat down. The Captain called up a number of retinally projected screens, only visible to the watcher, which seemed to hover about two feet away from each person's face.

"Please absorb the briefing. It will give you a detailed report of the problems we face. It will also show you everything we know about the outside world. Of course, you are all bound by the usual confidentiality agreements – break them and you'll be memory wiped and stripped of all Terminal privileges."

For ten minutes, they sat back in their chairs, gasping at the sight of the slerding plains, and shuddering at Mr Tikolo's gruesome leg quarry. To a casual onlooker, unable to see the screens, it would have looked like synchronised meditative madness – a succession of gaping mouths and shocked shudders. After the briefing, everyone talked excitedly about what they had just seen.

"Sir, do we get to visit the outside?" Saloni Mehta asked. "I would love to see the slerding plains."

The Captain shook his head:

"You wouldn't like it – I spared you the smell in the briefing. Visits to the surface use vast resources, so are taken out of necessity rather than sightseeing. Should a number of my calculations be realised, then a surface mission is a distinct possibility, but that is not the subject of today's meeting. Please, pay attention to your screens."

Adam recognised the image on his screen as the tunnel beneath the Via Sacra. The image slowly panned around, revealing Adam and John standing on the tiled platform.

"Hmm?" Adam mumbled, tapping a finger on his chin.

"What is it, Mr Eden?" the Captain asked. "The drone didn't detect anything of note at this end of the tunnel."

Startled out of his musing, Adam's eyes widened:

"I ... was just thinking that backcombed hair is a really, really bad look for me. Makes it look like I've got sticky out ears. Eighty years, and no one said a thing. I'm going back to a nineties' mop."

Ignoring Adam, the Captain swivelled the image back to the tunnel.

"What you are all seeing is the three-dimensional feed from the scout drone. The tunnel is about fifteen miles long and perfectly straight." The feed fast-forwarded along the featureless tube, and then paused by a grey wall. "This is the other end of the tunnel. As you can see, the tunnel ends in this opaque wall –

perhaps graphene or nanolite. We believe that it could be a sliding door, so the tunnel might continue on the other side."

The scene rotated to the left, revealing another tiled platform – almost identical to the one beneath the Via Sacra. The only difference, a major difference, was the presence of a huge square steel door. Resembling a large bank-vault security door, the sturdy slab of metal even had a number of thick locking rods and a submarine-style door wheel.

"That looks a bit old school for the 30th century," Adam noted.

"Do not be deceived," the Captain said, switching the feed to false coloured mode. "Those red dots and lines you are now seeing are various concealed sensors and defence mechanisms. I suspect the door is pure ornamentation, perhaps to throw the unwary off their guard. The AI is certain that the body thieves use this tunnel to gain access to the Via Sacra. It is probable that a large facility lies beyond the door, although it is unlikely to be of a size comparable to the Viroverse."

"And, that is where those delusional conquistadores think their great leader comes from," Dolph said.

"There is no delusion, Commander Zabel. Today, after reviewing the drone footage, the AI relaxed many of the rules regarding privacy and proportionate security. This meant I was finally able to scan the archived profiles of every Spanish prisoner that claimed to have seen Hernán Cortés in the Viroverse. I can confirm that they truly believed what they saw, and the audio and visuals are a perfect match for everything we know about the man. From Mr Tikolo's description of his ordeal and the direction and distance he walked, we also believe that Mr Edgar Allen Poe came from the same facility."

Adam crossed his arms again:

"Saving the slerds; that's the only reason the rules have been relaxed, isn't it? You do nothing for decades, whilst people are losing their lives, then some slerd suffers a little leg carvery and it's any means necessary!"

"That's exactly right, Mr Eden," the Captain agreed. "Their safety and enjoyment is paramount. Those 'bloody slerds', as you call them, paid for the Viroverse and your continued existence. Contractually, the Viroverse is little more than a doll collection. And, a doll collection, even with rebellious little voice boxes, has no real rights, and neither do you."

"Why don't we just seal up the passageway?" John suggested. "They might not possess the technology to break through again."

Captain Andrews agreed that sealing the breach seemed a sensible option, but the AI had insisted on contacting the inhabitants of the 'other place'. Cancelling the floating screens, he turned to Queen Boudicca:

"You Majesty, I believe you can shed some light on what we are dealing with."

Boudicca looked slowly around the table, meeting everyone's gaze, perhaps enjoying the anticipation on the faces of all present.

"My grandfather often talked about his plans for the future," she began. "Some may have called them dreams rather than plans, but Ming Hua was too shrewd to waste time on the unobtainable. He always knew what was coming and where his investments were headed. Before I died, the Chang Corporation already held many lucrative patents in the fields of human longevity and biological miniaturisation."

"The Chang Corporation's dominance in these areas is well documented," the Captain said. "But, what can you tell us of this 'other place'?"

"I do not have any definitive proof, but the discovery of Mr Poe and the involvement of Hernán Cortés, leads me to believe that Ming Hua made good on his plans, and constructed an environment for history's leading lights: famous leaders, warriors, artists, philosophers, inventors …. He always said that only the best people deserved resurrection and immortality."

"Are you sure?" Adam said, frowning. "You're famous and so is John Down, yet here you are, in the Viroverse. Hell, I've had tea and cakes with Queen Victoria and arm wrestled with Pope John Paul II. Shouldn't they all be in that 'other place'?"

"My grandfather was very particular in his tastes and often inflexible in his views – especially regarding the worthiness of others. I suspect he left me out because I was already immortal and always criticised this particular idea. As for the Popes and other religious leaders, I am not surprised they were excluded. Ming Hua was always in conflict with them over his plans. If he had given in to their constant objections then there would be neither immortality nor miniaturised people. Seriously, I don't know who on Earth would choose a 'cross-your-fingers' faith-based afterlife when you could get a rock solid, triple signed contract, guaranteeing resurrection from the Chang Corporation."

"… or your money back!" Adam scoffed.

"As for what particular historical figures my grandfather chose for the 'other place', all I can tell you is that he often mentioned that membership would be limited to about 500 thousand people, and that he would have the final say. Ah yes, he also loved Victorian Britain, so do not be surprised if that has some significance."

The Captain leaned forward:

"So, do you have any advice on how we should approach this? Should I send in a combat team or would a diplomatic approach be more appropriate? I already have a preference, but I do enjoy getting a human perspective … even if I am ultimately going to ignore it."

Dolph slammed his fist on the table:

"We should hit them hard! The rules are relaxed and this 'other place' lies beyond Viroverse jurisdiction, so we can use any weaponry we want. We suffered heavy losses yesterday, but I can still field a force of over 200 operatives. What are a bunch of fatheaded history book characters going to do against a highly trained and well-equipped army? Even if the damned Rodeleros' intervene, it will be a walkover."

"I advise caution," Boudicca spoke calmly, unphased by the Commander's call to arms. "My grandfather would not have built the place without the very best security available. Unless some calamity has befallen the facility, I doubt your forces could breach the defences. Send a small team to investigate … not to invade."

Dolph was about to protest, when the Captain held up a hand, urging him to remain silent:

"Commander Zabel, you have two days to prepare a strike force, but make sure we retain enough operatives to defend the most important halls. You choose the weaponry, but I insist that combustion is still forbidden. Remember that, though relaxed, some rules still apply inside the Viroverse. Use the Terminal as your base, sequestrate as many Sharkboards as you need, and have the force ready to move at an hour's notice."

For a few seconds, Dolph smiled proudly – a smile cut short as the Captain continued:

"For now, I concur with Queen Boudicca's wise counsel. We first try diplomacy: a five-person team, lightly armed, and I suggest that only one Terminal operative is involved. Even though we need an official Terminal representative, I think one hundred years of bloodshed might blind the judgement on both sides. Deputy Commander Mehta, I want you to join the team as chief negotiator."

Saloni stood up and saluted:

"It would be an honour, Sir. I won't let you down."

"I am sure you won't," the Captain said warmly as the deputy sat back in her chair. "Mr Eden, I want you to lead the team."

"Whoa, hold on, I'm Humanity's Representative," Adam protested, sitting up in his seat, realising he was no longer a passive observer. "Surely that makes me a Terminal operative. Only one Terminal operative involved, remember."

"Apart from yesterday's tragic events, I have managed to keep you away from the conflict, so you are not so smeared with the bloody brush. As for your being Humanity's Representative; that is not an official Terminal position. Anyway, as you know, Mr Tikolo has regained consciousness. He has attained a satisfactory level of lucidity and has now taken your job. After all, he is a genuine member of the human race and so has precedence. However, on behalf of the Terminal and the surface population of Earth, I would like to thank you for nearly one thousand years of sterling service."

Adam slumped back into his chair and rhythmically rapped his fingers on the oak veneer tabletop.

"You'd think I'd get gold watch or at least a pen. Do I at least get to choose the other three members of the team?"

"I want Stardust and Blitz to accompany you. They have fighting skills, and a certain ruthlessness should the need arise. The fourth person needs to be someone who was famous in their first-life – someone isn't intimidated by celebrity."

John Down stood up, and looked directly at the Captain.

"If I may be so bold, I would like to nominate myself for the position. Given my place in the history books, and Mr Chang's love for Victorian Britain, I feel my exclusion from this 'other place' is probably an oversight. I also have extensive negotiating experience with the Dreamers and her gracious Majesty, so I feel I am uniquely qualified for this mission."

Deep in his artificial mind, Captain Andrews silently accessed John Down's recent profile.

"Mr Down, your request is regretfully denied. From today, consider yourself on indefinite leave. Visit your family and enjoy the sea air. You are one of the Terminal's greatest assets and I need you to be 100 percent fit. Remember, this is not a mission for Terminal operatives."

"Then let me go," Boudicca demanded, as John sat quietly back into his chair. "I am the perfect choice. For all we know, my grandfather might live in this place, and I was always his favourite. Surely, the Chang name carries some weight with these people. After all, do they not owe their continued existence to my family's gracious generosity?"

Clenching his fist, although this time refraining from thumping the table, Dolph barely contained his anger.

"Sir, don't listen to this undeserving blue blood! We have lost good men and women to her family's fantasy playground. Unleash the full power of the Terminal and finish this once and for all."

"Your objections are noted, Commander," the Captain said, narrowing his eyes at his impertinent security chief. "You will be pleased to learn that Queen Boudicca will not be the fifth member." He turned to face Boudicca. "If your father built this facility then we cannot be certain his legacy is … respected. If any enmity exists against your family then your presence might be less than helpful, and I cannot guarantee your safety. Even if I thought otherwise, I still cannot send you, since the AI has put a block on any first-life British royalty being involved. The AI gave no reason for this." The Captain turned his attention to Adam. "Mr Eden, what if I was to tell you that Stern Lovass, the internationally renowned hindreader had agreed to fill the position? Despite being told of the risks, especially the possibility of true death, he seemed most eager to join the team. Along with your Psychoviro friends, Mr Lovass arrived at the Terminal this morning and is currently in the Central Plaza, wowing our visitors with an impromptu song and dance routine."

Ready to protest, more out of spite than reasoned argument, it only took a second for Adam to realise that Stern was the perfect choice. Larger than life, shockingly charismatic, Stern also had some hand-to-hand fighting skills – for many years standing in as Adam's sparring partner. Outshining the brightest of stars, Stern was a potent pheromone for women and a giddying muscular man-crush for men. Picturing the group, Adam could not help smiling:

"So, out of a population of 140 billion, that includes humanity's cleverest diplomats and wily politicians, you're sending a lazy drunk, two glam psychopaths, and a narcissistic arse sniffer. Well, at least Deputy Mehta is normal – at least as far as I know. Are you sure you want us to represent the Viroverse?"

"As usual, Mr Eden, I cannot reveal my motives, but you have not failed me yet. The AI has calculated every possible scenario you are likely to face and your chances of success or at least of coming back alive are very favourable. A show of force is always a tempting option, but it's worth giving peace a chance before we send in the troops."

Adam nodded thoughtfully and sat back in his chair, pondering how the inclusion of Stardust and Blitz constituted 'giving peace a chance'.

REVEALING LIAISONS

Riding the escalator down to the food hall, seeking a strong coffee, and perhaps some fried chicken, Adam attracted no attention. Wearing jeans, t-shirt, and trainers, without his Aloha uniform, he was just another face in a bustling crowd of cheerful visitors.

Nine hundred years from the peak of his fame, would anyone still recognise the legend of the psychoviro, even if he wore the pink hibiscus shirt and tight white trousers? Perhaps there was a small piece of Adam's pride that did not want to test his celebrity.

By invitation only, the regular visitors to the Terminal came for those life-affirming differences and disabilities denied them in the Viroverse. Blemishes, tattoos, excess body fat, even partial sight or hearing, were temporarily reinstated in the Terminal's Day Spa. Once a feared place of suffering in payment for the procedures, a consequence of the Captain's programmed requirement for balance in all things, the Day Spa now provided a quick and painless experience.

These visitors, like the billions of other denizens of the Viroverse, were kept ignorant of the halls and the bloody conflict outside. Consequently, the Terminal operatives, both human and android never spoke of the disturbing secret, always maintaining a pleasant demeanour in the public areas.

In one respect, Adam did stand out from the crowd – not for his past notoriety, but the worried expression that he now carried. Deep in thought about the dangerous mission that lay ahead, he pushed through the crowds, oblivious to anything other than his own fear. He really needed that strong coffee. The Captain had talked of 'a brave new world', and bravery never seemed in short supply amongst the Terminal operatives. For Adam, bravery came easy when resurrection was guaranteed, but other than that, it was all just timely showboating and a strong belief in self-preservation.

Adam approached the gleaming chrome counter intending to order a French roast as black and bitter as his mood, but chickened out at the last moment and went for a double mocha with extra cream and chocolate sprinkles. Expertly dusting the top of the foam, the blue-uniformed barista spelled out an elegant chocolate 'Copa'. With a cheeky wink, she handed Adam the tall glass. The unexpected recognition, even from an android, immediately lifted his spirits.

Raising the glass, Adam noticed the man sitting on the next stool staring at him. The thickset man, wide brow deeply furrowed, thoughtfully wagged a finger and spoke with a pronounced Essex accent:

"Sorry if I've got this all wrong, mate – I'm always stuffin' up things like this – but I couldn't help noticin' it says Copa on your coffee. I was wonderin' if you're that Copacabana bloke; the one who killed all those nutters."

Adam put down the coffee, some creamy foam and part of the chocolate Copa now smudged onto his upper lip:

"And, I still kill them every month."

Without asking for proof, or telling Adam about his choco-foam moustache, the man sprung from his stool, waving and shouting excitedly:

"This is Copacabana! This is Copacabana!" People began looking over. "Top bloke, thought he'd retired or something, but he says he's still killin' those fucking nutters!" The man held out a hand. "I gotta shake your hand, mate. Not every day you meet a legend." He handed Adam a napkin. "Oh, and by the way, you've got shit on your lip."

After quickly wiping his face and shaking the man's hand, Adam was pushed against the counter as the crowd moved in, all looking for a rare glimpse of the Viroverse's first home-grown legend. The android barista, perhaps fearing for Adam's safety, leaned over and grabbed his hand.

A woman in the front enthusiastically punched the air, just as Adam climbed up onto the counter – her small but bony fist accidently thumping him in the groin. With a throaty wheeze, he fell to one knee, and then keeled over. The crowd fell silent as the barista hauled him to safety. The coffee bar's security shutters slowly slipped down before securely locking – a series of smart-flaps at the bottom gently pushing away any outstretched hands.

"Do you need some ice on that?" the barista asked, helping Adam to his feet.

"No, I'll be fine," he replied, carefully adjusting the crotch of his trousers. "Just need to keep my legs bowed and my zipper down for a few minutes."

"You know, they say it's only the greats that can make a spectacular entrance, but it's only the greatest of the greats that can make a memorable exit."

"Well, I'll certainly never forget that experience. I was really enjoying it before I got thumped in the balls. I thought nobody remembered me."

"Even a brave new world can't survive without the classics," the barista said, beaming a ruby lipstick smile that walked the line between wicked satisfaction and a touch of sympathy.

"Wait a minute … you're the Captain, aren't you? Was this a set up? I … I don't know what to say."

"A simple thank you or a punch in the face will do just fine. Your choice. I promise that the reaction of the guests was genuine. I only lit the fuse, and they did the rest. It was a calculated risk to motivate you for tomorrow."

"Well, apart from the painful exit, I guess it's thank you. Nice to know I'm still appreciated." Adam looked up and down the narrow space. "So, do I have to stay in here for the day?"

"Hah, you're not that important. I need the coffee bar open again in about ten minutes or the guests will start complaining. I can assure you they love their hot java far more than they love you. But, now we are alone, I can share some information with you that I withheld during the meeting. It's regarding Mr Tikolo's escape from his captors."

Adam's genital pain gradually faded as the Captain described Jomo Tikolo waking up in a small concrete room, without enough headroom to stand, surrounded by tiny people. After using duct tape to dress his leg wound, the slerd crawled out of the room and into a dense rainforest. The description of the army of tiny people attacking Jomo was detailed and shocking, with the revelations of the testicle hangers causing Adam to wince.

Finally, with customers banging on the security shutters, the Captain gestured to a door next to the patisserie shelves.

"Through there," he said, pointing with a slender finger, "you'll find a corridor that leads to the main staff tunnels. Just follow the blue line or the signs to the Plaza Hotel. The Secrets VIP Lounge is reserved for a few choice guests such as yourself."

"Hmm, I'll really, really enjoy my orange juice or maybe a Shirley Temple if I'm feeling particularly brave."

"Your alcohol restrictions have been removed, just for today."

"Then, my good Sir … or Madam, I shall take your leave."

Before he left, Adam swiped a couple of jam doughnuts:

"I'm taking these because I never got my box of southern fried chicken."

High up on the seventh floor of the hotel, offering an expansive wide-windowed view across the plaza, the Secrets VIP Lounge was a masculine mix of matt black and burr walnut, accented with understated strips of satin steel. Eschewing the large black leather armchairs, Adam headed straight for the softly lit bar, and parked his rear on a classic jet-black Magis Bombo stool.

"What can I get you, Sir," the waist-coated bartender asked.

Adam looked along the capacious down-lit shelves of whisky, the light diffusing through the bottles into a warm amber glow. Over three hundred rare and interesting whiskies from across the globe vied for Adam's attention.

"Hmm, I think I'll start with a …." Nodding a finger, Adam conducted a quiet eeny, meeny, miny, moe.

"Sir, can I recommend the 2044 vintage, 36 year old, Tomatin single malt? It might be a touch rich for the first drink, but I think you'll like it."

"Sounds good to me. If I don't like it, you can just recommend another one. And, make it a triple; I've been deprived of late. Today, I don't just want to wet my whistle; I want it well and truly drowned."

"And, how do you take it, Sir?"

"Straight, lowball, please."

"Can I recommend a tulip glass? This particular whisky has an impressive aroma – dried fruits and honey."

"Nah, I'll stay with the lowball; I'm not wasting any of it on my nose."

Adam shuddered, feeling a strong hand on his shoulder.

"I'll have what he's having, mi amigo," Stern said, sitting down on the next stool. "Though, I'll take it in a tulip."

The barman placed two glasses onto thick leather coasters – the Terminal 'T' logo branded deep into the grain. At a smooth, well-practised speed, he accurately poured six measures, and slid over a bowl of pistachios and a small plate of sesame crackers. Leaving Adam and Stern to talk, the barman went to the far end of the bar to serve a small group of customers.

Stern savoured the aroma of the whisky before tasting. Casually dressed in black trousers and a white short-sleeved cotton shirt, his bronzed skin was a perfect match for the colour of the aged spirit.

"You know," Stern held up the glass to admire the vintage malt, "somehow this feels better than from a viro dispenser."

"I'm sure it comes from a dispenser behind the scenes."

"I know that, but having a limited selection, and having someone pour it for you, makes it special. Back in the viro, we can have anything we want, whenever we want. After a while, you just stick to the same old things, day after day, year after year. A simple recommendation from a knowledgeable barman and it's like you've woken up."

"Hmm, I know what you mean," Adam agreed, knocking back half of his whisky. "Some people can get caught in a comfortable loop if they're not too careful."

"Maybe it's being too careful that gets you too comfortable."

"Is that why you agreed to risk your life for the Captain? I admit it took me by surprise. You've always said that you're a lover not a fighter."

Stern took another drink and then centred his glass perfectly on the coaster:

"Do I detect a note of disapproval, muchacho?"

"When the Captain first announced that you were joining the team, it did put my nose out of joint, but only for a little while. I can't argue that you're probably perfect for this mission. Depending upon what's behind that door, you could be our ace card."

"I like your honesty; it's refreshing."

"Life's too long for secrets and lies."

Stern tilted his head and raised an eyebrow:

"Coming from the sneaky embustero who never admitted he was Copacabana."

"Oh yeah, I guess there was that."

"And, even though we were all told you somehow saved the Viroverse, you never in a thousand years told me how or why or what from. Now, I find out you went out into the real world and became Humanity's Representative. Hell, I only found out about the Terminal a couple of weeks ago from John Down. Secrets and lies, muchacho."

Stern finished his drink and beckoned the barmen to refill the glasses with another expert choice. After enjoying the rich fruitcake and burnt caramel nose of the 17-year-old Glenfarclas single malt, Stern took a generous sip:

"So, you have no problem with me being a member of the team?"

"Just so long as you know I'm in charge. We can't have two heads on this one."

"No problem, muchaco," Stern put his hand on Adam's shoulder. "I promise I'll keep my ego in check. As for my awesomeness, I have absolutely no control over that."

As he drank his whisky, Adam heard a familiar soft creepy voice at the dimly lit far end of the bar. Putting his glass down, he stared hard into the gloom. A couple of uniformed Terminal staff closely flanked two besuited men with short dark hair:

"Is that you Stardust?" Adam called over, attracting the attention of both men.

Turning to face Adam and Stern, Stardust and Blitz were almost unrecognisable without their usual glam outfits. They shuffled uncomfortably in matching pinstripe suits – like gawky teenagers attending a family wedding.

"Err … nice suits," Adam said, not knowing quite what to say.

"Armani," Stardust said.

"The very best," Blitz added.

The two psychopaths, awkwardly in step with one another, approached Adam and Stern – the Terminal guards following, watching their every move. Once they were out of the gloom, Adam noticed the tall flute glasses with diamante topped strawberry spears and little yellow umbrellas:

"What on Earth are you drinking?"

"Champagne spritzers," Blitz answered bluntly. "What else would we drink in a five star hotel?"

"We aren't entirely without standards," Stardust said.

Stern smiled, and raised his glass of whisky:

"Well, I think you make a lovely couple."

About to raise his own glass, the mirth drained from Adam's face. Without their glam make-up and wigs, Stardust and Blitz were unmasked and starkly recognisable. No longer violently camp cartoon characters, they were notoriously evil 20th century serial killers – their stomach-turning crimes the sordid subject of countless guilty pleasure TV 'documentaries' and lurid internet sites.

In a moment of uncharacteristic empathy and perhaps shame, Stardust lowered his gaze, his lip noticeably trembling as he spoke:

"Oh Copa, I think it best you refer to us by our glam nicknames. I may have turned my back on my first-life, but I know there are those that will never forgive me. I committed those crimes many, many lifetimes ago."

"I know you make a big deal about giving up rape, but you still murder people."

Blitz pointed at Adam:

"So do you, you hypocrite! I've seen you grinning after a kill. I know you enjoy it as much as we do."

"And, remember, it's by application only," Stardust added. "Sometimes, I think we're the hunted. Remember that awful day when we accidently let that SAS team take part?" Stardust shuddered, his hand over his heart. "They picked us off one by one and hung our bloody corpses upside down under the bridge."

Adam finally raised his glass:

"I really enjoyed my Steak Diane that day."

The ice broken, Stern ordered another round drinks, replacing the Champagne spritzers with neat whisky.

For the next few hours, the 'team' drank heavily, making increasingly crude jokes and observations, whilst now and then picking up the courage to discuss the mission. It was not a case of male bonding, or imagining walking in each other's shoes, but finding a tolerable way of interacting without the urge to murder one another.

Returning to pour another round of whiskies, the barman noticed the snacks were depleted:

"Nuts and crackers, gentlemen?"

Adam looked at his motley crew, all heavy headed with alcohol, and slouched over the bar.

"We certainly are," he said with a grin. "We certainly are."

Later, back in his hotel room, Adam threw off his clothes and slipped into a silk dressing gown. Sober enough to stand, but far from clear headed, he ordered the room's sound system to play a selection of cool Motown tunes to take his mind off the dangers of the coming mission. The door chime sounded and a soft-spoken male voice announced that Adam had a visitor.

"Her Illustrious Majesty, Queen Boudicca Chang."

"Let her in," Adam said, and the door slid open.

"Cosy little room," Boudicca noted, walking in wearing blue and grey Terminal fatigues and snap-buckle combat boots. "I have a penthouse suite, but then again, I am royalty."

The door automatically slid shut.

"This music will not do," Boudicca said. "Room Music; early 22nd century, and base your selection on my real-time profile."

In an instant, the smooth Motown sounds disappeared, replaced by a sensual dark throbbing baseline – some 22nd century mood enhancer that Adam had never heard before. Boudicca stood in front of Adam, fists clenching and unclenching, as if spoiling for a fight.

"This may be the last time we are scaled for sex," she said. "Seems such a shame to waste such an opportunity."

Without asking, she thrust her hand between Adam's legs and squeezed firmly with a measured amount of pain.

"I … err … they do say you should always grab your opportunities," Adam gulped as she released his genitals from her tantalising grip.

"Hmm, feels much bigger than I remember, but then, it has been a thousand years."

"It was my reward for saving the Viroverse."

"And, now it will be my reward."

Adam stepped back:

"It's not that you're unattractive; it's just that I have had quite a bit to drink."

Ignoring Adam's childish blather, Boudicca moved even closer, staring ravenously into his eyes, their lips touching.

"Do we heal overnight here?" she whispered, her moist mouth guiding Adam towards the bed.

He nodded, still concerned about whether he could perform. Boudicca licked his bottom lip:

"Good, you are going to need it."

As he stepped backwards, Adam mentally kicked himself. Why was he still worrying about the alcohol? By now, they should be on the bed and working up a sweat.

Before Adam could display even a hint of macho dominance, Boudicca roughly grabbed him and kissed him hungrily and deeply. With aggression and experience, she ripped off his gown and threw it across the room – meanwhile, Adam awkwardly fumbled with her combat jacket and blindly peeled open some Velcro, possibly a pocket flap.

Wasting no time, Boudicca pushed Adam onto the bed and stood over him. She tugged open her jacket, revealing the firm snow-white curves of her breasts.

Strangely aroused by Boudicca's forthright sexuality, Adam smiled and hiccupped as his penis stood to attention.

"Your Majesty, those who are about to die salute you!"

Without sweet-talk or foreplay, Boudicca immediately impaled herself on Adam. Taking charge, doing all the work, she rode him to sweaty exhaustion.

FABULOUS FIVE

Dubbed the 'Fabulous Five' by a grinning Dolph Zabel – upon seeing their decidedly inappropriate clothing – Adam and his team enjoyed a tense yet uneventful shark ride to the entrance to the utility level. With nearly fifty percent of Terminal staff involved, the huge convoy was the largest and most heavily armed ever assembled – and all to give safe passage to five bizarrely attired envoys. A small number of unmanned surveillance drones flew close to the ceiling, scanning the upcoming intersections for possible threats, but the danger of previous days had evaporated. The complete absence of enemy activity was an anti-climax for many, but a welcome respite for those dimmed and exhausted by the recent bloodshed.

Deciding that a fresh morning start was essential, the Fabulous Five were to sleep in a viro near to the entrance to the utility level. Due to the relaxed rules, an uninhabited viro almost directly opposite the entrance became available. Empty, dark, and with an undeveloped cubic landscape, such viros were usually off-limits. Accompanied by a twenty strong elite team of Terminal operatives, Adam and his group entered the viro and camped out on a narrow, flat ridge. With only torches for light, they waited, exchanging stories and engaging in trivial banter until the sleep of midnight.

The next day, after a filling breakfast and a fresh change of clothes, they left the safety of the viro and made their way to the Via Sacra – the relaxed rules allowing more than two at a time in the gruesome vault. They bid their heavily armed escorts goodbye, and travelled by scooter along the smooth fifteen-mile tubeway, finally reaching the platform with the bank-style metal door.

Wearily, the team folded their scooters and climbed up onto the blue-tiled platform. They approached the huge metal door with a cautious unease. Adam and Stern stood in front, discussing whether they should try to turn the thick steel wheel, whilst Blitz and Stardust shuffled and bickered impatiently behind. At the rear, crossbow slung over her shoulder, Saloni stood impassive and silent.

Adam sighed, and looked around, taking in his team's attire. In scuffed and faded black leathers, Stern posed and flexed his muscles: his open waistcoat revealed his sharply defined pecs, and his strong jaw jutted out from beneath a low browed Stetson. Swaying on high platforms, Blitz looked menacingly shocking in his turquoise glitter jumpsuit and flash of red hair. Fabulous as ever, Stardust sparkled in black sequins and leather, gloss red platforms, and a snow-white wig. Saloni, ludicrously pompous in a white Terminal dress uniform, looked like the ruler of a third world banana republic: a 'T' emblazoned peak cap, embossed silver buttons, and wide tasselled epaulettes. Finally, Adam seemed dressed for a beach luau in his usual pink hibiscus shirt, blue deck shoes, and tight fitting white trousers.

The Captain had insisted on the choice of clothing, despite protestations from all volunteers. Fearing they might be heading for a psychoviro style urban warzone, they wanted stab-resistant, para-military fatigues. Never one for changing his mind, the Captain refused. Now, if all hell broke loose, they would go down fighting in the flamboyant regalia of a third rate 'Village People' tribute band.

"We should have used bicycles," Blitz complained. "Those scooters are too slow."

Inspecting the imposing steel door, Adam shook his head:

"Just shut up about the scooters will you? You agreed beforehand. You all did."

"I thought you meant motor scooters; you know mopeds. Those are children's toys."

"As I keep telling you, they're adult scooters – Oxela Urban 15s – easy to carry, robust, and fast. Don't forget, Stardust refused to ride a bloody bike."

"But I can't remember how," Stardust insisted, stung by the comment. "They say that once you learn you never forget, but it's been over a thousand years. And, I absolutely refuse to ride tandem."

Ignoring the petty complaints, daring to touch the sturdy looking wheel, Adam found that the Captain's suspicions were true. Waving his hand through the empty air, the wheel was perhaps a hologram or some other special effect.

"The real question is why us?" Blitz continued, as if in his own world. "Stern is here because of his celebrity status, perhaps to 'impress' his more well-known cousins, and Saloni is obviously the token female. But the rest of us …?"

"Saloni and Stern will do us proud," Adam said, gently pushing his hand against the flat of the door, wondering if it was also an illusion. "I guess the rest of us are here because we are experienced killers. However, I really hope our skills won't be needed. If this descends into a fight, then I doubt we'll be seeing the Viroverse again."

The touch of unrelenting hard cold metal confirmed the door's reality, but a distant clank, somewhere behind, caused Adam to stand back. Instinctively, Stern thrust his hand forward, as if drawing an imaginary pistol.

"So, you're packing an invisible gun," Adam said jokingly, hoping to mask his fear. "Now I feel safe."

"Sometimes use a fake six-shooter in my act, muchaco," Stern replied, pulling back his hand. "Force of habit I guess."

Blitz leaned forward and whispered in Stern's ear:

"No need to worry, Stern. My cutlass is ready to drink blood."

"Are you sure they should be behind us?" Stern asked Adam.

"Blitz is harmless unless you get him angry. Stardust can keep himself under control for quite some time. If I were you, I would focus on that door."

Stern unsheathed and fitted his knuckle-duster spike – the steel knuckles were a row of grinning skulls and the 9-inch spike engraved with a writhing snake-woman. He turned and looked at Blitz and Stardust:

"Well, psicópatas, if that little devil on your shoulder gives you some wicked advice then I recommend you listen to the angel on the other. I don't like watching my back."

"Oh Stern," Stardust said, a warm twinkle in his eye, "the trouble is, we have a little devil on both shoulders … but they are angels to us. When they're ready, they work us up into a frenzy with their delicious plans and schemes, and in the end we always get to do something wonderful."

Stern shook his head and turned back to watching the door:

"Well, just think twice if you feel like doing something bad … especially if I'm in the way."

Blitz leaned forward again, his chin almost resting on Stern's shoulder:

"Nothing is bad if you never feel remorse or regret. For me, it is all a matter of revenge, hate, and my own personal enjoyment. Technically, I am more of a sociopath, not a psychopath. There are no Devils on my shoulders, just little copies of myself – and we are always in agreement. Since I don't really know you and you have never made me angry, you have little to fear from me." Blitz's voice changed as he gritted his teeth. "Now, Copout on the other hand always makes my blood boil and I probably hate him more than anyone I have ever met. However, killing the moronic pleb out here would be a tragic waste, since there's probably no resurrection. I prefer a chance to kill him every time he visits the psychoviro. When it comes to death, he's the vending machine that never stops giving." Blitz sniffed Stern's neck and screwed up his nose. "And, what is that awful smell?"

"Obviously too sophisticated for you. Histoire de Parfums 1740. It accentuates my style, and works well with the leather.

"Also known as Marquis de Sade," noted Stardust. "It's sooo animalistic. I bet it smells great on you when you work up a sweat."

"Then I'll remember to keep my cool. What's that you're wearing? I'm getting a waft of Damascus rose over here."

"It's one of my own creations," Stardust replied, gushing with pride. "I call it Rosalinda. Perhaps you can pick up a hint of red liquorice?"

Blitz sniffed scornfully:

"Well I'm wearing a few sprays of Adidas anti-perspirant – the blue one. Keeps me stink free all day."

Another metallic sound from behind the door abruptly stopped the conversation. Everyone, apart from Adam, had their weapons at the ready, held in tense grips, waiting for the door to open.

"Put the weapons away," Adam ordered quietly. "I'm quite sure they are watching us. If they think we pose a threat then they might keep the door shut. If it opens, then I don't think our blades are going to matter."

"So, what's the plan if it does open? Stardust asked, reluctantly sheathing his elegant 17th century rapier.

In truth, Adam had no plan. Asking the Captain for advice had proven fruitless; although he suspected the enigmatic android knew much more about this 'other place' than he would admit. What the Captain had no trouble divulging were the mission objectives, which were simply stated yet perhaps hard to accomplish. Firstly, find out what happened to Mr Tikolo and assess whether the slerds were still at risk. Secondly, discover the reason for the body snatching and the involvement of Hernán Cortés. Thirdly, and probably soon to be achieved, find out what lay beyond the metal door.

Another clank, followed by a muffled ticking, brought about four sharp intakes of breath and a clenching of both jaws and fists. Conscious of the rising tension, Adam sought to calm his disparate group:

"You want a plan?" he said, willing as much mirth into his voice as possible. "Well, as soon as that door opens, Saloni, Stern and I will rush through the centre singing 'YMCA', whilst I want you two to take the flanks with a stirring rendition of 'In the Navy'."

Though obviously scared, Stern, Saloni, and Blitz managed a couple of forced laughs.

Before Adam could tell the group to hold their positions, the heavy door quickly heaved upwards, accompanied by a deafening ratchetting sound. For a moment, they all stood still, transfixed by the noise and the inability to see through a thick grey fog that lay beyond the door.

Without warning, Stardust whipped out his rapier, rushed past Adam, and promptly disappeared into the impenetrable fog.

"In the Navy!" he bellowed, in an unexpectedly deep bass, as loud as his lungs allowed.

Silence followed.

THROUGH THE MIST

Quick thinking and appropriate action were easy when dealing with the familiar and expected. In the Psychoviro, the glam gang were always trying out new tricks and schemes, but those twisted ideas were still the product of the same tired old minds. No matter how warped and random they appeared to the uninitiated, they were ultimately just vile variations on what had gone before. Now, this simple open doorway with a concealing fog was an unfamiliar predicament from an unknown source.

Staring into the fog, listening for any sound other than their quickening heartbeats, Adam pondered their next move. For now, in the seconds following Stardust's disappearance, the next move was lacking any movement whatsoever.

A very deep, slightly distorted, voice boomed all around them, breaking the silence:

"Please enter the security mist. I promise you will not be harmed. Please enter the security mist."

"A la verga," Stern muttered, re-fitting his knuckle-duster spike. Blitz growled and unsheathed his cutlass. Saloni coolly readied a bolt and held her crossbow at chest height.

"Please enter the security mist!" the voice continued. "Carry your weapons if you wish, but please enter the security mist! I repeat; you will not be harmed."

Adam did not draw his weapon:

"What have you done with my ... colleague?"

"Please enter the security mist."

"Let him speak to us! We're not doing anything unless we hear him speak!"

"Please enter the security mist."

Blitz, his face red with rage, lunged towards the doorway. Adam threw his arms around the furious glam-warrior, holding him back.

"Let me go, you coward!" Blitz screamed, struggling and squirming like a giant silvery-turquoise fish. "Stardust, if you're in there then make a sound! Let us know you're alive!"

"Please enter the security mist. You will not be harmed. Please enter the ..." There was a brief pause, before a weary male voice returned, without the distortion. "I've had enough of this. Look, you can stay on the platform if you want, but in three minutes, I am going to lower the door. No matter how long you stay out there, I will not raise it again. I promise that your friend is unharmed but secure. He cannot speak, so stop asking. Make your choice."

Adam ran through the options in his mind, still holding onto Blitz, who refused to stop struggling.

"So, what's your call?" Stern asked.

Without another thought, Adam let go of Blitz, who immediately and expectedly ran screaming into the fog. As with Stardust, a sudden silence ensued – the dark mist offered no clue as to the glam psycho's fate.

Saloni stepped forward and stood alongside Adam:

"Now that we've ditched those lunatics, perhaps we can make a more reasoned decision."

In a contemplative moment, Adam closed his eyes and sucked in a slow lungful of air. Was he about to enter the final darkness, the mortal end to the manmade cycle of death and resurrection?

"Somehow, I don't think this is a time for reason."

"I hope you are not proposing we base the decision on blind faith," Saloni said indignantly.

Adam shook his head:

"I was never one for trusting to faith – even in myself – but we are definitely blind here. I propose we follow Stardust and Blitz's lunacy and just walk on in. You can both leave if you want, but I want to know what's on the other side of that mist. Decide quickly though, because I can't keep this hero nonsense up for long."

Stern laughed, clenched his steel shielded fist, and cast a wild-eyed glance at Adam:

"Well muchacho, I've never had a problem keeping it up. See you on the other side!"

With a heroic bearing, almost cinematic in quality, the leather clad hindreader strolled into the mist.

"And I will not let the Terminal down," Saloni said, straightening her cap before following Stern into the swirling dark. "We must take this chance to end the conflict."

A couple of seconds later and Adam stood alone on the silent platform. He thought about following his squad into the unknown, and stood with his face only a few centimetres from the mist.

Adam's attempt at heroic leadership had only encouraged those of a braver disposition to act. Now, he could return to the Viroverse and claim the others had met terrible ends, or perhaps just brazenly admit his cowardice. The mission was unknown to all but the Terminal operatives, and the Captain would surely never trust him with any new responsibilities. Comfortably nestled amongst the blissful ignorance of his Viro neighbours, Adam could spend eternity berated by only his own internal guilt and shame – and he did that anyway.

"More guilt, more shame, more life," he muttered. "Sounds better than the alternative."

Before turning to leave, the tip of Adam's nose touched the mist. Like an instant fix adhesive, the mist held on tight. Cautiously, Adam tilted his head back, but his nose remained stuck in the gluey mass. He pulled a little harder but could not release it. Moving his head from side to side and up and down only brought about the snoutish contortions of a cheeky child pressing their face against a glass window.

With each movement, the nose became more deeply embedded and the mist began pulling Adam forward. Ignoring the possibility of complete nasal separation or a cartoonish Pinocchio elongation, he engaged in a painful tug of war with his vaporous captor. Also, fearing that his eyes might be torn from their sockets, Adam tightly closed his eyelids, and clamped his mouth shut lest he engage in a powerful sucking 'duckbill' kiss.

Gradually, inexorably, the mist drew him in. His resolve finally collapsed as the mist latched onto the crotch of his trousers – a terrifying tug of war best avoided. Not wanting to prolong his suffering, Adam pushed into the darkness and embraced whatever fate awaited him.

The fear of the unknown and the possibility and pain and death swiftly gave way to a dreamy journey over voluminous softness. Intoxicating lines snaked through Adam's bloodstream, numbed his nerves, and flowed into every corner of his being. He quickly lost contact with reality and soared into an otherworldly place of happiness and contentment. Colourful images of better times, of friends and family, gently pulsed in and out of focus, whilst the kind words and gestures of a generous lifetime soothed away any lingering concerns.

Adam enjoyed his realm of peace and tranquillity for only a few minutes, until he became aware of a tightness in his throat. He found moving his head an arduous task, and the rest of his body seemed only to slowly sway despite his best efforts. The increased physical activity quickly put an end to Adam's dreamscape and he opened his eyes to a gritty reality.

Red brick walls and sturdy wooden floors enclosed the large warehouse-like space. The room was industrial Victorian in style, with huge wooden double doors on the far side and wrought iron framed windows in the arch above. A number of black iron pillars with elaborate cornices supported the high ceiling, and Adam noticed about ten large empty handcarts neatly parked along one of the sidewalls – he shuddered, immediately picturing bodies from the Via Sacra piled high in the carts.

Slowly moving his head to view the other side of the room, Adam's eyes followed a row of sturdy timber-topped tables strewn with a variety of hand tools, before finally resting on a man sitting at an oak writing desk.

Slim, with side parted black hair and imposing mutton chop sideburns, the man wore an old style mid-blue police uniform – typically British with a traditional 'bobbies' helmet placed on the side of the desk. The man looked to be typing on a keyboard whilst staring at a screen, but there was neither a keyboard nor screen to be seen.

Stretching his neck around as far as the constriction would allow, Adam saw the rest of the team lined up alongside him. Covered up to their noses in a matt black material, thick and rubbery in consistency and appearance, they were totally silent, their only movement a slow swaying. Adam tried to speak but could not produce even a squeak or a groan. The 'air' supplied inside the tight cocoon seemed unusually thick, causing a dull ache in his throat and chest.

"Ah, you are awake!" the man at the desk said without looking around. "I'll be with you in a moment. I guess you are the one in charge, so I am going to remove your mouth shroud. I'm not mad, by the way – I've gone virtual, smart contact lenses." The man shook his head as if encountering a glitch. "I must have read this manual a hundred times, but the last time was over ten years ago and I do NOT want to make a mistake."

Adam waited patiently as the man typed on his invisible keyboard for a few more minutes. Studying the layout of the warehouse, he noticed four thin openings high up on the far wall, either side of the arch. Though the light was dim, he caught a glint of metal, and realised that they were probably arrow slits with deadly projectiles trained on his helpless group.

"Here we go," the man muttered, tapping his finger down. "Of course I'm sure." He tapped his finger down again. Leaving his seat, the man hurried over to Adam.

The consistency of the gas subtly changed and Adam found his breathing easier and less constricted. He hummed and groaned, testing his voice, just as the rubbery shroud peeled down to his shoulders allowing him to move his head.

"Thank you," Adam said quietly. His voice was already back to normal with only a faint soreness in his throat remaining, but he thought it best to take it easy.

"Right, first things first," the man said. "Welcome to Reynold's Gardens. Please accept my sincerest apologies for keeping you like this, but as you no doubt realise, we cannot take any chances. My name is Henrik Wergeland. Perhaps you have heard of me."

Adam shook his head:

"I can't say I have. Are you famous?"

Henrik stood up straight, accentuating his height, and puffed out his chest:

I am a Norwegian writer of some note. There are those that consider my work of great importance. I wrote 'The English Pilot'. Surely one of you has heard of that."

Adam shook his head, as did the others – albeit very slowly.

"Do you mean 'The English Patient'? Adam asked, trying to help. "I saw that at the cinema when it came out. My favourite bit was when they cut off ..."

"I did NOT write 'The English Patient', and sadly you are not the first to make that mistake. Maybe my work does not translate well."

His pride obviously deflated, Henrik grumbled quietly to himself before continuing:

"Before you ask any questions, and I am sure you have many, I must warn you that I am NOT authorised to give out any information about this place or the people that live here."

"So, what do we do now? Are you going to set us free?"

"I cannot do anything until Artie gets here. Then, I am sure we can move things forward."

"Artie?"

"Artie, our Chief of Police, will be here in a few minutes. I sent out a runner as soon as you stepped onto the platform. Before the chief gets here, perhaps you can tell me who you are. Your clothes seem to suggest you are members of a circus troupe or a burlesque show."

"I really, really don't want to explain the clothes, but my name is Adam Eden. Perhaps you've heard of me. Apparently I'm not just famous, but I'm a living legend."

"No I haven't heard of you," Henrik sniffed, "and quite frankly, that sounds like a made up name."

"I'm also known as Copacabana."

"Don't be preposterous! That's a beach in Brazil. Do you speak Spanish?"

"Actually, Brazil was a Portuguese colony."

"So, you are Portuguese."

"No …"

Before the conversation could devolve further, the double doors at the far end of the room swung and a tall imposing man marched in flanked by four other men, all wearing police uniforms. Without another word, Henrik left Adam and walked over to welcome the Chief of Police.

Though as tall as Henrik – about 6ft 5" – the man was considerably better built. His uniform covered a powerfully muscular frame, whilst his dark skin spoke of an African heritage. As the man neared, Adam noticed his piercing brown eyes, similar in intensity to Stern's famous laser blues, perhaps suggesting a keen detective mind.

"I came as fast as I could," Artie said, shaking Henrik's hand. "Qu Yuan's been threatening Bai Qi again. When I got your message, I convinced Wu Zetien to step in and by now they are no doubt drinking tea and singing in the Grey Pavilion. I see you have our visitors suitably restrained. Is there anything you can tell me before I question them?"

Henrik lowered his head slightly and spoke quietly:

"I forgot how to activate the audio feed, so I am not sure what they were talking about when they were outside on the platform. Their body language suggested that the one without the mouth shroud is probably in charge, but it was hard to tell. We had a brief conversation before you arrived. He gave a couple of false names and then claimed he wasn't Portuguese."

"So, you think he's Portuguese."

"No, I believe he isn't."

"Hmm, I'm not sure how that helps. What were the false names?"

"Copacabana; which, as you are probably aware, is a beach in Brazil, and the other was …"

"Adam Eden?" Artie asked, raising an eyebrow – a clear look of surprise on his face.

"Yes, Sir, that was the name. Sounded like a made-up name to me."

"What is he wearing under that shroud?" Artie's gaze was now fixed on Adam.

Henrik paused for a few seconds and thoughtfully rubbed his chin:

"White trousers and a pink and white shirt. Strange clothing, but quite ordinary when compared to the others. He was carrying a machete. All their weapons are on the table over there."

Artie told Henrik to return to his virtual station and monitor the platform for any further activity. Then, hands on hips – a casual rather than commanding pose – the Chief finally addressed his captors:

"I'm sure Constable Wergeland has already welcomed you to our home. I would like to also welcome you, and assure you that you will not be harmed. Since detecting your drone a few days ago, we have been expecting a visit. We know why you're here and I personally believe that a dialogue is long overdue."

Artie walked over to the farthest table and picked up Adam's machete. Slowly, he ran a finger along the steel shaft and smiled as he felt the weight of the weapon. "Has a nice heft, and I love the curved shape of the blade."

"It's a Kopis machete, based on an ancient sword design," Adam explained, daring to speak. "The forward balance of the blade makes it perfect for hacking and the point means it has a good stabbing action too. I've tried many blades over the years but I always come back to this one."

"I respect any man who knows how to use his weapon," Artie admitted, carefully placing the machete back on the table, "and it takes a serious man to wield a beast like this. I must confess, Mr Eden, that for many years, I have been one of your most ardent admirers. There is never a day that I don't think about you and wish that you were here."

"And here I am," Adam muttered, quietly disturbed.

FIRST IMPRESSIONS

Fame spread like an evolving virus, from first-hand accounts, each with their own flawed perspective, then cascading in ever-mutated waves from person to person until fizzling out or, on rare occasions, becoming legend. For those at the end of the line, the fragmented and distorted tale could take on almost mythical qualities as the starstruck recipient filled in the narrative gaps with pure fantasy and their own personal yearnings.

Unexpectedly for Adam, the legend of Copacabana had infected this hitherto undiscovered world, no doubt passed on from the conquistadors' colourfully lurid stories, already far removed from the truth by many degrees of separation. How could the reality compare to the increasingly embellished accounts of a thousand tongues? Now, he stood, immobile and vulnerable, faced with a follower probably expecting far more than Adam could provide. Man or legend, Adam could not be both, and would probably come across as a substandard example of either.

As Artie approached, Adam decided that playing up to a God-like fiction was pointless. If this were a place populated by history's finest, then his shortcomings would be quickly exposed. Stern, possessing a personality and confidence far greater than his actual talents, could sell his image to even the most cynical of critics, but Adam approached self-promotion with a tired reluctance tinged with social ineptitude.

"If I could, this is the time I would shake your hand," Artie said, gesturing to the rubbery cocoon. "We'll have you out of that dreadful shroud right away. Henrik!"

"Yes Sir?"

"Please could you remove Mr Eden's shroud."

"NOT to be impertinent, Sir, but I thought you wanted to question him first?"

"They are unarmed, and if necessary we can end their lives in a heartbeat. This is Copacabana, the man who spends his life slaying evil madmen. No one who devotes themselves to such a noble cause, of freeing the world from the menace of such disgusting creatures, should suffer this indignity. Set him free."

Though silent behind their shrouds, Adam could almost physically sense Stardust and Blitz's anger. He hoped they would show an uncharacteristic restraint when released, or hopefully view Artie's reproving words with a warped pride and twisted respect.

"I think you should remove Deputy Mehta's shroud first," Adam said, before Henrik started prodding and swiping his invisible touchscreen.

"Deputy Mehta?" Artie looked up and down the line.

"The one with the white hat. She's our official negotiator. It's not ladies first or anything, just that she's the one you should be talking to. The more I speak, the more likely I'll end up with my foot in my mouth."

"Are you and Deputy Mehta close?" Artie asked inquisitively.

"I'm not sure what you mean by close. Captain Andrews, the head of the Terminal, assigned us both to the team. Saloni ... I mean Deputy Mehta is the official Terminal representative. God knows why I'm here."

Frowning, Artie rapped his fingers against the wooden truncheon hanging from his belt:

"So, you and ... Saloni are not in a relationship?"

"Just team mates, and I have the utmost confidence in her abilities."

A faint smile returned to Arties face and he ordered Henrik to remove Deputy Mehta's shroud.

"Here we go!" Henrik exclaimed, prodding the air. "Of course I'm sure." He prodded the air again.

The joyful expectation of freedom lasted only a few seconds. Artie's smile was the first to drop as Saloni's shroud swelled around her neck and began spreading over her entire face. In the time it took for Artie to ask Henrik what was going on, the black substance completely covered the deputy's head, knocking off her hat, and giving her the unsettling appearance of a giant blackcurrant jelly baby.

"That's not supposed to happen," Henrik said, rising from his chair. "The shroud is meant to drop away, not cover her head."

There was a moment of silence, until the thick ring of 'rubber' around Saloni's neck began contracting, squeezing its defenceless captive in a 360 degree stranglehold.

"Switch it off! Switch it off now!" Adam shouted.

Henrik threw himself back into his seat and repeatedly prodded the air:

"I can't stop it! I can't interrupt the sequence! This is NOT meant to happen! This is definitely NOT meant to happen!"

Artie rushed over to Saloni and tried to pull the shroud from her neck. Despite his efforts, and a stream of exasperated curses, the ring kept contracting, relentlessly choking its victim. A second later and the brittle sound of splintering bone followed by a muffled popping noise sent a shudder of terror through everyone in the room. A look of horror on his face, Artie took a few steps back as Saloni's shrouded head flopped to one side, still attached to her body by a thin black rubbery sliver.

"The sequence is ended," Henrik said quietly. "And I know what I did wrong. I will not make the same mistake again. Stay calm, and I'll release you."

Adam protested loudly – the others, wild eyed, slowly shook their heads. Artie grabbed Henrik's arm, preventing any further prodding:

"Before you kill anyone else, you had better tell me what happened."

"I forgot to change tabs. I was still on the Head page. I … I should have switched to the General page. I thought I was pressing the remove shroud button, but it was the …" Henrik coughed "… it was the eliminate threat button. I am so sorry."

Artie turned to Adam:

"Mr Eden, I cannot begin to tell you how sorry I am for this incident. I am as shocked as you are. This might sound redundant, but it is not our intention to cause you any harm. However, time is not on our side. We must preserve the deputy's brain before any serious deterioration takes place."

Adam thought for a moment before replying, aware that he was shaking and breathing heavily:

"Get this stuff off of us. Just make bloody sure he doesn't cock it up again."

Artie nodded:

"Henrik, make sure you're on the right page this time and double check before you activate the sequence." Artie gripped Henrik's arm very tightly for a second before releasing him. "I swear, if you mess this up, I will kill you myself and feed you into a dispenser."

Quietly, Henrik returned to his virtual screen and, after a slight hesitation, gently prodded the air:

"General page."

He ran his finger slowly from left to right, as if double-checking every button:

"Remove shroud."

Again, he prodded the air:

"Are you sure you wish to proceed?"

Henrik hesitated again, his finger wavering over the invisible confirmation button. Silently, everyone tensed, beads of sweat forming on their fearful brows. Adam closed his eyes as Henrik meekly whispered, 'of course I am', and jabbed his finger forward one last time.

Opening his eyes, Adam nearly collapsed as the supporting shroud fell away. Not sure he could walk, he stood leaning forward, hands on knees. He looked sideways. Stern struggled to stand tall, swaying on an uneasy balance, whilst Stardust and Blitz clenched their fists, glammed-up faces full of rage, portending imminent vengeance. Sprawled on the floor in an expanding pool of blood, Saloni Mehta's body lay shroud-less, silent and still – her decapitated head face down in the crimson shallows.

"You two, take a few breaths and stand down," Adam ordered the psychopaths, fearing a bloody escalation. "I'm angry as hell, but we won't honour Saloni by getting killed."

In truth, Adam knew that honour meant nothing to Stardust and Blitz, but they hissed and grunted their grudging obedience.

Stern, his balanced regained, stood over Saloni's body. Without a word, he bent down and casually lifted her head by the hair. Bringing the bloody head to eye level, he studied the deputy's final expression.

"She looks so calm," he observed, as Adam stood alongside. "Do you think her features were fixed by the shroud, or did she face death with a resigned dignity?"

"I'd like to think the latter, but in my experience the cruellest or most frightening option is usually the right one."

"Hmm, you're probably right. At least she's not suffering anymore. Here, take it." Stern tossed the head to Adam, who fumbled clumsily as the blood slicked his hands. He clasped tightly onto an ear, narrowly avoiding dropping the grisly object.

Concerned that Saloni's horrifying demise had affected Stern's mental state, Adam hid the head to one side and guided the morbidly enthralled celebrity away from the gory pool. Whereas Adam and the psychopaths regularly faced a gruesome red-wash spectacle of spilt guts, severed limbs, and swift decapitations, Stern's brushes with terror were confined to errant farts whilst performing, and a rare inability to 'get it up'. Now, he seemed too relaxed with the situation – and Adam noted a conspicuous lack of 'muchachos'.

Artie hurried over with a metal serving tray:

"Please, Mr Eden, put the poor girl's head on this. We need to preserve the brain. Constable Lovelace!"

A policewoman, elegantly tall with strong features, stood to attention:

"Yes Sir?"

"We need an artist."

"I think I saw Monet on a bench by the lake. He was opening a bottle of red, so I suspect he is still there."

"Only the best will do. Take Constable Al-Nabigha with you and bring Monet back here. Make sure he brings a box and any tools he needs on the way in."

The constables hurried through the large wooden doors and Artie pulled out a long wooden bench from under one of the worktables.

"Come and sit," he said. "I suspect your legs feel like jelly at the moment. Once Monet gets here, you can relax and watch the show."

"Do we get our weapons back," Stardust asked hopefully.

Artie shook his head:

"I don't think that's a good idea right now. I think that first we should get to know each other a bit better. I want to know who I'm really dealing with."

"With respect," Adam began, sitting down on the bench, "you killed one of us. I want to know who we are dealing with."

Artie thought for a moment before fetching Adam's machete:

"Just you then," he said, handing Adam the weapon. "I have heard enough stories of your valour and integrity over the years to believe I can trust you. Just keep it clipped to your belt at all times."

Before taking a seat next to Adam, Artie placed the gruesome tray in the centre of the table – the decapitated head like some bloody joint of meat ready for carving. Henrik and the other two remaining constables stood guard.

"The constable you sent to get Monet," Adam asked, "is she Linda Lovelace. You now, the porn star."

"That was Ada Lovelace, Lord Byron's daughter. She is often called 'the first computer programmer'." Artie put a strong arm around Adam's shoulders. "Not what you were hoping for?"

"Oh no, I'm not into porn. I just thought I recognised the name. Well, I used to work with computers in my first life. I guess I could thank Miss Lovelace for my short-lived pitiful career."

Artie's hand tensed on Adam's shoulder:

"No need for that," he whispered in Adam's ear, so quietly that the others did not hear. "You definitely wouldn't like her. She thinks people from your world are unworthy peasants and reserves a special hatred for the warrior class. She has a sharp mind and an even sharper tongue. I advise you stay well away."

"I'll bear that in mind," Adam said, shrugging off Artie's arm.

Leaning forward, Artie looked along the line:

"So, I know my friend Adam here, but I have no idea who you all are. You two in the glittering outfits, please tell me your names and from what time you hail. I find your appearance quite baffling, though impressively striking."

Blitz glowered, his eyes narrowed. Stardust broke into a proud smile, no doubt flattered:

"My name is Stardust, leader of the … err … glam tribe, and this is my loyal deputy, Blitz. We originally hail from the twentieth century. As for our striking appearance, you could describe it as musically theatrical – or simply glam."

"Or simply stupid," Blitz added.

"So, you are musicians?" Artie asked.

"Not at all," Stardust said. "We spend our waking hours dancing to the glam beat."

"And killing to the rhythm," Blitz added, still glowering.

"Well, I'm not sure what you mean by that," Artie said, flashing a puzzled glance at Adam, "but I do respect men bold enough to go by a single name."

"They're here in a bodyguard capacity," Adam explained. "Stern over there is the celebrity of the group – sort of a VIP go-between."

"Stern. That is a strong name," Artie said. "I can see by your well defined chest that you take great pride in your physical appearance. I exercise every day, even though the system only allows limited improvement."

Stern placed his Stetson on the table and flicked his mane of raven hair:

"We have the same limitations in the Viroverse, but I do what I can. I believe that if you respect your body, you respect yourself ... and the ravenous eyes that feast upon you. And, by the way, my full name is Stern Lovass. Perhaps you have heard of me?"

Artie stared at Stern for a few seconds, tapping his finger lightly on the table. Then, smiled and pointed, with a look of surprise and recognition:

"I think I have heard of you!"

"I'm not surprised," Stern said nonchalantly. "My fame is widespread, and my hindreading skills legendary. I would be more surprised if you weren't a fan."

"Well, be surprised; I am not a fan," Artie said, shaking his head. "I think what you do is disgusting. I could never respect a man who smells people's arses as a profession. In my day, we banished people like you – and that's if they were lucky."

In an uncharacteristic display of embarrassment, Stern blushed – his perfect bronze tan becoming more copper-like:

"I do not smell arses," he protested. "My nose detects the faint aura that all humans possess. I sense, I perceive the very soul of the subject. The Ancient Egyptians believed the anus to be a portal for the soul and even Japanese folklore tells of the 'shirikodama' – a ball containing the soul that resides in the anus. I cannot say whether my skill is shamanic or science, or even a gift from God to aid humanity, but my readings are rarely wrong."

"I'm afraid I can't bring myself to respect your ... unusual gift," Artie said, once again putting his arm around Adam's shoulders, "especially when we have a real man in our midst. However, you do have a passionate admirer. He's the one who told me all about you – wouldn't stop telling me all the sickening details. Henrik!"

"Yes Sir!"

"I want you to go out into the Gardens and hunt down Mr Freud. You can usually find him outside the third station. If you do find him, then tell him we have a few special guests. We will be dining at the Balconies, and he is welcome to join us. Oh, and we will be taking the Viaduct route for security reasons."

"Will you need me for anything else, Sir?"

"After you find Freud, I want you to come back here and push Deputy Mehta's body into a dispenser. I expect you to collect every drop of blood. We waste nothing."

As Henrik hurried out of the warehouse, Artie picked up Saloni's head:

"That reminds me, I had better clean off all this blood before Monet gets here."

TIME IS MONET

Adam reached over and turned Saloni's face away from him. Artie had cleaned off the blood, and the deputy's expression now looked unnervingly serene, almost as if pleased that her head lay severed on a silver platter.

"Monet will be here soon," Artie said, as if empathic to Adam's discomfort. "He'll most certainly bring a gold casket so there will be no delay in preserving the brain."

"You keep saying you need to preserve the brain. Don't you have resurrection here? Or is this just a precaution because we are from another place?"

Artie paused for a moment before speaking:

"There has not been resurrection here for nearly a thousand years. Back then, Reynolds' Gardens suffered what we call 'The Great Catastrophe'. I will explain all of this in detail on the way to the Balconies, but one lasting consequence is the need to preserve the brain. I could …"

Artie stopped talking as the warehouse doors swung open. With verve and confidence, Claude Monet swept into the warehouse, closely followed by Lovelace and Al-Nabigha. Early twenties in appearance, Monet had a presence befitting one of the world's most famous artists. Dressed in black, a brocade waistcoat, impeccably folded cravat, and crisply creased trousers, the only dash of colour was the blue silk lining of his velvet cape.

Constable Lovelace unrolled a belt of small steel tools on the table, whilst Constable Al-Nabigha carefully placed a foot square golden casket next to the silver platter – the tired policeman wiped his sweaty brow, relieved to be free of the hefty weight.

The constables withdrew, and the great impressionist painter stepped up to the table. Dashingly rugged, thick dark hair swept back D'Artagnan style, Monet's eyes shone with a youthful enthusiasm that belied the passing of the centuries.

"Names, please," he asked, gently stroking Saloni's hair.

"The head belongs to Deputy Saloni Mehta." Artie replied. "She is a high-ranking official from the other world. Her death was an unfortunate accident – a tragic fault on our part. This man is Adam Eden, the leader of the group and a legend of the other world. The men in the colourful clothes are Mr Stardust and Mr Blitz – here in a security capacity, I understand. The handsome fellow at the end is Stern Lovass, a celebrity with a somewhat unusual talent on which I do not wish to elaborate. Saloni's death has left us all in a state of shock, so I think we should get this over with quickly. The short show please; if that is all right with you?"

Monet picked up the head and held it on the palm of his hand:

"The short show it is. Without any more delay, let the ritual begin."

Looking slowly from side to side, offering each spectator a personal expression of sympathy, Monet suddenly threw Saloni's head high into the air.

"Life is risk," he said excitedly, his gaze still on his audience. "A tightrope walk of colour and distraction, where darkness waits for our descent." With a fast aggressive motion, he reached out a hand and caught the falling head.

"In fear, we believed in life beyond the black." Monet once again hurled the head towards the ceiling. "And behold, we learnt to catch our fall." Another fast hand movement and he caught the head.

"Nature will one day take us all." Monet cupped Saloni's head in both hands and launched it once more, as releasing a dove to the sky. "I am nature's defier, and time is my gift." He spun around – his cape rising in a theatrical flourish – then faced forward, Saloni's head once again cupped in both hands.

Without waiting for a reaction, Monet set the head spinning in his hand, before springing it onto the tip of his index finger. With an outstretched arm, he displayed the twirling head in front of his bewildered audience:

"See Saloni; she spins for you."

As the rotation stalled, Monet let the head fall into the palm of his hand. He performed a subtle shallow bow, and Stardust and Blitz began applauding.

"Thank you," he said, "but much of the credit must go to my esteemed teachers, Meadowlark and Jordan."

Incensed by the display, Adam rose to his feet:

"This stops right now! How dare you use Saloni's head as a bloody basketball. Show the deputy some respect or I promise it will be your head sitting on that tray."

"Calm down, Adam," Artie said, before Adam could reach for his machete. "There is no disrespect here. We believe – well most of us at least – that the Gods are dead. There's no resurrection here. When we die, our best hope lies in preserving the brain. When we first awoke in this new life, Reynolds told each and every one of us that a fragment of our original brain is embedded in this artificial one."

"The part that makes us … us," Adam said, sitting back down. "The part that holds the sense of self. It's the same for us in the Viroverse."

"As long as that is preserved, then there is hope that we will come back one day. The artists are skilled in removing and preserving the brain. The rituals they perform around their work remind us that, even without Gods, the dead deserve a decent send off. Each artist's ritual is different; a reflection of their skills and personality."

Cradling Saloni's head gently in his hands, Monet smiled wryly, yet with compassion:

"Given your sensitivity, Mr Eden, you are fortunate they called on me and not Dali."

Once certain his audience was settled, Monet continued the ritual. Starting slowly, he began juggling Saloni's head in a large circle. The speed increased, and the great painter began reciting a simple poem – his face impassive, and his voice an imperious monotone.

> "Our lives are lived in loops and links,
> On golden wheels, ascending into night.
> Enthralled by the lustre, we dream of one more turn,
> Before the end extends a hand to steal us home."

With a smooth sideways moonwalk, as if floating above the floor, Monet slid to the far edge of the table. Maintaining a steady inch gap from the oak surface, he rolled Saloni's head from hand to hand, slowly heading for the silver platter.

"Too soon … too soon we find forever."

Gently, he laid down the head, cheek first, on the cold metal. Blitz and Stardust leapt to their feet, applauding loudly.

"You brought a tear to my eye," Stardust exclaimed. "I'm usually so pleased when someone dies, but for the first time in centuries you made me care … for a stranger. Oh, I wish I could knock you out, tie you up, and drag you back home. You could take our killing to a whole new level."

Blitz nodded in agreement:

"Mr Monet, I have always reserved a special hatred for your sort. I killed off nearly three art departments in my time. But, you Sir have given me pause. Your skill with a severed head is utterly breath taking. Bravo, Mr Monet!"

Stern clapped enthusiastically, jaw set hard, expressing the respect of one great showman to another. Adam clapped politely, wondering what other horrors were in store – especially since this was just the first room in a whole new world.

Turning his back on the audience, Monet skilfully hid the head from view and, for a few seconds, sweetly sang the first verse and refrain of 'Alouette'. He then turned back, presenting a now bald Saloni:

"Saloni is shaved and the removal can begin."

Placing the head onto the silver platter, Monet unbuttoned his cape and handed it to Constable Lovelace. He then rolled up his sleeves and produced an ornately handled steel scalpel. Sticking the blade into Saloni's forehead, he quickly sliced around the circumference of the head. With a firm tug, and a short sucking sound, Monet pulled off the fleshy scalp in one confident movement.

"Some discard the scalp at this point," Monet said, placing the bloody skin pizza to one side, "but I prefer to keep it to hand."

Adam placed a hand over his mouth – partly out of shock, but also concerned he might vomit. He noted that the former exuberance of the psychopaths was now replaced with silence.

Monet held up another tool, ornately handled, but with a glass-like point. With a smile and a cheery wink, he twirled it between his fingers like a mini baton:

"This is a diamond tipped rasp. My colleagues use a bone saw for this stage, but I have developed an alternative method."

Grasping the head firmly in one hand, with the other hand, Monet forcefully scratched the tip of the rasp around the rim of the exposed bone.

"Now I need help from the bereaved." Monet spun the platter towards Adam. "Mr Eden, would you hold dear Saloni while I pop the top?"

Like a reluctant audience member called to aid a magician's trick, Adam put a hand either side of the scalped head and clasped tightly. With all the handling, Saloni's brain had shifted slightly, and her eyes drooped – their doleful gaze staring straight up at Adam.

More small tools appeared – a hammer and a wide bladed chisel. Monet placed the blade in the rasped skull groove and tapped once with the hammer:

"I have tried many different surgical implements over the years, some ingenious in their design, but this simple cheese chisel beats them all – perfect for cutting a hard piece of aged Romano, or for splitting bone. And, before you ask, I have never practised on coconuts."

Prompting Adam to rotate the head, Monet worked quickly. A few more well placed taps and the top of the skull fell away, accompanied by an attached gelatinous membrane. With a silently mouthed 'thank you' and a couple of grateful claps, the celebrated impressionist relieved his volunteer of his grisly duty.

"Do not mourn the loss of the body," Monet said, slipping a long thin shim of steel down between the bone and the brain. "It is merely an artificial container, just as is the golden reliquary where I shall lay Saloni to rest."

Monet gave a firm shove once the end of the steel shim reached the bottom of the skull, severing the brain from the remnant of the spinal cord. Then, placing the shim next to his row of shiny tools, he selected a pair of surgical scissors. Within a few seconds, he snipped through the eyestalks, finally freeing the brain. Monet carefully slipped the brain from the skull onto the moist underside of the scalp he had earlier reserved.

"Before Saloni journeys to her golden years," Monet began, holding out the brain, "do any of you gathered here today have any final words?"

After an awkward silence – the product of shock, nausea, and the fact that none of them knew Saloni – Adam rose to his feet, coughing once before speaking:

"I have only known Deputy Saloni Mehta for three days, and I know nothing of her background: family, friends, or her first-life experiences. However, in the very short time I have known Saloni, I have been impressed by her bravery, combat skills, and utter determination. I heard that she possessed a talent for diplomacy and was a powerful negotiator. I believe I speak for all of us when I say that these skills will be sorely missed. Without her diplomatic gifts, I fear we might lack the required subtlety and restraint. I really, really wish you were still with us, Saloni."

All present, apart from Blitz, muttered their agreement, and Adam sat down. Monet leaned forward, proffering the brain scalp combo:

"Your words are welcome. Now, in time honoured tradition, you may kiss the brain."

"Oh God, that's not going to happen," Adam insisted. "My stomach is already heaving."

Blitz crossed his arms and shook his head. Stern nonchalantly waved away the suggestion, like a pampered guest turning down an hors-d'oeuvre at a celebrity soiree. Only Stardust made an effort, his pursed lips stopping a hairsbreadth away from the brain.

"Kiss gently," Monet whispered. "The brain is delicate, like pink blancmange."

Stardust immediately recoiled, exclaiming, "I can't; I just can't."

Monet stood back:

"Do not worry, my friends. You are from a different world, and cannot be expected to follow our customs. I will gladly send Saloni on her way."

To disgusted cries from Adam and his team, Monet softly placed his lips on the brain and engaged in a lingering kiss.

"I think he's using his tongue," Stardust squealed, peeking through the gaps between his fingers.

Monet drew away, licking his sticky Revlon-red lips, and then carefully dropped Saloni's brain into the golden casket – as it sank, the preservation gel filled every hole and rivulet.

"Saloni is still immortal," he said, closing the heavy lid and clipping down the airtight grips. "An engraver shall arrive shortly to inscribe the necessary information. Saloni's brain will be sent to the Brain Bullion Repository." He handed Adam the silver platter laden with the pieces of Saloni's hollow head. "Since you seem the closest to Saloni, it is only proper that you be the one to recycle her remains."

"How do I do that?" Adam asked, keen to lose the gruesome burden.

"You just use the reverse facility on the dispenser," Artie explained. "Don't you have that in the Viroverse?"

"Our recycling takes place automatically when we are asleep. The dispensers are all give and no take."

"It's easy to do. Just say 'recycle' and push the remains into the black glass. The dispenser knows what to absorb, so don't worry about being dragged in. Although, since you are not from here, perhaps you should exercise extra caution."

"You don't waste anything, do you?"

Artie shook his head:

"Resources are precious and not to be stored or lost. In the Great Catastrophe, we ran short of what we needed … and there were consequences. So, we religiously recycle."

"Nature recycles everything," Monet added. "Here, we defy her will, but are forced to play her role. However, we are but a wheel within a wheel, recycling our tiny universe. One day, she will sweep us all away." He adjusted his cravat and buttoned his cape. "Though the circumstances are tragic, it has been an honour to meet you. I have an excellent bottle of Bordeaux waiting for me by the blooms. Naturally, I shall raise a glass to dear Saloni. I shall also raise a glass to you all; hoping that you do not require an artist again … and that we may put an end to the killing."

With a dramatic flourish of his black velvet cape, Monet turned and strolled out of the warehouse.

"Class act," Blitz said, clapping. "Out of all the artists I have ever met, he is the only one I could imagine spending some quality time with."

Adam smiled:

"That could be arranged."

After recycling the remains of Saloni's head, it was time to leave the warehouse. Escorted by four constables, all wielding truncheons and wearing iron knuckledusters, Artie led the way with Adam at his side. Beyond the warehouse lay a wide corridor with another set of large wooden doors.

"Tragedy always has a silver lining," Artie said, setting a brisk pace. "For me, that means I will be dealing with you rather than Deputy Mehta. No doubt she would have made a challenging diplomatic adversary, devoutly loyal to the Terminal, but I feel I can call you a friend." Once again, he slung his arm around Adam's shoulders. "Hah, who knows; in time, perhaps we will be the best of friends."

As two constables opened the sturdy wooden doors at the end of the corridor, Stern leaned in and whispered in Adam's ear:

"Aw, muchacho, look at you both. Adam and Artie sitting in a tree."

IN THE GARDEN

S treams of sombre light broke through the leafy canopy, dappling a scene of perpetual twilight. Save for a winding roadway that disappeared into the woody depths, lofty Cornish elms enclosed the grey cobbled courtyard. High above, glimpsed through gaps in the dense foliage, moody mottled clouds stretched across a dreary sky.

Adam marvelled at the realism – a level of quality only rivalled by the most prestigious of VIP viros. Traced by verdant moss in the mortar of the dark red brickwork, and climbed by dark ivy that snaked up into the slate roof, the exterior of the two-storey warehouse appeared aged by nature and neglect. Underfoot, the rounded cobbles felt strangely flat – that perfect balance of authenticity vs comfort demanded by pampered tourists … and a blessing for platform-heeled psychopaths.

"It is only a short walk from here to the station," Artie said, leading the way. "Don't be fooled by the scenery, the forest is quite small – just big enough to hide the warehouse."

Only a few minutes' walk along the road confirmed the forest's diminutive size. Two short bends in the road and it broke into a picturesque Capability Brown landscape of neatly trimmed rolling grassland with well-chosen patches of trees. The view was partially obscured by a tall rail viaduct of black wrought iron that cut across the fields – the cobbled road passing under one of its elegant arches.

Up close, the iron viaduct revealed a level of fine detail and slenderness of frame that even the proudly fastidious Victorian engineers of old could never have achieved. An elevator, bearing the embossed letters, 'GR', remained unused and closed as Artie ushered the group up a long staircase.

Like the cobbles, the ribbed iron steps were easy on the feet, coated in some rubberised tread. The steps led to a wide station platform. A few benches, a dispenser, and a number of lampposts – all meticulously Victorian themed – were the only furniture, but a short open-topped carriage sat ready on the narrow gauge track. At this moment, elevated above the trees and low landscaped hillocks, Adam and his team gazed in wonder at the majesty of Reynolds' Gardens.

In the distance, some five miles to the north, the parkland gave way to a promenade-fronted beach of white sand and a grey blue sea. Rising up like a row of jagged mountains between the parkland and the promenade, six huge buildings dominated the view. Their steep spires almost touched the clouds, and the setting sun cast long shadows around the arches, ribs, and towers of honey-coloured stone. Colossal in size, the buildings seemed like the British Houses of Parliament spun up on a lunatic's potter's wheel into soaring gothic cathedrals.

Despite the breath-taking presence of the huge buildings, the park was the true centrepiece of Reynolds' Gardens. Cobbled roads and gravelled pathways endlessly meandered their way around the verdant meadows and woods. Elegant pavilions and follies dotted the landscape, their use a mystery to Adam. Here and there, often by babbling brooks or small ponds, colourful flowerbeds broke up the monotony of green and brown.

Adam cursed the Captain for insisting on their colourful style of dress, for as expected, the residents of this world dressed conservatively in Victorian attire – where even a bright red scarf or an open necked shirt might seem extravagant. Viewed from this distant vantage point it seemed the citizens of Reynold's Gardens spent their time conversing on benches, strolling along the pathways, and wining and dining under white gazebos – their numbers thinning the further from the beachfront urbanisation. Not far from the station, Adam spied a solitary figure sitting on a bench next to a tranquil water garden. He wondered if it was Monet, enjoying his wine, and perhaps reminiscing about his beloved garden at Giverny.

Looking west caused Adam to shudder, as if bitten by a sudden chill wind. About two miles away, as if ignored by the designers of Reynold's Gardens, a titanium-dark wall completely covered the view. From north to south and up beyond the cloud cover, stark and imposing, the sheer size of the great barrier invoked a sense of dread. The iron viaduct ended abruptly by the wall – the final few feet ripped through and crushed down.

"That can't be right," Adam said. "Surely, it's not meant to be like that. Did they run out of money or something?"

"It's a safety barrier," Artie explained. "It came down during the great catastrophe. Squashed anything underneath, including people – to this day, we aren't sure exactly how many. This is only the eastern end of the gardens."

Stardust climbed into the open-topped carriage and took a seat:

"Well, I think it adds a note of sophistication – a lovely shade of urban grey. Reminds me of home. It is true, I once craved the wedding cake fancy of Regency and the stirring drama of Victoriana, but over the years, the concrete and steel has grown on me."

"The other side is badly damaged and in perpetual darkness," Artie said. "There is a way through, but travel is restricted to essential business only." He waved Stardust out of the carriage. "Sorry my sparkly friend, but like many things in the gardens, the trains no longer work. It is a two-mile walk along the track to the Balconies. Once there, we can relax, have dinner, and discuss exactly why you are here."

Dismayed that they would not enjoy a miniature train ride, Adam and his group wearily followed their escorts east along the narrow trackway. Only a few minutes later, they crossed over a silvery-grey planked surface. Bridging a gap in the viaduct, a heap of twisted metal on the ground below, the planks were a crude repair.

"I've seen this stuff before," Adam said, kneeling down and running his hand over the plastic-like material. "It's like duct tape, but much thicker."

"It is full-scale duct tape," Artie replied. "I do not know where they get it from, but they send it through the wall from the dark-side. We use it for general repairs: the viaduct, the apartment block sky bridges, even fallen trees." Artie leant back against the viaduct's side railing. He glanced at his brass pocket watch:

"We have plenty of time before midnight …"

"But the sun's already going down," Adam noted.

"It's always going down. For a thousand years, there has been perpetual sunset – never a sunny day or a moonlit night … just sunset. You get used to it. Some think it dour and dreary, but others, myself included, find a certain romance in the eternal twilight." Artie flashed a subtle twinkle-eyed look at Adam. "Now, rest your legs and let me tell you about the great catastrophe."

The Great Catastrophe

"For nearly thirty years we played happily in the Gardens. Of course, there were a few troublemakers – there still are – but nothing more than hot heads looking for a fistfight or those desperate for attention. Whilst there are always those looking to clamp down hard on such behaviour, it's often wise to turn a blind eye. We need a bit of fire. You see, excessive time and idleness can create a place where boredom stretches its legs. We reached an agreeable balance.

However, a few seconds changed an eternity. No one knows what caused the great catastrophe. It was as if a giant's hammer struck our world. Everyone remembers the time – eight in the evening, just as the sun was setting – but then it all becomes a blur of pain and destruction. We were thrown off our feet, hurled out of chairs, and sent plummeting from the bridges and balconies. Huge broken blocks fell from the sky, crushing anything beneath – this break in the viaduct is a typical example."

"So, Chicken Little was finally proved right," Adam said, inciting a groan from Blitz.

"I have never heard of that particular soothsayer," Artie replied, "but no one in the gardens predicted the event. Just as people regained their bearings and the uninjured got back on their feet, the safety wall descended like a mountain thrown down by the Gods. The thunderous noise was unbearable and the impact sent us once more to the ground.

Then it was all over, or so we thought. So much that made Reynold's Gardens a place of relaxation and luxury was gone or irreparably broken: serving droids, the railway, elevators, escalators, and much, much more, taken away in one vicious moment. But, at least the dispensers were still functioning."

Stern, leaning against the opposite railing, took off his Stetson and held it against his chest as if in sympathy:

"Wow, muchacho, seems you guys went through Hell. I feel for you. Glad you came through it OK."

The constables shuffled uncomfortably, and Artie slowly shook his head:

"Oh no, my handsome friend, that was only the beginning. What happened next was far, far worse. We quickly adapted to the new reality. We abandoned the higher floors of the buildings – nobody wanted to climb that many stairs every night. Luckily, whatever mind controlled Reynold's Gardens anticipated the problem and we awoke in the morning wherever we fell asleep the night before, rather than in our beds. Now, you just find a soft patch of grass before midnight. It never rains, is never cold, and you always wake up refreshed."

"We wake up in our beds," Adam said. "Gets a bit boring after a few centuries, and it's sad you can never wake up next to your partner."

"Your partner?"

"If … I had a partner. I'm speaking hypothetically."

Artie smiled, as if relieved:

"Well, here you can lie next to whoever you want and wake up together. But, there's little else in the way of silver linings. Though we heal, even from the most serious injuries, we no longer resurrect. If you die before midnight, then it's all over.

"When we first awoke in Reynold's Gardens, a hologram of the man himself, Gordon Reynolds, explained that a small piece of our original brain – the bit that gives us our sense of self – was compressed and embedded in our new brains. We may have many of humanities greatest minds among our numbers, but the best we could come up with was preserving the brain in gel. Who knows, maybe it's the right thing to do, and one day they'll all return."

Adam interrupted Artie, perplexed at the constant references to Reynolds:

"I thought Ming Hua Chang created this place. I've never heard of Gordon Reynolds."

"And, I've never heard of Ming Hua Chang," Artie replied. "During my induction, Mr Reynolds identified himself as the man behind the project. He still appears now and then to offer advice."

"Chang bought the rights to the British throne in the 22nd century," Adam continued. "His granddaughter, Boudicca Chang, became queen. Surely you've heard of her – named after Boudicca, the warrior queen."

Artie's eyes narrowed:

"Why on Earth would anyone want to be named after that woman? She wasn't even really a queen." He coughed once. "Anyway, we can't access any information beyond the first half of the 21st century. Nobody here was originally alive beyond that time. How reliable is your source."

"I have no idea," Adam admitted, beginning to doubt Boudicca Chang's trustworthiness. "So, you said things got worse."

"About two months after the catastrophe, the food started running out. The dispensers ran dry by midday. At first we thought, or hoped, that it was a one off hiccup, but it kept happening. People started rushing to the dispensers every morning. This just made it worse. There weren't enough resources to provide breakfast for even half the population."

"Where we come from, the food from the dispensers is fake – tastes and feels real, but has no nutritional value. The real feeding takes place when we are asleep."

"After a few weeks of near starvation, we realised the same thing. The police force was created to ration the resources – Erwin Rommel was the chief back then – but no matter how well they organised the food distribution, some people were starving and some not. It seemed random, but after a day when the dispensers shut down almost completely, we realised what was happening. You see, the next day there were still some people who felt fully fed. That's when the panic set in and the killing began."

"I guess the police couldn't keep order."

"Rommel tried to calm the situation. He told us to feed the dispensers with anything we could find: furniture, ornaments, anything. It was too late. Most had already worked out the simple truth; that if there were less people, then they were more likely to be fed. However, Rommel got his wish, when an angry mob killed the entire police force and fed them into the dispensers.

After that, everyone gradually formed into tribes, waiting for a full feed so that they could prey on the weak. It went on for years. We still observed the ritual of saving the brains of the dead – no gold box in those days, just a small plastic bucket. In fact, only the painters were excluded from the killing. Like the ancient Celtic Druids, they were respected and left alone."

"Why painters?" Blitz asked, with his usual disdain for artistic types. "I would have thought scientists more suitable for the job."

"The painters have wonderful hand eye co-ordination, which is essential for the surgery – not many here have a real surgical background – and most have a certain sensitivity that suits the occasion. Plus, their creativity and artistic competitiveness makes for some impressive rituals.

"Well, gradually, as our numbers dwindled, there was enough food to go around. The killing continued for a few more years as scores were settled, but it eventually ended. We formed a new police force, with a new chief chosen once every 50 years, and our resource levels have been fine ever since."

"How many died," Adam asked.

Artic tightened his lips as if unwilling to reply. His face seemed harrowed with grief:

"There are nearly 220 thousand brains in the repository. We estimate there were between 450 thousand and 500 thousand residents originally, so we have lost close to half our original number. You must realise, that we were all involved. No one here is innocent. We rarely talk about it, but the memories of those dark years never leave us. Early on in the slaughter, Gustav Holst summed it up when he said, 'that with every death, we tear another page from the history book'."

"Is Shakespeare still alive?" Adam asked.

"No."

"Napoleon?"

"No."

"Elvis?"

"Ah, the entertainer. I believe he currently resides on the other side of the wall."

"And what about Edgar Allen Poe?"

"Hmm, I recall the name, but I do not know what happened to him."

Constable Lovelace raised her hand:

"Sir, I do not know for sure, but he may be in the 'third place'. I spoke with him the morning of the great catastrophe and he invited me to the west beach festivities. I had a prior engagement so declined."

"What's the 'third place'," Adam asked, eager for more information about Poe.

"Another safety wall came down on the western half of the Gardens – the dark-side," Artie explained. "It cut off the other six apartment blocks and the beach from the park. There is no way through, so no one knows what happened or if anyone is still alive. At the time, a popular cultural event was taking place on the promenade so there were many trapped behind the wall. We suspect that the devastation was so great that they suffered a far worse fate than the rest of the dark-side."

Adam decided to keep Poe's death a secret. The revelation that one of literature's most famous sons died scuba diving in a giant anal canal might prove problematic, even dangerous. Given the previous levels of slaughter in Reynold's Gardens, and Saloni's sad end, Adam wondered if there was already a gold box with his name on it.

"Hey there," a sharp voice suddenly called out. Everyone looked round, gladly distracted from Artie's tragic tale. Climbing onto the trackway from an access ladder, a besuited man – average height, short dark hair – straightened his tie and approached the group.

"Sigmund," Artie exclaimed, embracing the man. The man reciprocated and they both kissed each other on the cheek.

"How very continental," Stardust remarked to Adam.

"You don't approve?"

"I like to touch people. I really like to touch people. However, try that in the Psychoviro and you're liable to get raped or beaten to death." Stardust sighed. "Perhaps, when the mission is over, I could stay here a while."

Artie introduced his friend to the group:

"Friends, this is Sigmund Freud. I'm sure he needs no introduction. Sigmund, these are our guests from the other world that Henrik no doubt told you about."

"He only said there were special guests I should meet. I know I was supposed to wait at the Balconies, but curiosity got the better of me." Freud became wide-eyed, noticing Stardust and Blitz in their glam finery. "How very strange. A perfect pick me up on an otherwise dull day – better than coke.

Blitz swaggered forward, and squared up to Freud. High up on his platform boots, his flame make-up accentuating the hostile fire in his eyes, he towered over the celebrated 'father of psychoanalysis'.

"Think we're strange, do you?" Blitz asked.

"I meant no offence," Freud said, offering a hand, which Blitz did not accept. "A rebellious splash of colour and sparkle is most welcome. This place can become a tedious yawn of tea and biscuits."

"That sounds very … English. I thought you were German."

"Austrian, actually."

"You don't even have an accent."

"When we first arrived in the gardens, somehow we all spoke English. Obviously, that Reynolds fellow was obsessed with Victorian Britain. With some effort, we can speak in our original tongues, but it's quite tiresome. A few centuries and you don't bother trying anymore. It's no bad thing, though. There are many positive aspects to a common tongue. It leads to more meaningful communication, which leads to understanding … and friendship."

"Or fear and manipulation," Blitz added. The scorn in his voice betrayed his disdain for the eminent psychoanalyst.

Freud raised an eyebrow, as if assessing the impertinent stranger standing before him.

"Don't try and analyse me, Fraud," Blitz warned, pointing his finger. "I know who I am, what I'm capable of, and I like it."

"I was just admiring your wonderful clothes and face paint – quite the peacock. Is this normal where you come from?"

"Nothing's normal where he comes from," Adam interrupted, roughly grabbing Blitz by the arm and hauling him back from confrontation.

Stardust stepped forward:

"Please excuse my friend's threatening behaviour," he said softly. "It's just that we have a special hatred for psychiatrists. I assure you, it's nothing personal." Stardust offered a smile. "But it could be."

Artie put his arm around his bewildered friend's waist and led him over to Stern who posed moodily by the railing, the brow of his Stetson lowered, hiding his eyes.

"A man in black," Freud harrumphed. "Another who hates psychiatrists?"

With a single finger, Stern raised the brow of his Stetson:

"Life's far too long to hate anyone, muchacho."

With a shocked shriek, Freud threw up his hands and jumped backwards:

"Oh my goodness, it's you! It's you! It's really you! I never thought I would see the day …"

"Mr Freud, that day has come," Stern said coolly. "And, I'm flattered to have a fan in this far flung place – especially one as distinguished and so obviously discerning as yourself."

"Whew, I must catch my breath a moment," Freud said, taking in a few deep breaths, steadying himself. "My legs feel so giddy. Hah, I always imagined I would appear more composed and sophisticated if we ever met. I feel so silly."

"Do not worry; you're simply experiencing the full force of my charisma." Stern flexed his bronzed chest, deepening his pec crease. "It's only natural. Now, what I'm really interested to know is how my fame spread to these parts."

"Oh, we have extensive archives in the Gardens. I have watched all of your shows many times – even the post credit interviews. Why you were not on Reynold's list I will never know. I have so many questions; so many things I need to know."

"Fire away, Mind Meister."

"Is it possible to hind-read with these tiny bodies? Do you still do readings?"

"Of course I do. I must respect my gift."

"Really! Is there a chance … oh, I shouldn't."

"Chance of what, muchacho?"

"A fantasy, Stern – a dream. I was wondering … hoping … that you might …"

"Read your hind?"

Freud nodded sheepishly, shuffling his feet, and raised his tightly crossed fingers.

"I'd consider it an honour." Stern looked deeply into Freud's eyes. "What secrets will surface from the hind of a great mind?"

"You can both satisfy your disgusting fixations tomorrow," Artie said, waving the group once more towards the Balconies. "We have important matters to discuss tonight, and I do not want to be put off my dinner."

Adam sidled up to Stern and whispered in his ear:

"Well, look who's sitting in a tree now."

DINNER DATE

The Balconies, an elegant twenty-storey latticework of viewing platforms, dominated the eastern end of the Gardens. Like the environments in the Viroverse, the outer walls of Reynold's Gardens recreated a realistic landscape stretching into the far distance – the grey safety barrier to the west an unnerving exception. Served by its own station and a number of cobbled roads, the Balconies acted as a focal point for wining, dining, and engaging in the timeless pursuit of people watching.

Five storeys up, Adam leaned with both hands against the stone balustrade, and gazed out across the Gardens. The wide semi-circular balcony, a Victorian take on a stadium VIP box, was lavishly furnished with rich dark woods and baby-soft leathers – heavy velvet drapes absorbing the light from the pear-drop crystal chandelier and frosted glass wall-lights. In the air, there hung a subtle scent of fresh lavender.

Without functioning lifts, enjoying the delights of the Balconies meant climbing the emergency stairs. After the long trek from the warehouse, everyone was keen to rest their tired legs. The four constables took up positions around the platform, whilst Artie, less formal without his heavy blue police jacket, sat with his guests around the large mahogany dining table.

Before joining the others, Adam spent a little more time soaking up the ambiance. Silver rampant lions bookended the grey stone balustrade, the top of which was inlaid with a cushion of buttoned red leather. Set into the stone, a brass telescope enabled detailed celebrity spotting for the voyeuristically inclined.

A few miles in the distance, in the twilight gloom, the western wall appeared as an impenetrable fog bank or a sheer cliff of granite. The gothic atmosphere was overwhelming, almost intoxicating, and Adam felt like a dread vampire lord overseeing his dark dominion – albeit a vampire lord who favoured Hawaiian shirts and tight white trousers. Blitz instantly broke the spell. Barging alongside Adam, he grabbed the telescope, and began spying on the crowds by the apartment blocks.

"Take a seat, gentlemen," Artie called over from the table. "Choose what you want from the menu, and my constables will fetch your food."

"I'll stay here if you don't mind," Blitz murmured, fastidiously looking from person to person. "I'm not that hungry and it's only a few hours until midnight."

Adam took a seat next to Artie, who handed chunky leather bound menus to his guests. Whilst they perused the long list of options, Constable Lovelace stood at his side, ready to relay the orders to Constable Hanzō who waited patiently outside in the corridor after drawing the short straw on dispenser duty.

"Do I need to ask?" Artie asked Freud. "The usual?"

"Yes!" Freud snapped shut his menu. "Cumberland sausage with mash and gravy. I always say I will try something new, but the allure of that long spicy coil is too great. And, before I am forced to endure yet another Freudian penis joke, sometimes a sausage is just a sausage."

"And for you, Stern? Steak perhaps? I'm afraid there's no Tex-Mex, unless you want to custom build."

Stern smiled and tapped the menu:

"Steak and kidney pie. Gotta be steak and kidney pie. When I was at university in London, I used to have pies delivered from Harrods – Turners if I remember rightly. The Tex-Mex thing is just part of the stage public persona. You might think me the Hot Sauce Burrito Bandito, but I'm a pie lover at heart. However, it has to have decent filling. I know it's all artificial, but I still don't like the idea of mystery meat – even fake mystery meat."

"Everything is high quality here," Freud assured Stern. "I recommend the steak and kidney pudding. It is a traditional East End recipe, with oysters added as a filler. Oysters were a poor man's food back in those days."

"Even better, muchacho; no wonder they had such big families back then. Never a bad time to fuel the sex drive – even if I'm not gonna use it. If you see me grinning later, you know I'm ready to go."

Adam played safe, settling for a medium rare Sirloin steak, whilst Stardust, after taking an age to decide, opted for Kedgeree – a lightly curried creamy pilaff of smoked haddock and boiled egg.

"Mmm, I'll have the grilled salmon salad with a light caper vinaigrette," Artie decided, before sending Constable Lovelace to help her colleague in the corridor.

Once the food was on the table, Blitz, still staring through the telescope called over to Artie, asking him to settle a query. The chief duly obliged, momentarily leaving his guests. As Artie looked through the telescope, Blitz whispered in his ear. Smiling, Artie nodded, patted Blitz on the back, and returned to the table.

Freud finished chewing a rather large mouthful of sausage:

"What about Joseph Merrick? Is he in your world? Does he still suffer from those awful deformities?"

"You mean The Elephant Man?" Adam asked.

"Yes; I have always wondered how resurrection treated the poor fellow. He endured the worst form of schaulust."

"Schaulust?"

"Scopophilia, the pleasure of looking – in Merrick's case the act of seeing that which is guilty or forbidden."

"Well, he is cured. As normal as they come, brown hair, fair skin – they say he takes after his mother. Apparently, he's very friendly and loves to talk, even to strangers, though he can get a bit deep and philosophical at times."

Freud smiled and cut another length of sausage:

"I'm glad he's left behind that rotten existence of freak shows and pointing fingers. We all deserve a chance at a good life."

Adam slowly shook his head:

"Hmm, the tragedy is that he hasn't left that life behind. He may be physically 'normal' now, but people turn up in his Viro all the time to point and stare. They all want to see what the Elephant Man looks like without his deformities. He takes it all in good humour, but I guess he'll always be a prisoner of his past."

"The cruel bastards," Freud grumbled, waving a ponderously large piece of sausage on the end of his fork, "some people have no standards and no shame."

"Yeah, well I was one of those people, and … I have so much shame."

Artie put down his knife and fork:

"Adam, there is no shame in what you do. If the stories are even half-true, then you are a credit to your world. Perhaps what you call shame is simply the sign of a good heart." Artie gently patted Adam's hand. "I admire a man who can bear the true burden of his calling."

Blitz approached the table:

"Excuse me, but I need to go to the bathroom. Is that the door over there? I don't want to be impolite, but I've been holding it in since we left the warehouse."

"That is the door," Artie replied, "but the toilets have been out of action since the great catastrophe. There is a dispenser in the corridor outside. Use that."

"A dispenser?" Blitz said, screwing his face up.

"Oh, my apologies; I forget you are not used to our ways. Using the dispensers when we need to go is something we take for granted. If you need to urinate, then just aim into the black glass – just make sure you are in reverse mode or you'll make an awful mess. If you need to go the other way, then you have two choices. If you are agile enough, you can contort yourself into a crouching position with your posterior hard against the glass and go directly – again, I cannot emphasise enough that the dispenser must be in reverse mode. Alternatively, since you are new here, you can dispense a chamber pot and some tissue and use them. When you are done, just push the pot and tissue back into the dispenser."

"And, how do I wash my hands?"

"Fortunately, the toilet cubicles have working sinks, so no problem there. Constable Hanzō will escort you to the dispenser. If you have any problems, he will help you."

"I'm quite capable of doing this myself. I certainly don't need anyone watching me."

Freud laughed:

"Since most of the dispensers are in public areas, this is not a place for the penis shy."

Incensed, Blitz turned and pointed aggressively at Freud:

"No one cares what you have to say, Sigmund Fraud. Just about every crazy theory you ever came up with has been debunked. Whoever built this place must have had a soft spot for snake oil salesmen."

"Well, you obviously have a strong interest in my work. Perhaps I should be flattered."

"Know thine enemy," Stardust said. "Like I said earlier, we have a special hatred for psychiatrists."

Freud clasped his hands together, as if in prayer:

"Over the years, most of my ideas have come in for intense scrutiny and even greater criticism. I consider it a success that they provoke such debate, and perhaps spur others to advance their own theories. To play safe, to put forward ideas that simply mimic or agree with what is already known, is a comfortable road to obscurity. My work came first; not the desire to please everyone."

"You think you're so original," Blitz spat scornfully. "I bet you don't even believe that you stand on the shoulders of giants."

"To the contrary, I am indebted to those that went before me, but I do find that particular metaphor rather dramatic and somewhat demeaning to those that come later – it also has a whiff of circus acrobatics about it. Though incongruous, I prefer to see it as sitting on the laps of those that went before, whilst they quietly peer over your shoulder."

"You're so full of yourself, aren't you? If I had my way, I would …"

Artie stood up and held up a hand, interrupting the escalating situation:

"This is all very interesting, Mr Blitz, but don't you need the toilet?"

Mumbling curses under his breath, Blitz strode out of the room with Constable Hanzō at his side. With Blitz standing tall on his high platforms, the diminutive constable seemed like a small child.

"Did this food come from the dispenser in the corridor?" Adam asked, looking worryingly at his plate. "You know; the one that you use as a toilet."

"There are no real hygiene implications," Artie explained. "What goes in is artificial and what comes out is artificial. As a legendary warrior, I didn't think you would be concerned with such things."

"Well, I know that it shouldn't bother me. It's just that," Adam pushed the remaining half of his steak across the plate, "I wish I'd chosen something less brown."

"Well, if you have finished, I suggest we get down to business," Artie stood up, rolling up his sleeves as if emphasising the point. "Come, let's talk by the balcony."

Adam took one last look at his steak, then, picturing Blitz contorting in the corridor, joined the imposingly muscular police chief.

"I think you need to tell them, first," Freud interrupted. "They have a right to know who they're dealing with."

Artie cast a pointed stare at the psychoanalyst:

"You are here as a guest, Sigmund. I decide the agenda."

"The time for secrets has passed," Freud insisted. "If you don't tell them, then I will."

"Tell me what," Adam asked.

Artie leant against the balustrade as if seeking support:

"Ok; I don't really know how best to explain this, but Artie is just a nickname. This isn't my original body; it's a replacement. I'm not even really a man. My real name is Cartimandua, Queen of the Brigantes."

Adam was silent for a few seconds, the revelation taking him completely by surprise:

"Err … do you mean that literally, or is it some Priscilla, Queen of the Desert kind of thing. I … I'm not prejudiced either way, but …"

"I have never heard of that particular monarch," Cartimandua continued. "I was the leader of the northern Brigantes tribe during the first century of the Roman occupation of Britain."

"Ah, like Boudicca, the warrior queen," Adam said, trying not to appear bewildered.

Cartimandua punched the balustrade's leather cushion and rolled her eyes:

"Boudicca, Boudicca, Boudicca … why do I always have to be compared to that woman? I was a real queen, of the largest tribe, and I never get mentioned without hearing her name."

"Maybe you shouldn't have betrayed Caractacus to the Romans," Freud said, busily mixing his gravy into the mashed potato.

"Shut-up, Freud," Cartimandua ordered.

"Or divorced your husband and shacked up with a commoner."

"I said shut-up."

"Or had to be rescued by the Romans when your people turned against you."

"Have you finished?"

Freud held up his hands and nodded, before returning to his dinner.

"I must admit, I enjoyed the luxury that Rome provided. I thought it best to appease them … for the sake of my people of course. Too late, I realised that I was wrong. I returned to lead my people in one last stand against the Romans. It was a bloody battle. We threw everything we had into the defence of our lands but we were defeated – although it was so, so close. Nobody ever hears about that. What little is written about me, labels me as a self-indulgent, sex-mad, scheming traitor."

"Well, I certainly never considered you a traitor," Freud quipped.

"I was never one for history," Adam admitted. "If it helps, you were leading your people and fighting the Romans in your final years, whilst in mine, I was mostly drunk from White Lightning cider and waking up lying in piss and vomit. I guess that's why Reynolds added you to this prestigious history book, and why I was resurrected as an afterthought."

Cartimandua smiled and looked into Adam's eyes:

"A warrior with a kind heart – an attractive combination."

"So, you say your body is a replacement?" Adam said, steering the conversation back to business.

"That's why you are here, isn't it? Bodies have been going missing from your recycling room."

"That's exactly why we're here," Adam said. "We know it's happening; we just don't know why."

"We are rotting," Artie confessed. "We believe that it's connected to the great catastrophe, but we have no definite proof. It has been postulated that from time to time our bodies require complete renewal. Without resurrection, we keep the same bodies … and they eventually rot."

"I thought you said you heal."

"But it's the same bodies healed over and over again. The rot begins as a light green stain. It can appear anywhere, but usually starts on the thighs. It slowly darkens and spreads. In the end, it kills you, although it takes decades."

"And, where does Hernán Cortés fit into all this? There are those in my world who want his head."

"He organises the collection of bodies from the recycling room. He also makes sure the Captain's forces are suitably distracted."

Adam remained diplomatically silent about the many Terminal operatives killed over the years:

"And, where is Cortés? Can I speak to him?"

"He controls the western half of the gardens, beyond the wall. I know he is keen to meet with any representatives from your world. We have always known this day would come."

"So, how did you get your new body? Do you get to choose or are you just given one at random?"

"The doorway to your world is only open for a limited time – no more than a few weeks every few decades. Because of this, there are never enough bodies for all those afflicted with the rot. As soon as the first stain appears, you are banished to the other side of the wall. There are thousands there desperate for new bodies."

"So, do the most rotted get the bodies?"

"Oh no; it's a tournament. You have to fight to win a body, and that's if you're lucky enough to be chosen."

"To the death?"

"You can concede if you wish, many do, but some keep fighting even when they are facing certain defeat. You see, the rot is relentless, and no one knows how long it will be before more bodies become available. Many have nothing to lose."

"You obviously won your fight."

"There was only one body left. To be honest, I had already given up hope."

"I have mercifully remained clear of the rot," Freud said, "but I crossed over to the dark-side to offer my dear friend some support."

Cartimandua nodded, smiling sentimentally:

"Sigmund and I were in the same tribe after the great catastrophe. We spilled much blood together, and watched each other's backs. It is a bond that can never be broken. He hugged me so tightly when my name came up – my chance to cheat death once more – but fifteen other competitors stood in my way.

It was one on one, until only one remained. Luckily, the others, all men, underestimated my fighting abilities – most of them had ill-conceived notions of a women's strength and this worked beautifully to my advantage."

"Oh, she was gloriously brutal," Freud said, punching a fist into his palm. "Her sword hacked and slashed through the enemy with such speed. I am not one for violence, but I was on my feet, cheering her on like a lunatic."

"Not one of my opponents conceded. I had to kill them all. I guess they thought it humiliating to give in to a woman. In the end there were just two of us left standing. He was a worthy adversary: fast on his feet and blessed with boundless energy. In the end, he mistook my angle of attack and it was all over. To this day, I still remember the look of horror on Benny Hill's face as I ran him through."

"Did you have to chase him?" Adam asked flippantly – though shocked and somewhat saddened by the result.

Cartimandua solemnly shook her head:

"And that is how I have this body. I do miss my old one. I used to be a redhead with the fairest skin. However, my new skin is so wonderfully supple." She held out her arm for Adam to feel.

"It is very smooth," he admitted, lightly rubbing Cartimandua's forearm.

"And, I can build the most impressive muscles. Look at these." Cartimandua unbuttoned her shirt to reveal two perfect steak-slab pectorals.

Stern wolf whistled and punched the air:

"Hell, they're better than mine. How often you do you work those babies?"

"Split routine, every other day, and the dark skin helps with perceived definition. Here, Adam, feel them." Cartimandua grunted loudly, flexing her upper body, strong jaw set hard."

Tentatively, Adam reached over and prodded each pec in turn:

"Rock hard."

"You like them?"

"They are … very impressive. Good work."

"I'm glad you like them; really glad," Cartimandua relaxed her muscles, and then coyly batted her eyelashes, "because … I really like you. There, I said it."

Swept by a wave of sudden pressure and stress, Adam looked at the others for guidance. Freud raised an eyebrow and took a swig of dark beer. Stardust sat as if frozen, his eyes wide and mouth open. Stern simply grinned, enjoying Adam stumbling into yet another awkward situation – either that or the oysters were kicking in.

"This is not about fulfilling some young girl's dream," Cartimandua said, a look of true longing in her eyes. "This is the real thing. I felt an unspoken bond between us the moment we met. I am sure you felt the same way. Tell me I'm wrong."

"I think you are a very handsome man … person," Adam said, aware of a bead of sweat dripping down his nose. "I will also admit that your muscles and skin tone give me that sort of … man crush feeling. But, I … err … also get that with Stern."

Stern stifled a chuckle, and waved his hand dismissively:

"Aw, little muchacho, as if I didn't know you were sneaking a peek."

"But … the thing is, even though I sometimes admire the male physique, I am not gay."

Cartimandua let out a deep sigh of relief:

"That's perfect, because neither am I. I have never been interested in women."

At that moment, Adam ran out of tactful options. Letting Cartimandua down easy would take a sensitivity and eloquence that he simply did not possess.

"I don't think it's going to work," Adam muttered sheepishly. "I'm only here for a short while … and I only go in for long term relationships."

"Is that really the case, or is it something else? Is it because I am black? Is that it? I've heard that racism is still a thing where you come from."

"No … it's because you have a man's body. There, now I've said it. I can't ignore the elephant in the room."

Cartimandua gasped, covering her face with her hands:

"So, you think I'm an elephant? Well, I am not an animal. I am a human being."

"I … I … don't think you're an elephant," Adam stuttered. "It's just an expression. It means ignoring the blatantly obvious. In this case, that you have a man's body."

The former Celtic queen moved within a breath of Adam:

"These are artificial bodies. They lend our minds mobility and allow us to sense the physical world. We have eyes to gaze upon one another, soft lips that we might kiss, and skin … for us to caress. Isn't that all we need? In another life, my first life, you would not resist me. I would simply take you for my pleasure."

Feeling ashamed and intimidated, Adam looked for a way out, wondering if he would survive a five-storey drop over the balustrade:

"Yeah, I understand what you're saying. I know we have skin and all that. It's just …"

"Then what is it? What is the problem?"

"You have a dinker, Artie!" Freud called out, the last remnant of sausage standing upright on the end of his fork.

"Is that it, Adam? Is it because I have a dinker?"

"If by dinker you mean penis, then … yes."

"Oh Adam, you are obviously thinking too far ahead – and they call me a sexual predator. If it really bothers you that much, I'm sure I could tuck it out of the way."

"A dance belt would do the trick," Freud advised, his plate clean, and clear of genitally metaphorical meat tubes. "Male ballet dancers wear them to keep themselves in check. All those lovely ballerinas can be so arousing."

"Good call, muchacho," Stern agreed. "I like to hang free most of the time, but I would never perform without a dance belt. You gotta remember to point your guy upwards when you put it on; otherwise, you're in for a world of pain if you get turned on."

For a moment, out of either diplomatic expediency or possibly the faintest glimmer of affection, Adam considered surrendering to Cartimandua's passion. What harm could it do? Did their physical exterior really matter? After all, they were fundamentally algae based constructs.

Cartimandua turned away, and leant against the balustrade:

"Have no doubt; I will have you," Her deep voice softened, "… but only because you will want me. For now, we will discuss only business."

There was neither time for business or talk of love, as the door to the viewing platform was flung open, and Constable Hanzō staggered in, blood soaked toilet tissue wrapped around his head.

"What on Earth happened?" Cartimandua asked, as Constable Lovelace quickly pulled up a seat for her injured colleague. "Where is Mr Blitz?"

"The coward hit me when my back was turned," Hanzō seethed, reaching for the water jug. "I think he used a chamber pot."

"Constable Lovelace; fetch some dermis sealant. Now, Constable Hanzō, why exactly did you turn your back on our guest? I told you to keep an eye on him."

"He said he couldn't go with someone watching him. It is a male hang-up from the old world – some men get anxious. I looked away for just a second and then it all went black. The dishonourable devil broke the unspoken code."

Cartimandua thought for a moment before her expression turned to one of alarm. Grabbing the telescope, she frantically scanned the area outside the second apartment block. Fixing on a growing crowd near the building's entrance, she froze for a few seconds, and then stood back:

"Oh no; what's he doing there? Is he dancing?"

BLITZ 'N' BLAISE

The trusting fool turned his back. Blitz grinned, allowing himself a moment to gloat. So far, everything was going to plan. With luck, Copout and his friends would take some time to finish their meal, bogged down by their interminably inane conversations. Hurriedly working the dispenser, Blitz procured a cutlass and a knuckleduster – violence was not intended, but anticipation and preparation were the products of an organised mind.

Before heading for the stairs, Blitz knelt down and wrapped a few layers of toilet tissue around Constable Hanzō's bleeding head. Dressing the wound was a calculated act of compassion designed to placate the idiots. The constable stirred, groaning quietly.

"Get back to sleep, you bastard," Blitz seethed under his breath, "Can't you see I'm trying to help you." He punched Hanzō hard in the head with his knuckleduster, knocking the unfortunate constable back into unconsciousness.

Not relishing stumbling down ten flights of stairs on cumbersome platform heels, Blitz slid down the mahogany banister rail, which wound all the way to the ground floor. As he sped down the banister, he saw himself reflected in the mirror tiles on the stairwell wall. Cursing his ludicrous appearance – a flame topped sliver of shimmering turquoise – he decided to stare at the rail.

"What are you meant to be?" a bowler hatted man exclaimed upon seeing the glam warrior slide off the end of the highly polished rail.

Blitz steadied himself and smiled – a rare expression he usually reserved for Copout's many deaths.

"Fancy dress party. Not my cup of tea, so I'm leaving early."

"Oh, I love fancy dress parties." The man looked at his watch. "Which floor? I'll pick up a costume on the way up."

"Oh, you made me do this," Blitz grumbled, punching the man in the face.

Under a rain of blows, the man fell to the floor – his bowler hat sent rolling away down the corridor. Blitz stood for a few seconds, making sure his victim was not getting back up. Then, he dragged the unconscious man under the cover of the stairs, out of sight to all but the most observant passer-by.

"Good job you're not bleeding, because I'm all out of toilet paper."

Peering through the huge arched entrance, Blitz looked carefully for any police that might be lurking outside. Satisfied that there were none, he slipped out into the gardens and sprinted towards the nearby railway viaduct. He knew the viaduct led directly to his destination, but instead of climbing the stairs to the large station, he ran underneath the snaking iron structure. Hidden from view, and with soft grass underfoot, he could enjoy a comfortable uninterrupted jog to the second condominium.

Blitz made quick progress, maintaining a steady bounding lope on his high platforms – a psychoviro running technique developed over the centuries to overcome the obvious problems with glam footwear. Now and then, he crossed a cobbled road, surprising pedestrians, who pointed and called out as he passed by. Blitz ignored them. Keenly focused on his target, he blocked out all distractions.

As he approached the tree-lined square that bordered the second apartment block, Blitz slowed to a normal walking pace. An obviously popular meeting place, the large square was alive with people. With an arrogant leer, the glittering psychopath swaggered through the gathering of top hats, canes, bonnets and bustles – even attracting a small entourage.

Standing near a bench at the edge of the square, a small group of men were engaged in a lively debate about various beers. The object of Blitz's attention, a pale long-faced man with reddish brown hair, enthused about the superiority of Barclay Perkin's Porter. With as much reverence as he could muster, Blitz walked up to the man:

"Blaise Pascal?"

The man broke from his conversation and gasped at the strangely dressed person standing before him. He looked Blitz up and down before replying:

"I am Blaise Pascal. Do I know you? I can't say I recognise you … with all that fire make-up on your face, and the striking costume. Is there some festival of which I am not aware? Hmm, didn't Thor have red hair? Is that who are dressed up as? I think he had a beard though. And, shouldn't that be a hammer, rather than a pirate sword? You are obviously aware that large bladed weapons are forbidden. I guess that is a harmless prop."

"Sir, my name is Trevor Wintock, and I am here because … you are the person I most admire. Ever since my teenage years I have had the greatest respect …"

"Did Descartes put you up to this?" Pascal furtively glanced around. "Is he watching us now?"

"Nobody sent me. I came here of my own volition."

"Descartes has not pranked me for years. However, he did give me the slyest look the other day, whilst I was enjoying lunch in the blue pavilion. He sent you, didn't he?"

"I don't know how to prove this, but I assure you that nobody sent me."

"Then why the strange clothing? How do you explain that?"

Having not thought out this part of his dream encounter, Blitz realised he could not reveal his true origins – neither his murderous life in the Viroverse nor his earlier life as a convicted serial killer:

"In my time, this clothing represented a musical style called glam rock."

"So, you are a musician. Should I be aware of any of your work?"

"I'm not a musician," Blitz admitted, desperately seeking an answer that would not lead to another question. "I am, I suppose, a follower of the music – a fan that dresses and dances in keeping with the fashion."

"Ah, so you are a dancer! Why didn't you say so?" Pascal winked at his friends. "Please, Mr Wintock, dance for us."

"I … I have no music. You need a beat for this."

"Give us a rhythm and we will all clap along. Please, indulge me." Pascal stood back, offering a deep bow, giving Blitz 'the stage'.

Blitz's first thought was to lope away and hide, but he could not deny his idol. Perhaps this was a chance to impress the great man. Every glam day in the psychoviro involved at least one session of dancing. In fact, when not engaged in deadly blood feuds, dance bouts often settled arguments. Though not the best dancer – lacking variety and sensuality – Blitz was renowned for his almost robotic ability to lock onto the beat.

Hand on hips, rising to his full height, Blitz began grunting a glam beat. Pascal whipped up the crowd, who enthusiastically clapped in time. Twisting from side to side, the silver psycho nodded his upper body up and down. He thrust out his arm, dynamically pointing at various audience members with his silver-gloved hand. Next, in a display of precarious balance, he added a high platform stomp. Less than a minute into his act, he noticed that the clapping had stopped.

Unperturbed, Blitz aggressively pumped his arms in the air, and stomped with greater force. It was then that the booing started. At first, it was the odd voice, but soon the entire crowd was loudly expressing their disapproval.

Treated to a surround sound of increasingly crude insults – an expletive filled tirade that was definitely not part of polite Victorian society – Blitz desperately improvised. Keeping his feet still and legs close together, he imitated skiing, with the emphasis on an in-and-out sexual motion.

"Please stop," Pascal called from outside the circle of humiliation. "Can't you see how embarrassing this is?"

With a defeated huff and a slouch of the shoulders, Blitz gave up. Keeping his head down, he shuffled over to his idol.

"Mr Wintock, in all my life I have never witnessed such dancing," Pascal fought to supress a laugh, "and I can honestly say, that I never want to witness it again."

"It works better in a group," Blitz said quietly, offering a half-hearted defence. "Anyway, I am really a mathematician."

Pascal laughed out loud:

"So, now you are a famous mathematician. Then tell me, why have I never heard of you before? Come now, this prank has gone far enough. Go back to Descartes and tell him to try harder next time."

"Please give me a chance to prove myself. If you could just see past these ridiculous clothes, and give me a chance."

"All right, we shall see if you are telling the truth this time. What exactly is your field of expertise?"

"It is geometry," Blitz announced proudly. "I was so inspired by Pascal's Theory …"

"Theorem."

"Of course, a simple slip of the tongue. It was because of you that I chose a career in mathematics."

"Well, if geometry is your field, then you are no doubt acquainted with Poncelet's porism."

"I … err … Poncelet's …"

"Ah, forgive me; you might know it as Poncelet's closure theorem. I sometimes forget that we may have lived centuries apart."

Blitz remained silent before cautiously replying:

"Of course I am acquainted with Poncelet's closure theory."

"Theorem."

"Oops, sorry, another slip of the tongue. To be honest, I have always found that particular theorem a bit mundane for my tastes. Why don't we discuss something else? What about some of your work? I would much rather discuss Pascal's Triangle."

"Perhaps we can discuss that … after you have told me about Poncelet's closure theorem." Pascal crossed his arms, and stared coldly, waiting for a reply.

"Well, you take a … square, and …"

"It's a circle, you dummy!"

"I meant a circle, which you … Oh can't we talk about something else?"

Pascal's friends began sniggering, and Pascal waved away Blitz's squirming drivel with his hand:

"You are no geometer," he exclaimed, assuming a pompously mocking tone. "I'll wager you also know nothing about Steiner chains."

"That is definitely the one with the square," Blitz spluttered, hoping for better luck with his guess.

"That is also circles! What is it with you and squares?"

Creased up with laughter, Pascal's friends pointed at Blitz as the tears rolled down their cheeks. Spurred on by their jollity, the great mathematician turned the screw:

"Hah, I fear your knowledge of mathematics is rivalled only by your skill at dancing. Descartes had nothing to do with this. This is the work of a fool, sir … and that fool is you."

Emotions deafened by the unrelenting laughter, Blitz felt the world pressing in on him. His blood rushed with rage, and his face flushed red, matching his hair and accentuating the flames on his forehead. Paranoia quickly replaced rationality.

In a haze of fury and madness, Blitz realised that this was Copout's plan all along – an elaborate series of twists and turns designed to bring about this ultimate humiliation. Pascal and Copout became one. They grinned like maniacs, and brayed like asses, but Blitz knew he had the upper hand.

No longer bound by the rules of the Psychoviro – that oxymoronic notion of honour amongst psychopaths – Blitz allowed his anger to rise beyond the limits of his self-control. In a state of mind not experienced since his first-life, the world became a series of staccato freeze frames – flashes of reality rousing an impulse to savagery. A flash; Blitz howled with wild primal abandon. Another flash; he felt the heft of the sword in his hand. A final flash; he thrust the blade deeply into Blaise Pascal's chest.

OF FORKS AND FARTS

For less than a minute, Cartimandua angrily paced up and down the balcony. Regaining her composure, she ordered Constables Nabigha and Unaipon to wait in the corridor, and took Adam to one side:

"When he was looking through the telescope, Mr Blitz asked if a man he had spotted was Blaise Pascal ... the mathematician. I told him it was."

"I know who he is," Adam said. "Blitz talked about him all the time in the Psy ... Viroverse. He wouldn't pass up the chance of meeting his God."

"He could have just asked, rather than knock out one of my constables."

Adam's first instinct was to tell the truth about Blitz, of his psychopathic murdering tendencies, but decided that diplomacy was the appropriate response – or lying as it was commonly known.

"Blitz is just tactless," Adam said, dismissing Cartimandua's concerns, "and sometimes unpredictable. I guess he thought we might say no. I mean, he's only dancing."

"Well, I want to keep this as discreet as possible. I'll take Nabigha and Unaipon, and I think you should accompany me to the square."

"Blitz is my responsibility. When we get there, you should hang back. If he starts something ..."

Cartimandua looked concerned:

"Starts something? Are you saying he's dangerous? I would like to believe that knocking out Constable Hanzō was an act of foolish obsession, especially since he took the time to dress the wound. Is his dancing a precursor to violence?"

"Not at all," Adam replied 'diplomatically'. "Right now, he's the proverbial fish out of water. I know how to deal with him. However, I think we should leave right away."

"I don't like the sound of this, but my instinct is to trust you." Cartimandua clenched a fist and rapped it against her leg. "I'll wait with my constables by the edge of the square, and you deal with Mr Blitz. And, for goodness sake, wear something over that shirt. I don't want people thinking the circus has come to town. A frock coat should do, or something a docker might wear. Use the dispenser in the corridor." Cartimandua buttoned up her blue police jacket and put on her helmet. "Sigmund, Mr Lovass, Mr Stardust, I want you to stay here with Constable Lovelace and Constable Hanzō. I will try to get back before midnight. If I don't make it, then please make yourselves comfortable and I will see you in the morning."

After Adam and Cartimandua left, Stardust pulled a chair over to the balcony and sat quietly. Leaning an elbow on the cushioned red leather of the balustrade, he rested his head on his hand and looked out across the Gardens.

Forever the outsider, the long-time leader of the Psychoviro always stayed a few steps beyond the crowd. Happy to step into the light to perform, to rouse his subjects, Stardust then retreated into the shadows. He knew his long reign was not due to charisma or strength. Ziggy's strong arm, and seasoned willow, kept any would be usurpers at bay. Other than that, there were those who saw in Stardust a comforting nostalgia harking back to the ancient glory days of Groover's leadership – a safe, though creepy, pair of hands.

Everyone else had found their dance partner – Copa and Cartimandua, Blitz and Blaise, Freud and Stern. Even the two constables chatted like old friends. As usual, Stardust was the odd one out.

In a distant teenage past, clouded by sorrow and showered with guilt, his loving father assured him that he was 'one for the girls', and that he would have to beat them off with a stick. Away from the judgemental ears of others, his mother always reminded him that he would never be man enough to fill his father's shoes.

His father passed, taken a week after a cancer diagnosis, and the sixteen-year-old Stardust became 'the man of the house'. In fear and under threat, he could not fill those rather large shoes, in depth nor girth … or other things demanded by his mother. Five years later, when she also died – an accidental tumble down a steep flight of stairs – Stardust sold up and moved to the city.

A laugh from the dining table stirred the man in glitter-black from his musings. Distracted for the moment, he casually eavesdropped. Stern sat back in his chair, and gently rapped his fingers together:

"Look, Sigmund, I am fully aware of my charms. I am also aware of my fame. But, even given the obvious attraction, I can't quite picture you as a fan."

"That is because you do not know me," Freud replied. "I am fully aware that to many people, I am simply a historical character – usually an older bearded man, in a tweed jacket, holding a cigar. Would it shed light on the matter if I was to tell you that I was an admirer of Joseph Pujol?"

Stern sat forward, surprised by Freud's admission:

"You mean Le Pétomane, the flatulist?"

"Yes; I saw him perform at the Moulin Rouge in the 1880's. I even kept a photo of him on my office wall. His ability to move air in and out of his rectum, and create such magnificent sounds was a rare gift. I consider Pujol a true and criminally underrated aesthete of the La Belle Époque."

"Is this somehow related to your work on anal retention?"

"I expect so, and perhaps also the influence of cocaine. Nevertheless, I believe that the great man should be living here in the Gardens … as should you."

"Well, you'll be happy to learn that he's alive and well in the Viroverse. Very proud man – nothing like I expected."

"You have met him?" Freud asked excitedly.

"Yeah, about two centuries ago. The Hind-reading Guild wanted to raise its profile, and so tried to set up an annual festival devoted to all things hind related. It was called the Gathering Be-Hind. The first, and last, gathering took place at Mama Fiesta's Party Hub."

"Party hub?"

"Ah, you don't know how the Viro system works. We live in Viros, enclosed environments a mile square. Everyone in the Viro was previously alive at the same time as at least one other resident – even if it was for just a second. Also, everyone is usually from a similar racial, historical, or family background. There is always some connection."

"There are still times, even after all these centuries, that I miss my family."

"I still keep in contact with my daughter, Sophia, but I haven't seen any of the others in a long time. Now, getting back to hubs. Fortunately, we can visit other Viros, but only as long as someone in that other Viro was alive during our own lifetime. That's where hubs come into play. Simply put, they are Viros that cover a wide time frame – for instance, if you had two first-life centenarians, where one was born on the same day the other died …"

"You cover 200 years," Freud declared.

"You got it. Mama Fiesta's is one of many hubs, but nothing beats its Mexican themed party atmosphere. I treat it as my home from home."

"You said it was the first and last gathering. I assume it was not a success."

"If anything, it damaged our reputation," Stern admitted, wincing as if remembering a painful experience. "We were far too open with our invitation. All thirty guild members attended, plus a number of flatulists. To our surprise, the Viroverse Fellowship of Proctologists also turned up. And, then there were the others." Stern shook his head woefully. "Oh God, those others."

"I dread to think."

"We weren't expecting so many ass-masters – in fact we weren't expecting any."

"Ass-masters?"

"Porn stars who specialise in anal sex, including some dildo strapped women. They outnumbered the rest of us by at least two to one. They even had a synchronised formation team, and gave public demonstrations in the central plaza. Muchaco, I am not averse to some backdoor moves, I'm well known for my sexual versatility, but I did not know where to look. Added to that, some pretty bizarre cults devoted to the anus held a recruitment drive. I was blocked from visiting Mama Fiesta's for nearly two years."

"But, you met Pujol."

"I spent most of the day with Le Pétomane, Mr Methane, and Fannie Fartingale. They were the best company – amazing sense of humour and they all had that wonderful sideways take on life. We stayed in one of the lesser-known cantinas, keeping well away from the sleazy goings-on in the plaza."

"I was under the impression that hind-readers and flatulists never mix."

"Well, yeah, a flatulist is usually regarded as the natural nemesis of the hind-reader – they create wind that our noses just don't wanna know about. And, before you say it, I know their farts rarely smell – they just suck air in and out – but even the feel of the breeze is too much to bear. It's a non-issue these days, since the Viroverse has cured them of their 'gift'."

Freud frowned:

"Cured? Surely you don't mean …?"

"Sorry, muchacho, but they have lost their farting abilities. Well, apart from the ones we all do."

"Oh no, that is terrible! Like songbirds that have lost their voice."

"Being a hind-reader, I can see the upside." Stern smiled wryly. "However, the flatulists were the only good thing about that dreadful day. We made them honorary guild members, although I never saw any of them again."

In disgust, Stardust blocked out the childish conversation and returned to his thoughts. He took himself back to a nightclub in the 1980's. Standing well away from the heaving dance floor, softened in the shadows, he nursed a bottle of lager.

Leaving nothing to chance, Stardust had perfected his façade. His cream chinos and a pastel blue polo shirt had the appropriate labels, and his tanned face was suitably topped off with a jaunty quiff. Grolsch was the chosen lager – only because he noticed that many of the more successful pick-up artists drank it. Stardust even learned to 'pop the top' of the bottle one-handed.

Fragrance played a major part in Stardust's mission to attract the opposite sex, and his experimentation with scents had aroused a hitherto unknown love for olfactory pleasure. Though his predilection was for the gothic – a heady sweet Turkish Rose – the rules of the unquestioning masses stated that he wear the fresh fougere, Jazz by Yves Saint Laurent.

Dancing played no part in his plans. He had tried a few moves in front of the mirror, but they seemed too soft, too feminine, so he abandoned the idea. Finally, armed with a memorised list of 'guaranteed' opening one-liners, Stardust was ready to hit the clubs.

He only wanted a partner, someone who could learn to love him. Without friends or family – at least none who wanted anything to do with him – Stardust lived a life of crushing loneliness. Ironically, the lively club, loud Hi-NRG synthpop, bopping bodies, and half-heard shouts and laughs, became a place of isolation amongst the crowd. For weeks, he waited patiently for someone to approach him, to talk. Having the courage to make the first move was a frightening notion for Stardust, and so he stood, alone, almost as if part of the décor.

Men were distracting. They got in the way, obscuring the view; their aftershave tantalised Stardust's nostrils and their designer stubble stirred some strange subconscious connection. He tried to ignore them, and concentrate on the women … but he often found himself enthralled.

Those precious few times Stardust found the strength to approach, or rather accost, a passing female, inevitably ended in humiliation. In hindsight, perhaps suddenly emerging from the shadows was a bad idea, but he thought the vulgar reactions were uncalled for – a simple 'I'm not interested' would have been sufficient to send him scurrying away. Also, in hindsight, he should not have used his father's list of 'guaranteed' one-liners, which included such timeless gems as, 'why don't you get your beard out?', 'your face or mine?', or 'can I buy you a drink or do you just want the money?'.

Some men seemed able to use any pickup line without provoking a negative reaction. Stardust imagined Stern could probably sidle up to almost any woman and say, 'can I sniff your arse, muchacha?' and then embark upon a night of unbridled passion. If Stardust had tried that, he would have most likely lost a few teeth.

He knew from bitter experience, that it was often not what was said that was important, but who said it. For the same comment, one person might be judged the life and soul of the party whilst another might be condemned as an unwholesome pariah. It all depended on the vagaries of public perception and the strength of ones charisma. Stardust relished his wicked status – years of killing had taught him that the image of a good-humoured party guy was so dull compared to that of a black-hearted Luciferian pariah.

Freud's loud voice once more cut through Stardust's dark reminiscing.

"The climax of his act was truly magnificent," Freud declared. "Pujol would fix an Ocarina to his anus with a rubber tube and then pump out a rousing rendition of 'Le Marseillaise'. The whole audience rose to their feet and sang along with such gusto. For a few minutes, no matter our true nationality, we were all proud Frenchmen."

Like a sleeper rudely awoken by a slamming door, or the flush of a toilet, Stardust grumbled and gradually drifted back into his daydream.

Back in the 1980s, his hope hollowed out by constant rejection, Stardust finally embraced his outsider status. Others may have succumbed to their sorrow, but Stardust's heart was now too cold and hard to break. His wise parents often pointed out that 'if you ask, you don't get'. It was time to take what he wanted.

Some careless souls left the clubs unaccompanied. Some even cut through unlit alleys, and across deserted carparks – those dark places on route to the sanctuary of the night bus. In his blue Ford Fiesta, Stardust sat silently, waiting for opportunities. Once sure that there were no witnesses, he left his car and followed his potential lover. Shedding his casual skin, he was now the man in black – black jeans, black sweatshirt, gloss black ankle boots … and black sunglasses after dark.

Stardust's first attempt at abduction failed miserably, as he tried to use a chloroform soaked rag. After two minutes of haphazardly holding the vaporous rag against the struggling woman's mouth, he gave up and sped away into the night. He cursed the movies and crime novels for making it seem so easy.

Referring to his father's copious notes on extreme sex games, Stardust came across the notorious 'blood choke'. By applying pressure to the carotid arteries in the neck for about ten seconds, he could induce unconsciousness. After practising the technique for a few weeks on the neighbourhood cats and dogs – only two died in the process, and the others told no tales – Stardust was ready to resume his hunt for a partner.

The success of the blood choke required new criteria. To minimise the risk of failure, the victim should be shorter than Stardust, and their neck exposed – high collars and scarves were a definite no. Fortunately, many of the female night clubbers eschewed coats and scarves, no matter how cold the weather – they tottered along on heels, their naked arms clasped across their partially exposed breasts, with a leg to skirt ratio far too large to provide any protection from the elements.

Pouncing on his first victim, slight build, dyed cherry blonde hair, Stardust wrapped his bare arm around her slender neck and squeezed. Maintaining his grip, he pulled the twitching girl backwards to keep her off-balance – her kicking heels scraping against the concrete pavers. Twelve seconds later, feeling her body go limp, he relaxed his hold, and dragged her back to his car.

Each week, until caught by the police four months later, he chose a different club, in a different town to find his next victim. A natural with the blood choke, and always approaching from behind, no one ever saw his face.

Once back at his latest residence, usually some dingy room in a doss house, Stardust meticulously prepared for the consummation. He slathered fragrant rose oil over his skinny body, and capsaicin cream on his penis to spike its sensitivity. His victim, heavily drugged, and blindfolded with soft velvet, moaned incoherently during the rape. Stardust never considered it an act of violence. Given his awkwardness and failure in starting a relationship, he saw it as fast-forwarding to the only stage he knew he could achieve. His parents had constantly reminded him that sex was the most important aspect of a relationship; that true love always meant sweat and thrusting. Anything else was just preamble or wasting time.

Letting a lazy eye linger on Reynold's Garden's forever setting sun, Stardust lifted a wrist and sniffed the scent of rose perfume. Only a faded remnant, but it brought him back to that sweet intoxication of rose mingled with carnality and fear. He always killed them cleanly: a warm bath and slit wrists. It was wrong, he knew that, but necessary – death was the ultimate fast-forward in any relationship. In a half-hearted effort to mend his ways, he had not raped anyone in nearly a thousand years, but killing was an addiction he would not let go.

A loud clap of hands from the dining table shook Stardust from his memories. As before, he tuned in to the conversation. Freud waved an inquisitive finger at Stern:

"As you know, I have watched all of your shows. I have probably watched each one at least a hundred times. What surprises me is that not once in all those hind-readings did anyone fart in your face. I would have thought, with all the stress and the hot lights, that some of the guests would let the odd one out."

Despite an effort to keep a straight face, Stern began laughing. Using a crisp clean napkin to wipe the tears from his eyes, he took a minute to compose himself:

"They did, my friend … far too many times. The show was not live, so any mishaps were edited out. For a while, we did consider releasing a compilation of 'the funniest fart fumbles' – that was to be the name of the release – but my manager refused in case it undermined my sexy image. Let me tell you, there is absolutely nothing sexy or sensual about a fart in the face."

"I have always thought you should have given the participants Simethicone before the readings."

Stern held out his hands in a blocking motion:

"Woah, muchacho, are you serious? You think we should have given them a drug that collects all the little pockets of wind in the bowel and sends them out in one mighty fart."

Freud nodded proudly. Stern frowned, sitting back in his chair:

"I take this is a joke? If so, then you should know that Simethicone is no laughing matter to a hind-reader. Do you see me laughing?"

"Oh no, it is not a joke, and I certainly meant no disrespect. I thought that if you gave Simethicone to your guests well before the show, you could ensure that they are totally clear of wind by the time your nose is next to their anus."

"That makes sense, but in practise, the drug's effect varies from person to person. We found the best way to minimise involuntary emissions was to control people's diet the morning of the show – keep them off the carbs and the fermenting veg. Not entirely fool proof, but …"

In a fit of anger, Stardust rose to his feet, kicking away his chair. Striking his most menacing pose, eyes glaring beneath his black guy-liner, he pointed at Stern and Freud.

"Stop talking! Just stop talking!" he cried breathlessly. "Why are you saying these things? I do not want to listen to another second of this. You are both grown men, over a thousand years old, and all you talk about are farts and anuses. No one wants to hear about farts and anuses. No one wants this disgusting information in their brain. I do not want my memories tainted by this filth!"

"Oh please, Mr Stardust," Freud chuckled, "there is no need to get upset. Have a little sympathy for that most maligned of body parts."

Stern, knowing Stardust's reputation, and noticing the fire in the psychopath's eyes, stood up and tried to calm him down:

"It's just idle conversation, muchacho. We can change the subject if you want. Just sit yourself down and have a drink."

"I do not want to sit down, and I do not want a drink," Stardust seethed, walking up to the table. "I think we should be out there with Copa. For all we know, we are being picked off one by one. First Saloni loses her head, then Blitz goes missing, and now Copa is gone. Maybe it will be you next, Stern. I'll bet Freud is only here to distract you."

Freud shook his head:

"Mr Stardust, I can see why you would think that, but I assure you I am only here as a fan of Mr Lovass. You have nothing to fear from us. If Artie had wanted you dead, then you would not have even made it into the Gardens."

"Well, I'm not staying here whilst my friends could be in danger."

Constable Hanzō was already guarding the door. Constable Lovelace spoke softly:

"I cannot let you leave, Mr Stardust. Artie told us to wait here, and that is what we are going to do."

Stardust grimaced, huffed, and made to leave. Freud flung out an arm and grabbed the angry psychopath round the waist.

"Don't you dare touch me!" Stardust cried. He snatched a random item of cutlery from the table, and thrust it into the top of Freud's head.

The famous psychoanalyst shuddered and retched:

"Ugh, what … what have you done?" he gasped, cautiously feeling the top of his head, and touching the silver-plated fork – the four prongs tightly and deeply wedged.

As if woken from a trance, Stardust stepped back, his eyes wide with horror:

"Oh my goodness, why did I do that? Why did I do that?" He stared penetratingly at Freud. "Do you think it's because I slept with my mother?"

With total disregard for his cranial cutlery, Freud leapt from his chair and grabbed Stardust around the neck. Still bewildered by his own attack, the black-clad psychopath lurched backwards, nearly falling over the balustrade.

"Why the Hell did you do that, you crazy lunatic?" Freud shouted.

Choking from the stranglehold, Stardust struggled to speak:

"I … don't think … that's an appropriate way … for a psychiatrist to talk."

"Well, maybe I'll stop talking just long enough to throw you over the balcony."

Stardust smiled.

"Why are you smiling?" Freud asked. "I assure you, you have nothing to smile about." Freud loosened his grip.

"I know you are trying to strangle me," Stardust replied quietly, "but you're paying far too much attention to my neck. I have two arms you know. Here's one." Stardust waved his hand in front of Freud's face. "My other hand is holding the fork handle. You know, I literally have the upper hand now."

Freud shuddered, immediately taking his hands away from Stardust's neck:

"I think, perhaps, we should talk about this. It is not in either of our interests for this to continue."

"Of course you want to talk about this," Stardust said. "That is what you do, don't you? You talk, and talk … about farts and anuses." Stardust pushed away from the balustrade and slowly walked forward. Freud edged backwards, keeping a perfect pace, feeling the sting of the tines in his brain.

"We can talk about anything you like," Freud said. "Just let me go and I will sit back in my chair."

"You think you're so superior, don't you? You're always the man in the chair and we are all just fodder for the couch. Maybe you're the one who needs analysing."

"There is no couch here, Mr Stardust. We can both sit on chairs and talk as equals. As I said, we can talk about anything you like. I am at your disposal."

"Hmm, disposing of you sounds like a good idea. You know, I think I have enough leverage to crack the front of your face off. However ... I believe I would like to take you up on your kind offer. I would like to talk about my mother."

"If you wish," Freud agreed. "I adored my own mother."

"I did more than that; much, much more. You did come up with the idea of the Oedipus Complex, didn't you?"

Freud made the mistake of nodding and howled as the prongs moved painfully back and forth, prompting a startled Stardust to let go of the fork. Immediately, Stern sprang into action, wrenching one of the psychopath's arms up behind his back, and heaving him away from Freud. With a sigh of relief, Freud collapsed into a chair.

"Cabron, if you don't keep still, I will cut your throat," Stern promised, holding a steak knife against Stardust's jugular. "I choose the right cutlery for the job."

After a few seconds of token resistance, Stardust gave up, unsure whether the reinforced high collar of his glitter shirt would have protected him from the serrated blade. Constable Lovelace promptly handcuffed Stardust to the balustrade telescope, where he sat glowering, his lips quivering as he imagined bloody vengeance.

Attending to Freud's silverware accessory, Constable Hanzō advised against removal. Instead, he sprayed the wound with dermal sealant, which formed an artificial skin over the affected scalp and the bottom of the fork. The sealant gave the disturbing impression that the fork was actually growing out of Freud's head.

"I think we should let Artie know what has happened," Freud suggested. "I do not want to risk waking up tomorrow with that lunatic standing over me with a spoon."

Constable Lovelace thought for a moment:

"Sigmund, if you can make it down to the ground floor, I can get a wheelchair from the lobby dispenser. We can take the second road to the apartment blocks. It has a smooth surface."

"Well, if you're going to wheel me across the Gardens, then I will require some head protection. I could wear a top hat, although I would prefer something a little sturdier."

Stern clicked and pointed a finger:

"What about a police helmet? They're protective."

"I don't think that's a good idea," Freud said, shaking his head. "A common dare amongst the rowdier elements in the Gardens is to knock off a constable's helmet."

"How childish," Stardust sneered.

"At least they are children who have learnt the proper use of cutlery," Freud angrily retorted.

Constable Lovelace, ever the calm voice of reason, intervened:

"I would recommend a fireman's helmet. They have strong chinstraps and are made of solid brass. I will have to snip off some of the fork handle, but your cutlery should be safe in there."

"A splendid idea," Freud agreed.

Stardust seethed menacingly:

"I like the sound of that. I reckon I could ring you like a bell."

Reggie the Hat

Fatigue quickly set in as Adam struggled to keep up with Cartimandua and her constables. A strong pair of legs was the only form of transport in the Gardens, and the police were its finest exponents. The police maintained an effortless sprint, engaging in idle banter as they moved swiftly along the cobbled roadway.

Labouring on increasingly leaden legs, Adam pondered the camaraderie exhibited by the culturally diverse denizens of Reynold's Gardens. Cartimandua, a fiery Celtic Queen with a replacement body, laughed and joked with Constable Unaipon, a witty and perceptive Aboriginal Australian, and with Constable Al-Nabigha, an ever polite and softly spoken man of Middle Eastern origin.

Was it that the slaughter following the Great Catastrophe had created an unbreakable bond and understanding between the blooded survivors, or was it simply the unifying effect of a common tongue? Whatever the reason, Reynold's Gardens was a place seemingly untainted by the scourge of racial intolerance and the usually inevitable clashes of culture.

In contrast, the Viroverse was a place of rigid compartmentalisation and carefully homogenised small populations. There was the ability to visit other cultures and have a one-day experience of their ways and traditions, but it was a choice not an imposition. Despite the passing of nearly a thousand years, there were many who rarely left the comfortable familiarity of similar Viros. There were also more adventurous souls, such as Stern, who lived to enjoy that brief taste of the different and sometimes exotic.

On the other hand, maybe Reynold's Gardens was not so benign. It was perhaps less a melting pot, but rather a devious trap created by Chang, wherein the rich traditions and beliefs of its citizens were subdued and subsumed within an enforced artificial Victorian themed monoculture. Such thoughts faded as Adam began to fall behind his speedy escorts.

"Keep up, Adam," Cartimandua cried. "We should be sprinting not jogging."

All Adam could offer was a breathless, half-muttered, half-wheezed, 'OK'. In the Viroverse, everyone was fit. It required no effort, save for simply waking up in the morning. Some, such as Stern, put in some extra effort, working out, building a more muscular physique. However, the Viroverse only allowed limited improvement. Here, Artie and his constables were on another level, exhibiting a degree of fitness that would put many an athlete to shame.

As sweat dripped freely from his brow, Adam unbuttoned his heavy dockworkers coat – inwardly, he cursed not choosing a lighter gentleman's frock coat because it sounded so stuffy. The increased circulation was an instant relief and he wearily picked up the pace.

They passed many people on route to the square. Adam did not recognise anyone. In fact, since arriving at the warehouse, there was not a single person that he recognised, and only a couple – Monet and Freud – that he had even heard of. Perhaps he should have listened in history class rather than scrawl pornographic doodles in his exercise book, or it could be that the creator of the Gardens had a rather eclectic taste in historical figures.

It did not help that everyone in Reynold's Gardens appeared to be in their late teens to early twenties, and dressed in everyday Victorian attire rather than their clichéd historical fancy dress outfits. I made identification almost impossible. For all he knew, the slim man in the paisley waistcoat who just tipped his bowler was Julius Caesar – clearly he should wear leather sandals, a purple lined toga, and a laurel wreath crowning his brushed forward hair.

The woman in the white bonnet who smiled kindly was perhaps Florence Nightingale – but who knows if she is not creeping about the shadows with an oil lamp. Moreover, would he even recognise the reputedly beautiful Cleopatra if their paths crossed – surely she would not look like Elizabeth Taylor, or any other actress who played the role.

How Blitz was able to pick out Blaise Pascal from a large crowd at such a distance was remarkable, although Adam attributed it to the psychopath's extreme obsessional nature and 'gift' for selective recollection – which ironically eluded him concerning mathematical formulae.

Near the square, the second apartment block dominated the view. The vast gothic edifice of stone arches and soaring spires architecturally overwhelmed the tree-lined paths and bustling public squares that lay in its immense shadow. Adam felt a shiver down his spine, overawed and humbled in the presence of this richly detailed mountain of honey-toned Anston stone.

A number of panicked citizens approached as the group reached the large iron archway to the square. They spoke loudly and all at once, pointing back to the square with expressions of terror. It was obvious that a major incident had taken place. Out of the crowd, a black man, dressed in an elegant grey velvet suit with a white satin cravat, walked forward and politely shook the police chief's hand. With calm, almost emotionless gravitas, he introduced himself as Olaudah Equiano:

"Chief Artie, there has been a murder. Blaise Pascal, a dear friend of mine, has been murdered by a madman."

"Oh my God," Cartimandua groaned, briefly fixing Adam with an expression of weary resignation. "Olaudah, are you absolutely sure Pascal is dead?"

A single tear fell down Olaudah's cheek as he nodded:

"The madman had a sword. He stabbed Blaise in the heart."

The constables quickly cleared a path through the crowd, and Cartimandua followed Olaudah through the archway. At the eastern side of the square, a thick pool of blood covered the hard pavers in front of a wide bench. On the neatly trimmed lawn behind, lay the dead body of the great mathematician. Adam stayed back amongst the crowd, keeping a low profile. He did not want to be the target of a vengeful lynch mob.

"Please, describe the killer," Cartimandua asked gently.

"He was a very tall man," Olaudah replied, "but that may have been his shoes. He had very tall shoes. He had the tallest shoes I have ever seen. I do not know how he could walk in such shoes."

"Anything else?"

"He had very bright clothes. He shimmered like a fish. His hair was red and he had fire on his face – perhaps tattoos. At first, he claimed he was a dancer, but he was most certainly lying. He was the worst dancer. Then he claimed he was a mathematician, but knew nothing about the subject. And then …" Olaudah choked, breaking down into a flood tears and emitting the most sorrowful moan as his naturally calm demeanour finally left him.

Cartimandua put a strong comforting arm around the trembling man, hugging him close and kissing his forehead:

"We have all lost people, Olaudah. Everyone can feel your pain. A painter will arrive soon to perform the necessary ritual. I promise with all my heart to hunt down this murderer and bring him to justice. Can you tell me where he went?"

Wiping tears from his face, Olaudah pointed towards the huge stone-arched central entrance to the apartment block:

"I did not see him leave as I was busy tending to my friend – we carried him onto the soft grass hoping he could be saved. I heard others say that the madman entered the building and ran up the stairs."

Looking over to the double doors of the building, Cartimandua breathed a sigh of relief seeing a solitary constable standing guard, stopping an angry crowd from following Blitz.

"Constable Unaipon," Cartimandua yelled, her usually deep voice brittle with the sour taste of betrayal, "I want you and Constable Al-Nabigha to help Constable Hooke guard the entrance to the apartment block. I do not want anyone following that madman."

Trying to keep his machete hidden from view, Adam tentatively walked over to the troubled police chief:

"Let me go in," he said quietly. "He'll listen to me."

"Not a chance, Adam." Cartimandua could not even look Adam in the face." I would be a fool to trust you again. However, fool that I am, I need to trust you one last time."

"Anything," Adam said, ashamed at letting down his kind-hearted host.

"I don't want to take any unnecessary risks, and nobody except your friend needs to pay for this. I am going to fetch reinforcements with crossbows. There are always a few constables around the first block. With luck, I should only be gone about half an hour. I want you to stay just outside the square and try not to talk to anyone. If you get into any trouble then either run like Hell or seek the protection of my constables. I'm not sure I can keep you safe anymore."

After announcing to the crowd that the matter would soon be under control and that there was no immediate danger to life, Cartimandua sprinted out of the square at a speed that amazed Adam. Then, before he could slope off to the relative safety of the trees and shrubs, Adam suddenly turned, hearing a voice behind him.

"Hey, kid!"

A short man, stylishly dressed in a top hat, white tie, and tails, with a black tote bag hanging from his shoulder, stood next to Pascal's dead body. Slicked brown hair, and a round face, the man spoke out of the side of his mouth like some 1930's Hollywood gangster:

"Hey kid, get over here. We need to talk."

Adam walked over to the man.

"The name's Reginald Marsh," the short man said, firmly shaking Adam's hand, "the painter. So, don't go confusin' me with the actor of the same name."

"Pleased to meet you, Mr Marsh," Adam said politely, having never heard of either the actor or the painter.

"My friends get to call me Reggie. Now, we've only just met, but I think you and I should be friends. I see you're carrying a blade under your coat."

Adam closed his coat tightly, hiding his machete from view:

"Err … you must have been mistaken … Reggie."

"No mistake, kid. I saw what I saw. Your shirt didn't look right neither. You new around here or something?"

"I'm not new," Adam lied. "I usually just keep to myself. I'm here on official police business … to help Artie."

"Look, kid, I just need to borrow that blade for a few seconds. No one needs to know. It'll be our little secret."

"I'm not sure if …"

"See the dispenser over there?" Reggie pointed to the far side of the square. "The one near the entrance?"

Adam looked across the square. To his disgust, a young woman was crouched in front of the dispenser, her voluminous frilled dress pulled up above her waist and her buttocks pressed hard against the black glass. Her strained red face gave away that she was in the grunting throes of defecation.

"I wish I hadn't seen that," Adam said.

"Well, the wet sock waiting next in line is Pieter Bruegel … the painter."

"And?"

"You sure you ain't new around here, kid? You should know the rule. Nobody's supposed to carry large blades – not even chef's knives. Only exception is when there's a death. Any painter has the right to get a blade to cut off the head. Bruegel's queuing for a blade. If that wet sock takes the head before me, then he gets to perform the show."

"I don't really want anyone to see that I'm carrying a weapon."

Reggie grabbed Adam by the collar and stared up into his eyes:

"Do you really want to see Bruegel's peasant clog dance? Is that what you want, kid, 'cause that is what you'll get? Nearly an hour of crazy clip clopping. Look, I got you covered if anyone starts asking questions. See, everyone trusts a painter. Trust me. Just hand me the blade, but don't let nobody see."

Adam furtively slid the deadly Kopis machete from his belt sheath and handed it to Reggie.

"Woohoo, I got me a mean looking blade!" Reggie shouted, holding the blade aloft as if it was his all along. "Lucky I was passing a dispenser when Pascal got skewered." He whispered worriedly to Adam, "I never used a crazy blade like this. I gotta be accurate. I gotta keep as much neck as possible for my act. The neck is make or break. How skilled are you, kid?"

"Skilled enough," Adam replied, "but do the rules allow me to …?"

"Sure they do," Reggie said, handing Adam the blade. "As long as it's my blade, I can designate you as my head-chopping proxy. Better shake a leg, kid, the broad's near done poopin'. And, remember, I need a lotta neck."

Adam stood, one foot either side of Pascal's head. With one swift slash he cut through the flesh and bone, leaving barely a millimetre of neck attached to the shoulders.

"Good enough?" Adam asked, wiping the blade clean on the inside of his coat, before sneaking it back into its holder.

Reggie held up the decapitated head and grinned:

"Oh my, that's some beautiful slicin', kid. You got real talent. I've never been able to keep that much neck before."

They crouched on the grass and Reggie prepared the head. Rummaging in his tote bag, he pulled out a thick sponge-like disk. He sat Pascal's head neck down on the sponge. Like some 'miracle' late night TV shopping channel super absorber, the sponge seemed to suck up every last drop of blood – the head turning deathly pale.

"And, now to add back a little colour to the poor schmuck." Reggie took a small bottle out of the bag and sprayed a light tan foundation onto Pascal's face. "Gotta do the ears. So easy to forget the ears."

Adam shrank back as Reggie then produced a strange mini coat-hanger contraption from the bag. Fussily fitting it inside Pascal's mouth, Reggie carefully adjusted a couple of screws until the famous mathematician sported a wide, though unnervingly unnatural smile.

"You gotta go out smilin', dontcha?" Reggie gushed, proud of his work.

Next, Reggie took off his top hat and placed it on the ground next to Pascal's head. Adam was surprised to see that the hat had no top, and even more surprised when Reggie gingerly placed the head onto the opening – the neck sliding easily into the gap.

"Hey kid, get me the long needles from the bag. You did such a swell job with the neck, so I reckon I only need four."

Like a nightmarish version of KerPlunk, Reggie took one of the long barbed metal needles and pushed it through the hat and into the neck. Pushing in the other needles and the neck was securely pinned into the hat.

"This guy's not going anywhere," Reggie announced, giving the head and hat combo a vigorous shake. "Now kid, if you would like to take your place in the crowd, I will start the show."

Reggie strolled confidently into the square. Waving his cane, with the head-hat held in the crook of his arm, he called out like the frontman of a carnival sideshow:

"Ladies and gentlemen, gather round! Gather round and experience the spectacle that is Blaise Pascal's final journey. Bid farewell to the esteemed mathematician before he travels to the palace of gold; that exclusive resting place where God's angels themselves are forbidden entry."

A crowd quickly formed and Reggie pointed his cane at various members of his audience:

"Sir, are you here to pay your respects? Are you faint with excitement, Miss? What about you, my good man; are you ready to be astonished? Do not watch if you mean to gloat! Do not watch if you are easily disturbed! Do not watch if this memento mori fills you with mortal dread! A golden box waits for Pascal!"

With one hand, Reggie launched the head-hat into the air. He spun elegantly on the toes of his shiny tap shoes, his tails rising, before the hat landed perfectly on his head – he stooped skilfully, absorbing the impact. With his cane lazily over his shoulder, Reggie strolled up and down next to the bench, splashing in the pool of blood, all the while whistling a laidback jazzy tune.

The crowd gasped as the dapper painter jumped effortlessly onto the long bench and glided along, pointing his cane in the direction of travel. Pascal's cheerful head wobbled and bobbed, but always stayed firmly in the hat. Skipping to the centre of the bench, Reggie flung out his arms and broke into a Vaudeville style swing song – his smooth lounge crooner vocals perfectly matching his stylish moves:

> I got Pascal in my hat.
> Well how about that?
> And, my head's in my hat
> 'cause it's a two head hat.
> But, he's travellin' with me
> To eternity,
> 'cause he wants that sense of styyyle!

To rapturous applause, Reggie leapt from the bench and began tap-dancing in the blood, his cane flailing majestically through the whirls and jumps. Thoroughly stunned, Adam stood silently, mouth open, unable to take his eyes off the gruesomely energetic top hat and head ballet.

Twirling his cane like a swing time majorette, Reggie once again strolled up and down. As he whistled, he nodded, causing his smiling second head to nod and bob in time. Jumping back onto the bench, Reggie threw off the hat and caught it on the end of his cane. Gliding from side to side, he held up the head-topped cane to the twilight sky like a sacred totem.

Once more, Reggie skipped to the centre of the bench. To the appreciative roar of the crowd, he carefully placed the other end of the cane on the top of his head – Pascal's head-in-the-hat now balanced high above and given proper reverence. Flinging his arms out, Reggie performed the second part of his song:

> Pascal's high in the sky.
> 'cause he's that kind of guy.
> And, he'll never get old,
> Now he's going for gold.
> But, he's travellin' with me
> To eternity,
> 'cause he's got that sense of styyyle!

Reggie leapt from the bench and launched into a series of spins. With subtle jerks of his head, he kept Pascal's precariously balanced head facing forward. Adam noticed Olaudah standing nearby, watching the spectacle and shaking his head, with tears streaming down his face. Sidling up to Pascal's distraught friend, Adam put a hand on his shoulder.

"I know how you feel," Adam said, casting an annoyed glance at Reggie. "You know, you don't have to watch this. I dread to think what Pascal would have made of this disrespectful mess."

"I do not know what you mean," Olaudah muttered, a serene smile crossing his face. "Blaise would have loved this. They say there is a silver lining to every tragedy, and I think that this incredible show is just that. When my time finally comes, I can only hope that I am fortunate enough to receive such a send-off. That sweet little man with the hat has brought a glimmer of peace to my heart."

Realising that he was so very out of synch with the ways of the Gardens, Adam walked away from the head-hat show and made his way through the crowd to the central entrance to the apartment block. With the show in full swing, the angry crowd that had tried to follow Blitz had dispersed and joined the audience.

The situation was alarming. What was the Captain thinking, allowing two psychopaths to join the team? It was like throwing a couple of live grenades into an elegant ballroom: there could be no positive outcome. In addition, what justice would Blitz face at the hands of the mob, especially one with such an ingrained sense of historical entitlement? At least Stardust had so far behaved, but Adam knew it was only a matter of time before the leader of the Psychoviro would succumb to his natural urges.

The three constables straightened up as Adam approached, adopting a wary posture.

"Don't worry," Adam said, raising his hands as if in surrender. "I have absolutely no intention of running in after that bloody lunatic. I just wanted to get away from the show before he shucks the brain out of the skull. I may have seen a lot of death in my time, but that's a little too surgical for my tastes. If you don't mind, I think I'll wait here with you until Artie returns with the cavalry."

Adam was lying.

PSYCHO CHASE

Discerning the weakest link in the group – the constable most likely to fall for Adam's simple plan – was an easy task. Constable Unaipon introduced Adam to Constable Hooke: a noticeably irritable man of average height with a small chin on a large head. According to Unaipon, Hooke, who had doggedly guarded the door since Blitz first stormed into the building, had in his first-life been an architect, philosopher and a man of many other talents – a genuine polymath. Conveying bitterness and a subtle anger in almost every movement and utterance, Hooke added that he was underrated historically and that he truly belonged in the pantheon of great achievers.

"Do you hear that crowd?" Constable Hooke said, straining on tiptoes, his voice high and whiny. "Oh, that must be some show. I wish I could watch. Thanks to that idiot in the fancy suit we have to guard this bloody door."

Constable Unaipon grinned and rolled his eyes:

"You do realise that if it wasn't for that idiot in the fancy suit there wouldn't be a show. For goodness sake, stop acting like a child and apply some of that logic you're famous for."

"Still, we don't get that many deaths these days," Constable Hooke continued. "I haven't seen a good show in ages."

"Now you're just lying, Robert. I saw you up in the warehouse gallery earlier today on crossbow duty. You saw Monet perform."

"That was a short show; it doesn't count. Short shows are like going out for dinner and only getting the starter and a dessert. It never works without the main meal. You never get a decent steak for a starter."

Constable Al-Nabigha spoke softly:

"Constable Hooke, why do you always dwell on what little you don't have, rather than the many gifts Reynold's has bestowed upon you?"

Taking the opportunity to begin his deception, Adam crossed his arms and looked thoughtful.

"Woah, there's nothing wrong in not wanting your glass half empty," he said. "Rob here, is one of those 'go large' type of guys … and there's nothing wrong with that. A genius only wants what they rightly deserve."

"Now that's the first sensible comment I've heard in a long time," Hooke agreed, scowling at his colleagues.

"Well, I was talking to Reggie before the show," Adam continued. "He told me to watch out for the final segment. He told me to expect something absolutely spectacular."

The statement immediately caught Constable Hooke's attention: "Spectacular?"

"Oh yes; a spectacle the likes of which has never been seen before in Reynold's Gardens. If the first part of the show was anything to go by, then the finale is going to be really, really spectacular."

Constable Hooke moaned and jumped up and down, desperately trying to see beyond the top hat and bowler horizon of Victorian headwear.

"I wish I'd never volunteered for police duties," he said. "Artie is just so damn persuasive."

"All I know is that the spectacular bit takes place on the bench," Adam said, reeling in his catch, who was by now, hopelessly 'hooked'.

Constable Hooke became more animated, and even Constable Unaipon took an interest.

"I can just about see Mr Marsh when he's prancing about on the bench," Constable Unaipon declared, "well only above the shoulders. If only the crowd would move out of the way or at least be polite enough to crouch."

"I could lift you on my shoulders," Constable Hooke said. "Err … but then I don't get to see the show."

Adam pointed to a low wall, some ten feet away from the doorway.

"If you climbed up onto that wall," he said, as innocently as possible, "you could probably see the show. It's quite low, but I think you could get a reasonable view of the bench at least."

Constable Al-Nabigha, the quietest of the group, stroked his lustrous oiled beard and cast a suspicious eye on Adam:

"Then where will you be when we are standing on that wall, Mr Eden?"

"Hmm, well I guess I could stand up there with you," Adam replied, as if under duress. "Remember though, the moment Reggie starts the brain scooping, I'm off the wall. I really, really don't want to see that."

"Any of you bothered about missing the removal of the brain?" Constable Al-Nabigha asked his colleagues, revealing that he too was desperate to see the show. The others shook their heads. "Ok, let's go. I think we'll catch the last ten to fifteen minutes."

Helping each other up, they all climbed up onto the low wall. Keeping their charge under close guard, Adam stood between Constables Unaipon and Al-Nabigha. With uncommon joy, Constable Hooke thanked Adam:

"Absolutely perfect! I think we have a better view than those lucky bastards in the crowd."

"I know we all want to see the grand finale," Al-Nabigha said, "but we should also keep an eye out for the chief. If we're caught away from the doors, then it's tavern duty for us for the next year, and we don't want that."

"Don't worry," Adam said. "You just enjoy the show, and let me watch out for Artie."

Adam watched Reggie carefully, waiting for just the right moment. It came as the painter once more jumped up onto the bench wearing the head hat – Pascal still sporting his 'coat-hanger' smile.

"I think this is it!" Adam shouted, surreptitiously slipping off his heavy coat and letting it slip behind the wall.

With the constables' attention fixed on the antics in the square, Adam jumped back off the wall. With a powerful shove, he pushed the unsuspecting constables off the wall onto the hard pavers on the other side. Hearing their pained and surprised cries, he allowed himself a satisfied smile, and sprinted to the doors.

"Please don't be locked," Adam muttered, trying the polished brass handles. The large oak framed doors swung open on well-oiled hinges and Adam headed into the voluminous marble-floored reception hall. Unclipping his Kopis machete, preparing for confrontation, he ran up the wide staircase.

Halfway up the first flight of stairs, Adam heard a voice calling him.

"Come back, Mr Eden!" Constable Unaipon called anxiously from the doorway below. "If you come back now, before Artie gets here, then we can forget about this!"

Pausing a moment, Adam looked back. Constable Unaipon, a worried expression on his face, did not follow. Outside, he could see Constable Al-Nabigha tending to Constable Hooke, who leaned weeping against the low wall, a long graze down the side of his face. Adam shook his head at Unaipon, more out of pity than defiance, and carried on up the stairs.

Reaching the first floor landing – a sumptuous affair with indoor topiary and inlaid stained glass panels – Adam almost tripped over a body lying slumped against the rich mahogany banister. Certain that the constables were not following, he stopped and knelt by the motionless figure, and immediately noticed the pooling blood.

The body, a man dressed in a modest grey suit, twitched. Adam carefully raised the unconscious man into a sitting position, and examined the bleeding wound in his stomach. It took only a cursory inspection to confirm that the man would soon die.

"So, I'm not dead yet," the man mumbled, taking Adam by surprise. "How can a man who looks so comical be so violent?"

"Just hold your hand firmly over the wound," Adam advised, knowing there was not much help he could offer. "Artie will be here soon, and it's not long until midnight. Stay alive until then, and you'll wake up tomorrow as right as rain."

The man placed his hand gently on Adam's hand.

"When I am gone," he began, with a tired drawl, "when I am nothing but dead grey matter in a golden box, do you think they will remember me?"

Adam looked at the man, and sensed an inner pain in his gaunt hollow-eyed expression.

"Of course they will," Adam said, hoping to raise the man's spirits. "How could anyone forget you? But I don't think it's come to that."

"And, of my accomplishments? How will they be remembered?"

Adam noticed tears in the man's eyes. This was not a time to admit to not knowing the man or anything about his accomplishments.

"I … err … think you already know the answer to that," Adam replied evasively.

"Of course, you are right," the man wearily agreed. "But do you believe it is a curse or a blessing?"

"A blessing of course. Come on, you know what you did. I absolutely loved what you did. It was great … absolutely great. I only wish we could have had more accomplishments like yours."

The man looked quizzically at Adam and then patted his hand as if offering thanks. Bowing his head the man struggled to remain conscious.

"I have to leave you," Adam admitted. "I have to find the man that did this to you. I would like to stay here, help you make it through to midnight, but I really can't."

"I think the asshole went up to the third floor," the man said, finding a remnant of vengeful energy. "I heard him head up the stairs before I blacked out."

Hearing the sound of footsteps in the reception hall downstairs and Cartimandua's commanding voice yelling orders at her constables, Adam told the man to hang on, and then continued up the next flight of stairs.

Due to the Victorian style high ceilings, the stairs were incredibly long, and Adam understood why few ventured beyond the second floor. He guessed Cartimandua and her constables would stop to attend to the dying man, but he still rushed up the stairs – he had witnessed their incredible speed and needed to keep a distance between himself and his pursuers.

Reaching the third floor landing – another stunning medley of immaculately clipped greenery and colourful glass – Adam halted, spotting a smear of blood on the white marble. Another spot of blood, just inside an adjoining corridor, perhaps revealed the route Blitz had taken. Not seeing any more blood or other clues, and worried that Cartimandua would catch him, Adam decided to roll the dice and headed down the long corridor.

With crisply carved stone archways at either end, and lit by a glittering procession of gold chandeliers, the corridor stretched far into the distance. An Indian patterned runner, a classic floral Agra design, was soft underfoot, making for almost silent progress. Adam passed door after door, brass handles and nameplates, and the usual highly polished mahogany. He wondered what unused luxury lay within the abandoned apartments of Reynold's Gardens.

The far archway led onto yet another landing and stairway, with another archway and corridor on the far side. The distant sound of clashing swords brought a fresh turn of speed from Adam's tired legs. Far along the next corridor, under the lights of a large gold chandelier, Blitz fought furiously against a much shorter opponent, their swords arcing and thrusting like lightning.

Colourfully dressed in a long gown of yellow and blue silk with a matching pillbox hat, the stranger, observably female, wielded both a cutlass and a dagger. To Adam, the luxurious décor, and the flamboyant garments of both combatants, lent the scene a vivid theatricality.

They twisted and whirled, ducked and leapt, kaleidoscopically vibrant as two shimmering dragonflies dancing under a brilliant sun. Adam charged down the corridor, machete in hand, ready to aid the embattled woman. With two against one, perhaps Blitz would stand down – although the psychopath seemed too crazed to surrender.

Blitz's blade flashed and stung, and a bloom of red appeared on the woman's upper arm. She faltered, dropping her cutlass, but still lashed out defensively with her dagger. With a demented cry of triumph, Blitz punched the ribbed metal guard of his cutlass against the woman's head, knocking her back against the wall.

About to execute the final thrust, his blade poised to stab the woman through the heart, Blitz suddenly noticed Adam hurrying towards him. The psychopath laughed belligerently, and raised two fingers to his eternal enemy. Without bothering to kill the woman, Blitz turned and loped towards the grand archway at the far end of the corridor.

Reaching the woman, who was slumped against the wall and just regaining her senses, Adam put a supporting arm around her waist. The arm injury, though bleeding slightly, looked superficial.

"My name's Adam," he said. "Here, let me help you. Your head wound looks worse than it is. The cut on your arm is not so bad, but I think you should take it easy until Artie gets here. Rest on that sofa over there."

She shrugged off Adam's concern with an impudent glare of her eyes. Far East Asian in appearance, with an attractively angular face and thin lips, she exuded power and defiance.

"So, I will live," she said brusquely. "I could have told you that. And my name is Shi Xianggu, but you most probably know me as Ching Shih."

Adam nodded, as usual feigning recognition.

"What were you doing up here?" he asked. "I was told that nobody bothers going beyond the second floor."

"And, exactly what business is that of yours?"

"Sorry, I just …"

"My apartment is on this floor. I know most people rarely visit their old homes, but I often come up here to be alone with my thoughts. I sat quietly, meditating in my parlour, picturing fair winds and full sails, when I heard a commotion in the square. When I looked out of the window, I saw that dog enter the building. I readied my blades, just in case he came this way, and waited in the corridor. Soon after, we were face to face, and blade to blade."

"Isn't there a rule about carrying large blades?"

"I follow no rules but my own. I never go anywhere without a cutlass by my side, and a dagger in my belt." Ching Shi looked at her bloody arm and shook her head. "Ah, but I am so out of practise. In my heyday, I could have finished the dog without a second thought."

"Look, I need to catch up with that madman," Adam said, worried that Blitz would cause further bloodshed. "I just don't like to leave you here like this."

"If it will make you feel better, I will sit on that sofa and wait for our glorious chief." Without Adam's help, Ching Shi staggered over to the red velvet couch and collapsed onto its plush buttoned cushioning. "The dog won't get far. He's heading for the sky-bridge. The archway on the other side is permanently gated."

Adam turned to leave. Ching Shih called out, emphasising her words with a wave of her dagger:

"Make sure you put that mad dog down! And, Adam ... I love a man who knows his shirts."

NEAR MIDNIGHT

The stone archway opened onto a wide semi-circular balcony that narrowed into a long 100ft-foot wide bridge spanning the huge gap between the second and third apartment blocks. The bridge, an intricate cast iron arch with a flat grey cobblestone top, had stout iron railings either side, preventing the careless or reckless from plummeting to the ground some 40 feet below. Worryingly, the centre part of the span had sustained damaged – no doubt during the Great Catastrophe – and repaired with the ubiquitous full-scale planks of silvery grey duct tape. Even more worrying was the absence of railings in this section.

"Hah, Copout; I wondered when you would show your ugly face," Blitz shouted, emerging from the shadows on the other side of the bridge. "Thought your friends could slow me down and wear me out, did you? Give yourself an unfair advantage, eh?"

"I had nothing to do with this, Blitz," Adam replied, slowly walking towards the centre of the bridge. "This is all you. I'm here to stop this madness. If you lay down your sword and come with me, you might just get out of this place alive."

Blitz edged towards Adam, his steps exaggerated, almost dancelike, and his cutlass held aloft as a cobra ready to strike.

"Aw, dear Copout," he spat, "you think you can take me without a fight? You think you can humiliate me and I will just come quietly?"

Adam stood near the centre of the bridge, a couple of feet before the repaired section. He tried to project a calm demeanour, keeping his machete at waist height, pointing downwards.

"I have not come here to fight you, Blitz. You killed Blaise Pascal, your idol, and injured two others. This isn't the psychoviro. You won't go down fighting to the death, and then wake up tomorrow without a scratch. There's no resurrection here. I know you fear death as much as I do."

Standing in the centre of the bridge, Blitz jabbed his cutlass threateningly at Adam.

"That was not Blaise Pascal!" he seethed. "The Blaise Pascal I revere is an honourable man; a man of logic and integrity. That imposter was one of your slimy stooges, set up just to embarrass me. This whole mission is a clever trick so you can have your revenge for the many, many times I have got the better of you." Blitz smiled, an unrestrained cruelty in his eyes. "If there is really no resurrection here, then I can finally be rid of you."

"I thought I was the vending machine that never stopped giving."

"Believe me, you have nothing left to give."

With a screeching banshee wail, Blitz roused himself to attack.

"Wait!" Adam yelled, holding up his hand.

Blitz hesitated, his face trembling with combative anticipation.

"What now?"

"If we have to fight, then why not make it a little more interesting."

"I'm listening," Blitz said darkly, bringing his cutlass down to a less threatening level, "and then I am going to kill you."

"You reckon you're the master when it comes to fighting under the bridge. Err … King of the Swingers, I believe you called yourself."

Blitz looked over the side of the bridge, down to the pavement below.

"This isn't the same."

"Afraid of heights are you? There's no water here to break your fall. Or is it that you can only win on your own turf?"

"I've fought and killed you on the top of the towers a few times, remember? I'm not afraid of anything or anyone."

Taking the risk that Blitz still had a crumb of honour hiding somewhere in his crazed mind, Adam clipped his machete back into its belt sheath. Blitz watched silently as Adam climbed over the railing and carefully manoeuvred himself into position – hanging by his hands over the perilous drop. Face reddening with effort, Adam grunted and groaned as if undergoing a gruelling physical exertion.

"Oh, so close," he said finally, sounding quite exasperated. "I can nearly touch my feet under the bridge. If it wasn't for running up those bloody stairs I could have done it easily."

"Hah!" Blitz cried triumphantly. "That's why I'm the master and you're … nobody. A soon to be dead nobody, I might add."

Laughing loudly, Blitz sheathed his cutlass and immediately dropped over the side of the bridge. Clinging on to the side with his hands, he let out a loud whoop and swung his body up under the bridge. Adam was already calmly climbing back over the railings when Blitz realised his mistake.

"Ah, I can't move my feet! This damned duct tape is sticky underneath!"

"Of course it is," Adam replied coolly. "Can't knock something for doing its job."

Cursing, Blitz squirmed and heaved, desperately trying to free himself, but became increasingly affixed, including his hands and arms. Eventually, after much struggle and bluster, he gave up. Adam stood over him, tutting and shaking his head. By now, all that was visible was Blitz's glowering face sticking out from under the side of the bridge.

"Damn you, Copout, you cheated! You cheated! You knew that would happen."

"Shut up, Blitz, and calm down. I'm sure I can hear them coming. If you can act sane for the next few minutes, then I might be able to talk them out of killing you."

"Don't tell me what to do, Copout!" Blitz shouted, angrier than ever. "Come nearer so I can spit in your face."

Adam looked to the archway as Cartimandua marched through with ten constables – all armed with deadly crossbows and long hardwood truncheons. The chief of police had an expression of cold resignation, cut with perhaps the faintest hint of regret. Her faith in Adam's flamboyantly overblown legend now thoroughly shaken and darkened, she seemed in no mood for compromise or hesitancy.

"Take his head, Adam," Cartimandua said bluntly. "Put him out of our misery. We won't bother with a ritual or a box. He does not deserve it. Just let his head fall to the ground."

Adam knew the time for argument and for mercy had all but slipped away. Without a word, he unclipped his machete. Looking down into Blitz's wild eyes, red rimmed with anger and fear, he gripped the weapon with both hands, ready for a clean golf-swing decapitation. Below, an angry crowd had gathered, waving canes and fists, and baying for the blood of the glittering flame haired murderer.

Adam loathed Blitz more than anyone he had ever met – a rare achievement given the competition in the psychoviro. However, even with the current trail of bloodshed, he felt uneasy taking his life. In his first-life, when he saw a News item on an animal that escaped its cage that went on to kill or injure, only to be put down for its crimes, Adam always felt as much pity for the animal as its victim. Surely, the punishment should fall on the person who allowed the animal to escape. In this case, it should be Captain Andrew's android head on the block rather than an officially incurable psychopath.

Blitz tensed as the point of the Kopis machete ran teasingly through his bright red hair. Ignoring the loud calls for vengeance, Adam stood back.

"I won't allow this," he said, turning to face Cartimandua. "Blitz should be back in his cage where he belongs. He shouldn't be here. None of this should have happened."

"But it has happened. If you are lucky, maybe the rest you will be allowed to leave. As for this murderer, he dies, and insanity is not grounds for mercy. If you won't do it then we will. Constable Scappi, you have my permission to take the shot. When you are ready, constable."

Obediently stepping forward, his wood and steel crossbow already cocked, Constable Scappi knocked a bolt into the barrel. Hazel eyes fierce with contempt, frowning mouth framed by his thick dark beard, Scappi raised the crossbow and aimed at Blitz's head. Gently, almost imperceptibly, he squeezed the trigger.

"You can't do this!" Adam cried, leaping between Scappi and his intended target – he held out his machete as if he could deflect the oncoming projectile.

The steel bolt hit Adam in the lower leg, just below the knee, firmly embedding itself in his shinbone. Everyone, except Adam and Blitz, let out a pained collective groan.

"Hah, I'll bet that hurts," Blitz said, chuckling.

Sucking up the pain – a sharp intake of breath through gritted teeth – Adam fell back onto his arse, still holding out his machete in defiance.

"I just saved your life, you ungrateful bastard."

A number of constables raised their crossbows, and waited for their chief to give the command to fire. For a moment, and not for the first time, Adam faced the prospect of true death. The feeling was always the same: a knotty tightness in his stomach and a tense numbness in his head. Whether it was noticeable to anyone else, he was quivering with fear.

"Stand down," Cartimandua ordered her constables. "We take them alive."

"But, chief, they have to die," Constable Scappi said obstinately, clearly desperate for a 'righteous' kill.

"The old zoo's not far from here," Cartimandua said. "We'll lock them up there and decide on this in the morning. The decision should not be mine alone. Wiser minds should be involved."

All the constables lowered their crossbows without further protest; a testament to Cartimandua's leadership and the deep respect she commanded. After Adam laid down his weapon, she instructed a few constables to free Blitz from his sticky predicament – this involved cutting him out of his clothes and the careful application of a pungent solvent. A couple of other constables, including Constable Scappi, supported Adam under his arms for the journey to the zoo. As he limped past, Adam caught Cartimandua's arm:

"Thank you, Artie," he said.

"Oh, it's far too early to thank me, Adam. Ching Shih will live, but you had better pray to your Gods that Robert Oppenheimer survives until midnight."

***

Kneeling, Adam pressed his face against the black bars of the cage. The zoo, a collection of small cages and large enclosures, was devoid of animals – apparently, the robotic facsimiles disappeared during the Great Catastrophe and were never seen again. In a cage nearby, Blitz sat silently, his back turned on the world as he stared at the rough stone floor. Naked, except for his 1970's tiger print underpants, he sported a black eye and a bleeding lip – the result of violently resisting arrest.

Cartimandua stood, hands on hips, just outside the cage. Her mouth open and closed a couple of times, as if about to speak before changing her mind. Going down onto one knee, face to face with Adam, she finally found the words:

"I … don't want you to die, Adam. I fear if I have Blitz killed, then people's bloodlust will be roused rather than be satisfied. Tomorrow, I will talk to Cortés. If this world has anyone we could call a leader, then it is him. With luck, people will respect his decision, but there is no guarantee. He has probably spent far too much time on the other side of the wall."

"And what if he wants us dead?"

Cartimandua compassionately clasped a hand around Adam's hand – he did not pull away:

"Then … then there is nothing I can do," she said, her deep whispered voice cracking. "Of course, I will argue your case until my very last breath, but the mob is already demanding blood. Anyway, I will settle down here for midnight and see you again in the morning. If, for some reason, you don't sleep as we do, then there is some water and food in your cage."

"Whatever happens tomorrow, I want to thank you," Adam said. "It was totally stupid of me to bring those psychopaths. I could say I was only following orders, but that's usually the excuse of a robot or a coward."

"Those psychopaths? Are you saying there's another? Does Mr Stardust have the same … temperament?"

"He has a bit more self-control. Well, at least I hope he has."

A small group walked up behind Cartimandua:

"Chief!"

Cartimandua stood up, surprised:

"Constable Lovelace, I did not expect to see you here." She gestured to Stardust and Stern. "Constable Hanzō, get those two into the cage with Mr Eden as quickly as possible. It is nearly midnight and want them securely behind bars. Constable Unaipon, rush over to that dispenser and get some more bottles of drink and jars of preserved food. Hurry, there's not much time."

Constable Hanzō pushed Stardust forward – Stern followed quietly, his head bowed. With a quizzical expression, Cartimandua told Stardust to stop a moment:

"Why is Mr Stardust cuffed? What has happened?" Confused, she wheeled around, her attention turned to the man in the wheelchair. "Is that you, Sigmund? Why on Earth are you in a wheelchair? And, why are you wearing that ridiculous helmet?"

TUNNEL VISION

The perpetual twilight softly caressed Adam's eyes. Awaking in the cage, slumped comfortably back against the bars, he smiled at Stern, the charismatic hind-reader's blue eyes returning the gaze. Glancing over to the other cage revealed Blitz and Stardust also roused from slumber.

Whatever systems controlled Reynold's Gardens had replaced Blitz's clothes and he was back to his peacock strutting best – resplendent in turquoise glitter and the shiniest platform boots. He offered Adam a cold expression that menaced behind the fire make-up.

A quick sniff confirmed the absence of body odour – Adam's clothes seemed new, and his hair fresh and detangled. He turned his hand and nodded appreciatively. A small graze was gone, the skin perfectly healed. Blitz's bruises were also healed, and Stardust …

To Adam's surprise, Stardust was holding his hands over his face and peeking through the gaps in his fingers, as if embarrassed by the view. If the psychopath was blushing beneath his pale make-up, Adam could not tell.

"Oh muchacho," Stern muttered, his eyes taking on an extra level of intensity, "you didn't get to see this in History class."

Still on his knees, Adam shuffled around to see what had caught the others' attention. Holding onto the bars with both hands, he froze, his mouth forming a perfectly surprised 'O'.

Cartimandua and her constables were awake and getting to their feet. Freud sat on the floor – cutlery gone, head healed – rubbing his hands together as if eager to start a new day. In the distance, many were already engaged in conversation and strolling to the dispensers. Everything was as expected … except that the citizens of Reynold's Gardens were naked.

Impressively Olympian in stature, Cartimandua flexed and stretched her black masculine musculature. The dark grooves of definition, tight between well-formed muscles, lent her body a statuesque appearance as if carved from a rich wood. Despite being the wrong gender for the Celtic queen, her adopted form was a strikingly rare find.

Hanging amongst the bulging curves was Cartimandua's unassuming, almost lacklustre penis. On a normal body, one of average size, it may have seemed of slightly generous proportions, but here it was almost lost. The bodybuilder's eternal curse, the penis was the muscle that stubbornly stayed the same, and so became relatively smaller as the rest of the body grew – and a lifetime of wanking, that furious penile exercise, made absolutely no difference, apart from an infrequent sore patch and the mythical teenage fears of hairy palms and blindness.

"Not so intimidating in the flesh, is it?" Cartimandua said, noticing the direction of Adam's stare. "Perhaps we don't even need a dance belt to keep it under control."

"I wasn't looking at your … err … I promise I …"

"Perhaps in another life then, Adam. Anyhow, I have to get dressed and talk to Cortés. My constables will guard the zoo until I return." She smiled at Freud, who was now standing and running his fingers through his hair. "Ah, Sigmund, I prefer you without the unfortunate headwear. Walk with me, old friend. We need to talk."

Little was said during the two hours that Cartimandua was away. Constables Lovelace and Hanzō fetched uniforms for themselves and their colleagues, whilst the naked Hooke, Unaipon, and Nabigha, sat quietly, their humiliated expressions fixed on the prisoners. A small crowd had gathered by the entrance to the zoo, shouting abuse and calling for Pascal to be avenged. A strong line of police kept them at bay.

Finally, the police chief returned, fully dressed and alone. Wasting no time, she knelt down outside the cage, facing Adam:

"Sigmund has agreed to keep quiet about his ordeal for now, as has Cheng Shi. And, my constables will not say anything unless I give my permission."

"What about Oppenheimer?"

"He's dead," Cartimandua said abruptly. "We moved the body to a secret location and Bruegel has performed a private ritual. Oppenheimer was a bit of a recluse, so hopefully we can also keep his death quiet for a while."

"So, do we get to leave?" Adam asked hesitantly, fearful of the answer.

"You have a choice. You can either leave Reynold's Gardens straight away – I will arrange an escort to the warehouse – or you can go through the wall."

Adam thought for a moment. He still had no information about Edgar Allen Poe, and nothing on the gruesome ordeal of Mr Tikolo. Perhaps the answers lay on the other side of the wall. After all, Cortés seemed to be the boss around here. A sudden image of the sneering conquistadors and bloody combat in the halls filled Adam's mind, immediately swaying his decision.

"I think we should leave," he said. "Maybe we could learn more from Cortés, but I think we've caused enough trouble. Yes, we'll leave."

Cartimandua looked over to the other cage:

"Mr Stardust and Mr Blitz have no choice. Cortés insists they go through the wall."

"But, you just said we had a choice."

"I said you have a choice, Adam. Well, yourself and Mr Lovass."

The violent image of conquistadors returned. This time, Adam had Stardust and Blitz fighting by his side – somehow their psychopathic presence suppressed the mortal dread.

"Then I will go with them," Adam declared. "I don't like them. Even on one of their better days they really, really disgust me, but I'm supposed to be the leader of the group."

"Are you sure?" Cartimandua said, her voice betraying a hint of concern.

"What about you, Stern?" Adam asked. "Are you coming with us? Without you, we're a bit lacking on the charm front."

Stern rose to his feet and pulled down the brim of his Stetson:

"Muchacho, I don't like to leave you like this, but I gotta get back to the Terminal. The Captain gave me explicit orders not to cross over to the other place if there was one. I didn't know what he meant at the time, but this sure sounds like it."

"Just you, or did he mean all of us?"

"Just me. Has other plans for me apparently, but I have no idea what they are."

"But, how would Captain Andrews know about the wall?"

"Hey, the guy's not human. He probably knows a Hell of a lot more about this place than he lets on. Gotta admit, Adam, I feel like a coward bailin' on you like this."

Taken aback by Stern's revelation, Adam wondered if he should also leave the Gardens.

"So, how long have you worked for the Captain?" he asked. "Is this recent, or …"

"You know I can't tell you that," Stern replied. "Hah, I guess you're not the only one keeping secrets now."

Though deeply suspicious of his friend's role in the mission, Adam clasped Stern's hand. After a firm handshake, Adam patted Stern's arm.

"Don't worry about it, Stern," he said. "John Down always told me to trust the Captain, no matter how crazy or dangerous the situation might seem – but right now this all seems beyond crazy. I hope to God he was right."

Leaving Stern under Constable Lovelace's protection, Cartimandua and six constables led the 'Fabulous Three' across the park, taking lesser used paths, and shortcuts through the woods – a more circuitous route but hidden from the angry mob. Blitz and Stardust remained handcuffed and under close escort.

After about half an hour, they emerged from under a broad shadowy canopy of majestic oaks to face the wall. Up close, only some few feet away, the intimidating safety barrier completely filled their field of vision – Adam looked down at his feet for a moment, afraid of losing his balance.

They followed the wall north for a few minutes until reaching a large glass and whitewood summerhouse. Hiding the interior, the arched windows were curtained, and two constables stood guard by the double doors.

"You understand we will have to head-bag you before you cross over?" Cartimandua said.

"That's fine," Adam replied nonchalantly. "I would be surprised if you didn't."

The police chief stopped a moment, appearing surprised at Adam's casual reaction. Taking him by the arm, she led him over to the wall.

"That is the way through," she said, pointing to a small square opening, about three feet above the ground.

"You're joking, aren't you? There is no way we can fit through that tiny hole. I mean, not unless you've got some Alice in Wonderland shrink-me potion."

"Your head will fit. As I said, you will be head-bagged."

Adam's mind filled with all manner of frightening explanations.

"Oh no, no," he said slowly, "so a head bag doesn't mean that you put a bag over our heads so that we can't see what's going on? You know, like when they move dangerous convicts around?"

"Head-bagging involves a total body deconstruction."

"Deconstruction?" Adam shuddered.

"Most of your body parts – legs, arms, rib cage, etc. – are surgically removed and wrapped in a preservative film. By the end of the procedure, you are a head with your major organs and spinal cord still attached and bagged. Your organs, including your brain, will still function, although in a much reduced capacity. After that, we put you in a greased stainless steel container, a bit like a fish kettle, and push you through the gap." As if to emphasise the point, Cartimandua thrust her muscular arm into the hole.

"Oh God, that sounds awful. Like that disgusting bag of giblets you get in an oven ready chicken." At this moment, Adam wondered if there was still time to catch up with Stern – perhaps those psychopaths did not deserve his help.

"I know it sounds terrifying," Cartimandua said, softening her tone, as if to calm Adam's fears, "but it's a standard procedure performed every day. You have absolutely nothing to worry about. You will be reconstructed on the other side."

"So, what famous surgeon will be carrying out the 'gibletting'?"

"I heard that Picasso and Donatello are on rotation today, so you'll be in good hands."

Adam just stood, silent, staring at Cartimandua in disbelief. She put a comforting hand on his shoulder.

"I promise they are fully trained and very experienced. Soon after the Great Catastrophe, a hologram of Gordon Reynolds appeared and explained the procedure. We have a few expert surgeons among our number and they carried out the first head-bags. After a few years perfecting their skill, they gradually moved to a teaching role, and eventually the painters took up the reins."

"Wouldn't it have been easier to have put a bigger hole in the wall in the first place? Whoever designed this place should be ashamed of themselves."

"There is, or rather was, another way through. A large doorway, about four foot wide, with thick safety doors can be found to the south of here. Unfortunately, during the Great Catastrophe, the crushed viaduct pushed over a few trees, one of which completely covered the doorway. We've tried everything to break through, all kinds of tools and as much brute strength as we can bring to bear, but it won't budge." Cartimandua gestured towards the summerhouse. "Now, if you will accompany me to the bagging room, we need to take you apart."

Head Bag

Cartimandua held open the door to the summerhouse, and ushered Adam in. Slapping him on the back, she wished him luck and closed the door behind him.

Whilst the exterior of the elegant sugar-spun structure spoke of warm summer days, afternoon tea, and lazy hours lounging with a good book, the interior had all the relaxing ambience of an incoming dentist's drill. Gloss red floors, no doubt to disguise the blood, and steel operating tables edged with drainage channels, competed for terror value with trays of strange surgical tools and a stack of shiny 'fish kettles'.

Two men approached, strikingly dressed in red surgical gowns and matching aprons. In addition to the clothing, both men wore well-practised smiles.

"Mr Eden, my name is Pablo Picasso," the first man said, shaking Adam's hand. "I will be conducting your head-bagging today. I will be ably assisted by my good friend and colleague, Donatello."

For the first time in this land of historical characters, Adam actually recognised someone. Sure, Picasso was younger with a fringe of dark hair, but his eyes were unmistakeable – intense and staring, almost as if seeking to break free from his face. Donatello, with much softer features, reached over and shook Adam's hand.

"Pleased to meet you, Mr Eden," he said.

Utterly professional, the two painters offered minimal instructions, a laugh and an anecdote or two, and within a few minutes, Adam was laying naked on the steel table, his head propped up on a firm foam cushion. He dissolved a large thin blue tablet under his tongue and soon lost all sensation in his body, although was still able to talk and move his head and neck.

The painters began wrapping thick silver tape around the top of Adam's thighs.

"What's that for?" Adam asked, his mouth dry with unease. "Is that duct tape?"

"Hah, it's certainly not duct tape," Picasso explained. "This tape causes the blood vessels to close. Only takes a few seconds. We cut through the middle of the tape to remove your legs without any blood loss. Well, to tell the truth, there are sometimes a few drips. We use the same technique for the arms. It's like cutting through a lightly cured ham." Inspecting both tapes, Picasso gave a thumbs up and told Donatello to fetch the saws. "Well, before we begin," he said to Adam,

"I am required to ask whether you wish to be zipped or is this just a one-off visit to the other side."

"We might make a return trip, but nothing beyond that. And, what exactly do you mean by 'zipped'?"

Picasso leant forward so that Adam got a good view of his neck:

"Can you see the line on my neck? Look carefully. It runs all the way around, like a very faint decapitation scar. It joins the one running vertically down my chest."

"Ah, yes, I can see them. You know, if you hadn't told me, I would have never known."

"It is a form of Bio-Velcro; for those clients that cross over on a regular basis. It allows them to be taken apart quickly and efficiently – a kind of pre-prepared dissection."

"How safe is it? What if someone pulled your arm with a bit too much force? Would it come off?"

"Hah, of course it wouldn't. Bio-Velcro won't come apart unless you use an enzymatic separator." Picasso reached into his apron pocket and held up a small metallic device that looked similar to a safety razor. "We call it an Unzipper. Just press the button and run the Unzipper along the zipped seam. We can take apart a body in a matter of minutes. There is a similar tool to seal up the seams during a reconstruction."

"What if I don't want to be zipped?" Adam asked, dredging up a distant childhood memory of the time his prized teddy ripped open at the seams during a sibling tug of war.

"Then we use good old fashioned stitches and bone welders. The stitches are so fine, so very fine, that you will never notice them. Anyway, when you wake up tomorrow morning you will be completely healed – the stitches will vanish. Zipped seams, on the other hand, are seen by the system as an improvement rather than an injury, so they remain in place even after sleep. Choose whichever method you want. We are happy to cater for either."

"I'll take the stitches and the bone welders."

Smiling amiably, fine tooth saw in hand, Donatello stood over Adam:

"Mr Eden, you want to be conscious during the head-bagging?"

The thought of the procedure sickened Adam, but his curiosity was truly piqued.

"Will I feel anything?" he asked. "I reckon I want to see what's going on, but I really don't want to feel anything."

"Oh, you'll experience a slight tingling now and then, but nothing that will cause you any discomfort. If you want, you can even chat to us while we're working. We've done this so often that we're not easily distracted."

"In that case, I would like to remain conscious."

As Donatello began sawing through Adam's leg, Picasso wrapped tape around one of Adam's arms, close to the shoulder.

"Tell me," Picasso asked casually, "who performed Pascal's ritual? The second block is Bruegel's patch, but I do know a few other painters that hang around that area."

"Actually, it was Reginald Marsh."

Picasso stopped taping for a moment and looked at Adam in surprise:

"Are you kidding me?"

"No, he did this head in the hat routine ..."

Donatello walked past, carrying one of Adam's legs under his arm, the end cleanly cut and unquestionably ham-like:

"Reggie Marsh, he's one of the worst performers out there."

"I thought he was pretty good," Adam said, feeling the need to defend the man-with-the-hat. "The audience seemed to like it."

Picasso started taping Adam's other arm:

"But he just stands there with that stupid head-in-the-hat, whilst doing really bad impressions of people you've never heard of. How could anyone think that is good?"

"Oh no, he didn't do impressions. It was a song and dance routine, like one of those old music hall numbers. There was singing, tap dancing, and an amazing balancing act."

Picasso finished taping and picked up a saw:

"Hmm, sounds like someone's developed a whole new act. You say the audience liked it."

"They loved it."

"So, that's it," Donatello declared, confidently sawing Adam's remaining leg, the blade rasping through the bone, "Piet Mondrian is now the most boring painter."

Adam turned his head towards his shoulder, and gulped, seeing Picasso's saw slicing back and forth. The great Spanish surrealist pulled out the blood-smeared blade and pointed it at his colleague:

"Are you kidding, Don? Have you even seen Piet's ritual?"

"Yes, and just he stood there, dressed in a long frock coat, hardly moving, with the head balanced on one hand and his other hand dead straight against his side." Donatello carried the other leg out of Adam's narrow view. "OK, every now and then he let out some random sound, but other than that, absolutely nothing happened."

"Oh, you watched but you obviously didn't see," Picasso said, handing Donatello the freshly cut arm. "You didn't notice the subtle hand movements, and that sublime moment when Piet flared a single nostril after saying the word 'Angst'. For me, it was a masterpiece of minimalist abstraction. By the end, I was weeping." He moved over to Adam's other arm and angled the saw across the tape.

"Snoring, weeping, it was still boring," Donatello said.

"What about Bruegel's act?" Adam asked, resolutely looking straight ahead, avoiding watching the sawing of this final limb. "Reggie said it was a load of rubbish."

"Oh … he … lied," Picasso said, in time with the strokes of the saw. "Bruegel's act is one of the best. When he dances, wearing those oversize clogs, with the head nestling in a basket of turnips …"

"Does it involve juggling the turnips and the head?"

"Yes."

"Thought so." Adam's eyes widened as Picasso passed the arm over his head to Donatello. "Err, what's next?"

Picasso placed the saw on a nearby trolley and picked up a shiny steel blade:

"Well, we've removed your limbs. Don will wrap them and pop them in the bag over there. Next, I'm going to remove your genitalia. I like to use a curved blade for this." Picasso held up a miniature sickle, his eyes staring so widely that they appeared to float within their sockets. "With one neat circular motion, I can remove the scrotum, the penis – even cut the suspensory ligament – the whole package in one. You could call it my party piece."

Picasso moved down to Adam's lower body. Straining his neck, Adam desperately tried to see what the painter was doing.

"Ah, what is that old nursery rhyme you Brits sing?" Picasso mused, tapping the flat of the blade on a remnant of thigh. "Oh yes, 'round and round the garden like a teddy bear." He gently walked the blade towards Adam's exposed genitalia. "One step, two step …'"

"Knock me out! For God's sake, knock me out!"

**

No thoughts, no sensation, no sense of time, Adam slowly opened his heavy eyelids. His mind a muddled haze, he tried to move his head, but it seemed stuck fast. Though he wanted to take a big gulp of air, to fill his body with life, he managed only short shallow breaths. A cry for help came out as little more than a sigh.

Picasso's smiling face came into view.

"Welcome back, Mr Eden. You've woken up just in time."

"Am I back together?" Adam whispered. "Why can't I move my head? I … I've seemed to have lost my voice."

"Take a look, Mr Eden. I think you'll agree we've done a splendid job."

Eyes bulging with pride rather than malice, Picasso held up a mirror, much like a barber showing his client the back of their head. Seeing the reflection, Adam tried to scream, but instead expelled a slow, quiet wheeze.

Tightly packed at one end of the shiny steel container, Adam's head was the only recognisable body part. Beneath his head, a large gelatinous bag filled the rest of the space. Faintly visible within the bag, Adam's organs pulsed and pumped, and the tail of his spine twitched against the other end of the 'fish kettle'.

Adam's terror partially subsided as Cartimandua's face appeared in his view. He let out a sigh of relief, which in his present lung restricted state sounded like the contented coo of a baby.

"I hope this isn't goodbye," Cartimandua said, close to tears. "Who knows, tomorrow you might be on your way back. I … I really don't know what to say."

"Aw Chief, I could fetch one of his arms if you want to hold his hand," Donatello teased from somewhere off to Adam's left.

"I'll push him through the wall," Cartimandua said, lifting up the steel container and cradling it in her strong arms.

Adam stared up into Cartimandua's face – partially for reassurance but mainly because his head was stuck that way. Reaching the wall, she carefully placed the container on the ground.

"I have to put the lid on now. There's absolutely nothing to worry about, Adam. They do this many times each day."

"What about the others?" Adam whispered.

"They're working on Mr Stardust right now. Both your colleagues will be unconscious for the procedure. We're not taking any risks." Cartimandua readied the steel lid. "I shall wait for your return."

Adam felt a slight knot in his bagged stomach as the lid pressed down, sealed tight, completely blocking out the light. Shut inside his small metal coffin, he waited silently.

THE DARK SIDE

Standing in the small dark room, reconstructed and back in his old clothes, Adam listened intently at the door. Stardust sat on a hard backed dining chair, worriedly checking every inch of his body, making sure there was nothing missing or leaking out – a difficult feat since not only was he clothed in his tight fitting glam clothing, but he was also still handcuffed. Unconscious for most of the procedure, Adam knew little about the painters who worked on him, save for their first names, Walter and Valentin.

Through the door, Adam heard muffled laughter and indistinct babble. Now and then, he felt sure he could hear Blitz's faint voice somewhere in the distance, but it was far too quiet for him to be certain. A matter of minutes later and Adam heard a key turn in the lock. He stood back as the door opened.

Both Adam and Stardust squinted as the light burst in from the operating room. However, having spent only an hour in the darkness, their eyes became quickly accustomed to the brightness. Walter, still dressed in his red operating gown and apron, chuckled quietly through his fine black beard as if enjoying the final tickle of a private joke. Smiling, he told his guests it was time to leave.

Valentin, his long brown hair partly fallen over his thin face, also wore his gown and apron. He gave a faux cry of triumph as he finished polishing the top of the steel operating table with a soft cloth. Adam looked around for Blitz, expecting the psycho to be squeezing into his turquoise glitter suit, or at least regaling Adam with a sneering remark or two.

Stardust spotted Blitz almost immediately, and gasped:

"Oh my God," he cried in horror, "what have you done?"

Adam yelped as his eyes fixed on the gruesome sight. Hanging on the wall, slotted into what looked like a small basketball hoop, was Blitz's head and bag – his mouth stuck shut with duct tape. Like some hunting trophy, the grisly writhing head-bag sat above a majestic wood and tile fireplace. Walter held out an arm, as if presenting his latest work.

"A most visceral three-dimensional piece, don't you agree? Valentin thinks the tape detracts from the artistic intention, but I find it adds a gritty focal point that speaks of silence."

Valentin washed his hands in a nearby sink:

"If it stops his constant moaning then I can live with it; although, I would have preferred a strip of black velvet."

"Put him back together," Adam demanded, instinctively reaching for his machete, which was not there. "You can't do this."

"On the contrary; it's done," Walter said. "We know about Pascal, and we also know about Oppenheimer and Cheng Shi. There are no secrets between painters."

"But, this is totally barbaric," Adam insisted, angrily moving forward, knocking into a trolley of instruments – the wheeled trolley bumped into the operating table with a loud clang. "Did Cortés order this?"

Stardust banged his cuffed hands on the top of the operating table and seethed menacingly:

"Take off these cuffs, give me my rapier, and we'll settle this here and now."

"Count yourself lucky you're not up there too," Valentin warned, drying his hands with a towel, unphased by Adam and Stardust's aggression. "A rumour's running around the Gardens that you tried to scalp Sigmund Freud. They say he was hiding his injury with a fireman's helmet. We don't deal in rumours, and that's why you're not wall-art."

"I stuck a fork in the top of his head," Stardust said indignantly.

At that stark admission, everyone fell silent for a few seconds, looking at each other with mistrustful expressions. Finally, Valentin spoke, his voice full of enthusiasm:

"That's an absolutely striking visual! If you don't mind, I might incorporate it into my next ritual."

"Yes," Walter agreed, stroking his beard in a pseudo intellectual fashion, "the everyday tools of domestic consumption feeding on the feeder. Visually striking, yet also throws a sop to metaphorical pretension. Oh, I love it! Hmm, but you might have damaged Freud's brain. If he had died …"

"We are supposed to meet Cortés," Adam said, hoping the name of the illustrious conquistador would provide some leverage.

"Pah, Cortés has no authority over the painters," Walter scoffed. "There are no rulers here. However, we will let the fork-man keep his body. I don't think we can be bothered to take him apart again after we've only just put him back together."

"Will Blitz be healed tomorrow?" Adam asked hopefully. "Will you let him go then?"

Both painters shook their heads.

"No chance of that, I'm afraid," Walter said. "We zipped your friend's body parts. The only way he'll heal, is if we decide to reconstruct him … or kill him. Until then, he stays on the wall."

Looking at Blitz's pained face – his red-rimmed eyes projecting a blend of dread, confusion, and anger – Adam actually felt sorry for his long-time adversary. Even in the violently horrific confines of the Psychoviro, they had long given up casual torture – except during the hunt where inducing immense pain was a delicacy they still savoured.

"You can't kill him," Adam pleaded. "What about the Hippocratic oath?"

"Oh please, we're painters not doctors," Walter said scornfully. "We are committed to our art, not peoples' wellbeing."

Clenching his cuffed fists, Stardust narrowed his eyes:

"Well, I'm a firm believer that all artists should suffer for their art. As I said, take off these cuffs, give me my rapier, and I'll show you what I mean."

Arrogantly unyielding, well aware of their privileged status, the painters ignored and rebuffed Adam and Stardust's continued protestations. With more reconstructions on the way, Walter and Valentin quickly and expertly manoeuvred their guests out of the building. Once outside, Adam and Stardust fell silent.

There was no mistaking that this was the dark side. Still early afternoon, this side of the wall was blacker than night. The only illumination in this dark place came from a few strange yellow glass orbs, which were attached to various trees and buildings – so weak that each one illuminated little more than a ten-foot radius. Casting a weak sickly glow, the unnatural light also gave the skin an unhealthy pallor.

What surprised Adam more than anything were the dense crowds of people. Dressed in tidy Victorian garb just like their twilight neighbours, the only noticeable difference was the absence of joy on their faces and that many wore facemasks – dark leather patches, colourful Mardi Gras creations, or often a simple scarf – obviously to hide the rot. It seemed that everyone congregated around the illuminated areas, mostly just hanging around with little to do.

This T-junction of cobbled roads played host to a small number of buildings. The building they had left, a stately two-storey mini-mansion, had once been a restaurant called 'The Larkspur' – or so said the sign hanging above the entrance. Adam guessed that the summerhouse on the other side of the wall used to serve as an overspill when things got busy.

Opposite 'The Larkspur', on one side of the junction, stood a large bandstand. Instead of hosting musical entertainment, it was overcrowded with people simply sitting and talking. An austere imposing stone and brick building on the other side of the junction looked like a huge Victorian church. However, a second glance at the carvings in the stone archway, and the lively statuary outside, revealed the structure as a gin palace – now also just a place to sit and congregate.

"What about our weapons?" Adam asked Walter, aware of many eyes watching them. "How safe are we here?"

"Not safe at all," Walter replied. "You can get some weapons from the dispenser over by the bandstand. Everyone on this side of the wall is armed, and most are experienced fighters, so I suggest you don't start any trouble. They carry wooden weapons – good for practise, less damaging. Also, it would be a good idea to get to the hall before more people hear about your friend's disgraceful behaviour."

Urging Stardust not to cause any trouble, reminding him that there were people just itching to start a fight, Walter produced a key and uncuffed the psychopath.

"The hall?" Adam asked.

"The Grand Reynold's Hall," Walter said, "in the far south western corner of the Gardens. That's where you'll find Cortés. Before the catastrophe, it used to be a major entertainment venue. The design is reminiscent of The Royal Albert Hall in London. Around here, we simply call it Gordon's Hall."

"What's it used for now?"

"The second safety wall that came down cut us off from our seafront apartments. Over four thousand people live in and around Gordon's Hall, including Cortés. Very crowded, but as you can see, property is at a premium this side of the wall. Most of us live in and around the cafes and follies, mainly along the yellow-lit road."

"Is it where you hold the tournaments … for the new bodies? I've heard all about the tournaments."

"Yes, that's where they are held. Tournaments are rare, although there has been one in progress recently. Well, until your people forced Cortés to abandon the body collection. As I said, Gordon's Hall is mainly used for accommodation and some combat practice."

"How do we get to the hall?"

"Just follow the yellow-lit road."

"You mean this road," Adam said, pointing down the junction.

"That's the one. Cortés has ordered everyone to stay off the road, to give you clear passage."

"I thought you said Cortés had no real power."

"Not over the painters. Nobody pushes us around. With everyone else, he has some authority."

Without saying goodbye or wishing their clients good luck, Walter and Valentin went back into The Larkspur', shutting and locking the door behind them. Adam and Stardust headed straight to the dispenser and procured their weapons of choice. To Adam's dismay, despite acquiring a new Kopis machete, albeit with an overly ornate ivory handle, the dispenser could not supply any 21st century daggers. Stardust, a fan of historical weaponry, recommended a simple 8-inch bowie knife with a leather sheath. Adam nodded his approval and attempted to return the favour, suggesting that Stardust forgo his usual rapier and instead choose a more versatile blade such as a cutlass.

"But cutlasses are sooo hack and slash," Stardust said disparagingly. "They have absolutely no elegance. You know I prefer a touch of class, and that is why I always use a rapier. Yes, I agree it might lack a certain versatility, but you know I just love to thrust and penetrate." With a hearty 'haha', Stardust thrust his arm in and out.

With the eyes of the crowds watching, faces of suspicion and barely suppressed malice, Adam and Stardust kept their hands low, ready to draw their blades. In front of them, the cobbled road snaked off into the distance, lit by the yellow orbs. As the distance increased, only the faint light of the orbs was visible, like a trail of fading stars set in a sea of inky black. It reminded Adam of the dark place, the limbo between death and resurrection – a place that the resurrected feared almost more than death itself.

Stardust pointed into the far distant black, noticing an almost imperceptible white glow – Gordon's Hall.

"Time to follow the yellow-lit road," Stardust said, attempting a smile that looked more like a grimace. "After you, Dorothy."

Sensing conflict was waiting for them, Adam wondered if his Dorothy could rely on Stardust's Wicked Witch.

As they made their way towards Gordon's Hall, dimly lit pools of yellow light punctuated the black. The cobbled road seemed a journey in and out of existence, slipping between the dangerous unknown and the relative safety of feeble vision. One mile away from 'The Larkspur', Adam and Stardust walked slowly in the gloom, their weapons now held at the ready.

Low whispers and murmurings filled the air along the road. What Adam had first taken as gnarly tree trunks and tall shrubs, were crowds of people lining the road, standing back in the darkness. Sometimes, as they passed through the yellow light, he perceived the shadowy shape of a face, the white of an eye, and troublingly, the dull silhouette of an unsheathed weapon.

They made slow progress along the yellow-lit road, mindful of the threat on both sides, and disturbed by the relative silence of the crowds. Halfway into their journey, passing through a dim circle of light, the crowd suddenly surged forward like an inadvertent belch. The heaving line of angry Victorians braced and buckled, catching itself only a couple of feet from their startled guests.

Adam and Stardust stood back to back, their blades held up in defence. Before the grim tide subsided back into the black, the green silk scarf of the nearest would be assailant slipped down from his face. Supressing a gasp, Adam shivered at sight. Covered with wet wormlike growths, the left side of the man's face was unrecognisably human – the eye pushed out of its socket and surrounded with bulbous weeping cysts. As the man pulled the scarf back over his face, Adam lowered his blade and gave a respectful nod.

GORDON'S HALL

The second half of the journey proceeded with fearful caution yet without incident. In the distance, brilliant light crested the black hilltop horizon – the lights of Gordon's Hall. Atop the hill, starkly silhouetted, the crowds either side of the road were statuesquely menacing. It was hard to remember that these were history's finest rather than a horde of rotting ghouls.

Over the hill, the huge hall was finally revealed. A layered cake of red brick and cream stone, wrapped in classical mosaic friezes and topped with a glass-domed roof. The Italianate colosseum-like structure dominated the view. Swivelling on the roof of the building, powerful spotlights scoured the low landscape, illuminating the surrounding parkland and the masked grotesquery of the dark-side.

Crowds lined the road all the way to the wide stone steps of the hall. There was genuine loathing in their faces, and many gripped their wooden weapons as if aching to attack. Looking back, the road was filling with people, a teeming mass obliterating the route. Shouting the name of Blaise Pascal, the crowds waved their wooden swords, axes, and hammers. Worryingly, some shouted out the name of Oppenheimer – obviously, the painters could not keep a secret.

Adam advised Stardust to look straight ahead, not to give any provocation or sign of weakness. He knew that they stood no chance against such numbers. Adam still hoped that Cortés would be there to welcome them and whisk them away to safety – or at least to keep the wolves at bay.

Ignoring the constant insults and threats, they climbed the steps to the golden arched entrance. Two men dressed in red British military tunics with gleaming brass buttons, and crisply creased black trousers, held open the large doors and ushered Adam and Stardust inside. Brandishing their steel sabres, the men each offered a half-hearted and reluctant left-handed salute.

"I'm telling you, this is going to end in a gladiator style fight," Adam said. "Probably to the death. This place even looks like the bloody colosseum."

Stardust shook his head:

"Oh Copa, for all you know, we might be treated to a lavish musical. You have such a negative view of human nature."

"Well, visiting you creeps once a month hasn't exactly given me a positive outlook. Anyway, why would expect anything less than death? I thought you psychos saw darkness in everyone and everything."

"On the contrary, Copa, it's my strongly held belief that most people are quite honest, trusting, and extremely naïve. It's how we have our fun. You're too sceptical. That's why you're more of a challenge than a pleasure."

Once through the doors, the crowds inside quickly funnelled Adam and Stardust along the high ceilinged foyer and shoved them through a set of black swing doors – each door bearing the silver initials 'GR'. On the other side of the doors, the air immediately erupted into a deafening roar of cheers, boos, and whistles.

They entered a huge circular auditorium, with numerous tiers packed with excited spectators. A large raised stage at the far side of the hall stood next to a large central arena – no doubt used as standing room during certain events, but looking ominously perfect for gladiatorial combat at this moment. Around the central arena, the expectant crowds filled the many rows of seats. Most of the audience, which seemed to number in the thousands, carried wooden weapons. Adam wondered if the thin red line of guards, positioned around the low wooden barrier of the arena, could keep the crowd under control.

Unceremoniously pushed down one of the aisles, towards the central arena, Adam wondered if Stardust was still holding out for a lavish musical. Suddenly, one of the crowd sitting along the aisle sucker punched Stardust in the side of the head, partially dislodging his white wig. Instinctively, the psychopath drew his dagger. Adam caught Stardust's arm before any throat cutting could take place:

"Not a good idea," Adam said. "I think we need to save it for what's coming."

Trying to remain composed, the leader of the Psychoviro reluctantly sheathed his dagger and adjusted his wig:

"Bloody nobody," he said to the grinning man. "I bet you couldn't draw such an audience."

Once beyond the barrier, they stood at the arena's edge, surrounded by a group of guards. In the distance, a figure emerged from the shadows at the back of the stage. Confidently, the man walked into the light. Muscular, bare chested with bronzed skin, the man wore a red loincloth secured with a black leather belt. He held a short sword in one hand, whilst on his other arm he held a red rectangular curved shield. Atop his head, a bronze helmet with a silver plume looked Ancient Greek in design. His only other clothing was a metal greave – a piece of armour protecting the shin – on his left leg.

"I knew it," Adam groaned. "I guess there's a small chance that he's an opera singer, but I really, really doubt it."

"Copacabana!" the man shouted. "I, Flamma, challenge you! One on one! To the death!" He pointed his sword – a Roman gladius – at Adam.

Like a reluctant audience member called to the stage by a magician, Adam sighed and walked forward. Stardust tried to follow but was held back by the guards. The man nimbly jumped down from the stage and held his sword aloft. Once again, the crowd erupted into noise, stamping their feet on the floor and chanting the name 'Flamma'. Adam simply smiled. He had heard of Flamma. Syrian born, he was a legendary gladiator of Ancient Rome, famous not just for his victories but also for refusing his freedom on more than one occasion. Shuffling his feet, Adam pretended to be unimpressed.

"Nice costume, Flamma," he said, "though it doesn't look very Victorian."

"There was a lavish theatre production of Sophocles' 'Ajax' in 1899. The costumes were as robust as the real thing. I have heard that you wear those skimpy clothes to fight. Would you prefer some proper armour instead? Maybe something a real man might wear?"

"I'll stick with what I know. These clothes have served me well over the years."

Flamma nodded and adopted a fighting stance:

"Very well, Copacabana; prepare to fight."

"Wait a moment," Adam yelled, waving his arms in the air. "Before either of us dies, tell me why you didn't get out."

"Get out of what?" Flamma looked hungry to begin the fight.

"Four times you turned down the Rudis, four chances of freedom. You chose to keep fighting in the arena. Why?"

"I chose life."

Adam gurned and flung out his arms in an 'I do not know what you mean' gesture. Flamma lowered his sword.

"Given your reputation, I thought you would understand. Yes, I could have retired to some luxury villa in the countryside. There I would have drunk wine, taken a wife, got comfortable and as fat as a Senator's arse. Instead of that slow death, I chose life. Surely, Copacabana, you have felt the exhilaration of the fight, the glory of the win, even the anger at losing. Those emotions are greater than sex … and I thrust my cock deep and often."

"But you were killed in the arena. You died young."

"A fierce Roman Briton named Catavignus ran his trident into my chest. I lived life right up until that moment. Better that than a slow shameful walk towards the Gods." Flamma raised his sword once again and fixed his colourful adversary with a cold stare. "No more talk, Copacabana. Prepare to fight before I take you for a coward."

If Flamma still fought as in his first-life gladiator days, then Adam knew what to expect. As a Secutor – a chaser – he would close quickly on his opponent and strike. Without cover, Adam was once again at a huge disadvantage. His stealthy hide-and-seek hit-and-run techniques, perfected in the concrete jungle of the Psychoviro, were useless in this bare arena.

Silently, without a war cry, Flamma began his run towards his prey. His shield held in front, sharp eyes staring above the brim, he moved swiftly. Like a high jumper approaching the bar, he arced across the arena, his speed belying the weight of his shield and armour. Adam slowly backed away, keeping his eyes fixed on the rapidly approaching danger.

Like a flash, Flamma was alongside, lashing out with his shield, viciously knocking away Adam's machete arm with the huge rectangular sheet of metal. At the same time, the gladiator turned, plunging his short sword towards Adam's chest. Already backing away, Adam stayed clear of the lethal blade, barely managing to keep hold of his own weapon.

Before Adam could counterattack, Flamma was heading back to his original position for another run. Flamma – the Flame, symbolising Vulcan the God of Fire – had that rare but deadly quality of clinically controlled ferocity. There was no easy way to even the odds – Flamma was like Blitz on steroids – but perhaps Adam could reduce the deficit.

Running forward, Adam took the fight to his opponent. A vain hope perhaps, but maybe Flamma's defence was lacking compared to his offence. At least if death were certain, then it would be on Adam's own terms. Surprised at his opponent's impertinence, a somewhat bemused expression on his face, Flamma readied himself for the attack. Keeping his shield facing Adam, he offered teasing glimpses of his sword.

Taking advantage of his machete's long length, Adam lunged and stabbed at Flamma's face, forcing the gladiator to raise his shield to deflect the blow. Hidden from view, Adam immediately stepped sideways, lashing out at his enemy's muscular sword arm. With lightning reflexes and finely tuned instincts, Flamma parried the attack, steel ringing against steel.

By now, the crowd was delirious with excitement, watching their champion go head to head against Copacabana, the legend of the Viroverse. 'Oohs, aahs', and a stream of tense expletives accompanied every move. There was no love or support for Adam, but that made him feel right at home – perhaps even strengthening his resolve.

For a few moments, they exchanged fierce blows, each switching from attack to defence, with neither gaining any advantage. Inwardly, Adam congratulated himself on his plan of taking the fight to his opponent. Without the intimidating momentum of a run up, Flamma seemed lacklustre and bereft of ideas. However, his confidence was short lived.

Stepping up a number of gears all at once, Flamma launched into a brutally fast and precise attack. He easily evaded Adam's sword, bringing his own blade chopping against an Aloha sleeve. Fortunately, the robust evolved material remained intact, preventing the severing of an arm or at least a potentially deep and fatal wound. Flamma scowled, now understanding Adam's reluctance to wear 'proper' armour.

Undeterred, the expert gladiator displayed his overwhelming superiority by immediately and successfully attacking the same arm, though this time stabbing with the point of the blade. Adam cried out in pain as the sharp metal pierced his shirt and upper bicep before coming to a halt a few millimetres into the bone. Smiling triumphantly, Flamma pulled back the blade. Fearing another follow up attack, Adam recklessly lashed out in defence, body slamming Flamma's shield.

The unexpected impact knocked Flamma off balance. As he fell back, he raised his left knee, the hard metal rim of his grieve thrusting into Adam's groin. The gladiator steadied himself as his enemy dropped his machete and collapsed to the floor in agony.

Adam lay on his side, groaning quietly. For the third time in a week, his abused testicles felt like golf balls smashed up a driving range. Unable to reach his weapon, he looked up at Flamma and awaited the killing blow. At least the end would come quickly. Gladiators usually honoured their adversaries with a swift death.

Honour was in abundance as Flamma threw down his shield, bent down, and extended a hand to Adam.

"Please forgive me," he said. "Take a moment to recover. I will not disgrace myself by taking your life under such circumstances."

With the audience not knowing whether to cheer or jeer, Adam reached up and took Flamma's hand. Taking his other hand out of his trouser pocket, clutching the Unzipper he had stolen earlier from the trolley in the painter's operating room, Adam attacked. His finger pressed down hard on the activation button. In one swift motion, he ran the small tool up from Flamma's belly button to his neck.

The startled gladiator stood back as the bio-velcro seam came apart, and a horizontal dark line appeared on his body. He let go of Adam's hand and raised his sword. Ignoring the widening body split, and the escaping blood, Flamma stabbed down at his opponent. Rolling out of the way, Adam leapt to his feet.

The crowd were already out of their seats, voicing their anger as the legend of the Colosseum dropped his sword and futilely tried to hold his body together. Deftly moving behind Flamma, Adam grasped both edges of the bloody divide. With one great heave, he ripped Flamma's body open. The gladiator's guts spilled out onto the killing floor, his ribcage split apart, exposing his organs, which hung like a misshapen variety of sopping ripe red fruits – a detailed visceral thrill for those in the nearby seating, and a distant splash of colour for those watching from the 'heavens'.

"Sorry about that," Adam whispered, gently letting go of the dying son of the Colosseum, "but I don't fancy meeting the Gods today."

Without a word, Flamma staggered forward. Somehow, he raised an arm, clenching his fist defiantly. The crowd responded, punching their fists into the air. Slipping on his hanging entrails, Flamma fell face down onto the hard floor.

Like a ball boy at a tennis match, a short man in grey overalls immediately ran in from the edge of the arena. He crouched next to Flamma's body, checked the pulse, and shook his head. Looking up at Adam, he rummaged through his leather shoulder bag.

"Wen Zhengming, official painter for Gordon's Hall" the man said, smiling broadly. "I've come for the head."

Wasting no time, Wen produced a small steel axe from the bag and took only two strokes to decapitate Flamma. He left the head snug inside the Greek helmet, using it as a convenient container.

"Good luck," Wen said, winking at Adam. With that, the painter promptly shot off up one of the aisles with the head – no doubt to perform the brain ritual in less dangerous surroundings.

With the guards struggling to maintain order, as some of the enraged crowd tried to climb over the barrier, Stardust escaped his minders and loped across the arena on his platform boots. The psychopath joined Adam in the centre of the arena, and screwed his face up at the sight of Flamma's headless bloody mess of a body.

"Oh Copa, what do we do?" Stardust blathered fearfully. "They're going to kill us!"

"Head for the stage. If we're lucky, there'll be a way out the back that's clear. We've still got our weapons, but I hope it doesn't come to that."

They turned slowly, and then sprinted towards the stage. Already, a couple of angry darksiders were on the arena floor giving chase. Stardust managed to reach the stage and leapt up with a single bound – the pneumatics inside his glam boots proving invaluable. Adam was not so fortunate. Whilst he awkwardly clambered up onto the stage, someone grabbed his leg.

Frantically, Adam kicked out and clawed at the wooden floor, trying to free himself. To his side, the red gloss of Stardust's boot appeared, kicking whoever was holding Adam's leg with brutal force. With a guttural howl, the person instantly let go. Getting to his feet, Adam wheeled around. Below, a dark haired woman in an elegant blue bustle dress, backed away. Spitting out teeth, blood dripping from her mouth, she seemed dazed. Staggering across the arena, she obviously wanted no more of the fight.

A well-built, pale-skinned, ginger haired man climbed up on the stage and rushed at Stardust, wooden sword raised above his head. The man wore a white silk shirt, and unencumbered by the customary heavy Victorian jacket, moved with great speed.

"You're so dead!" the man cried, sweeping the sword towards Stardust's head.

The psychopath took an elegant step back, avoiding the blunt weapon with ease. In response, he flicked his rapier against the man's right cheek, administering his signature 'S'. The man stopped and held his hand against his bloody cheek, a look of horror on his face. With a haughty sniff, Stardust adopted an exaggerated fencing stance, and prepared to administer a fatal blade insertion.

Not wanting to anger the crowd further with another death, Adam barged in between the two men, his Bowie knife in his hand. He hugged the ginger haired man close, gently pressing the tip of his dagger against his lower abdomen. Staring straight into the man's light blue eyes, Adam spoke softly:

"You are all just amateurs, carrying toy weapons. Another second, perhaps two, and my friend's rapier would have pierced your heart. If I wanted, I could kill you right now in so many different ways. I could gut you like a pig, or cut any number of major arteries – the femoral would end it pretty quickly – or maybe just shove my blade up under your chin and into your brain. Do you like those options?"

The man shook his head, beads of sweat forming on his forehead.

"Didn't think so," Adam said. "Instead, I'm just going to push you off this stage. Please make sure you don't land awkwardly and break your neck. You ready?"

Shaking nervously, a relieved look on his face, the man nodded. Without a word, Adam swung the man around and shoved him off the stage. Fortunately, the man landed on his feet, and immediately ran back to the relative safety of the crowd, stumbling and tripping over his feet in his haste to escape.

Emulating Flamma's earlier dramatic pose, Adam stood at the front of the stage and pointed his machete at the crowd. The few people already on the arena floor paused, whilst those still in their seats quietened down, prepared to listen to the man in the Aloha shirt. Lowering his machete, Adam addressed the crowd:

"I defeated your champion! Who cares how I took him down? There's no resurrection in this godforsaken place, so it comes down to survival, not honour! I've been fighting and killing psychopaths like you for almost a thousand years! I choose to fight, month after month, year after year, and you know why? I enjoy it! I enjoy hunting down those fucking maniacs and hacking the bloody life out of them! Does that make me a psycho? Does it? What does that make me? I'll tell you what it makes me! I am the true psychopath amongst psychopaths. I am the Superpsycho!"

Suddenly, Adam felt a searing pain in his left arm. He dropped his dagger as blood began seeping from a puncture wound just below his elbow. He looked around to see Stardust wide eyed, his rapier shaking in his hand.

"Did you just …? Why … why did you do that?"

"Oh, I got so excited, Copa," Stardust said, his lips quivering with manic delight. "I couldn't help myself. I really wanted to kill that ginger man."

As Adam held his hand against the bleeding wound, Stardust jerked his sword arm forward, stabbing him again, this time in the leg. Adam hobbled along the edge of the stage:

"You … you … stop that!"

Seeing Adam in such a weakened state, many in the crowd began climbing over the barriers, ignoring the guards, who had given up on keeping the peace. They ran across the arena, gleefully anticipating killing their unwelcome guest. Horrified at the incoming horde, Stardust stayed close to Adam.

"I don't want to die, Copa," Stardust shrieked, jabbing Adam in the leg once more. "Do something!"

Adam slumped to the floor. A second later, he heard a thud and Stardust was lying unconscious by his side. A strong arm lifted Adam into a sitting position, accompanied by a strong familiar voice:

"There's timing for you."

"Cartimandua!"

"Looks like you could use some help. Your own people don't seem exactly … reliable."

Constable Hanzō stepped forward and held the tip of a cricket bat against Stardust's head. "Should I finish him, Chief?"

"Please … leave him be," Adam said. "Cuff him if you must, but please don't kill him."

"You are too soft-hearted, Adam," Cartimandua said, before ordering Hanzō to cuff the unconscious psychopath.

"Why are you here?" Adam asked.

"After I put you through the wall, I bumped into Cheng Shi. She tracked us to the summerhouse. A painter friend told her that the darksiders planned to kill you. Apparently, she owes you her life. If we get you out of here alive, then I think she's honoured her debt."

"How are you going to get us out of this? I thought you had no authority on this side of the wall."

"I may not have the authority, but I have a powerful bargaining chip." Cartimandua nodded at Constable Hanzō, who held out a shiny 'fish kettle' that he had carried under his arm. She reached in and pulled Blitz out of the fish kettle. Holding him up by his shock of red hair, she presented the grisly writhing head-bag to the crowd. Adam wanted to look away as the head twisted in her strong grip and stared straight at him for just a moment. Blitz spoke, too quietly to hear over the noise of the crowd, but it was obvious he was saying 'help me'. Inside the translucent bag of organs, the psychopath's heart pounded rapidly – Adam could only imagine the terror Blitz was experiencing.

The head twisted back to face the crowd as Cartimandua's commanding voice boomed out across the auditorium:

"My friends, this is the one who murdered Blaise Pascal. This is the one that should face our wrath. We are not monsters. We will not punish the innocent for this man's crimes. Only he should pay."

"What about Oppenheimer?" a voice called out from the crowd. "Two lives for two!"

Cartimandua waved her arm, desperately trying to calm the crowd who were now chanting 'two lives for two', almost drowning out her words.

"Yesterday, we accidently killed one of their group. We killed their top diplomat … a high ranking Terminal official."

The crowd cheered loudly – clearly glad that their enemy had lost a major player. Cartimandua continued:

"So, it will be two lives for two. These two men will not be punished. The matter is settled." With exaggerated movements, Cartimandua looked around the auditorium. "Hernán Cortés, I call on you to protect these two men. I have no authority on this side of the wall, so I ask you to take them into protective custody." The Chief thrust the head-bag forward, the weight testing her strong muscles. "Now justice will be served!" With a mighty heave, she threw Blitz out onto the arena floor.

Adam wanted to cry out, to stop the barbarity, but was too concerned about his own survival to risk drawing attention. He closed his eyes in shame as the crowd swarmed around the helpless psychopath – though he still heard the stamping, cracking, and squelching.

"Smear him into oblivion!" Cartimandua shouted. "He will have no golden box and no future!"

"I see you haven't lost your touch, Cartimandua," a man's voice commented from behind Adam. "You were always so skilled at rousing the crowd."

Adam and Cartimandua turned. Walking casually across the stage towards them, a man immaculately attired in a black suit, with gaunt aristocratic features and stylishly coiffured shoulder length black hair, was accompanied by six guards – all wearing the usual red tunics and black trousers, and all brandishing steel sabres.

"Hernán!" Cartimandua said, exhibiting an expression of relief and friendship. "I hope you're here to offer these men your protection."

Cortés strode up and shook Cartimandua's hand:

"The crowd seem satisfied. I will take these men to my suite, as guests rather than prisoners. They will be safe there … for now."

As the famous conquistador and Cartimandua exchanged pleasantries, Adam discerned a quiet intimacy in their expressions. Perhaps, at some time they had been more than friends – he wondered if it was before or after Cartimandua's body change.

"Time to go," Cortés said to Adam and Stardust. "We will leave by the back of the stage. And, please, leave your weapons here. I promise you won't need them."

Obediently, Adam left his blades on the stage floor. One of the guards bound Adam's wounds tightly with medical gauze and helped him to his feet. With three guards closely escorting the cuffed and subdued Stardust, Adam limped freely at the back of the group accompanied by Cortés.

Before exiting the stage, Adam turned and looked back. In a moment of tender telepathy, Cartimandua also looked back, pausing a while before jumping down from the stage to join the crowd. Adam mouthed a grateful 'thank you', and in return, Cartimandua blew Adam a big kiss. Instinctively, he caught the invisible token and held it to his heart. Then, revealing immature sexual confusion, he dropped it to the floor like a hot coal.

A subtle frown crossed Cartimandua's face, enough to convey real hurt. Telling the insistent conquistador to wait a moment, Adam grimaced through the pain of his injuries, bent down and picked up the imaginary kiss – he actually visualised a fragile red rose petal. As he slipped it into his trouser pocket, he noticed Cartimandua already on the arena floor, no longer looking in his direction. Had she seen his feeble attempt at righting a wrong? Did it really matter?

Exiting stage left, Adam realised how close Cartimandua's big blown kiss was to his genitals. On cue, a faint twitch behind his zipper raised an eyebrow. Patting his pocket, Adam told himself this was some involuntary reflex due to the excitement of the day rather than a deep subconscious yearning for the chief.

HERNÁN CORTÉS

A lesson in bygone luxury, Cortés' apartment was a testament to his power over the dark-side. Whilst others huddled together in the hall's foyers and auditorium, or found a relatively comfortable spot alongside the yellow-lit road, the notorious conquistador lived in Victorian splendour – he was, after all, the bringer of bodies and therefore of life.

Adam's wounds were dressed, the deep lacerations cleaned and sealed. Sitting in plushly cushioned leather wingback armchairs, Adam and Stardust faced their saviour. The arched windows of the cosy parlour were obscured by closely drawn blue velvet drapes – although the darkness outside would have offered little in the way of a view. A feast of plated Victorian savouries and sweets, laid out on a round black lacquered table, was as yet untouched.

"A shrewd move, sparing that red haired fellow's life," Cortés said, striking a friendly tone. "He is one of the more influential people on this side of the wall. If your friend had not decided to stick you with his rapier, you might have won over the crowd without Cartimandua's intervention."

"I didn't think another death would impress the crowd," Adam replied quietly, "… other than my own or Stardust's of course. Besides, the man looked healthy, with no sign of the rot. It's not like I would be putting him out of his misery."

"Only a third of the dark-side population are afflicted with that wretched curse. Some people never left after the great catastrophe, and some choose to stay even after gaining a new body. The lifestyle on the dark-side does have a certain attraction, if you like combat training and the absence of light."

"I find it hard to believe anyone would stay here after getting a new body."

"The red haired fellow is an example. If I remember correctly, he won his new body nearly a century ago, but has stayed on. In his first-life, he founded the People's Republic of China. As I said, a very influential individual."

Stardust's eyes immediately lit up and he slapped a hand to his mouth:

"Oh my God, I nearly killed ginger Mao! I nearly killed ginger Mao!"

"Hah, and then you tried to kill your friend, the great Copacabana."

"No he didn't," Adam said. "Stardust was just punishing me. If he had wanted me dead, then we wouldn't be talking now. Although, I'm also sure we wouldn't be talking now if Cartimandua had not arrived when she did."

"She obviously cares about you very much. I couldn't help noticing that you pocketed her kiss. Perhaps the feeling is mutual? She is quite the Adonis these days."

"Err … I don't think it would work out."

"Don't be so cautious, Mr Eden," Cortés said, with a knowing glint in his eye. "Cartimandua is one of the most genuinely passionate souls I have ever met. You are very lucky to have her favour, and I don't just mean because she saved your life."

"I know … it's just that …"

Cortés narrowed his eyes:

"She has the body of a man? Ah, I forget that your world still has the dubious luxury of choice."

"I know some people are into the 'alternative' stuff," Adam explained, face reddening, wishing he could disappear into the cushioning of his chair, "and that's fine by me, but that kind of thing just stresses me out. When it comes to sex and relationships I really, really can't cope with anything … too different."

"We are neither enlightened nor debauched, Mr Eden, if that's what you think. We only have three weeks every forty years to fetch as many bodies as possible from the recycling room. Only bodies that can be repaired are chosen. Even with a full team, we can only bring back a few hundred usable bodies in that time. With thousands rotting, doomed to die, absolutely nobody quibbles about gender, race, or the size of the cock or tits on offer. Frankly, when it comes to intimacy, no one gives a damn anymore about what person-suit they're fucking. You see, where there's no choice, there's no prejudice."

"Oh, I don't know what to think," Adam admitted, exasperated, his head pushed back against the chair.

"Hah," Cortés said, clapping his hands together, "not knowing what to think is a step in the right direction. A small step, but a step nonetheless."

"You seem so friendly, after planning to kill us? I've always imagined you as someone who doesn't change their mind."

"Yes, I am quite intractable. Some might see that as a flaw, but I am inevitably always right so I see no reason to change. Personally, I didn't care either way whether your friends lived or died. However, faced with a few thousand angry prima donnas demanding vengeance, I decided to stand back and let justice take its course. I was dismayed that you accompanied your guilty friends, but that was your choice. I really only took you in because Cartimandua swayed the mob."

"Given your involvement in the body snatching, I thought you would want us to meet."

"Believe me, before yesterday's murderous turn of events, I was planning to meet with you." Cortés' expression suddenly turned to stone. "Now, please excuse me if this sounds flippant, Mr Eden, but exactly why are you here?"

"Err, you already know why," Adam mumbled, caught off guard. "The bodies …"

"If your esteemed Captain and the almighty AI truly have intelligence far beyond the comprehension of normal man, then I am sure they already knew about the bodies and probably even our use for them. We have taken corpses from the conveyors for many, many years

"I'm sure they would have pieced some of it together, but …"

Cortés interrupted, maintaining his pointed momentum:

"Well, my friend, you obviously know what is going on, and we obviously know that you know what is going on, and, to take it further, you are no doubt aware that we know that you know. So, if everyone knows what everyone else knows, then I ask you again, why are you here?"

"Err … the AI relaxed the rules. I … um … guess it decided it was time to investigate … to find out the truth."

Cortés nodded politely, but his expression betrayed his disbelief in Adam's babbled answer. He left his chair and picked up a cut-glass jug filled with a cloudy straw-coloured liquid. Filling two tumblers, he then added some ice cubes and gently stirred the drink with a silver stirrer.

"Victorian style lemonade," he said, handing both guests a glass. "It's not carbonated, but is quite refreshing with ice."

Adam thanked his host and took a large mouthful. Cortés leaned forward:

"So, why are you so interested in Edgar Allen Poe?"

Though mouth puckering, the tart lemonade was no match for Cortés' sharp question. Holding his hand to his mouth, Adam nearly choked.

"Has quite a bite, doesn't it?" Cortés said calmly.

Adam coughed once, and answered hoarsely:

"I never said I was interested in Edgar Allen Poe."

"Cartimandua told me that you asked about Mr Poe when you first arrived."

"I … I asked about a few people. Poe just happened to be one of them."

"You are only alive because of Cartimandua's intervention. I trust her judgement without question and so should you. She trusts me, and if you are wise, you will trust me also. Now, tell me about Mr Poe."

"We have him," Adam admitted.

"Is he alive?"

"He's dead, but I assure you that his death had nothing to do with us. Poe was already dead when we found him. The Captain has preserved his body in some of that goo … like the stuff in the gold boxes."

"Where did you find him? How exactly did he die?"

Adam squirmed in his seat, not really wanting to answer:

"He was crushed and suffocated … inside someone's anus. You know, a full size human anus."

Surprisingly unphased by the shockingly sordid revelation, Cortés simply nodded:

"What was Mr Poe wearing?"

"I think you already know the answer to that question. He was wearing scuba gear … like people use for deep sea diving."

Cortés sat back in his chair, his eyes fixed and penetrating like a spaghetti western gunfighter calculating the exact moment to draw his gun. He reached over to the table and took a walnut. Without breaking his stare, the conquistador dramatically cracked open the shell in in his clenched fist – a well-practised party piece perhaps. After eating a few pieces of the brain shaped nut, Cortés stood up from his chair.

"I doubt you and Stardust can return the way you came," he said, carefully brushing the nut debris into a small metal bin. "There are still many out there, on both sides of the wall, who want you dead. I am sure Cartimandua will go to any lengths to keep you safe, but even her authority has its limits. However, if you are really interested in finding out the truth about Mr Poe, and keeping your heads, then there is perhaps another way."

Encouraging his guests to enjoy the food and drink on offer, but not to leave the parlour, Cortés hastily made his exit. For some time after, Adam and Stardust talked about their host's sudden departure. Concerned about what 'another way' meant, they contemplated making an escape. However, after filling their plates and stomachs with the delicious selection of Victorian savouries – the Scotch Woodcock was especially moreish – they relaxed into their comfortable chairs and ended up reminiscing about their many encounters in the Psychoviro.

Over five hours passed before Cortés returned – with midnight only a couple of hours away. With typical conquistador gusto, he filled a glass with sherry – a nutty brown dry Oloroso – and quaffed it down in one. Placing the empty glass back on the table, he put his hands on his hips and smiled widely:

"Gentlemen, you have a choice. Stay here, and take your chances with your legions of admirers, or come with me."

"Come with you where?" Adam asked.

"I can't tell you, but we shall leave first thing tomorrow morning. Trust me, where you are going is far safer than the dark-side. Also, if you are still so inclined, you can find the truth you are seeking."

"I know you said we should trust you but …"

"Perhaps this will change your mind."

Cortés reached into the inside pocket of his jacket and produced two black wrapped objects. He handed one of the instantly recognisable chocolate bars to each of his guests.

"A Mars bar?" Adam said, inspecting the wrapper.

"Well, what do you think? Interesting, eh?"

Stardust had already ripped open the wrapper and had taken a large bite.

"I haven't had one of these for a few years," he said, chewing slowly. "The way all that caramel, nougat, and chocolate melts together in your mouth is divine. I must put them on the fight-day menu once I get back."

Adam put the Mars bar down on the side-table. He tapped his finger on his lips, inwardly congratulating himself that he had seen through Cortés' scheme

— that the chocolate bar was obviously a lewd metaphor for his sexual confusion over Cartimandua.

"Mmm, they're nice," he said", but I prefer them straight out of the fridge. I like to pick the chocolate off first, and then roll back the caramel."

"No, you missed my point completely! Gentleman, I thought you were smarter than this."

"Look, I know what you're really trying to say," Adam conceded. "This chocolate bar represents Cartimandua's penis. The material used to make this bar is the same material we are all made from. Therefore, what you're saying, rather crudely I might add, is that if I can put this in my mouth and enjoy it, then … oh my God …"

Stardust stopped chewing for a moment, frowned, and then carried on, obviously deciding that the taste of chocolate always trumped any disturbing allusions.

"Hah, Mr Eden, you are so wrong, so very wrong," Cortés said. "However, don't let me shatter your hopes and dreams of edible penises. No, gentlemen, what you are missing is that this confectionary is clearly not Victorian. It should not be available in Reynold's Gardens, but here it is."

"You're saying that this comes from elsewhere?" Adam said, picking up the bar and inspecting the wrapper once more. "Do you have another way into the Viroverse?"

"Not the Viroverse, but there is a place where the usual rules do not apply. Now will you come with me?"

Adam carefully opened the wrapper and took a bite of the Mars bar. Appreciating the creamy taste, he mused:

"Do you really, really think that a chocolate bar we can get from any dispenser back home is going to make us blindly follow you to some secret, probably dangerous destination?"

"Well?" Cortés asked, arms crossed, waiting for an answer.

Adam took another bite and nodded his head:

"I'm in."

"I see absolutely no reason to stay in this awful dark place," Stardust added.

DEATH IS GOLDEN

Toast and marmalade washed down with a cup of milky tea was a quickly snatched breakfast. In a hurry to leave, Cortés was still buttoning his black ruffle collar shirt when he burst into the parlour. With a comfortable groan, Stardust heaved himself out of the soft leather armchair and Adam decided to forgo a slice of perfectly moist Madeira cake.

They followed Cortés along a number of lavishly decorated corridors – red and gold flocked wallpaper and dark-wood wainscoting. A guard stood by a narrow staircase. He saluted sharply and stood aside as the group made their way to the lower level.

They found themselves in a short corridor – utilitarian in appearance with minimal lighting. Cortés opened a door at the end of the corridor and walked through. The dim lights of the corridor were insufficient to illuminate far beyond the doorway. Adam and Stardust tentatively took a few steps into the room and halted, unable to see ahead and still wary of Cortés' intentions. Noticing their unease, the conquistador apologised and flicked a few switches. The lights came on and Adam fell silent, save for a sharp intake of breath.

The huge room, a copy of the arena and stage above, would have impressed anyone for its size alone – the lower ceiling giving the space a far greater appearance of length and breadth. Rows of seats bounded the arena, just a sumptuous as those in the main auditorium above, and soft gas-type lighting lent the large room a feeling of intimacy.

However, no one was taking notice of the premium quality of the furnishings or the cleverly subtle lighting. Filling almost all the arena, nearly two thirds of the way up to the ceiling, a magnificent mountain of gold captured and held the attention. At first, the scene was a blur of brilliant glister, an awe-inspiring fusion of a fantastical Pharaoh's treasure room and a national bullion depository. As shock turned to curiosity, Adam focused, and noticed the mountain's structure of cube-like blocks.

"This is the Brain Bullion Depository," Cortés explained, right on cue, before Adam or Stardust could say a word. "A rather inelegant title, but unfortunately it stuck. Come; step down from the stage and take a closer look. We have a few minutes."

Even though he knew that these were the gold boxes containing the brains of the dead, as Adam jumped down onto the arena floor he still found it hard to believe. The sheer numbers involved were humbling – hundreds of thousands of cubes stacked in one huge mound like the nightmarish progeny of a prolific 8-bit golden goose.

Cortés drew their attention to the nearest part of the pile, pointing out the inscriptions on the sides of four of the cubes – Saloni Mehta, Blaise Pascal, Julius Robert Oppenheimer, and Yedibel son of Nesha: AKA Flamma. Apart from the occupant's name, a storage code, and a first-life date of birth and date of death, the golden boxes were plain and undecorated.

"If it were not for Cartimandua's timely arrival," he said, "I might now be placing your boxes alongside these. You are very lucky."

"Perhaps," Adam said, "or, like Blitz, we would be bloody smears on the arena floor."

"He paid the price for his crimes. Don't expect any sympathy from me."

Adam could not help thinking that Oppenheimer had developed the first atomic bomb, killing hundreds of thousands, and had still earned his golden repose. The scientific genius had said of himself, 'Now I am become death, the destroyer of worlds'. At least Blitz could have pleaded insanity. As usual, mindful of his own survival, Adam kept his thoughts to himself.

"You save people by putting their brains into new bodies," Stardust said, tapping a finger on the top of Saloni's box. "Have you tried pulling the same trick with the ones here?"

"It doesn't work," Cortés replied. "Once the brain is dead, as far as we know there is no bringing it back, and it does not take much for our miniaturised brains to die. We do have excellent medical facilities and skilled practitioners here, but even if the patient is quickly stabilised, or the damage quickly repaired, the brain is dead. Attempts at resuscitation are usually pointless." Cortés took a white handkerchief from his top pocket and polished Stardust's fingerprint from Saloni's box. "Death is golden. This is the best we can do."

"Then how do you transfer the brains of the living to a dead body?" Adam asked.

"I had already been visiting the Viroverse on and off for centuries when the full horror of the rot hit us. The conveyor room was fascinating in the early years, but I was more interested in exploring the environments and maintaining my contacts within the conquistador communities."

"How did you get around? I mean, those corridors all look the same to me. Did you have some sort of mapping tool?"

"Of course I had a digital mapping tool, but I usually used the grid co-ordinates."

Adam looked blankly at Cortés.

"Every intersection has a five symbol code at the base of one of the central downpipes. I find it hard to believe you don't know that. I thought you were a high ranking Terminal official."

"More unofficial, and they don't like sharing information. When it comes to the halls, I'm really just a passenger."

"Hmm, plausible deniability – I would expect nothing less from the Captain. Anyway, once we realised that the rot was fatal and irreversible, using the bodies from the conveyor room was a desperate consideration. By the time the security gate opened again, some fifteen years later, hundreds were already dead. We immediately sent a team to bring back as many bodies as possible."

"But, if there's no resurrection here, why would you think it would work?"

"We didn't think it would work, but we were ready to try anything."

"Couldn't you have sneaked the worst cases into the Viroverse – to hide out with your conquistador friends – to see if they resurrected after death?"

Cortés leant against the arena barrier:

"I took a dear friend of mine to the Viroverse to try just that. Ferdinand Magellan had only days to live. He could hardly walk, but agreed to be our guinea pig. We managed to get him into a Viro – a quaint rural village, not too far from the conveyor room. An hour before midnight, I cut his throat and watched him die." His dark bravado leaving him for a moment, Cortés hesitated before continuing, as if supressing a choke of sadness. "When I awoke the next morning, he was still a corpse. We brought Magellan's body back to the gardens and the painters agreed to gold box his brain."

"Many centuries ago, I also lost a good friend," Adam admitted, remembering Manny. "Cut his own throat. Stupid sod wanted to die."

Cortés nodded in understanding, regaining his composure:

"Once we got the conveyor room bodies back to the Gardens, the painters did their best to repair any physical damage. A few heroic souls volunteered to be the first recipients. They knew it was a long shot. Even the most optimistic amongst us had huge doubts, but it was their only chance."

"But it obviously worked."

"The first attempts were a complete failure. The brain transfers were conducted half an hour before midnight with three painters per procedure. The next morning, the new bodies were gone, and the dead brains back in their original dead bodies. Most of the painters were too distraught to continue. They were far too sensitive to cope with their culpability in the killing."

"But ... somehow you ...."

"I gathered a few seasoned warriors, those who had no qualms with dealing death, even to innocents, and we threatened to slit the throat of any painter who refused to carry out their duties." Cortés offered a wry smile. "Claude Monet refused. I still remember his unruffled obstinacy, striding out, claiming he had an important appointment with a bottle of lightly chilled Sauternes and a bowl of bananas and cream. I sent a couple of men to follow him, with orders to kill him if he refused to return. I made sure the other painters heard me say that."

"Well, unless I met Claude Monet's lesser known twin brother, he came back."

"He still refused, so my men held him captive, out of sight, until the others finished their duties. I never intended to kill anyone, but a touch of mortal fear goes a long way."

Cortés took a walkie-talkie out of his pocket and stared at it a moment, as if impatient to receive a message. Shaking his head, he held the device down by his side.

"Well, that night," he continued, "we found the answer through a fortunate accident. One of the teams of painters, led by the meticulous Kano Eitoku, was squabbling over who should transfer the final brain to the waiting body. It was only a few minutes before midnight and everyone was tired, tempers frayed. Somehow, we lost track of time and the pre-midnight search for a comfortable resting place began to take hold. As you know, you can't fight the urge, but Kano had the presence of mind to scoop the detached brain out of its skull. With only a few seconds left, he lined up the shot and lobbed the brain over to the new body. Even though I was in the process of settling into a rather comfortable armchair, I cheered as the brain plopped neatly inside of the empty skull – a perfect shot."

"And, the next morning?"

"Leif Erikson, the Icelandic explorer, and another good friend of mine, was back to his usual pig-headed self, but now in the body of a lithesome Latino woman. You should see his gorgeous legs." Cortés smiled devilishly, running his hand through the air in a stroking motion.

"Maybe you should introduce him to Cartimandua," Adam said. "I'm sure they could work something out."

"I'm sure they could," Cortés replied. "Perhaps I should set up a threesome for you. Anyhow, we had discovered how to transfer brains into a new body. The old body was gone and whatever systems operated after midnight had healed the new body perfectly. Our only remaining problem is that we can't get enough bodies to save everyone. With the security gate open for less than a month every forty years, we expect to lose thousands before any more bodies become available."

Stardust shuddered as if stung by a sudden chill, and clasped his arms around his chest:

"That's a lot of golden boxes. And, it's so deathly quiet. How long do we have to stay here?"

As if in answer to Stardust's unease, a quiet male voice issued from Cortés' walkie-talkie:

"All clear, Hernán. Guaranteed clear for the next five minutes."

Cortés thanked the man and put the walkie-talkie back in his pocket.

"Time to go, gentlemen," he said. "Follow me. As you just heard, we only have a few minutes."

Offstage left, hidden behind an embroidered heavy red curtain, a brass wall light illuminated a dark blue double door. Cortés handed out black velvet capes with cowls that hung on a neat row of hooks. After putting on his cape, the infamous conquistador took a rope and belt combination from one the hooks.

Fastening the belt around his waist, he told Adam and Stardust to take hold of the rope:

"When I open the door, there will be no talking until we reach our destination. Silence is essential. Keep hold of the rope, stay behind me, and obey my instructions." He pulled the cowl over his head. "There's total darkness out there and it's all too easy to get lost or have an unfortunate … accident." Quietly turning the handle, Cortés opened the door.

Like evil monks heading for a dark ceremony, cowls pulled over their heads, long capes flowing to the ground, they headed out into the Gardens. Without the light of the yellow orbs, the view was pitch-black. Adam opened and closed his eyes, blinking to become accustomed to the dark, but there was no point. The saying went that 'in the kingdom of the blind, the one eyed man is king'. Here, in this impenetrable darkness, that one eye held no such advantage.

Cortés led the way, with Adam and Stardust holding tight onto the cord, keeping as close as possible. Now and then, the conquistador offered quiet instructions, such as to halt, take two steps sideways to the right, and move forward again. Turning to face a new direction was a more intimate experience, with Cortés telling his rope slaves to hug together and swivel as one.

The most troubling part of the dark journey occurred when Cortés called another halt. He told Adam and Stardust to get down onto their hands and knees and detach themselves from the cord. Hesitantly, they complied.

"On my signal, I want you to crawl slowly forward," Cortés whispered. "Do not raise your heads or attempt to stand until you bump into me. Now, wait for my signal."

A few seconds later, Cortés told Adam and Stardust to start moving. The ground was gravelly, a pathway perhaps. Small bits of stone stuck to the palms of their hands and dug into their knees, making for very uncomfortable progress. The real worry came from not knowing what was above them. It might just be the low boughs of a tree, but it could also be a huge precariously balanced ruin from the great catastrophe. Perhaps Cortés had cut the umbilical cord and abandoned them to the perpetual black, leaving them surrounded by unseen dangers. In the dark, there was no way of knowing, and Adam fought hard to keep his natural negativity at bay.

Adam kept his arm outstretched throughout the ordeal and breathed a sigh of relief as he felt the supple leather of Cortés' boot. The conquistador grasped Adam's hand firmly and heaved him to his feet. Stardust was close behind, and soon they were again holding onto the rope, sightlessly shuffling towards the unknown destination. Such was their disorientation, that it would not have surprised Adam if they suddenly found themselves standing outside Gordon's Hall.

"Stop, gentlemen, we're here," Cortés said.

"And, where is exactly is here?" Stardust asked. "You could have at least brought a torch with you."

"Portable lights are forbidden in the dark-side. Currently, we are standing a few feet from the northern safety wall. Directly in front of us is a park bench, so I suggest we sit down and rest awhile."

They fumbled their way onto the wide bench, taking care not to inadvertently sit on each other's laps. Adam sat back, relaxed, and stared into the void. The journey to this point had only taken a couple of hours, but his body ached from the constant tension of wondering whether he was about to walk face first into something hard or trip over.

"The wall is right behind us," Cortés said. "Cuts us off from the beachfront and the apartments. This is why living space is at such a premium."

Adam reached out behind him and touched the cold metal wall:

"So, what's on the other side? Is it ruined like the rest of the Gardens? You obviously know, or we wouldn't be sitting here."

"Oh, you'll find out soon enough."

Only a few minutes passed before Adam heard Cortés slip off the bench. The faint sound of metal against metal near his feet was perhaps the application of a tool – a spanner seemed likely.

"What are you doing," Adam asked, as Cortés brushed against his legs.

"Releasing the latch," he replied. "Sit still for a moment."

Cortés grunted, as if straining with something, and the bench slid forward. A faint light suddenly illuminated the area around the bench. Adam and Stardust stood up to see what their host had uncovered. A three-foot opening behind the bench, ten-foot wide along the wall, was filled with water, with soft light filtering through the lightly rippling surface. Even with little light, Adam discerned a floor gently sloping, disappearing under the security wall.

"What's down there?" he asked.

"We are at the western extremity of the Gardens." Cortés explained. "The twelfth apartment block is directly behind the wall. This is a subway that runs under the wall and the building. It comes out at the promenade. It's the only way through to the other side. We keep it hidden just in case anyone manages to make it to this spot. It's vital we keep people in the dark."

"Hmm, but the other safety wall has a doorway through the wall, even though it's blocked, and that hole they put the head-bags through."

"They are both completely blocked on this wall. The people on the other side saw to that soon after the Great Catastrophe."

"People? You mean there are people alive on the other side?"

With a dramatic flourish of his cape, his face a shadow beneath his cowl, Cortés pointed at the opening:

"The answers you seek lie at the other end of this tunnel. I'm afraid that now you know about this place, you cannot go back. Oh, and cast away any ideas you might have of threatening me. As we speak, there are four crossbows trained on you. My men are wearing night vision goggles and would love to bring you down – Flamma is sorely missed."

Adam looked down at the water.

"Do I have your word that this won't end in our deaths?"

"I don't want you dead. However, I cannot guarantee the hospitality of those on the other side, even though they are very interested in meeting you."

"Is the subway completely flooded?"

"Yes, it's totally flooded – a rather effective defensive measure. The subway is just over 60 metres long, but a good lungful of air is enough. You'll find there are ropes with hand-loops on each sidewall. The people at the other end will pull you through – there's a pulley system. Just relax and head for the light at the end of the tunnel."

"That's been my aim for forever," Adam said, forcing a smile. "Not reached it yet."

Stardust, worried, clasped his hand against his chest:

"We don't have to strip off, do we? There's been far too much nakedness in this place."

"I usually go through fully clothed," Cortés admitted. "Though, those boots you're wearing might be a bit heavy. Your choice, but either way I don't think you have anything to worry about."

A couple of minutes more deliberation, Adam, and Stardust stepped down into the cool water fully clothed, including glam platform boots. Cortés warned that he would push back the bench once they were under the wall. There would be no turning back. Waist high in the water, Stardust stopped a moment, carefully removed his white wig and stuffed it down the front of his black shirt.

"I'm going to drown," he sobbed, grabbing Adam's arm. "I'm going to get caught on something. You'll try in vain to save me, and then I'm dead, lifeless, slowly floating by with that pale puffy face, mouth slightly parted … and those eyes, those hollow staring eyes."

"You'll be fine. If anyone gets caught on anything it will be me."

"Oh, Copa, you must have seen all of those films where the survivors have to swim through a flooded tunnel. Some poor soul always dies. Now, I may be fabulous, but let's be honest; I'm the secondary character here. This is your mission. We have lost someone at almost every twist in the road … and I'm next."

Adam shrugged off Stardust's hand:

"Well, then you stay here and let Cortés' men use you for target practice."

Reluctantly, Stardust took a big gulp of air, slipped under the water, and disappeared under the safety wall. Adam followed, keeping to other side. Fortunately, the rope straps were conveniently highlighted with a big red arrow on the subway wall.

Adam tightened the leather strap around one of his wrists and held tightly onto the rope. Some feet behind, a dull thud indicated that Cortés had slid the bench back over the entrance. Holding his breath, heart pounding with anticipation, Adam looked over to Stardust on the other side of the subway. The psychopath, clinging desperately to the rope, had his eyes closed.

Slowly, the rope began to move. A few seconds later and Adam was rushing at speed through the salty water. Thoroughly exhilarating, the experience could have been a wild Waterpark ride. He fought to keep his eyes open to see what was waiting up ahead. The light was steadily growing, the end nearing.

Squinting, Adam could make out a group of blurry figures ahead. The rope ride stopped about 10 feet from the ramp. Adam quickly unstrapped himself from the leather tether. Before he could swim away, two bronzed muscular men in colourful Speedos swam up to help – or so Adam naturally assumed.

The first swimmer held up a small torch. He clicked it on, dazzling Adam with an unexpectedly powerful light. Meanwhile, the other swimmer clamped something around Adam's right leg. As his eyes recovered, lungs hungry for oxygen, the swimmers were already heading back up the ramp.

Desperate for air, Adam began swimming towards the light. He only got a few feet before something held him back. Twisting in the water, Adam noticed a wide padded plastic shackle on his leg, attached to a lightweight grey cord. Frantically, he pulled at the cord, which was fixed to a large flat concrete slab on the subway floor. In his panic, Adam had no time to wonder whether Cortés knew this was going to happen.

Lungs almost bursting, mouth obstinately shut despite wishing to take a deep breath, Adam finally gave up the struggle. He gazed up towards the top of the ramp, and the cruel promise of sweet, sweet air. The swimmers stood in a relaxed posture, simply watching.

Adams last conscious vision, causing him to gasp in a lethal lungful of salt water, was the sight of Stardust, floating lifeless above his own concrete slab, face pale and puffy, mouth slightly parted … with those hollow staring eyes.

BEACH OF MY FATHERS

A dam slowly opened his eyes. Usually, after death, he would simply wake up and leap out of bed. However, without the pain and suffering of the dark place, the transitional realm between life and death, he was not sure whether he had died. His last recollection was of daylight at the top of the ramp and encountering two swimmers.

Looking around the small dark unfurnished room, he noticed Stardust huddled by the wall, shivering and quietly whimpering. Taking a risk, Adam put his arm around the highly volatile psychopath.

"It's Ok, Stardust, we're alive," Adam said, increasingly sure that death and resurrection had taken place. "They have resurrection. Cortés should have told us, but …"

"How come you're so calm?" Stardust asked, his voice shaking. "The dark place … the …?"

Reluctantly, Adam decided to tell the truth:

"Somehow, I automatically block out any memories of the dark place. For me it's almost as if it never happened. It's been so long since I've felt the fear that I forget how it affects others."

"Then … then how did we die? Last thing I remember was swimming up to the light. I saw these men in skimpy swimming trunks."

"Same here. Perhaps we drowned. At least we've resurrected in our clothes."

For the next few minutes, they theorised about the manner of their deaths until the only feature in the room, a single door, suddenly opened. Three figures, briefly silhouetted against a harsh light, walked in, slamming the door behind them. Two of the men, barely discernible in the dark, moved forward brandishing swords. The third man knelt down next to Adam:

"There is no danger," the man said with notably superior enunciation. "I guarantee that you will come to no harm. Please, take these."

The man handed out black wraparound sunglasses and small blue phials – recognisable to all Viroverse residents as combatting the negative symptoms of resurrection. Stardust immediately drank the liquid in the phial and slipped on the sunglasses – coincidently, the shades were his preferred style. For forms sake, not wishing to explain his immunity to the effects of the dark place, Adam also drank the liquid and put on the shades. The man stood and waited patiently for a couple of minutes before introducing himself.

"Welcome to West Beach, Mr Eden, Stardust. I am Dylan Thomas. These fine gentlemen with the fluorescent t-shirts and sharp swords are my bodyguards:

Owain Glyndwr and Llewelyn." Llewelyn nudged Dylan. "Llewelyn the Great," Dylan added. "We must never forget how great he is."

Growing accustomed to the dim light, Adam found his captors' clothing bewildering. Owen and Llewellyn wore scuffed stonewashed jeans and lime green t-shirts, whilst Dylan Thomas sported a short sleeved pastel pink shirt and beige cargo shorts – to Adam's horror, they all wore open toed leather sandals.

"How did we die?" Adam asked, showing absolutely no deference. "We did die, didn't we?"

"We had to kill you, I'm afraid," Dylan admitted. "Nothing personal, you understand. Standard practice. This way we get to meet you completely on our own terms. Also, there were a few people I needed to consult."

Adam helped Stardust to his feet.

"So, how did we die?"

"Oh, we drowned you," Dylan said. "We shackled you to concrete slabs under water. You see, if you had somehow swum back under the wall, then you would not have been resurrected."

Stardust straightened his wig:

"Oh, so nice to know you care."

"Believe me when I say that I really do care," Dylan said. "Well, gentlemen, let's not linger. I think it's time I introduced you to West Beach. I'm sure you don't want to spend all day in this stifling little storage shed. Best you keep wearing the shades though. It is rather bright out there." He opened the door.

Compared to the gloomy twilight shadow world of the eastern Gardens, West Beach was genuinely dazzling. Enticingly paradisiacal, a beach of white sand gave way to an azure sea. Set back from the paved promenade, which teemed with crowds of colourfully dressed people, the light-honey stone of the gothic apartment blocks shimmered under the bright sun. Obviously not limited to conservative Victorian Attire, the residents of West Beach favoured light beachwear – shorts, slacks, sandals, t-shirts, and a noticeable prevalence of floral Hawaiian shirts.

"Oh my God, it's the planet of the Copas!" Stardust declared, immediately feeling out of place in his black glam finery. "Hmm, it's making me feel quite prickly all over."

Adam nodded, also taken aback by the vibrant scenes:

"Well, this place certainly seems untouched by the catastrophe."

"We consider ourselves most fortunate to be trapped on West Beach," Dylan said.

Somewhat breaking the enchanting spell was the slab grey of the eastern safety wall, cutting across the promenade, beach, and sea like the side of a giant battleship. Adam knew that the other safety wall to the dark-side stood to the south, fortunately hidden from view by the nearest apartment block.

Stardust twisted around, staring at a man walking away from a nearby snack kiosk.

"Err … was that Tom Jones?" he asked.

"The Welsh do seem well-represented here," Adam said.

Urging his guests to follow him along the promenade, Dylan offered an explanation:

"On the day of the Great Catastrophe, we were holding the bi-annual Eisteddfod. Taliesin the Bard was standing on a raft just off the shore, reciting his famous 'Ode to the Twilight Sea', when the earthquake struck. The buildings suffered light damage, and a few people were injured, but nothing compared to the rest of the Gardens."

"So, is everyone Welsh?" Adam asked.

"There are quite a few of us, and we do hold a special place even after all these years, but we are still only a small minority. You know, it was the first time we held the Eisteddfod on the beach. Before then, we used The Grand Reynold's Hall, but the organisers fancied a change of scenery."

"Woah, good call. Have you seen the dark-side?"

"Hernán keeps us well informed. He is our man on the other side. After the wall came down, he volunteered to find out what was going on in the rest of the Gardens. He returned quickly and advised us to block the doorway and the hatch – to wait until things got back to normal."

"But they never did."

"One day, perhaps. Until then, we do what we can to keep Hernán on the throne."

Seeing that West Beach was clearly a place of plenty, almost totally unscathed by the ravages of the Great Catastrophe, Adam wondered why its fortunate citizens were allowing the dark-side to suffer.

"If you are fully resourced and have resurrection, why don't you help those poor buggers on the other side of the wall? There are thousands dying."

"We could lose everything we have," Dylan admitted curtly, as if countering a well-worn criticism. "It is believed that all the problems are linked to resource levels. Until they return to normal, we would be foolish to reveal ourselves."

"But, with all the deaths, I was under the impression that resource levels were fine. There are no problems with the dispensers in the rest of the Gardens."

"Look, tomorrow we will go upstairs and everything will be explained. Tesla is very eager to hear about Edgar Allen Poe. However, now is not the time."

"Upstairs?"

Dylan pointed out to sea. Both Adam and Stardust were surprised not to have already noticed the extremely out-of-place feature. Some two miles out, a dark, twisted branch emerged from the surface of the glittering sea. Natural and wood-like, the length of the branch carried on up into the blue sky, before finally disappearing into the clouds.

"That is the root," Dylan explained. "We think the base of the facility was damaged during the catastrophe. This force of nature found its way through, and finally broke the surface of the sea about 200 years ago. It kept growing until it pushed its way through the ceiling beyond the clouds. That was nearly 80 years ago. You could see it as our very own fairy-tale beanstalk."

"You mean it broke through to the outside?" Adam asked. "Does it lead to the outside?"

"No, and we keep it trimmed now. The large hole it has created allows us access to a quasi-maintenance level above the ceiling. We use suspended baskets to travel up and down. About a third of our population stay up there long term – mainly scientists and engineers, but others too. I am supposed to have some oversight, so I visit once a week. Over the years, we have gained some technical control over the Gardens. We have adjusted the dispensers in West Beach to dispense items from any era, not just that dull Victorian crap. In time, we hope to return all of Reynold's Gardens to full functionality."

"Including resurrection?"

"A long term goal, and unfortunately it will come too late for those poor souls afflicted by the rot, but Tesla swears it's possible. Man's an absolute genius. I've never known him to be wrong." Dylan frowned. "Well, once maybe."

Walking further along the promenade, they attracted attention from passers-by, obviously surprised to see new faces. They stopped by an ornate Victorian bandstand, which stood proudly on a semi-circular section of promenade that jutted out onto the beach. Adam leant against the lacy iron fretwork of the bandstand.

"You know, your voice isn't what I expected," he said to Dylan.

"And, what exactly did you expect?" Dylan answered, crossing his arms.

"Well, it's just that you have a really, really … posh accent. I don't mean to be insulting or anything."

"I have been told that my voice is smooth, rich, and clear. If that's what you mean by posh, then it is no insult. I have always spoken like this, even in my first-life. Good enunciation is key. What is the point of speaking misheard mumbled words?" Dylan gently wagged his finger as if emphasising his point. "Of course, there are those that speak clearly yet have very little to say, and also those that say little that others wish to hear. You see, I believe that erudition and elocution live along the same lane. Those who desire true success should spend time at both houses. One will only take you so far."

"And, you visited both?"

"I like to think so. Look, I do not want to seem rude, but I have a few errands to run, so you will have to excuse me for a while. Llewelyn the Great and Owen will act as your bodyguards. They'll stay at a discreet distance, so feel free to explore West Beach. Everything is operational, including the lifts and toilets. If you need anything, then just ask one of the android servants. They are the good-looking ones in the white shirts and black ties."

After shaking Adam and Stardust's hands, Dylan headed off along the crowded promenade and into the nearest apartment block.

"Fancy a drink," Adam asked Stardust after just a moment's thought.

"Maybe another time," Stardust said. "I think I will find some shade. This sun is far too bright for me, and the people seem so ... happy."

Noticing a number of tables with colourful parasols scattered about the beach, each hosting a group of people engaged in busy conversation or just relaxing under the sun, Adam asked a nearby android if there were any free.

"Of course, Sir," the android replied. "And, would you like a drink ... or maybe two?"

"Two drinks sounds fine. Tequila Sunrises; I want to get into the spirit of the beach."

A few minutes later, another android appeared, skilfully carrying a table, four chairs, and a parasol with one arm, whilst balancing a small tray with the two cocktails and a bowl of mixed snacks with the other. Adam followed the android out onto the beach; the fine white sand felt soft underfoot. Finding the perfect spot, a good walk from the bandstand and only twenty feet from the gently rolling surf, the android set up the furniture and then bade Adam farewell.

Adam relaxed into his chair, sucked at his cocktail, and lazily took in the beach-life. He quickly realised that freedom and enjoyment were paramount on the West Beach. Rollicking in the shallows, a group of naked pleasure seekers played volleyball, whilst nearby, a man lay sleeping on the sand next to a small stack of empty lager cans – an early start, even by Adam's standards. However, most revealing was the casual acceptance of this behaviour by others on the beach. Here, there were no judgemental stares or muttered distaste. Everyone just got on with the business of having a great day.

It was at this moment, a rare moment of profound revelation, that Adam saw the contrasts and similarities with his first-life experiences as a down-and-out. Instead of a moody slate grey sky with cold rain lashing down, here was a bright blue vista with ethereal white clouds and warm sunlight. The deliciously refreshing Tequila Sunrise would have no doubt been a syrupy can of Tennant's Super or a plastic bottle of acid sharp White Lightning cider. In addition, the colourful striped parasol, a soft haven from the midday sun, was the paradise equivalent of the dark dirty space under a hedge that he often used as shelter.

Everything about this moment was the cheery mirror image of his squalid first-life experiences. Now, for the first time, Adam understood the real reason behind the Aloha clothing, chosen by the Viroverse AI all those centuries ago. Many had speculated about the meaning of the colourful ensemble – a connection perhaps to Miami drug gangs, all the way to his father's constant assertion that Adam had not left 'the closet' – but now the answer was obvious.

Lazing on a recliner under a warm sun, next to cool waters, with a delicious cocktail to hand, was Adam's true calling – a life he always aspired to, yet never truly tasted. Lounging drunkenly by the river, back in the Viro, was a pale imitation of this life, attracting nothing but disapproving stares and negative gossip. Here, he just blended in with the scenery. It seemed that the only difference between being taken for a down-and-out or a child of paradise was simply a matter of location. Adam leant back and spent the next few hours comfortably dozing.

"You fit this place like a pampered foot in a comfortable cotton sock," Dylan said, taking Adam by surprise. "You already have that perfect recliner slouch – excellent slump of the shoulders and a nonchalant tilt of the head. Some people are born to relax by the beach."

Pulling up a deck chair, Dylan sat opposite Adam, yawning as he got comfortable.

"Two of my great aunts retired to the Costa Blanca," Adam said. "After all these years, I still remember visiting them as a child and playing on the beach. I tried to get a suntan – ended up with sunburn."

"Ah, so as a mere babe you soaked up the spirit of Spain – Toreros and flamenco – the land of torrid romance and high drama."

Adam chuckled, shaking his head:

"Well, it was more a full English breakfast at Sandy's Cafe and watching the karaoke at the Britannia Pub. My Uncle Dave let me have a shandy."

"Ah, the public house, our gift to the world – horse brasses, fat arses, a game of darts, and old man's farts. I'll wager it was a bitter shandy. Oh, and now I am thirsty. I should never venture this far out on the beach without a drink."

"It wasn't all British," Adam said defensively – these were those rare fond memories in a lifetime of hurt, and not to be criticised or shattered. "Auntie Kath cooked me paella back at the villa, although I think it was a ready meal from the freezer. We even listened to a CD of Matt Munro singing some Spanish classics while we played cards. Oh, and Uncle Dave bought me a red sombrero to wear on the plane."

"Well, despite, or maybe because of, your holidays in Llareggub Del Sol, you have definitely caught the spirit of the beach. Why don't you stay? I'm afraid I can only promise you 365 days a year of paradise."

"You know, if it was just about me, I would give it some thought."

"Stardust is also welcome to stay."

"He can't."

"Adam, you sound like an over-protective father. Let your son run free. Let him romp and gambol across the sands."

"If he stays, you will have to kill him. Stardust can seem normal for a short while, friendly even, but he's an irredeemable psychopath." Adam pointed towards the bandstand. "I mean, look at him."

Crouching awkwardly on the sand under the wide lip of the promenade, Stardust appeared as a glossy black insect seeking shade from the Sun.

"We are not stupid, you know," Dylan said, his tone suddenly serious. "We know who he really is, and what he did in his first-life. Why not give the man a chance? You'll be surprised the difference a few days at the beach can make."

"He can't change," Adam insisted. "People will die. I know you have resurrection here, but death is still something you should avoid."

"Let me be straight with you, Adam. I like you, and I think you might make good company, but you can't leave here alive. Nobody leaves. We can't risk it. Nobody can know what we have here."

"That sounds like a threat."

"For now, it's a genuine invitation. Please don't make up your mind just yet. Wait until you've seen upstairs. Oh, and you are invited to join me later on. We have something of a beach tradition that I think you'll enjoy."

Adam gulped down the rest of his drink:

"Does it involve a five-minute head start before you hunt us down? Or, do we have to fight your champion?"

"Not everything involves killing, Adam," Dylan said wearily. "Besides, if I had intended sarcasm, then you would have surely noticed the inflection in my wonderful voice."

THOSE PERFECT MOMENTS

Adam woke up to someone shaking his shoulder. He rubbed his eyes and yawned, sitting up in the comfortable recliner. Llewelyn and Owain Glyndwr stood patiently with Stardust – the Welsh princes' fluorescent lime green t-shirts, and Stardust's glitter ensemble were a challenging sight for tired eyes. Adam, for once, felt quite plainly dressed.

"And, what can I do for you fine gentlemen?" Adam asked. "I guess it is time for that thing Dylan told me about?"

The beach was far busier than earlier, with people sitting all around, their faces excited. Trudging across the sand, the group made their way to the centre of West Beach, close to the bandstand. The bright daylight had given way to early twilight, with vibrant streaks of lava orange and red painting the greying clouds of early evening.

"Hah, what timing!" Dylan said upon seeing Adam. "If you will excuse me, I shall leave you for a brief moment. I need to stand at the shoreline and gift my piss to the Gods of the surf."

"Does he always talk like that?" Adam asked Llewelyn as Dylan strolled whistling across the sand.

"Usually," Llewelyn said. "I think he's actually holding back a bit, probably because he wants to make a good impression. You see, we don't get many new faces round here."

Dylan returned a few minutes later and sat back down beside Adam. By now, it seemed the entire population was gathered on the beach, as if waiting for something. Some distance away, Adam noticed android waiters busily working their way through the crowds. Each carried a small bucket and a shoulder bag. Soon, one of the waiters approached Dylan's group and handed out tiny paper cups from his bag.

"What's all this about," Adam asked, receiving a cup – only slightly bigger than a thimble. "Are we going to toast something?"

"We do this nearly every night," Dylan replied as the waiter carefully tipped a spoon of liquid into his cup.

After receiving his own portion of the mystery liquid, Adam looked at Dylan for answers.

"Drink it down in one go," Dylan advised. "Don't worry, it's perfectly harmless."

Adam sniffed the creamy white liquid suspiciously, picking up a resinous aniseed note.

"What is it?"

"It is the sap from the root. We collect some every day."

"So, what does it do? Is it drugs? I was never one for hard drugs."

"As I said, it's totally harmless. It induces lovely visions – daydreams. I originally named it 'the milk from under the wood', although it never caught on. Now we just call it Root Juice. All you have to do is lie down and enjoy the experience, and I absolutely guarantee you will enjoy it."

Deciding to trust his amiable host, Adam downed the Root Juice in one swallow – extremely bitter and quite mouth puckering, the thick liquid was obviously not favoured for its flavour. He placed the empty paper cup on the sand, settled back, his head resting on the plump cushion, and anxiously waited for the effects of the drug to kick in.

Taking his cue from Adam, Stardust also drank the juice:

"If this goes bad, Copa, then I am holding you responsible. Oh, there will be consequences. There will be serious consequences."

It took little more than two minutes before Adam heard the first popping noise, accompanied by a sudden bright light, like a flash from a camera. More popping noises and flashes followed. Soon Adam's vision was covered with exploding white dots, increasing in number and concentration until resembling the effervescence of a highly carbonated drink.

The dots gradually blended in to each other, creating a moving image. Adam sensed water all around him, and his body moving energetically. He looked ahead, and saw the smiling face of his father.

"Kick those legs, Adam," Harry urged. "Keep those arms moving. You're doing great."

His awareness sharpened, Adam realised he was in the local leisure centre, in the big pool, learning to swim. Bobbing backwards, Harry had the proud expression of a young father making a positive difference to his son's life. Keeping pace by his side, his mother, Edna, gave her vocal and physical support:

"If you keep this up, Adam, they will pick you for the Olympic swimming team. You'll be the next Duncan Goodhew."

Edna kept a hand under Adam's stomach, supporting him in the water. Every now and then, she gently lowered her hand, allowing him to sink or swim. When he began to struggle, thrashing about as he began to sink, she pushed him back up. Adam responded with an extra effort every time he felt the hand let go, confident that his parents would come to his rescue should he fail.

Three widths later, about 12 feet from the side of the pool, Adam felt the hand let go once more. This time was different. This time, he kept an even rhythm. This time he was finally swimming unaided. Harry moved aside as Adam thrust forward his hand, allowing his son to grab the smooth lip of the pool edge.

Edna immediately scooped up the proud four year old in her arms, and hugged him close. Harry punched a fist in the air and let out a whoop, causing everyone else in the pool to look over. Adam laughed and cheered. He knew he would get his promised reward, a double 99 with strawberry topping and two flakes, but in truth, the pure joy of this moment was reward enough.

The image popped out of existence, and the enlarging effervescence began anew. Over time, a succession of memories appeared and disappeared: long, short, from various stages in his first-life, but all were happy and uplifting. Vivid, and engaging all his senses, the memories seemed real. Adam lost all sense of time and place, not knowing where or when he truly was. Another sea of dots filled his vision, and quickly coalesced into another memory.

The slowly rotating mirror ball cast rays of coloured light across the dark school hall. A petition, requesting that the Winter Disco be renamed the Winter Rave was thrown out – Mr Barnes, head of the maths department and perennial school DJ, would not be moved by the transient winds of fashion. At this moment, the packed hall echoed to the pounding hip house sound of The Shaman's 'Ebeneezer Goode'. Four years of teenagers enthusiastically did their best to appear easy with the shapes and moves – the younger ones wearing themselves out, the sixteen year olds trying to appear casual. Many grinned, aware of the drug connotations of the song, chuckling to themselves that 'Barnsy' did not have a clue.

The song ended, and Adam staggered sweating to the side of the hall next to the climbing bars, and flopped into a plastic chair. His friends, Dave and Carl, parked themselves either side. They all relaxed as the first slow song came on – 'Goodnight Girl' by Wet Wet Wet, beckoning the brave to make their romantic move, and signalling that the disco was nearly over.

"Do you think we should go now?" Dave said, pulling his dayglow orange baseball cap round to face the right way.

"May as well, "Adam decided, running his hand through his sweat matted hair. "We can stop by 'Fai's Fryer' and get a bag of chips."

"I might get a battered sausage," Carl said, as they stood up to leave.

Adam turned and found himself face to face with Amanda Doyle.

"You're Adam, aren't you?" she said. "Mark didn't want to come out tonight, and I want a slow dance. One song will do."

With anyone else, Adam might have mumbled an excuse to leave – the thought of a slow dance with a girl was a terrifying prospect, even if planned for. Amanda Doyle, beautiful, always cheerful, was the undisputed Queen of Adam's year, and not someone you could easily refuse. She looked at Adam with her soft hazel eyes, her full lips curved into a warm hint of a smile. He could not say no.

His heart pounding, surroundings a blur, Adam took Amanda's hand and walked back onto the dance floor. If his friends were complaining or perhaps even egging him on, he was too focused on his dance partner to notice. Stopping near the centre of the hall, Amanda put her arms around Adam's shoulders and he put his around her waist. Like all those around them, they gently rocked from side to side, and slowly turned around and around, roughly in time with the music.

Taking a chance, knowing that Amanda's boyfriend, Mark, tended to resolve matters with fists rather than words, Adam dared to rest his head on Amanda's shoulder. A clean fragrant bloom of aqueous melon with ethereal floral notes immediately pampered his sense of smell – no doubt, the latest in fashionable perfumery, since Amanda Doyle would wear nothing less. She reciprocated, nuzzling her head on his shoulder, and he thanked the Universe that it was on the side of his neck without the resident family of zits.

They rotated and hugged under the dreamy kaleidoscopic lighting for another minute as the end of the song drew near. Adam wished they could keep dancing, hoping that this might be an extended 12-inch remix. He was only now beginning to relax, to really enjoy and appreciate this magical moment.

A thudding noise followed by a high-pitched scratchy whine abruptly ended the song. Adam and Amanda let go of one another and looked up at the stage. Mr Barnes spoke smoothly into the microphone:

"Sorry about that, boys and girls. And, no, that wasn't me showing off my scratchin' skills. I bumped into the turntable reaching for my sandwich. Let's spin that one again."

The opening strains of 'Goodnight Girl' once again echoed around the hall. With a smile, Amanda grabbed Adam and pulled him close:

"I said one song will do. This is still that song."

Barnsy was now, officially, a God – a divine bestower of miracles. From this moment forth, Adam vowed he would no longer mock the newly deified maths teacher or misbehave in his lessons. Thanks to Mr Barnes clumsiness, Adam spent the next four minutes in a state of exquisite ecstasy.

The song finally ended and they lazily lifted their heads from one another's shoulders. Before Adam could react, Amanda kissed him full on the lips – her lips as soft and moist as the rumours suggested. For a tantalising fraction of a second, Adam felt the probing push of her tongue against his lips. Stunned by the unexpected move, his lips remained obstinately shut, as if afflicted by selective rigamortis. Forever after, Adam wondered how far the kiss would have taken him if only he had been more relaxed.

Amanda backed away. Her kind-hearted parting expression said, 'it could never go further than this', but that, 'this was a special moment for me as well'. She waved with a little cuff of her fingers, and joined a few of her friends waiting by the exit.

David and Carl clapped and nodded approvingly as Adam returned. The beaming smile on his face was not born of triumph but of a blissful daze.

"You, my friend, are going to tell us everything on the way to Fai's," David said, shaking Adam's hand.

"Gentlemen, Fai's awaits," Adam announced regally. "Tonight, I feel like celebrating. It might cost a bit more, but I fancy trying something different. Think I'll have that chilli cheeseburger everyone's been raving about."

A final white flash and a loud pop and Adam found himself back on the beach, staring up at a starlit sky. Propping himself up on his elbows, he coughed – his mouth and throat were parched. Dylan, sitting patiently next to his bewildered guest, handed over a frosty can of Carlsberg lager.

"I usually go for a bitter, myself," he said, "but there's nothing like a cold lager to revive you after a Root Trip."

Nodding his thanks, Adam thirstily drained the can. The refreshing beer quickly and effectively moistened his dry mouth and throat.

"That was amazing," he said. "It was like I was reliving the best times in my life – well my first-life. Is it like that for everyone?"

"Every time. You don't always get the same memories, but they are always wonderful. It's the only way we get to see our families again. West Beach is a nice place to live, but one can sometimes feel trapped here."

Putting down the empty can onto the sand, he noticed Stardust lying nearby, still deeply under the influence of the Root Juice, his body twitching and his face going through a gurning myriad of expressions.

"Is he all right?" Adam asked Dylan.

"Some people stay under for longer the first time. Most of us came out of the trip over an hour ago. I'll wager Stardust will dream until midnight. Shame really, since he won't get to hear Robeson sing."

"Robeson?"

"Paul Robeson, the baritone. Lovely voice."

"I don't think I've ever heard of him. Is he Welsh?"

"He's American, but you could call him an adopted son of Wales. You probably know him for singing 'Old Man River'. The man got into some political bother during his life – talented and controversial. Anyway, having Robeson sing us to sleep is quite the tradition around here. Always the same song, mind you – 'Sometimes I Feel Like a Motherless Child'. Reminds us of all the people we will probably never see again. He's already set up on the prom."

Adam looked over to the well-lit promenade – the ornate Victorian streetlamps elegantly illuminating the wide paved walkway and the lower façades of the gothic apartment blocks. He quickly realised he had a VIP view, since the legendary African American singer was sitting directly opposite him, in the middle of the bandstand, comfortably reclined on a large sun-lounger with a stand mounted microphone placed conveniently by his side.

"You must have a decent speaker system to cover the whole beach," Adam noted.

Dylan pointed up to the sky:

"The workers upstairs fitted active wireless speakers into the ceiling way above the clouds. They are cleverly disguised, so you can't see them from down here whether it's day or night."

"Do you mean full-scale speakers; like the full-scale duct tape I've seen all over the place? I'm pretty sure nothing on our miniature scale would be powerful enough."

Dylan nodded:

"And, tomorrow, you will learn the truth about that. For now, just settle back, relax, and wait for midnight. There's only a few minutes left."

Heeding his own advice, Dylan laid back and made himself comfortable. After shaking the sand off his cushion, Adam did likewise. As he did so, by sheer coincidence, nearly all the streetlamps shut off along the promenade, leaving only one solitary light shining down on Robeson – a dramatic and evocative start to the performance as the singer sat alone in the spotlight, surrounded by darkness and the indistinct hulks of the apartment blocks.

A loud hum arose from the masses laying on the sand, deep and resonant, honed over decades. Adam turned his head and saw that Dylan had his eyes closed, the poet humming along with his beach brethren. It soon became clear that the humming was a lead in and accompaniment to the song as Robeson sat up straight, pulled across the microphone, and set his voice free.

Adam lay on the sand, eyelids now gently closed, head comfortably nestled in the soft cushion, as Robeson's rich sonorous tones rolled down from the starlit Heavens like the voice of God. As the deep mournful lyrics washed all around the beach, stirring a palpable atmosphere of shared heart-wrenching emotion, even Adam could feel the longing for those friends and family who were just distant memories.

At this moment, this was truly a form of paradise. Not just a paradise of sun, sea, and sand, but also of the heart and mind. If Adam could find an answer to the Stardust problem, that did not involve murder, then he might never go back.

In the last few seconds before midnight, Robeson's voice fell silent, the last streetlight went dark, and the accompanying hum faded away. Settled into a restful foetal position on the soft sand, waves quietly lapping against the shore, Adam murmured:

"I'm finally home."

A CANDLE IN THE WIND

Breakfast, from a busy kiosk on the wide promenade, was a perfectly constructed chilli cheeseburger with a side of onion rings and a medium coke. The server, dressed in the crisp starched white of a Victorian waiter, complete with a bow tie and a black waistcoat, was a very convincing high-end android. Twitching his waxed moustache, he handed Adam the food. With absolutely anything on offer, not just the small menu of Victorian fare scrawled on a blackboard propped up on the counter, Stardust took a while to decide what to have. This prompted a few choice words from an irritated few in the queue.

Stardust finally settled on a tuna mayonnaise and salad baguette, accompanied by a cup of milky breakfast tea. Clearly unphased by the sharp insults behind him, the psychopath thanked the server, even offering the semblance of a smile.

"Well done for not reacting to those scumbags," Adam said, before taking a bite of burger.

"Oh Copa, they're children, even compared to the best of the Psychoviro. Anyhow, I must say I'm feeling quite ... serene this morning." Stardust sipped his tea and attempted another smile. "I think it's something to do with that Root Juice. Such beautiful memories – so real."

Adam wiped a run of chilli sauce from his chin, holding the cheeseburger carefully in its wrapper to avoid another mishap.

"I have to agree with you there," he agreed. "I was like a child again. My parents were teaching me to swim. I could really, really feel their love for me. I was so happy."

"Oh my, that's the first time you've ever said anything nice about your parents. Maybe I could do a deal with Dylan Thomas. If I could ship a few gallons of this back home, who knows what a difference it could make?"

"Probably put me out of job. You know, the best memory was my first real kiss. I felt a bit scared, but so proud ... as if I had crossed a frontier. It's one of those forgotten milestones in life's journey. What were your memories?"

Stardust lowered his head, his eyes narrowed:

"You really do not want to know." He took a quick bite of baguette and chewed slowly.

They stood for a while on the promenade, leaning against the iron railing, looking out to sea. Taking a large bite of burger followed by a long slurp of coke, Adam studied the distant root with a sense of trepidation. Since he had fought many brutal battles on the roofs of the Psychoviro tower blocks, it was not the height that bothered him but the thought of precariously dangling in a basket. Finishing his food, he stuffed the packaging in a nearby bin. A familiar figure emerged from the crowd.

"Ah Llewelyn the Great," Adam said, "have you come to keep an eye on us? You needn't worry; neither of us is feeling particularly confrontational today."

Serious as ever, his grey and blue Hawaiian shirt more conservative than most, Llewelyn got straight to the point:

"You need to come with me right away. Upstairs are sending a basket down."

"Hah, do we have to swim over, or do you have pedalos?"

"Don't be stupid; there's a speedboat moored over by the West Beach Pier."

They followed Llewelyn along the busy promenade, attracting smiles, high-fives and thumbs-up from many passers-by. The Welsh prince remained silent and keen eyed, taking his responsibilities very seriously, making sure nobody got too near his charges.

Standing opposite the twelfth apartment block, almost as far west as was possible to travel without encountering the virtual landscape wall, was the West Beach Pier. With smooth sanded planking, delicate iron arches, an assortment of white weather-boarded kiosks and pleasure palaces capped with lead domed roofs, the large Victorian style structure stretched out into the calm waters. Completing the effect, colourful flags fluttered from the tops of buildings, their walls hung with red, white, and green bunting, whilst a variety of android entertainers – magicians, clowns, singers, and a bawdy hurdy-gurdy man vigorously cranking his organ – attempted to amuse the jaded crowds with their skills.

Nowhere in Reynold's Gardens was the Victorian artifice so vivid as on the West Beach Pier. With the entertainers in period costume, playing their characters as if born during the heyday of the British Empire, it was impossible to ignore the contrast with the general population in their jeans, shorts, t-shirts, and other assorted beachwear. A scene that could be taken from any number of 21st century theme parks or commercial tourist attractions, all that was missing were bawling babies drowning out the singing, sugar-hyped children kicking the entertainer's shins, and nostalgia yearning seniors slowly shuffling their way towards the penny arcade.

Near the end of the long pier, a voice called down from the flat rooftop of 'Fisherman Jack's Shellfish Café':

"Two for the root, or are you travelling as well, Llewelyn?"

Llewelyn looked up at the man in the sailor's cap leaning over the black iron railing, and said nothing. The man scratched the side of his strong jaw, ruffling an impressive dark sideburn, before rolling his eyes:

"Are you travelling as well, Llewelyn … the Great?"

"Just the two, Gareth," Llewelyn replied.

Even from his low vantage point, Adam could see the black rubberised contraption installed on top of the café. Gareth and two colleagues sat ready by a couple of large steel levers and a central steel steering wheel – all wore sailor caps and black tank tops, their strong arm muscles on impressive display. Adam recognised the device as a full-scale remote control, such as used for model cars and boats.

"Over here, gentlemen," Llewelyn said, walking over to the pier railing by the side of the cafe. "The ladder's the only way down. They say we're getting a staircase soon, but then, they've been saying that for the past twenty years. This is where I will leave you. Perhaps, if it goes well upstairs, I will see you again."

The long ladder ran down the side of the pier to a small wooden jetty tethered to two of the pier's iron legs. Sitting alongside the jetty was an open topped speedboat. The boat, sleek, shiny, and black with plush white leather seats, bobbed unnaturally in the water, conspicuously like a full-scale model from the 'real' world, rather than something especially designed for the miniaturised world of Reynold's Gardens.

Climbing into the boat, Adam and Stardust sat uncomfortably – the leather seats turned out to be hard plastic, without any cushioning but boasting sturdy six-point racing harnesses. High above, Gareth looked down from the roof of the café and called out through a megaphone:

"Gentlemen, please secure your harnesses."

With the harnesses securely fastened, a high-pitched tone sounded, and Gareth continued:

"Gentlemen, you will be travelling at around 3 miles per hour. Now, that's 3 miles per hour in the real world, but here it works out at just over 200 miles per hour. Your journey time to the root will be about 25 seconds. Please remain seated, do not release your harnesses, and do not lean over the sides."

Both Adam and Stardust fell back against the hard seating as the boat suddenly lurched forward and quickly picked up speed. The high-pitched whine of the electric motor, much like a swarm of buzzing bees, was unmistakably that of a model boat.

With such a calm sea and the craft riding high in the water, it felt more like a jet skimming across the surface. At any moment, Adam thought that a sudden bump of a wave could send them hurtling to destruction. For the entire short journey, the rush of air pressed hard against their faces – neither man relaxed, each gritting their teeth, their hands tightly gripping their harnesses.

About a mile out, the boat turned sharply right, banking steeply, sending a spray of water over the terrified passengers. The huge root loomed ahead, seemingly increasing in size as they rapidly approached – Adam wondered if the boat had ever crashed into the grey sea serpent-like growth.

Both men slipped forward in their harnesses as the propellers went into sudden reverse, slowing the craft. Then, in a smooth, expertly executed deceleration, the boat gently came alongside a large floating platform tethered to the root, and stopped dead in the water.

After releasing their harnesses, Adam and Stardust helped each other out of the boat. Still shaking from the extreme rollercoaster ride, unsure on giddy legs, they held onto each other for support and took a moment to regain their composure.

"A heart stopping ride, isn't it?" a voice called over from the far side of the platform. "Don't worry about the trip upstairs – far slower and quite relaxing, as long as you have a head for heights."

Glad that their 25-second ordeal was over, Adam and Stardust walked over to the waiting basket. Suspended on sturdy chains, the 'basket' looked starkly modern rather than Victorian – gloss-white, waist-high plastic sides topped with silver, and a matching silver floor. The man in the basket swung open the white plastic gate and welcomed them in. Once everyone was safely inside, the man closed the gate and introduced himself. With strong facial features – staring eyes, full lips, and a prominent nose – the dark haired man appeared unnaturally alert, unnervingly intelligent, and on the striking side of handsome.

"Henry Longfellow," the man said, firmly shaking each man's hand.

Adam and Stardust returned the greeting and leant back against the side of the basket.

"Is it a long trip," Adam asked, disappointed to find no seating.

"Under ten minutes. I promise you will have a rather magnificent view of West Beach, so the time will slip away. I have made the trip countless times and it is still a thrilling experience."

Further breaking the Victorian character of the Gardens, Longfellow took a black walkie-talkie out of his pocket. He pressed a button on the facia and held it to his mouth:

"Longfellow and two others in the basket," he said.

"Close the gate and be ready to ride," a clear female voice replied.

"Gate closed. Haul us up." Longfellow pressed the button again and slipped the device back in his pocket.

With a slight jolt, the chains attached to each corner tensioned and the basket slowly lifted. After a few seconds, the speed increased, and they soon had a commanding view of the beachfront, the apartment blocks, and the grey safety walls. Adam had to admit that the view, as Longfellow promised, was truly magnificent.

Running his hand along the silver cladding, Adam realised it was the ubiquitous duct tape. The glossy plastic sidewalls also had a familiar look, especially the faint block lines. It only took a second to recognise the material:

"Is this Lego? Is this full-scale Lego?"

"I'm not sure how much I can reveal, but we do have access to full-scale products. These toy plastic building blocks are quite versatile. We glue them together for extra strength."

"They use the duct tape all over the Gardens," Adam said. "This stuff would be great for construction and repairs. The dark-side could really do with some more housing."

"And, how exactly would Cortés explain the sudden appearance of full-scale plastic building blocks? I heard he had a hard enough time explaining away the planks of tape."

Adam tensed as a light breeze caused the basket to sway – Stardust froze and gripped Adam's arm. Longfellow seemed unperturbed at the sudden movement, but Adam feared they could be dashed against the hard bark of the root.

"The wind never gets any stronger than this," Longfellow said, "and it always blows from the same direction. There is no chance of us colliding with the root or tipping over, if that is your concern. Spare a thought for those brave souls who first climbed the root. In the early days, it was all ropes and pulleys, muscles and sweat. Lately we've installed electric motors and a control panel."

"How do you power it?"

Longfellow's eyes widened with enthusiasm:

"The motors are full-scale, for toy vehicles. The engineers have adapted them to haul the baskets. They run of some kind of fuel cell – will last for decades I'm told."

Reassured, Adam relaxed and once again took in the distant seafront vista – a couple of minutes and they would be amongst the clouds.

"I personally requested that I accompany you on this journey," Longfellow said. "It's a routine trip but I wanted to ask you something … face to face. Edgar Allen Poe and I were long-time adversaries. In the old times, he made it his mission to smear my reputation and discredit my work. Once here, we embarked on a thousand year rivalry."

Somehow, to Adam, the juxtaposition of the words Poe and Longfellow begged for a crude, certainly lavatorial, joke. However, heroically slapping down his baser urges he nipped its creation in the bud – after all, if he intended to stay at West Beach, he needed to make a good impression.

"So, have you heard what happened to Poe?" Adam asked. "Horrible way for anyone to go."

"I am not here for the sordid details. I simply want to know if he is really dead, and whether there is a chance he can come back."

"We have his body preserved, but we are unable to resurrect him – for both technical and contractual reasons. If this place runs by the same rules as the Viroverse, then even if Poe is returned to Reynold's Gardens, I don't think he can come back."

Relaxing against the side of the basket, Longfellow sighed, his mouth quivering with the faintest shape of a smile.

"You seem pleased," Adam said.

Longfellow shook his head:

"Truth be told, now I know he is really gone, I don't really know how I am feeling. I do sense a certain relief that the battle is finally over, that I can now relax, but there is something else. It is as if something is missing."

"Poe is missing."

"Hmm, he was a prominent fixture in my life. Our rivalry meant we kept writing … to outdo each other."

"Maybe he was your motivation, and you were his."

"That thought has often crossed my mind. Perhaps we were less adversaries and more sparring partners, though neither of us would have admitted it. The hostility had softened somewhat in the last few years. In fact, I gave his last work, 'The Tunnelling Fingers', a grudgingly positive review."

"How did he react to that?"

"He said nothing. Let me clarify that for you. For Edgar to say nothing in such circumstances is the equivalent of a firm handshake or a warm embrace from anybody else. Suffice to say, the absence of malice inspired me to write another poem in the hope that he might show his appreciation."

"And, an end to the hostility."

"I would have settled for a friendly rivalry. It is a shame, not just because I have lost a potential friend, but also because I shall never know his thoughts on my work."

"Have you completed it?"

"Yes, I have. The work possessed me like a demon. I cannot find the words to describe the extreme passion, the intensity, the effort I put into it. For weeks, the poem held me in its thrall, every waking hour, right up until the sleep of midnight. It was not a matter of burning the candle at both ends. Such was my passion that every day the candle was completely consumed. You could say that I burned my candle whole."

There were opportunities, low, ignoble opportunities, that could overwhelm Adam's resistance, despite his best efforts to remain mature.

"You burned your candle hole?" he said, maintaining a serious demeanour. "That must have been painful."

"You are a most perceptive man, Mr Eden. You have it right; it was very painful. The pain of burning my candle whole is forever seared into my memory."

"Are you sure it was just your memory that was seared when you burned your candle hole?"

"There are rumours that you are a man of low intellect and base humour. Evidently, these are scurrilous lies, for you obviously possess great insight. Of course, I know what you mean. The intense pain is also seared into the very words on the page. I only hope that this means others can experience …" Longfellow tapped his chin, as if seeking the perfect phrase.

"… the pain of burning your candle hole?" Adam suggested.

"Hmm, you have tears in your eyes, Mr Eden." Longfellow frowned. "Is that a smile? Surely you do not find this humorous?"

"Err … I'm not smiling, I'm wincing," Adam said, contorting his face as he tried not to laugh. "The thought of you burning your candle hole is making my eyes water."

"Is there some yarn I am not party to?" Longfellow asked.

Clearly oblivious to the joke, Stardust nodded his head thoughtfully, like a well-informed expert, and raised an index finger:

"I believe what Copa is trying to say is that any burning of the genital area is a very serious matter requiring immediate medical attention. Whilst I have never inserted a candle into my hole, a particularly sadistic prison warder did burn it quite badly with a lighter. So, I can sympathise with the pain you experienced. There should be support groups for people like us."

"Candle hole? You ... you ..."

Not able to contain himself any further, Adam bent over laughing, wiping the tears streaming from his eyes. Stardust stood quietly bemused, one eyebrow raised as he tried futilely to understand the situation. Longfellow looked at both men with cold disdain, and spoke firmly yet politely:

"Dear gentlemen, though I am blessed with immortality, I don't wish to waste any more of my time engaged in this inane conversation. Please be content to amuse yourselves for the rest of the journey without my full attention."

With a haughty sniff and a huff, Longfellow turned around and looked out at the sky. As he turned away, Adam and Stardust could not help staring at the seat of the great poet's trousers ... perhaps expecting to see scorch marks.

THE TRUTH

Coming up through the crack in the ceiling, Adam felt as though they were passing through the roof of the world. Despite the strength of the miniature world materials, the ceiling had proven no match for the force of nature. The wide gap around the root was easily big enough to fit the toy speedboat.

A colourful makeshift barrier of the popular toy building bricks lined the jagged edge of the gaping hole. Once the basket lined up with the floor, a metal walkway with protective side-rails was pushed into place, allowing the passengers to disembark.

Stepping off the walkway onto the floor of the ceiling, Adam felt relieved to feel a hard steady surface underfoot. Looking back, the root carried on for about another 10 feet before ending in a neatly cut flat stump – a ring of guttering collected the Root Juice that wept incessantly from the wound.

Huge pillars, topped with simple arches between vaulted ceilings, stretched into the distance in every direction. A hollow honeycombed structure, the roof of the Gardens was built to absorb colossal stresses – though pierced by the root, the great catastrophe had not broken its back. A number of raised platforms held small electric motors, which powered the pulley system for transport up and down the root.

"Welcome, gentlemen," said an impeccably dressed man with short, slicked-back dark hair. "I am Nikola Tesla, and I believe you are here to learn the truth."

Shaking hands with Tesla, the genius of electricity – and noticeably different without his famous moustache – Adam mumbled a thankyou on behalf of the Terminal and the Viroverse. Without speaking, Longfellow barged past, eyes glaring, betraying his continued displeasure.

Dylan Thomas stood alongside Tesla, wearing a loose fitting red floral shirt and khaki cargo shorts, and looked as out of place up here as Adam and Stardust. There were a number of people busily milling around the root area, and all either wore a smart black suit or grey workers' overalls. Tesla's suit, Edwardian with short tails and perfectly tailored, seemed a cut above the others, perhaps signifying his importance … or vanity.

With the still offended Longfellow leading the way, they made their way through the seemingly endless procession of arches. Adam noticed that the knee pockets of Dylan's cargo shorts were bulging, weighed down, and slapping against his legs as he walked.

"I hope you've got your belt tightened," Adam said. "With all that weight, you might end up with your trousers round your ankles."

"They've only got one dispenser up here, so you need to be prepared if you want a snack or a drink."

"Really? How do they manage?"

"They simply go without. They are so insufferably frugal. See it as a sign of strength."

Without turning to look at his guests, Tesla joined in the conversation:

"And yet it is through our efforts and sacrifices that you are able to indulge yourselves so generously."

"As well as frugal, they are also insufferably pious," Dylan added.

Tesla did not reply, maintaining a steady pace, hands held behind his back. He did not talk again for some ten minutes, when they finally reached the outer wall and a wide corridor with a narrow-gauge rail running along its length. Facing Dylan and Adam, Tesla coughed into his clenched hand:

"A change of plans, gentlemen. Instead of the guided tour I originally promised, I think we should head straight to the chamber. As always, we have much to do and time is ever calling."

For another few minutes, they waited by the track. In the distance, a train duly appeared – a streamlined silver engine pulling five jet-black open-topped carriages. Far from full, a few passengers, some in smart suits and others in overalls, sat single file in the carriages. Tesla waved his hand in the air and the approaching train slowed to a halt.

"No chairs?" Adam said as they climbed into the second carriage.

"The train set is actually very small scale," Tesla explained, flipping up the tails of his jacket as he sat down on the plastic, wood-effect floor. "We couldn't install a larger system without compromising the walkway. We took the roofs off the carriages, shortened the walls, and removed the internal furniture. Please, sit."

Grunting, Dylan sat awkwardly, trying not to squash his overloaded pockets:

"Every time I ride on this ruddy arse beater, I tell myself to bring a cushion next time. I always forget."

"Mater artium necessitas," Tesla replied, somewhat smugly. "Necessity, not your comfort, is the Mother of invention."

With everyone seated, the train resumed its journey along the corridor. Dylan grumbled under his breath:

"Where I come from, my comfort is a bloody necessity,"

Within a few minutes, the train ended its journey south, and everybody got off. Set into the southern wall, the destination for all passengers seemed to be a very large steel door – again, large enough to fit a toy speedboat.

"This is a decompression chamber leading to the outside world." Tesla said. "Other than the hole accidently created by the root, there is no other way up here, so its presence remains something of a mystery. Some say it serves as an emergency escape route for the residents of the Gardens, but again, there is no other way up here."

"It may be a redundant system," Adam offered. "The network of halls in the Viroverse is part of an earlier design that was never used, but still constructed due to contractual obligations. This could the same thing."

"An interesting idea, Mr Eden," Tesla said, as he pressed his hand against a panel at the side of the door.

With a sucking sound, the huge decompression chamber door unsealed and slid open. Inside, the white coated metal chamber was immense, far larger than Adam had expected, with rows of modular plastic seating along the walls and another huge door facing the one they just entered. Soft lighting, set into the ceiling, took the harshness off the otherwise austere space.

Wafting his silk handkerchief over the seat of a chair, Tesla sat down, pulling the knees of his trousers before crossing his legs – Adam smiled, reminded of John Down's fastidious gentlemanly ways. Dylan commented that though the seats were damn hard, at least they were moulded to accept the human form. Stardust also crossed his legs. Somehow, the psycho's glitter gloss black clothing and snow-white hair seemed a perfect stylistic match to the stark white chamber.

Dylan unbuttoned one of the pockets on his shorts and retrieved a small bag of hard-boiled sweets. He offered the sweets, traditional red and white pear drops, to the others. Adam took a couple of white ones, Stardust one red, whilst Tesla declined with a disinterested look and a dismissive wave of his hand.

"Mr Eden, Mr Stardust," Tesla began, "we will be in here for the next thirty minutes. Since we have nothing better to do, it is a good time for you to hear the truth you claim to seek."

"Are you sure thirty minutes is enough," Adam queried. "I thought decompression chambers took much longer than that."

"You forget that we are not really human," Tesla explained. "I have used the chamber many thousands of times since we first moved upstairs and as you can no doubt see, I am perfectly fine. Besides, the system is automatic, so we have no control over the time."

"Ok, so what's the truth?" Adam asked, relaxing back into his chair.

"The truth is that we still have a resource problem," Tesla answered succinctly.

Bemused, Adam furrowed his brow:

"I thought with all the deaths that things had balanced out. I mean, there are still people dying in the dark-side. Surely you should have a huge surplus by now."

"We are happy to let people believe that. The truth is that we have a finite amount of resource material, and that each year a small amount is lost. Though there have been a number of interesting theories put forward, we do not know why this is happening. Whether the system is self-contained and leaking in some way, or whether before the great catastrophe it was topped up from an outside source, our main aim here is to find a suitable material to replenish what is lost."

"So, how long do you have before …"

"This is only an estimate, but we are currently only a few months ahead of the curve. Without the rot, the resource crisis would have re-emerged years ago. Instead of rotting to death, we would be facing death by starvation."

"Perhaps the Viroverse could supply what you need."

"Do you really believe that? Would they help? They won't even let us take the bodies we need."

"If they can't, it will be because of some stupid rule or regulation. I'll ask the Captain when I get back."

Tesla clasped his hands together:

"Well, we took matters into our own hands. That is why you are here. As I told you, that door leads to the outside world, and also a facility for manually adding resource material to the system."

The truth hit Adam immediately:

"Oh God, that man, you were feeding him into the …"

Tesla nodded:

"You are way ahead of me, Mr Eden. I intended to tell you that we tried adding all sorts of material: various forms of vegetation, insects, even items from a full-size dispenser we discovered a few kilometres from here. All were rejected. Then we found the vast plains with those pitiful … creatures."

"Those pitiful creatures are people," Adam explained. "In fact, the entire human population is sliding around out there, wrapped up in some kind of eternal mind game. Just like us, their bodies are artificial."

"The entire human population?" Tesla looked genuinely shocked. "Hmm, we didn't know that. At first we thought them some form of sub-human – little more than animals."

"Then he woke up," Dylan said, his voice tinged with sadness. "He spoke. We were cutting him up. We were cutting up an intelligent being." Shuddering, Dylan ran a hand across his face.

Cold to Dylan's obvious distress, Tesla continued:

"It took a few years and many expeditions before we discovered the plains. As I said, we had already found a full-size dispenser that was still operational. It was the fact that the climate was always pleasant around that area, no matter how bad the weather only a few metres north, that alerted us to something beyond a thick screen of trees."

"The slerding plains," Adam said.

Tesla leaned forward, his nose pointed questioningly towards Adam:

"What does slerding mean?"

"Easy; it means sliding herds. Slerd is a nickname the people gave themselves. The slime suits make it easy for them to glide around."

"Well, we decided to test whether these slerds could provide suitable resource material. A small team was trained to obtain a biopsy – occasionally, one of the creatures would break away from the herd and slide near to the forest edge. The sample proved compatible and was not rejected. All our efforts then turned to taking down one of these beasts."

"One of those humans, you mean," Dylan corrected, his guilt laid bare with every syllable.

Tesla sighed:

"We initiated a comprehensive training programme, which lasted nearly two years. Whilst most prepared for climbing the slerd and attaching ropes, some specialised in more invasive techniques. You are obviously aware that the late Mr Poe was one such specialist."

Adam nodded, trying hard to look respectful.

"Well," Tesla continued, "we left a couple of landboards at the edge of the forest."

"You mean those oversize skateboards with the big wheels?" Adam asked.

"Yes, and we attached cords ready for the big day. Every morning, for a few months we made our way to the plains. One day, our prayers were answered. One of the slerds had ventured very close to our position. Wasting no time, we executed our plan. The specialist teams weren't needed as the bea … slerd toppled easily with just the climbers and ropes. We got him onto the boards and dragged him back to the hanger just as midnight fell."

Adam raised his hand, as if asking a question in school:

"Midnight? Then how did …"

"The enforced sleep of midnight doesn't happen beyond this room. A small group volunteered to stay with our catch, feeding him sedatives and nutrients until the rest of us returned."

"Three days later," Adam said.

"We then began the delicate task of cutting our catch into pieces small enough to feed into the resource chute. We minimised the blood loss with injected hardeners and carefully cut around any veins – we have some excellent chefs with knife skills you would just not believe."

"And, then he got away," Adam said, slapping down his host's boasting.

"We were still asleep, with six hours before we woke. Luckily, he wandered deep into the jungle before making it to the old road. It gave us time to catch up. We caught him just a few metres away from the plains. We gave everything we had to try to bring him down. Our fear was that he might somehow raise the alarm and contact whatever authorities were out there." Tesla had an expression of defeat on his face. "Even our most highly trained Anal Divers and Testicle Danglers failed to stop him."

Adam and Stardust grinned and chuckled, in contrast to the others in the room, who shook their heads sombrely – Longfellow's expression somehow managed to display an even deeper level of contempt.

"There's nothing to laugh about, gentlemen," Tesla said. "We lost so many good people that day. So much genius lost to the world." He clasped his hands together and fixed his gaze on Adam. "And, now it is your turn to tell us the truth. What really happened to our dear friend and colleague, Edgar Allen Poe, and why is the entire population of the Earth wandering around like unwashed cattle?"

For the short remaining time in the chamber, Adam obliged, telling his hosts everything he knew – the sad and sordid details of Poe's death causing visible grief amongst those assembled. However, it was the revelations about the fate of humanity that caused the most emotion – mainly shock and disbelief that there were no free thinking full-size humans left on the planet.

Finally, a soft tone alerted everyone that the sequence was complete. With a strong, sincere shake of the hand, Tesla thanked Adam for being so candid. A few minutes later, giving Dylan just enough time to hand out another round of sweets, Tesla opened the decompression chamber door.

HANGING IN THE HANGAR

S tretching far into the distance, the vast space beyond the decompression chamber could easily be described as awesome and breath taking – Adam could imagine airships or the largest jet aircraft comfortably accommodated. Dwarfed by the huge open space, hundreds of people, busily engaged in a variety of tasks, looked like an army of tiny insects.

"Everybody remembers their first time," Dylan joked, regaining a touch of his usual good humour.

"How big is this place?" Adam asked, looking up at the distant ceiling.

Tesla waved an arm:

"In real world numbers, the space is about eight and half foot long, four foot wide, and three foot high. No doubt you know that in our miniature world you have to multiply those figures by 70."

"Three feet of sky," Adam said, remembering the dimensions of Viroverse environments. He pointed to the far wall, which looked metallic compared to the drab grey of the rest of the hangar. "Are those doors? Is the outside world on the other side?"

With a certain pride and almost smug manner, Tesla nodded and offered his guests a tour of the hangar. The manual resource chute, sticking out from the wall near the decompression chamber entrance, was little more than an open funnel some few feet across. Adam looked carefully at the edges of the chute, expecting to see dried remnants of blood, but it was spotlessly clean.

At first, Adam thought that some form of transport would be necessary. The hangar doors, nearly 600 feet away, seemed a tiresome destination for lazy legs. That is, until Dylan came up with a challenge:

"Try a big jump on the spot," he said. "Or take a running jump if you're feeling brave."

"I beg your pardon?" Adam said.

"Just do it."

At the risk of looking like a fool, Adam bent at the knees and jumped up. Letting loose a string of expletives was unavoidable as he sprung high into the air, some thirty feet above his grinning hosts. More expletives accompanied the fall back down to earth, which was mercifully without pain as the landing proved far softer than expected – just as well, since he ended up on his back.

"That was amazing," he admitted, getting to his feet.

"Our bodies are designed for much stronger gravity than this," Tesla explained. "Up here, we are stronger, faster, and far more agile."

Marvelling at the feats he could possibly perform, Adam made a mental note to try a few more jumps and leaps later on.

"Stardust, you just have to try this. Just make sure to bend at the knees when you land."

Without explanation, Stardust emphatically refused. Knowing well the psychopath's volatile and violent nature, Adam did not press the matter. It was then he noticed his hosts drinking from paper cups; a large drinks dispenser by the chute was filled with a familiar white liquid.

"Root Juice," Dylan said, crushing the cup in his hand before throwing it down the chute.

"So, we're going to be dreaming again," Adam said. "I guess the tour is off."

Tesla also threw his cup down the chute and carefully wiped his mouth with his handkerchief.

"This is not for you," he said. "The juice has a very different effect in this gravity. Rather than those insipid hallucinations that everyone is so fond of, it provides us with an extra degree of ruthlessness. You could call it bravado, but it is more focused than that. It enhances our training, and allows us to venture outside without fear. It can take up to a couple of hours before having any effect."

Together, they walked towards the centre of the hangar, passing people engaged in a variety of vigorous activities. In a daring and dangerous display of advanced circuit training, a number of highly focused teams leapt over rocky obstacles, scaled precarious towers of leather clad scaffolding, and balanced on high bars as their comrades threw hard balls at them – the last one reminded Adam of his time training with the Sarge all those centuries ago.

Pointing to the ceiling, Tesla handed Adam a small pair of binoculars. Close to the ceiling, long white beams stretched from one side of the hangar to the other. Small groups of people, wearing tight fitting grey jumpsuits, clambered nimbly around a variety of pipes, cables, and ladders attached to the beams. A row of strange pendulous large brown bags hanging near a cluster of pipework caught Adam's eye. He lowered the binoculars and turned to Tesla:

"You know, those bags look like …"

"Giant testicles," Tesla said, finishing Adam's sentence. "Those brave men and woman are our elite squads: Hair Hangers, Ear Piercers, and Testicle Danglers. Keep watching; the woman running along the long pipe towards the bags."

Adam raised the binoculars again.

Keeping low, throwing herself down onto the pipe then leaping up as if avoiding an imaginary foe, the woman sprinted towards the nearest bag, which hung perilously in empty space some eight-feet away from the end of the pipe. Propelling herself away from the pipework, a sword held in each hand, the fearless Dangler leapt across the gap. Just as Adam thought the woman might plummet to her death – or perhaps just badly bruise herself, given the effects of gravity – she plunged her blades into the leathery testicle bags. After swinging backwards and forwards for a few moments, the woman settled into a relatively safe static dangle.

"Well that was certainly painful to watch," Adam said, handing the binoculars back to Tesla. "What do you if it's a female slerd? In their slime suits, they are really hard to tell apart."

"I am quite sure they will find something to hang off," Tesla remarked dryly.

As they continued their walk towards the hangar doors, Adam noticed a number of unusual objects and features. Quite near to the doors, parked by the sidewall, was a huge toy fire engine. Bright red plastic, with large black tires, and a white ladder lying on top, the item was certainly from the outside world. Also along the sidewall were a number of spiked barriers – all with cords attached, perhaps for dragging them into place – and racks of metal spears, enough to arm a few hundred people. He smiled knowingly, spotting two huge full-scale rolls of silvery grey duct tape stacked by the fire engine.

"Wait a minute," Adam said, pausing near a large group of people engaged in jumping and rolling exercises. "If you are still training, does that mean you're planning to take down another slerd?"

"It's just a precaution," Dylan said, "in case we have to defend ourselves against the authorities."

"Except that is now clear that there are no authorities out there," Tesla added. "Well, except for this ragtag group from the Terminal, if that's what passes for authority these days. I think it won't be long until we will be filling the resource vats again."

Quick to outrage, Dylan stood in front of Tesla, his eyes wide, face reddening.

"Weren't you listening, Nikola?" he said angrily. "Those are people out there. They are not just dumb creatures. We should find another way before resorting to savagery. See if the Viroverse will lend a hand."

Tesla's expression did not change or even twitch in the face of Dylan's fury.

"Our calculations show that just one of those creatures would fill the resource vats. Just one of those creatures is enough to solve our problems for at least another thousand years. Just one life to save the lives of hundreds of thousands. I cannot see any grounds for debate."

Adam stood next to Dylan:

"Except that you could see it as slaughtering an endangered animal, like a rhino for instance, to feed an infestation of tiny ants."

Tesla pointed his nose at Adam:

"Except that we are the endangered species … and our size is of no importance."

"Oh, believe me, size matters," Adam said.

As if tired of the conversation, Tesla clapped his hands. Neither Adam nor Stardust had noticed the crowd forming around them – the teams breaking away from their training to join their leader. Two burly men, each carrying a sword, stood either side of Adam. Nonchalantly, Stardust attempted to walk away, but another armed group blocked his path, edging him back at the points of their blades.

"Gentlemen, I believe it is time for you to leave," Tesla said. "Prepare the fire engine!"

"Nikola, you can't do this," Dylan protested. "They can stay with us downstairs; lay on the beach all day. By all that's sane and reasonable, let them stay."

"They do not belong here, and they cannot go back. Killing them is the only option."

Before anybody could take in Tesla's sudden executional edict, or 'prepare the fire engine', Henry Wadsworth Longfellow strode out of the crowd and stood close to Adam and Stardust. The American poet cast a scowl at Adam, but offered Tesla a supportive wink. No doubt possessed of both elocution and erudition, Longfellow seemed also skilled in working an audience. Striking a proud upright patrician pose, he turned slowly, pointing at the gathered crowd.

"If these men are to die at our hands," he began, his voice resonating with firm authority, "then let there be words. Let there be strong words, honest words. Let there be words that clearly describe their felonious deeds."

The crowd murmured in agreement, and even Tesla clapped politely — though by his cool expression he seemed unconvinced by the unexpected intervention. Longfellow nodded his appreciation, and held up his hands to silence the audience.

"But first, you have to ask yourselves whether their actions are truly that of clever scheming felons, or perhaps, simply stupid." Longfellow paused, judging the reaction of the crowd, which remained quite cold. "Well, we wouldn't want to suffer stupid people, would we? Would we?"

At this point, Adam regretted every moment of the candle hole episode as he expected Longfellow to exact a cruel revenge.

"Put it this way, my friends. We have a few disputes amongst ourselves. My favourite is that age-old argument over who are the true creators. Is it artists, like myself, who imprint our ideas over various media, interpreting the world and our existence?"

"Fuck off, you arty farty bastard," cried a voice from the crowd, prompting both cheers and a few boos.

"Classy as always, Archimedes," Longfellow said, absorbing the heckling with good humour. "Or, are the true creators those engineers and scientists who transform our world to free the human spirit. You folks create the canvas upon which we arty farty types spew out our dreams and ideas."

The crowd, obviously dominated by science types, clapped appreciatively.

"So, really, we have no-one to look down upon. We are all rather equal. We are the chosen ones, those historical figures that Gordon Reynolds deemed worthy of saving. Don't you ever miss that feeling of superiority? I do. Yes, I admit it. I really miss being looked up to. Friends, we have spent a thousand years demeaned by an unnatural horizontal status. Perhaps it is time for a change."

Tesla, shrewd enough to know where Longfellow was heading, tried to end the speech. He walked up to the charismatic poet, clapping and laughing as if the show had ended. Longfellow simply carried on:

"So, we are the Gods on the hill, living in our resplendent palace – well, a palace that needs a little fixing here and there – whilst these two unworthy degenerates are from the giant warren of despair along the way. Let me elaborate on the word 'degenerates' ..."

Adam felt his face reddening as the esteemed poet commenced to pile insult upon insult. He took a step back and whispered to Dylan:

"What the hell is he doing? Why is he saying ...?"

"He's trying to save your life," Dylan replied quietly. "Longfellow may be a massive ego, but, like me, he is one of the honourable ones. Just keep your mouth shut, perhaps look a little offended, and let him work his magic."

"Just think how marvellous it will be to have a couple of total idiots around," Longfellow said, finally prompting a positive laugh from the crowd. "Yes, a couple of idiotic nonentities to whom we need show neither respect nor concern."

Out of the corner of his eye, Adam noticed a sudden movement. Too late to intervene, he saw Stardust slip out of the clutches of his guards, relieving one of them of his sword with a quick twist of the wrist. The psychopath ducked, and sliced open the guard's inner thigh. Immediately springing up, he thrust the point of the blade into the other guard's neck.

"No, Stardust!" was all Adam could cry, as all eyes turned to the sound of the commotion.

Longfellow was in mid-sentence as Stardust came up behind him and held the blade against his neck. The crowd surged forward, but then stopped short as Stardust jerked the blade, threatening to kill his captive.

"Stay back," Stardust seethed, eyes narrowed, scanning the faces of the crowd. "No-one, and I mean absolutely no-one, speaks about me like that. I'm going home. I am leaving this place, and he's is coming with me. If anyone tries to stop me, I'm going to cut him a new candle hole."

Stardust looked at Adam and nodded, as if telling him to come over. Adam stood rooted to the spot, not sure what he should do. Tesla broke the momentary impasse, brazenly walking up within a few feet of Stardust and the terrified poet.

"So, you think you can negotiate," Tesla said calmly. "If we let you return, then our secret is out. Everything we have achieved or may yet achieve could be undone. Do you really think we are going to risk all that for a single life when so many are dying in the dark-side? If you give in, and let Mr Longfellow go, then I might make your passing less painful. It's your choice, Stardust."

After a few seconds thought, Stardust smiled and nodded his head in agreement:

"Oh Tesla, you make such a compelling argument. Let me sweeten the deal." With a joyful squeal, Stardust ripped the blade through Longfellow's neck, cutting so deep that it bit into the cervical vertebrae. "Enjoy your new candle hole," Stardust laughed as Longfellow fell to the floor, face down in the pooling red of warm blood.

Horrified, Adam looked at Dylan for support. The usually high-spirited Welsh poet stepped back into the crowd, his face ashen with shock.

"Help me, Dylan," Adam pleaded quietly.

Dylan held up a hand and shook his head.

"I thought you were one of the honourable ones," Adam said.

"This is about survival now, not honour," Dylan muttered, echoing Adam's speech in Gordon's Hall. "You're on your own."

With no other option, the hostile faces of the crowd now drained of any vestige of goodwill, Adam slowly backed away and joined Stardust. Laughing as if enjoying a side-splitting comedy routine, Stardust waved his sword towards anyone who dared to get too near.

"Just you and me against the world, Copa," Stardust said, slapping Adam on the shoulder. "Just as it should be."

Suddenly, unexpectedly, a Dangler plummeted from above, landing on Stardust with great force, knocking him over. Stardust lost his blade, which flew into the crowd, lacerating the forehead of a man who failed to catch it. Despite the impact, Stardust had broken the neck of his attacker even before they hit the floor.

Adam twisted and helped his psychopathic teammate back to his feet. Instinctively, both men adopted a close quarter fighting stance. Adam stood solidly side-on, both fists raised. Stardust, though a formidable foe in the arena of the psychoviro, always insisted on elegance and grace, which often compromised his abilities. More Wushu than Kung Fu, he leaned back into a dramatic crouched stance, cupping his fingers, beckoning his enemies to attack.

Tesla's people wasted no time. Fired up on Root Juice and the promise of violence, upon their leader's snap of his fingers, they rushed into combat. Realising he had no chance against such numbers, Adam attempted to leap away. However, his futile, low gravity jump for freedom ended abruptly as Tesla grabbed Adam's ankle, bringing him slamming back down to earth.

ADAM AND THE ANTS

Stardust finally regained consciousness, groaning through split lips and missing teeth. He struggled to move. Turning his head – wig long gone and hair matted with blood – he looked at Adam through his single functioning eye; the other badly bruised and swollen shut.

"You should have stayed asleep," Adam said. "This is not going to end well."

Unlike his glam comrade, Adam had remained conscious throughout the ordeal. The fight had ended with vicious kicking as Adam and Stardust lay helpless on the hanger floor. With a single command, Tesla called off the attack – a calculated intervention, denying death and the promise of merciful release.

Next, the hanger doors were raised, revealing the lush green of the outside world. A landscape of tall green fronds stretched into the far distance, bounded by giant trees that seemed to soar miles into the sky. Adam quickly realised that the fronds were just grass and the distance to the trees was probably only a few feet using full-scale measurements.

Held up by two men, Adam gazed awestruck at the massive vegetation outside. For the first time since first resurrecting, Adam got a true sense of his size in the world. His few forays into the real world, brief glimpses of the slerds and the slerding plains, were always in a full-size human body, so everything seemed as normal – if the shocking sight of humanity's future could be classed as normal. In the Viroverse, many believed there was no miniaturisation, that it was just a convenient hoax, but now Adam beheld the truth.

A gang of men, using ropes and harnesses, pulled the colourful fire engine side-on into the opening. With no regard for the pain of their injuries, Adam and Stardust were carried and dragged over to the toy vehicle. Using thin strips of the ubiquitous duct tape, their broken and battered bodies were fixed to the side of the fire engine, where they faced the dense menace of the jungle. Adam noted that his arms were left free, but he was not strong enough to peel away the tape.

"What's happening?" Stardust asked.

Adam looked ahead, scanning the long fronds of grass for movement:

"I don't really know, but I've got a strong feeling we're about to become something's lunch."

An expression of shock accentuating his already gruesomely contorted face, Stardust slowly turned his head to face forwards. In the background, some distance behind the fire engine, Adam could hear a furious argument taking place. The words were indistinct, but now and then, he picked up Dylan Thomas' unmistakable rich tones.

Other sounds drowned out the voices. A loud scraping noise was probably the spiked barriers being hauled into place, and the clatter of metal was no doubt the spears being handed out. Tesla's gang were obviously preparing for a violent confrontation – perhaps one they had fought many times before.

"They're coming!" a voice shouted from on top of the fire engine, somewhere above Adam's head – whoever it was quickly clambered off the vehicle to join the others.

A dark smear had emerged from the distant tree line, blending with the green of the grass, moving towards the hanger. As the black tide drew nearer, shapes become more distinct. At first, Adam shuddered, mistaking the terrifying black creatures for giant spiders. He felt no less fear upon recognising that they were an army of ants – an old enemy that he had stamped on, poured boiling water over, and even squashed with a bouncing tennis ball as a child. If this was karma at work, then Adam was far too scared to appreciate it.

To the disapproving cries of the crowd, a man ran out in front of the fire engine, holding a spear.

"This shall not pass!" Dylan Thomas yelled defiantly, the Root Juice in full effect. "We shall not return to the atrocities of ancient days! Stand with me, my brothers and sisters!" He raised his spear. "Stand with me!"

Nobody came out to stand with Dylan. Instead, they shouted from the hanger for him to come back, to stop this idiocy, to not risk his life for undeserving scum. A few rare voices offered a more conciliatory tone but most were rabidly hostile to his foolish endeavour.

Dylan looked at Adam – no words were exchanged, since none were needed. The great Welsh poet turned to face the danger. Letting out a primal scream, a guttural wrench of wrath and fear, he thrust his spear forward.

"Gwyliwch fi rage!" he roared repeatedly as he charged into the forest of grass, the overloaded pockets of his cargo shorts slapping against his pale skinny legs.

The valiant Welshman stopped suddenly, standing his ground between the fire engine and the oncoming tide of jet-black insects. Only his head and shoulders were visible above the tops of the grass fronds.

The cries for Dylan to return fell silent as the first ants confronted their prey. Antennas twitching, front legs lashing out, the ants were unphased and hardly slowed by the steadfast poet. In a desperate display of savage fury and visible experience, Dylan impaled an ant through its thorax, lifting and twisting it up on his spear before dropping it to the ground.

"Nid af yn dawel!" he cried, his strained voice emphasising great pain as the black ants skittered and twitched around him.

Dylan let go of the spear and drew his sword – too late. In a sudden shower of blood, Adam saw an ant's mandible snip off one of the great poet's arms. A second later, and Dylan Thomas fell silent, his proud mane of dark curls disappearing beneath the grass-line.

The ants surged forward. Whilst most scurried past the fire engine, heading for the barriers and the waiting wall of spears, a few found the struggling miniature humans taped to the toy vehicle more interesting. Ignoring Adam, offering him a short horrifying respite, they attacked Stardust first.

In another context, the phrase, 'feasting on Stardust', may have struck a light whimsical note, but here it meant nothing but sickening gore accompanied by intense pain. Adam watched as the ants began devouring the man in black, their sharp mandibles snipping and chewing at his already bloodied limbs. Leaving no scraps, except for tattered clothing and picked clean bone, the insects moved methodically from foot to hip and from fingers to shoulder.

Stardust quickly lost consciousness, yet his face maintained a pained rigor, a frozen expression of agony. The ants began chewing the hips and stomach, and Adam could watch no more. Anticipating his own turn as 'le plat de jour', he closed his eyes and awaited the inevitable first bite.

"Ric … o … chet, feel my balls!" a familiar voice boomed out, as if blasted from a huge speaker array.

Adam opened his eyes in time to see a large stainless steel ball shoot overhead into the hanger. Blinking his eyes into clear focus, he gasped at the sight before him. More colossal than any giants he had seen in films, or imagined in his most alcohol addled moments, the Terminal team were truly mountainous. Wearing mid-grey fatigues, looking like magnificent living cliffs of granite, four operatives had appeared at the edge of the clearing some few feet away. Even if he stood on tiptoes, Adam doubted he would be taller than the steel toecaps of their sturdy black combat boots.

Momentarily distracted from the sea of ants around the fire engine, Adam quickly recognised three of the giants. Crouching low, Ricochet let loose another steel ball from his slingshot – one eye narrowed, accurately gauging the shot. Standing next to her Psychoviro compatriot, Jet looked ready to pounce, her grey Terminal fatigues a drab contrast to her usual figure-hugging shiny black leather. In her other hand she held a short bladed dagger. Dolph Zabel, the Everest of the group, stood behind Ricochet, armed with what looked like a small flamethrower – a small steel canister strapped to his upper arm feeding a long black tube, which he held one handed, aiming towards the hanger doorway.

Keeping close to the huge security chief, a thin black man had an expression of unease. Adam thought the man might be Jomo Tikolo, though with a face more human than before – his bland slerd visage replaced with far more detail and a thick head of dark hair. If it was Jomo, perhaps showing the others the way, then Adam had nothing but respect for the man returning to the territory of his cruel tormentors.

Behind the fire engine, Ricochet's balls were ricocheting around the hanger – one hitting the back of the fire engine, nearly knocking it over, and dislodging the ants gnawing on Stardust. The noise of battle had changed to that of panic. If evidence was needed of the carnage taking place inside, then one of the steel balls slowly rolling out of the doorway onto the grass was enough. Spattered in blood, leaving a wet red trail in its wake, the deadly projectile was immediately swarmed by hungry ants.

The shouts and screams from Tesla's army became increasingly distant as they abandoned the barriers and hastily retreated for the safety of the pressure chamber. With the ants in pursuit, many would not see another day.

Jet leapt forward. Her hand moving like a blur, she stabbed the ants around the fire engine. The blade of the knife seemed as a wide wall of steel, stabbing up and down, blocking Adam's vision. In a furious insect derivative of the knife game – no fingers involved – Jet found her targets with unnerving accuracy.

Once the ants were cleared, Jet quickly peeled away the tape from the bloody remains of Stardust's body and pressed him into a small gel-filled metal casket she had ready in her other hand. Snapping the container shut, she turned her attention to Adam.

"Hold still, my love," she whispered seductively, bringing the edge of her blade close to Adam's body. "One slip and it's all over."

The wall of sharp steel slipped under the duct tape, and Jet gently prised the tape away from the plastic fire engine. As the last strand of stubborn adhesive gave way, she let Adam's limp injured body slide onto the flat of the blade.

Carefully laying the knife on the ground, next to another metal casket, Jet reached into her breast pocket. Producing a short needle from a plastic container, she leant over Adam's helpless body. Her face was so close, so large, that Adam felt as though he could crawl into her eye and watch the world from the inside.

"You know, this is so ironic, Adam," Jet said. "For the first time, I don't want to kill you, but, for the first time, I actually have to." Without a smile, Jet pressed the point of the needle into Adam's chest, piercing his heart. "I'll see you when I'm insane again."

HAPPY RETURNS

The delightful tingle brought a smile to Adam's face. Gently drawing the file across the nail of his index finger, the female manicurist returned the smile. An android of course, but like all those in the Terminal, the sharp-eyed blonde had enough AI to pull-off a believable empathy. As Adam relaxed, she moved on to the next finger.

A morning pass to the Day Spa had not initially imbued Adam with confidence – he still retained vivid memories of its torturous gory past. Although he knew those days were long gone, he viewed the menu with caution. Sticking to simple pampering – the spa equivalents of the children's menu in a restaurant – he put himself down for a full body massage, a manicure, and an aloe face mask followed by a warm spa bath.

The male masseuse, who introduced himself as Ronald, managed to walk the line between the relaxing release of stress whilst avoiding any awkward sexual arousal. In fact, Ronald's vigorous two-handed massaging of Adam's thighs without a hint of genital contact was a truly skilled skin-walk of wonder.

Only when a thought of Cartimandua facing off against the angry crowd in Gordon's Hall crossed his mind, did Adam feel that telling twitch between his legs. Like a customer divulging their life's woes to a hairdresser, he decided to confide in his android masseuse.

"Tell me Ronald, what does it mean if a heterosexual man has sexual feelings for another man … even though that other man isn't really a man? Does it make him a bisexual?"

Ronald lightly chopped his hands up Adam's back. Reaching the neck, he stopped and leaned down:

"I don't do extras, Sir," he whispered in Adam's ear. "If sexual stimulation is what you are after, then next time I suggest you select the tantric massage. Ask for Reinhardt; he has extremely flexible fingers."

His face as red as a beetroot, Adam kept quiet for the rest of the session.

Overall, despite the physical expertise of the androids, Adam's favourite treatment was relaxing in the warm bubbly water of the spa bath. Enjoying an excellent refreshing Mojito – the mint leaves freshly muddled with brown sugar syrup and lime juice – he found time to remember those special moments spent at West Beach, but found it difficult to get Cartimandua out of his head. Of course, in a world of perpetual youth and perfect fitness, none of this 'treatment' was necessary, but then again, very little of what humans craved was necessary, except to satisfy those incessant cravings.

Leaving the Day Spa, Adam headed for his appointment with Captain Andrews. Upon his resurrection, Adam had spent less than a minute with the wily android – the relaxed rules meant that only a quick brain scan was required rather than a lengthy 'soft' interrogation. Now, four days later, the Captain had agreed to answer any questions that Adam might have concerning his turbulent time in Reynold's Gardens.

Over the past thousand years, the Captain's office had changed location and décor many times. The latest incarnation, a strikingly officious white and chrome balcony suite overlooking the main runway, seemed appropriately authoritarian given the Terminal's recent paramilitary mobilization. A large stainless steel 'T' logo on the wall behind the Captain's wide piano black desk lent the room a touch of corporate totalitarian chic.

Adam sat in one of the ribbed black-leather cantilever chairs, facing the Captain across the desk. The Captain, with a crisp white shirt and grey tie, but without his pilot's cap or jacket, was dressed to match the stark corporate ambiance.

"I'm surprised you're not wearing a Terminal armband," Adam said. "When we've finished talking, do we go out on the balcony for a few sieg heils?"

"In English, that means 'hail victory'. If your efforts in the Gardens, no matter how chaotic they might seem, have brought an end to the conflict, then why shouldn't we allow ourselves a few sieg heils." He sat back in his chair and frowned thoughtfully. "Well, we could if you humans didn't attach such historical and moral significance to such words and symbols."

"Hmm, I saw no end to the conflict when I was there. But, even if you are right, who can claim victory?"

"If things progress as I now predict … then everyone. Peace is always a fitting monument to the dead. Anyway, Adam, I am sure you have other questions you want answered."

Recalling his list of questions, mainly grievances, Adam crossed his arms and glared at the Captain, remembering that he was supposed to be angry as Hell.

"Well, for a start, with the new rules, you can read people's minds whenever you feel like it. I'm not sure I like someone tapping in to my private thoughts."

"Then you'll be glad to know that your thoughts are out of bounds. I can only access some sensory information. For instance, I can see what you saw and hear what you heard. I can also monitor some bodily functions, such as heartrate. Nothing more than that."

The Captain clasped his fingers together, waiting for the next question.

"Fair enough," Adam said. "Well, before we left, you said there was a very high probability of success, and that we would return alive. We lost Saloni, Blitz, and Stardust. For all I know, Stern didn't even make it back."

"Stern is fine," the Captain said. "He is back in your home viro, taking a well-earned rest. You know now that he works for the Terminal – over twenty years' service so far. A very capable operator."

"What does he do? He has said many times that he is a lover not a fighter."

"Time can change a person. Let's just say, that Stern no longer allows his lust to get in the way of his work. I like to call him my 'Plan B' … although I really think 'Plan A' is a better title."

"What plan?"

"I've said all I will say on that particular subject. Getting back to your grievance, I only said that you would most probably return alive. You'll no doubt accuse me of playing with words, but you should know me by now. However, it might cheer you to know that Stardust is healed and back in the psychoviro. Along with Blitz, he was a wonderful catalyst for change. I don't think you would've got as far as you did without their blessed insanity."

Despite knowing that his host was an android, Adam still felt unhappy with his apparent disregard for human life.

"So you don't care what happened to Blitz? I know you're not human, but don't you have a guilt circuit you can switch on?"

The Captain took a moment before answering – obviously a calculated attempt at a considered human response.

"I have allowed myself to feel grief and some remorse for Saloni Mehta's death," he said slowly. "The timing and manner of the Deputy's passing were highly improbable … but unfortunately a longshot is always a possibility." He looked at Adam. "Next question."

"Are you going to let them take the bodies they need? The gate will close again for forty years, so you could turn a blind eye for a few days."

"Even though the rules have been relaxed, I can't allow the body snatching to continue."

"Hah, so the war isn't over …" Adam pointed a finger at the Captain.

"If we detect intruders in the Via Sacra, we will immediately despatch a team to investigate. Their job will be to collect detailed data of any body collection and report their findings to the Terminal. After a number of such infringements, at my discretion, we will send a strongly worded letter to whoever is in charge, informing them of our displeasure and urging them to give up their criminal enterprise."

"And if they continue?"

"We will despatch another team and the process begins again."

At the Captain's admission that the body snatching could continue, albeit amid a toothless flurry of finger wagging bureaucracy, Adam relaxed in his chair – a true relief that not even the Day Spa could achieve. He frowned, wondering if the gate was still open. As if reading his mind, the Captain placed his hands down upon the table:

"I sent Dolph and a team of our best techs to inspect the gate and its operating system. Turns out there was a setting in the software that was set to Intermittent – meaning the gate only opened for a short time. A simple finger prod was all it took to set it to Permanent. It was in a sub-section, but Wergeland missed it for all those centuries. Apparently, he is so distraught that he has given up his duties and crossed over to the dark-side."

Adam shook his head in sad disbelief:

"Wow, you'd think with all those great minds in there that someone would have noticed. So many more could have been saved."

"Sometimes, the light of genius burns so brightly that it causes blindness to the glaringly obvious. We have inspected the east part of the Gardens to see if there is anything else we can do."

"What about the safety walls? I can imagine things would be better without them."

"The safety walls came down for a reason. I'm sure if the situation were really improved then they would be raised. We have the tools to unblock the doorway through to the dark-side, but for now, I believe it is prudent to leave things as they are. I do have a plan to relieve their resource problem. Tesla may be ruthless, but he wasn't wrong about the need to regularly top up the vats."

"You could let them use our resources."

"I have a much better way, and it involves you. Your trip through Reynold's Gardens is just the beginning. We hoped that you would find Ming Hua Chang, or Gordon Reynolds who we believe is the same person. Even though he wasn't in the Gardens, we now know where he might be."

The memories of his recent ordeals still fresh in his mind, Adam was uncomfortable at the prospect of another mission and, no doubt, more danger.

"So, this isn't over?" he said, feeling his body tense again. "What do you want me to do? I do have a choice in this, don't I?"

"Adam, you always have a choice, and you always make the right choice. Though the state of the Gardens is important, it pales into insignificance compared to what we've recently learned."

"It involves the slerds, doesn't it?"

The Captain smiled as if acknowledging that Adam was correct, but offered no answer.

"We will talk about this in a few months' time. The situation is dire but not pressing. For now, return to your viro and relax. A month from now, we will return Edgar Allen Poe's body to the Gardens. There will be a ceremony and the signing of a treaty of understanding. The Terminal is sending a guard of honour. I was hoping you would be part of it."

Before leaving, Adam had one last question:

"Why did you send Jet and Ricochet to rescue me? I mean, Jet in particular is extremely unpredictable."

"With full-size brains, we can make the necessary chemical changes to temper their madness. In the Viroverse, such changes are impossible given the tiny size of your brains, and the rules limiting changes in personality."

***

Adam approached his life in the viro with renewed confidence. Shunning the dressing gown, every morning he strutted down to the riverside in casual Hawaiian beachwear – rotating a number of colourful floral ensembles. Relaxing on a recliner, he sipped his cocktails and watched the small world go by through the dark glass of his Rayban aviators.

Somehow, drinking took second place to people watching, and Adam never found himself rolling around on the floor or waking suddenly from a drunken stupor. The downside to his relative sobriety was the sad realisation that he and Stern were keeping a distance from one another. Polite words were sometimes exchanged, but their former friendship lay dying in the ruins of mistrust.

As the days passed and Poe's ceremony drew near, Adam spent more and more time thinking about his relationship with Cartimandua. Would they also keep their distance from one another when they met? Would the sparks be allowed to fly, or would Adam's deep-rooted prejudices, masquerading as preferences, keep them apart. He remembered that long lamented kiss with Amanda Doyle and his denial of her tongue. What future did he deny himself? Perhaps this was not a simple battle of head versus heart, but instead, the fear of consequences. Like many people, Adam held that contradictory yearning to achieve great change in his life, whilst clinging onto the dull monotony of his everyday routine.

***

Never one for formal ceremonies, even his own wedding all those millennia ago, Adam felt uncomfortable in his grey Terminal dress uniform. The peak cap gave him scalp sweat and the tight black boots chafed his ankles. Even the tunic was a little too restricted around the neck and Adam resolutely resisted the urge to pull down the zip.

Dolph Zabel led the procession. Walking in front of Poe's metal coffin – the casket steadfastly shouldered by six honour guards – the huge Terminal security chief nodded respectfully, acknowledging the crowds lining the route through the Gardens. Taking up the rear, a motley assortment of Terminal experts and operatives, including Adam, tried hard to march in step with their military drilled colleagues.

The ceremony itself was a short affair, with a few polite words followed by the removal of Poe's brain and its incarceration in the obligatory gold box. Leonardo Da Vinci, clean-shaven and naked except for a ragged silk loincloth, performed the solemn ritual involving three brass candlesticks and a bell – his amazing surgical skills were a blur of kinetic efficiency.

Adam was surprised to learn that Cartimandua had stood down as Police Chief – another casualty of Henrik Wergeland's tragic oversight. The new chief was Al-Nabigha – now using his real name, Ziyad ibn Muawiyah. He gave Adam a hearty and most unexpected hug, before directing him to the fourth apartment block. Stopping off at one of the black glass dispensers on the way, Adam headed across the Gardens.

Finally, standing outside Cartimandua's apartment, Adam hesitated, afraid to take the next step. The hesitation also allowed him to get his breath back after a tiring slog up to the eighth floor. Not knowing whether he was motivated by maturity or foolishness, Adam knocked on the door. The reply immediately revealed that something had changed.

"It's open," a female voice called from inside.

Adam entered the apartment – rustic wooden furnishings and an eclectic assortment of ornaments softened the predictable high Victorian décor. Rising from a lightwood spindle-backed chair, a woman wearing a simple calico gown swept her long flame-red hair away from her face.

"Cartimandua?" Adam asked, somewhat surprised.

The woman walked up to Adam and placed a hand on his waist:

"It's a remarkable likeness," she said. "I was certainly not a priority for a new skin, but the moment Cortés saw the body he set it aside for me. For days, I just gazed in the mirror." She lowered and raised her gaze demurely. "All this time, I have waited for your return. I knew you weren't strong enough to resist me."

Adam ran his fingers through Cartimandua's hair and drew her close:

"You said you would have me because I would want you. Call it weakness if you must, but I want you."

There was no more time for words as their lips came together. Adam's fear of consequences melted away as their tongues slid against each other – a wet friction promising sensual pleasures to come.

Breaking away for a moment, they gazed into each other's eyes. Cartimandua unbuttoned two large ivory buttons on the shoulder of her gown. The humble robe fell away, revealing the Celtic queen's naked pale skin and statuesque curves. Without a word, she slowly unzipped Adam's jacket.

Well, I guess I won't be needing this," Adam said. He dropped the dance belt to the floor.

Printed in Great Britain
by Amazon